NEITHER CASTLE WALLS NOR COURTLY CUSTOMS CAN CONTAIN THEM. . . .

For they are the warrior princesses, their domains anywhere in their world where they are needed, their duty to champion those in need, to defend their people against mortal—and immortal—enemies. Ride with them now on such thrilling adventures as:

"Hunger"—Her father had been the king of Thessaly before the goddess cursed him. She was his daughter, the only treasure that still remained his. But even a princess has a price. . . .

"Boudicca"—Her husband slain, her tribe threatened with conquest by the Romans, she alone had the vision and the strength to challenge the might of an empire. . . .

"Three-Edged Choice"—The child of noble blood, she had chosen a career far different from that to which she was born. But she would soon find out whether she had chosen wisely. . . .

WARRIOR PRINCESSES

WARRIOR PRINCESSES

edited by
Elizabeth Ann Scarborough
and Martin H. Greenberg

DAW BOOKS, INC.
DONALD A. WOLLHEIM, FOUNDER
375 Hudson Street, New York, NY 10014

**ELIZABETH R. WOLLHEIM
SHEILA E. GILBERT
PUBLISHERS**

First Printing, May 1998
1 2 3 4 5 6 7 8 9

ACKNOWLEDGMENTS

Introduction © 1998 by Elizabeth Ann Scarborough.

My Princess © 1998 by Elizabeth Moon.

Marimba: A Retelling © 1998 by Janet Berliner Gluckman.

Hunger © 1998 by Nina Kiriki Hoffman.

Boudicca © 1998 by Morgan Llywelyn.

Pestilence © 1998 by Michael Scott.

Three-Edged Choice © 1998 by Ru Emerson.

The Jewel of Locaria © 1998 by Jacey Bedford.

Warrior of Ma-at © 1998 by Kathleen M. Massie-Ferch.

Common Ground © 1998 by John Helfers.

Twelve-Steppe Program © 1998 by Esther M. Friesner.

The Road to Vengeance © 1998 by Mickey Zucker Reichert.

The Dreamway Princess © 1998 by Bill Ransom.

Become a Warrior © 1998 by Jane Yolen.

Golden Years © 1998 by Lea M. Day.

The Sword of Undeath © 1998 by Felicia Dale.

The Little Landmaid © 1998 by Sara Young.

She Wants Things © 1998 by Bruce Holland Rogers.

One Tree Hill © 1998 by R. Davis.

Strays © 1998 by Megan Lindholm.

Debriefing the Warrior/Princess © 1998 by Elizabeth Ann Scarborough.

CONTENTS

INTRODUCTION
by Elizabeth Ann Scarborough

Not all princesses are damsels in distress, need rescuing, or even live happily ever after. Quite aside from Wonder Woman and Xena, history has several examples of warrior princesses who are far from the dainty and pampered passive aggressive stereotypes. Rather than waiting for their princes to come, these women waded into battle and bailed out themselves, their kingdoms, and maybe a prince or two in the bargain, unless, of course, he was the enemy.

The warrior princesses in this anthology include several historic and mythic figures. Morgan Llewelyn has chosen one familiar to most of us, Boudicca, and lets the druid who first forecast the charismatic queen's fate tell how it unfolded. Michael Scott selected for his subject another ancient warrior princess, Scathach, the warrior who tutored the Irish hero Cuchulain in battle. Michael mentioned that Scathach was probably the role model for Xena, since, like the fictional Xena, Cuchulain's tutor was once so cruel she was known as "The Pitiless" but later in life mellowed, reformed even, until she fulfills a somewhat gentler role in the story included here.

Janet Berliner has also taken a figure from history and legend, the African warrior princess who was also a musician and gave her name to a musical instrument, Marimba. Nina Kiriki Hoffman's princess in "Hunger" uses her only weapon and currency, her body, to try to save her father from the curse of an angry god in a fascinating take on an ancient Greek myth. Kathleen M.

Massie-Ferch's "Warrior of Ma-at" is an ancient Egyptian princess who might well be a historical figure as well. The princess in my own story is a familiar one who started out, perhaps, as one of those stereotypical blonds awaiting rescue, but by the end of her short life had become a legend who fought many a valiant battle to be allowed to champion crusades she believed in, and to me echoed the life of another, more ancient, British legend.

Besides the British, the Greeks, the Irish, the Egyptians, and Africans, we have three princesses from the New World—Bill Ransom's orphaned Lula Kax fights her way through the horrors of South American wars to reclaim her identity as a leader of her people. In "She Wants Things," Bruce Holland Rogers reminds us that not all princesses are *good* princesses. In the contemporary story of the self-appointed (or is she?) Queen of the Strays, Megan Lindholm's ragamuffin royal models herself on the Amazon warriors of old to save her own spirit and that of the stray cats she protects from being crushed by an ugly reality.

The royalty of the Middle East and the Hordes is represented in a hilarious story by Esther Friesner. A similarly tongue-in-cheek tone is adopted by newcomer Lea Day in the letter from her Greco-Roman viewpoint character to her warrior princess mum about what happens to warrior princesses who do not have the luck to die in battle.

Elizabeth Moon's "My Princess" is well drawn by the warrior-writer (and mom) in such a way that one feels that this is what a warrior princess is *really* like. In "One Tree Hill," by R. Davis, the horrible cost of war and love is at the story's center. Jane Yolen's dark fairy tale, "Become a Warrior," reminds us that people, even princesses, have reasons for becoming what they become. Ru Emerson's princess Liatt, as Ru says, "Isn't very nice but she has Reasons."

Sometimes it's fate, rather than reasons, that create a warrior princess, however, as is well-illustrated in

Felicia Dale's "The Sword of Undeath" in which a pacifistic princess inherits a truly double-edged sword.

Fate likewise plays a large part in creating as warrior princesses the protagonists in newcomer Jacey Bedford's "The Jewel of Locaria" and Mickey Zucker Reichert's "The Road to Vengeance," although the roads taken by the princesses in the stories ultimately turn out to be vastly different.

Perhaps the most fantastic princesses in the collection are those in the stories of John Helfers, whose princess allies herself with former enemies of another species, as does The Little Landmaid in the maiden voyage into fantasy fiction of Sara Young.

The collection is bookended by Elizabeth Moon's unglamorous but valiant fictional "My Princess" and my own take on a very glamorous but nevertheless valiant real-life princess in her imagined afterlife. From beginning to end, the anthology runs the gauntlet (if not gamut) of real and imagined warrior princess victories and defeats in such a way that the term "princess" takes on a singular nobility not necessarily associated with it in the past. Let the battles be joined!

MY PRINCESS
by Elizabeth Moon

Elizabeth Moon first gained prominence in the fantasy field
with her Paksenarrion trilogy, *Sheepfarmer's Daughter, Divided
Allegiance,* and *Oath of Gold.* She has revisited the
world of Paksenarrion in two subsequent novels. She has
also written science fiction, collaborating with Anne McCaffrey
on the novels *Sassinak* and *Generation Warriors.* She
lives with her husband and son in Texas.

The princesses in fairy tales are so young and beautiful—or,
if plain, gifted with unusual virtues that
bring them love and the admiration of their people.
The princesses in fairy tales die young, tragically, or
live happily ever after, with or without a prince. In
those rare tales (more folk than fairy) of warrior princesses,
these are also young, beautiful, brave . . . the
poignancy of putting such rare fragile beauty in mortal
peril is part of the charm.

In reality, the warrior princesses are unlikely to be
beautiful or any more fragile than the average of mortal
flesh, and when they die in battle, no one weeps
over the tragedy in terms of roses lost to untimely
frost, or delicate crystal shattered by ruinous barbarians.
Not for them the wails and tears, the spontaneous
outburst of songs; not for them the flowers piled
against a palace wall.

I was thinking of this while cleaning my princess'
tack, using an old toothtwig on the clotted blood and
sweat. Her sister, the Rose of the Kingdom, or her
other sister, the Lily of the Morning, neither one of

those could walk down the street without a murmur of adoration. They wear the royal clothes well, those two, and smile at everyone, reaching out with gentle hands to touch the shining heads of children, the gray curls of grandmothers. They are beloved, with reason. If they should die before their time—a stupid expression, that, because the time to die is when you die— songs will be sung for them, and enough tears shed to float the bier to some enchanted island.

Her Highness, my princess—though, in truth, they are all my princesses, I claim her especially—would likely die in this war, despite her skill. She would have a funeral, of course, when it was convenient, and her mother would commission a bard to write her a song, and crowds would gather (would be gathered, if necessary, by the household guard) to line the processional way. But her touch is iron and steel; her comfort remote to those she protects. She is not beloved, who strides along with a ringing of bootheels, whose very glance is dangerous, out of a face plain and tanned as the flap of a saddle.

I finished the bridle and hung it on a peg. In parades, her parade horse wears the fancy bridle and saddle with the royal arms set onto every possible location. It's not my job to polish that; the royal stables have an entire staff to care for the royal tack, keeping gold and silver and ruby enamel bright. My job is, like my princess', less showy and more dangerous. It is my responsibility to see that the gear her warhorse wears is whole and sound in every part.

I had been doing this for eight years now. She was a tense, awkward youngster when she came to us, and I was assigned to her—to her horse, actually, though to me it is the same thing. She rode old Ponder then, who had been her father's warhorse—steady, reliable, and—though she did not know this, as indeed neither did her father—voice-trained by the troop commander so that if she should stray into an excess of peril, the horse would bring her home.

We never had to use the command, though. From the first, she showed herself steadier in danger than before it—unusual for any, and especially for princesses. In that first battle—a skirmish, really—she was white to the lips but did exactly what she had been told, unlike her cousin who, eager for glory, spurred his horse into a deep bog and had to be rescued at the cost of fourteen lives.

Now she fights as well as any other eight-year veteran and her eyes have that look which only veterans acquire, and which nothing but a long peace can take away. Fate has not granted us a long peace—or much peace at all—since my princess was twelve years old and first learning to toss the lance. She does not command all our armies, but she has earned command of some few squadrons of cavalry. Where she commands, the enemy has never raided unscathed; her vigilance has held them at bay even when others slackened their guard.

"Mol—" Her Highness called me. I tucked the rag I was using into the sack that held a lump of saddle soap, twisted the toothtwig into the thong, and went to her.

"Milady." She does not like formal address on the field, and though we have all been ordered by His Grace the noble Duke to address her so, when he is not there we do as she wishes . . . or somewhat closer to it, since she would prefer to be called Captain only.

"I thought I felt the saddle shift a bit today—would you check with the saddler about restuffing?"

"At once, milady." I glanced up at her face. Five days before, I'd been in the capital, where her sisters had greeted me as they ought . . . her sisters with the flower-faces, the shining hair, the smiles and graces that everyone associates with princesses. My princess looked more like a queen in exile, weatherworn and dangerous. The word princess fit her as ill as a ball gown would, these last years.

I took the saddle to the saddler, who hummed over it and gave me a sharp glance, as if he suspected me of pilfering wool from its panels. Then he waved me away, and I went back to my work. The bridle, done . . . and I had checked the stitching of the reins. The breastplate, the girths, the crupper and breeching on which the barding hung. While old Festus had the saddle, I could get at the rest of the harness, and by the time I was done, afternoon had dimmed into evening. Beyond the torchlight, I could see nothing.

I cleaned my hands carefully and went out of the tent to find that Festus had set the saddle on the stand outside. I moved it under cover, and checked every stitch. Then I took saddle and harness to the horse tent where Warning's groom was rubbing the last of the day's mud out of the gray horse's hairy fetlocks with handfuls of dry straw. Festus would have checked the fit, but I was the one who had to be sure every strap of the harness fit.

Warning snuffled at me, hoping for a tidbit, but the groom scolded him. Grooms are jealous, always convinced that the horses they care for become somehow their own. I suppose it's natural, but I have no affection for the tack that is my care—only for the princess whose life it may save. Or not.

Festus had done his usual good job; the restuffed saddle fit Warning's back perfectly. I unrolled the rest of the harness, and tried it on. This would have to come down a hole, but—I considered—as the new stuffing compressed, it might need to be shortened again. I made a note, a knot of horsehair, to remind myself to tell Her Highness that in the morning.

Then I set everything ready for tacking up and went to get my supper. I've heard men complain about the food, but I carry as much flesh as ever, and can stay the march with younger men. War is not for delicate feeders. I took my hunk of ill-baked bread, my bowl of soup more full of cabbage and onion than I like, and squatted near the fire. It was coming on to autumn again; up here in the hills, the nights could be cold. Long habit let me notice how the sentries were placed, and how alert they were—good enough, this chill night. I relaxed a bit and ate my supper. *She* would eat in her tent, with her officers around her, and long after I fell asleep in a pile of straw, she would be awake planning for the morrow.

It had been so for almost eight years. I went to my bed expecting it to be so for the next eight, unless she were killed in battle, which was likely enough. That prospect disturbed me; I would be assigned to her flightier cousin, no doubt, and despite my deep respect for the entire royal family, I could not like that scatterbrain.

To bed at war, I wakened to peace—or so the heralds declared, riding into camp in the black belly of night with torches flaring and trumpets sounding. We all roused, thinking at first it was an attack; I had Warning half-saddled when the real message got through to me. Peace. A treaty with our old enemies, sealed by the marriage of my princess' sisters to the sons of their royal houses—entirely traditional. It would not last; we all knew that. But for now—at least until after the wedding and bedding and birth of heirs—we would have peace.

I pulled the war saddle off Warning and waited, uncertain whether she would ride back to the capital tonight. Usually she told me herself which tack to use, but this night word came by her bodyservant. She would ride Sudden, not Warning, for his speed; she wanted the lighter gear; she would leave at dawn. I checked that tack, and lay down again for the brief time left me. I could not sleep. Uneasy in my mind, I wondered why, when the peace that we had all desired had come at last.

By the first light, I had Sudden tacked and warmed up for her; unlike Warning, the chestnut has a cold back and needs to be settled or he'll buck when mounted. After getting the kinks out of him, I laid the wool horse-cloak over his back and walked him up and down outside her tent until she was ready. It is not my fault that I heard the voices, for I was where I should have been following the orders I had been given.

"No," my princess said. I had heard her say no to things before, but this had an intensity beyond the usual, beyond *No, we'll attack through this gap,* or *No, I'm not tired.*

Rumble, rumble, the deep voice of a man whose natural register was even lower than mine.

"But Your Highness must understand the importance of this treaty," said another, more tenor than bass.

"It's different for my sisters," my princess said. I stumbled over air, jerking Sudden's lead, and the horse threw up his head. I soothed him and walked on, but closer to the tent walls. That much is my fault, if you want to apportion fault. "I cannot—" my princess said, her voice going rough as it did when she held the dying, her throat closing against sobs. "I gave all that up—he can't ask now—" They have betrothed her, I thought, though I could hardly believe it; no one trains a falcon, then cages it like a songbird and expects sweet music.

"You will become used to it," said the tenor voice. "It is your duty."

"My duty," she said, "is to my troops and to my country."

"You have the order reversed," the deep voice said. It was almost familiar, that voice; I would know it in a moment, or if it spoke louder. "Your duty is to your sovereign, who represents your country. Your duty to your troops ends when you are relieved of command."

I almost snorted, letting out a tiny huff of air that Sudden heard and danced to. I quieted him again. Before she answered, I knew her answer, and it came.

"My duty to my troops will never end," she said, her voice ringing out now into the cold still air. "Their

bodies have stood between me—between all of us—
and the enemy these eight years."

"Well, in a ceremonial sense, of course that's true,"
said the tenor voice. "But your immediate duty—"

"Is to return and obey your sovereign's command,"
the bass voice finished.

I glanced around. A surprising number of soldiers
found it necessary to do their morning chores within
earshot, though I was closest, having the best excuse.
I locked eyes with the color sergeant; his mouth
tightened.

"And I am here," the deep voice said. "And my son—"

His noble grace, the duke, that's who that was, and
his son was a lordling only year older than my princess, with half her experience and the reputation for
being just a little slow to engage the enemy. At one
time gossip had linked their names, but we could not
imagine our princess wedded to such a man, and nothing had come of it.

Her voice was tight with anger when she spoke
again. "And your son is to command these troops?"

"Yes, Your Highness," said the tenor voice. I
glanced at the sergeant again; his face might have been
carved of gray stone in that early light. I saw someone
move between the tents, away from hers, and knew
that word would pass. The tenor voice went on, when
it would have been better silent. "This commission
was given by your gracious mother herself; I shall en-
deavor to live up to your example."

Oho. So the tenor was the son we'd heard of. They
must have come while I rested, in the deep night—
had I dozed, not to hear them?

"It may seem strange at first," the duke said, in a
tone he probably meant to be soothing and fatherly,
though I knew how it would rasp my princess' nerves.
"But you will be relieved of this unnatural strain, this
hardship, this danger. In peace and safety, you will
regain your—" He paused; I could have laughed, almost, as he realized the corner into which he'd maneu-

vered himself. Whatever he said now would be wrong, would insult her—regain youth, beauty, charm? Were these not part of the definition of princess, whether a live princess displayed them or not? "Your peace," he said finally.

"Peace." Her voice rasped on the word, steel on stone. I dared to lead Sudden past the opening to her tent, and glance in past the sentries. In the lamplight, she still looked what she was, and the duke looked like what he what he was, all courtier. "And you trust this peace, my lord? You trust our enemies so much?"

The men's voices dropped again, and I could not hear their words clearly. I could guess much, but I had no proof. And then she came out, pulling her gloves on, her face as still as on any other morning. I held the stirrup for her to mount; she looked down at my face, a long look. "Thank you, Mol," she said. Then, to the duke and his son who had followed her out. "I want Mol to come with me, to help me at the changes of horse."

"I will need him," the duke's son said. "To see to my tack."

My princess looked at me again, and something flickered behind her eyes. Not fear—I had seen her afraid, in those first years, enough to know what her fear looked like—but something related to it. Wariness perhaps. Calculation. "Take care of Warning," she said to me. "Very good care." Then she gathered her reins, and with the escort behind her spurred to a gallop on the way back to the capital.

The duke stayed to breakfast and the midday meal, making sure that everyone knew his son was in command. Then he rode away with his entourage, off to the northeast. The duke's son was not ill-looking, but I did not like the way he ordered me to saddle Warning, or the way he threw the reins to me when he dismounted after exercising the horse. He had a taste for formality; though it was normal for a new commander to hold an inspection, he went at it as though he expected to find some serious problems which the enemy had not noticed. Eight years, I thought to myself, and he thinks we are still green?

The duke's son had brought his own warhorse, a roan stallion, but continued to use Warning daily. He rode well enough, with dash I would say, but sat more on his left hip than his right; his horse's saddle showed the characteristic flattening. When I took it to Festus to be restuffed, the duke's son reproved me. I had not asked permission. I ducked my head and apologized, glancing aside at the miniature he had put on his desk in her—in his—tent. He had married a sweet-faced girl, if that picture had much likeness, a girl who probably thought he was handsome. I suppose he was—I tried to be fair, but I could feel, as any veteran would, the slow unraveling of the troops, the loosening of strands our princess had knit tight. We obeyed, but day by day obedience became more form than spirit. We said nothing to each other—what was there for soldiers to say about this, that lay too deep for words?—but I met more and more in other eyes the mood I felt behind my own.

The first flurries of snow blew down from the higher hills, and the duke's son ordered a retreat to the lowlands, only a day's march from the capital. He did not leave behind the pickets she would have left; he trusted the wedding truce. I heard that some of the captains argued, to no avail. I said nothing; no one would listen if I spoke.

Some days later, we moved even closer to the capital. As an honor to my princess, some of the troops she commanded would be paraded at her wedding. We knew now who she would wed. Not a king's son, after all, but a noble's son from the kingdom to the east. That king had no unmarried sons; she would marry a cousin.

I could not imagine it, my princess in a wedding gown, pledging herself to a man who, by all accounts, had never taken the field.

In the city there was no escape from rumor. Her sister princesses were seen almost daily, at one celebration after another: balls, receptions, even walking through the market scattering alms. Their cheeks were rosy in the chill air; they moved as gracefully as reeds in the wind. She had not been seen since she returned. Locked up, some said, to force her to submission. Secluded while serving women did what they could to repair the ravages of eight years in the field. It would take years, a woman in the market square said in my hearing, to reshape her figure, bleach her complexion, and teach her womanly skills and graces.

I thought of the spears and swords her skill had turned aside, her grace in the saddle. I wanted to hit the woman, but she was a commoner, a cheesemonger by her apron, and she had but said what many thought. They did not think how she had served them, in heat and cold and danger, for those eight years—they only compared her to her pretty sisters.

We saw the bridegrooms to be, as well. Two were princes of the blood, from the enemies of our west and south: a slim light-haired fellow hardly taller than I, with a sweet but dangerous twist to his mouth, whose cool blue eyes lingered too long for my taste on the details of the city's walls and gates. And a brown-haired man, somewhat stocky but not fat, who moved like soldier when he walked and had a scarred left hand. Rumor had it he had been wounded twice in battle; his personal guards bragged in the taverns that he was braver than any. Then there was my princess' bridegroom: stoop-shouldered, with a disgruntled expression that made it clear he thought the others had the best bargain. I saw him smile only when flattered.

The more dangerous rumors were harder to find, but being sure they existed, we searched the more diligently. For what reason was our princess being sacrificed?—for that is what it was. What other purpose had the most noble duke, our commander-in-chief, for removing her from command of the east, and putting his son there—and then marrying her to that eastern lordling? Those of us most interested spent our last coin on drink and herbs to find out, and the truth we found at last chilled us to the bone. Treachery within treachery . . . was the whole world rotten but her? She would not live to see a child grown, though she might live to bear a few, if that itself did not kill her. But no more, for her, the open air and fields, not even the joy of the chase.

Finally, only ten days before the weddings, I saw my princess again. She came into the stable yard, where I was polishing the duke's son's tack, and I did not recognize her at first. She looked thinner and softer, tricked out in women's clothes; she wore a tight-laced ruffled dress and a fur-trimmed cloak, and low boots with pointed toes. Her hair was piled up, with loose tendrils blowing . . . I realized that most of it was false, since she had not time to grow out her warrior's crop. Her face looked strange, until I saw that she had been made up to look less brown. In the chill wind outside, her own color splotched through the powder and paint.

She knew me, though, and came near. "Mol," she said.

"Your Highness." In this courtyard, only formality would serve, and I was well aware of those who watched and listened.

"Warning?"

"Is well, Your Highness," I said.

"He rides him?"

I knew the lack of name was intentional. "Yes, Your Highness. But he is not a bad rider."

"That's good." Her eyes shifted away, very unlike her old direct gaze.

"I'm . . . sorry," I ventured, very low. She looked at me then, a glance as sharp as a dagger; I almost flinched.

"You . . . know?"

"Yes, Your Highness."

"It won't work," she said, as softly. "He doesn't want me; I don't want him. I can't—it's too late, after all that's—"

A voice called querulously from the doorway. She glanced over her shoulder, the only furtive movement I'd ever seen from her. It was her husband-to-be, hunched against the chill like a vulture. She did not move toward him, but stood erect, tense. He came out, calling her name again.

"You'll be late," he said. "And this wind, my love, will roughen your complexion." He looked at her as men look at ugly women.

I head her growl, such sound as she had made once when she found one of our men had been mutilated. Not loud, but intense. I glanced his way; he had not heard it.

"What do you do here?" he asked, coming closer. "Who is this fellow?"

"Mol," she said, with no resonance in her voice. "He cared for my tack in battle. I came to thank him for his care, that preserved my life those years, and to thank my troops—"

"Surely you need not come yourself," he said, with a chuckle I wanted to push back down his throat. "You have servants now, to carry such messages—"

"And to see my old horse," she said. "Since you say I will not need him—"

"No, indeed," he said, agreeably enough, looking around. "We breed fine horses at home, fit for a lady's pleasure. You shall have a nice mare for your excursions and, when you no longer wish to ride, a matched team for your carriage."

She had stiffened at *no longer wish to ride;* her gaze slid past mine, toward the stable opening. "Warning is here?" she asked me abruptly.

"Yes, Your Highness," I said. I could feel the man's

gaze on my bent head. "Left aisle, fifth stall." I almost
told her where her war saddle was hung, but did not.

"What a name for a lady's horse," the man said.
"You will be glad, I'm sure, to ride gentler beasts. But
let us go and see your . . . Warning . . . one last
time. I understand that women are sentimental about
such things."

Because I was looking down, I saw the knuckles of
her sword hand whiten, the tendons standing out in
her wrist. I dared not look up, dared not meet whatever expression she had found to answer him. They
walked off; I saw that he was trying to offer his arm,
and she was not seeing it . . . deliberately, that much
was clear. From behind they looked as ill-matched a
pair as Warning and Sudden in double-harness. Her
shoulders were still broader than his, despite the
weeks she had not practiced; the lady's boots she wore
forced her to a shorter stride, but she swung her leg
from the hip anyway.

When they came back across the courtyard, she neither looked at me nor spoke, but one of her hands
flicked, as if something had stung her. I knew by that
she would return.

No one walked the castle grounds at night unchal-
lenged. No women came out after dark at all. I sat
with my back propped on a sack of corn, restitching
the reins to the roan horse's bridle, and listening to
the evening noises. No one walked by night unchal-
lenged, but by day the bustle increased, with more and
more wedding guests crammed into the city, with more
and more servants crowding the workspaces. Hard to
do anything without being observed, but harder yet to
keep track of all the newcomers. Eight of us, this evening, were sharing the lamplight in one small alcove,
all working on tack. I glanced around. Festus the saddler replacing the saddle flap. Two foreigners, cleaning
a tangle of bridles. Three more grooms from the old
troop, mending halters and other gear, and one palace

flunky soaping a harness. This wasn't the place to clean harnesses—they had a separate shed for that—and he wasn't doing it right anyway—so I assumed he was watching us. When he left, the harness still half-cleaned, it was clear he'd decided we were harmless.

We were supposed to sleep in the loft, but it was noisy up there—half the grooms snored, I had complained repeatedly—so I slept on the ground floor, on a pile of sacking. With the city so full, no one scolded me for this. I lay there, looking out the stable door, listening to the horses shift and stamp or make water. So it was I saw the kitchen boy edging along the wall before dawn, a shadow against the torches across the courtyard.

"Mol . . ." came the soft voice.

"Um." I swallowed the natural thing to say; here it would be fatal.

"I . . . cannot marry him. I must get away." She sounded apologetic; they had shamed her, who had never turned away from danger before.

"I know," I murmured into her ear. I nearly choked on the scent they made her wear, like a tavern wench's. If the guards got close enough, they'd know she was no kitchen boy. I told her the little I could, and sent her back in only a few minutes. We could not get past the gates at night, or against arms. Yet Festus and the color sergeant and I had an idea which might work—or at least might give her a better death than the one she faced in that dull lordling's birthing chamber. She nodded, when I'd finished, and pressed my arm with a hand still strong enough to hurt.

The duke's son had planned to ride his own roan stallion at the head of the troops, but the stallion came up lame that morning. The duke's son bit his lip, annoyed, and told me to saddle Warning. He did not like her saddle, but he had not told me to have another stuffed to fit Warning's back. I took her war saddle off the rack, and checked it over a last time.

Strap by strap, buckle by buckle, I fastened the harness and gear onto the gray horse. Into the saddlebags I put the required supplies, knowing the sergeant would inspect them.

The duke's son mounted, narrowly missing my head with his boot as he swung his leg over while I held the stirrup. "I wish this horse fit my saddle," he said irritably. "I'll have to get a new one."

He would indeed. I ran a cloth over his boots with extra care.

After he rode off, I knelt in the stall and pulled out the hair I'd run through the roan stallion's front leg, through the space between bone and tendon. I hoped he would recover quickly. Then I mounted and rode out to join the troop. At least they had let her name the men she wanted to have parade before the crowd. All, except the duke's son, were ready.

The crowds cheered her sisters, their breath steaming in the cold air. In their furred hoods, her sisters looked indeed like the flowers they had been called. She, in her carriage, looked nothing like them; the crowd's cheers were perfunctory for her, and louder for her escort. I rode beside the carriage horses, eyeing the postilions on the nearside of each pair. They rode well enough, but not like cavalrymen—and they would not expect what was coming.

We were just turning into the market square when I saw Warning flinch. The duke's son's heavy hip had done its work, pressing hard enough to force the sharp flint through the cloth sack Festus had made for the saddle panel. We had argued, Festus and I, over how much padding to put in; the horse must not buck on mounting, but must feel the stone before the procession ended. The duke's son sat deeper, and Warning flinched again. I hated doing this to a horse, but—we had to unseat the duke's son without actually touching him. We needed that confusion. I glanced again at the postilions and let the fingers of my right hand, held down at my side, flick twice. I did not look at my

princess. She was not an eight-year veteran for
nothing.

The next turn was to the left, around the square,
and I knew the duke's son would slip to his inside
hip; he always did. Warning flinched, then hopped; the
duke's son, as I expected, yanked on the reins and sat
back heavily, clenching his legs. Warning whirled, and
half-reared. Behind him, the color sergeant said,
"Warning—look *out,* sir!" and Warning went straight
up and came down bucking. The duke's son stayed on
for two bucks—one more than I had bet; I'd lost three
silver pence on that—and then rolled off. The color
sergeant cut Warning off neatly in front, but his wild
grab at the reins went carefully astray.

"Warning!" My princess called, in her old voice,
and the gray horse broke into a canter toward us,
kicking out when anyone tried to grab the loose reins.
I whirled my own mount, spurred, and he kicked the
lead carriage horse and postilion square on. As Warning came by, I slid off, all apologies, and ran to him.
A hand under the near side of the saddle, and the
pesky flint in its bag came away, into the front of my
uniform. I held reins and stirrup while the princess
lunged from the carriage onto his back, skirts all a-
tumble. Warning steadied, without the flint gouging
his back; my companions, meanwhile, had dismounted
all the postilions, and cut the traces of the carriage
horses, who fled plunging into the crowd.

Faster than it takes to tell it, we were charging past
the rear of the procession, the crowd scattering. Our
princess slashed at her skirts with the dagger I handed
her, and by the time we cleared the gates, she was a
ridiculous figure indeed with a ruff of skirt and under-
skirt around her waist and torn white silk hosen on
her muscular legs, the beribboned sleeves of her wedding gown blowing, her wig hanging by one remaining
ribbon. She yanked it off her head and threw it away,
grimacing as a lock of her own hair came with it.

Beyond the gate we vanished, people said later, but

sixty armed men and a warrior princess don't really vanish. She had more respect among the farmers whose land she'd protected all those years, where she'd insisted that we could not take even a stray chicken for dinner without asking. So we made it to the forest, and before she was quite frozen, she had changed into the clothes we'd brought for her. I don't think any of us, man or woman, veteran or novice, thought for a moment of those glimpses of her body we had seen then.

My princess died far away from court and crowds; the only flowers on her grave are those wildings that seeded there from the bunches I lay on it. You would ask, I know, of what she died, and when, and the number of her wounds. You would ask if she ever married, if she had children, if she lived to old age. You would like to know how her sisters fared, how her own land survived, if it did. You would make a tale, perhaps, of the gallant swordswoman, or the poor misguided girl, or the wild adventurer. But I tell no more than this: her death, like her life, won my respect, and I do not give that easily.

MARIMBA: A RETELLING
by Janet Berliner

In her twenty-five years as a writer, editor, and publishing consultant, Janet Berliner has worked with such authors as Peter S. Beagle, David Copperfield, Michael Crichton, and Joyce Carol Oates. Among her most recent books are the anthology *David Copperfield's Beyond Imagination,* which she created and edited, and *Children of the Dusk,* the final book of *The Madagasacar Manifesto,* a three-book series coauthored with George Guthridge. Currently Janet divides her time between Las Vegas, where she lives and works, and Grenada, West Indies, where her heart is.

As I have done many times in my writings, I thank *Vusamazulu Credo Mutwa for his book,* Indaba my Children.

Mutwa's father was a Zulu, a former Catholic cate-chist, his mother the daughter of an Induna, *a High Witch Doctor, who was also a custodian of the Tribal Relics and a guardian of the tribe's history. For the most part, Mutwa was raised as a Christian, but in the late '50s he renounced Christianity and underwent the "Ceremony of Purification." Then he began training as a witch doctor and prepared to take over his grand-father's role of Custodian of the sacred Tribal Relics. He is a medicine man, a storyteller, and a fine writer. I wish that I could meet him, but all my efforts to do so have been in vain. Should he read this retelling, "This is for you, Vusamazulu Credo Mutwa. I hope it adds in some small measure to the music of your people."*

*   *   *

In the absolute silence of a star-tossed midnight, the surface of Lake Nyanza shone like a mirror beneath the summer moon. The lake was the heart of the Earth. Reflected in its image was the most beautiful woman the world had ever seen. Her perfect face looked as if created in *mushragi*—ebony—by the finest of carvers. Her skirt of tanned leopard skin was short and revealed legs that were surely the envy of the Goddess of Beauty. She wore bracelets of copper and carved ivory and a necklace of copper rectangles, etched with the tribal secrets of wisdom. Her hairstyle was the oldest in the Land of the Tribes, upswept into dual lobes to create the "ears of the caracal" and decorated with carved combs and cowrie shells which matched those sewn into the hem of her skirt. As for her breasts, they were round and firm, like those of a young girl, though she was far more than a hundred summers old.

Holding the woman upright stood a man in excess of seven feet tall. Although he was not Masai, his admiration for the tribe he had once ruled with Evil had led him to assume their aspect. His hair was plaited and tied above his forehead. The cord which tied it went around his head to a second hump of hair behind and beneath his skull. His ears were double-pierced to hold the weight of heavy copper earrings. He wore a simple loinskin, and a band of python around his forehead. Eschewing the necklace of claws and teeth usually worn by Masai warriors, he chose a single decoration—a broad ivory band, embedded with copper oblongs that matched those in the woman's necklace. In his hand, he carried an *assegai* tipped with *ligwadla* rock, a huge bow, and a quiver filled with stone-tipped arrows.

Behind him, the man could hear ghastly sounds. They came from the Forest of Killima-Njaro, which housed the demons of Hell—the *Dija-Nwana* or Night Howlers, the Fire Brides and Night Eaters, the Viper

Maidens with long rodent tails and the eyes of cats. Once, the lake had been the gateway to earthly lands both terrible and strange; the forest had been the playground of lions and leopards and birds. Nearby, there had been villages whose children came of strong men and beautiful women with high cheekbones.

This was no longer so. It would be again after the man and his love descended into the waters, but for now the demons were all that remained. Having feasted upon the humans, they had followed the Words of Tribal Wisdom—they had hunted and destroyed each other, so that only the strongest among them survived.

They were fearless, these demon survivors, but not even they would dare approach this man and this woman. Not now. Not ever.

"It has been a hundred summers, Beloved," the man said, though he knew the woman would not hear him. "Tonight, *Ma,* Mother of the Stars, will release you into this world of sight and sound. Then she will guide us to the golden sanctuary she has prepared for us in the depths of Lake Nyanza."

The woman did not stir, nor could she see herself—or him—in the mirrored surface of the lake.

Gently, the man pulled the woman down beside him onto the warm earth. As he held her in his arms, *Ma* brought him the gift of knowledge and he was able to travel back a century and see the truths of their lives. He spoke them aloud though she could not hear him, wishing he could have passed them on to their hundred sons and fifty daughters, and to their children's children . . .

. . . The Evil Ones thrived, all but their leader who was known as Nangai the God Immortal. Nangai could truly thrive only if he fed a little each day upon the blood of a Human Immortal and it was too long since he had found such a meal. There was, in fact, only one such left to him in the land, and that was a woman. A

Warrior Princess, beautiful and beloved by her people, and so clever that she had, till now, been able to elude him.

But no more.

Nangai lay in his dark cave and, in his mind's eye, looked out upon Lake Nyanza where a long canoe steered steadily toward him through the hot and humid night. In it rode five people. One of them was the woman who would give him back his left arm that lay as a useless stump against his side; she would cure the sores that festered all over his body, even as new blisters erupted, and heal his right arm which had never recovered from the wound inflicted by the poisoned arrow of *Mulungu* the Father of Light when he drove Nangai from the Land of the Gods.

Not that he was afraid of disfigurement or of pain, Nangai thought, or that he knew why he wanted to continue with life, except that it was what he did. He lived, he ate, he ruled over the Evil Ones.

He stumbled to his feet and moved toward the lake. When he saw himself reflected in its waters, he grimaced at his own hideousness. Then he raised his head and watched the canoe approach.

From his perch in the canoe, the elderly wizard-lord of the Wakambi saw Nangai. He smiled smugly, for it was he who had ordered Marimba to be drugged during the Festival of Odu her Father, he who had proclaimed himself Chief in Marimba's stead, he who had sent Nangai a dream message, asking for protection on this journey and immortality upon delivery of the comatose woman at his feet.

"I am wiser than the crocodiles which house our ancestors," he told his three cohorts, knowing that they had no choice but to agree with him. One of them was also a woman who, though she lacked his power, was as evil as he.

"You are indeed wise, my Chief," she said.

The self-appointed Chief shuddered. Hearing himself addressed as Chief was a new enough sensation that it still brought him pleasure; hearing it from Marimba's daughter-in-law, her son Kahawa's least favorite wife, added extra spice.

"Thanks to you, our lives will soon be sweeter than the honey from my apiary," Luchiza added, rare words of praise from the son of Motengu the Headman, who was also the first beekeeper in the world.

Mbongo the one-eyed, whose only virtue was that he had none, said nothing in words, but his chuckle resounded into the silence, and he nudged his foot against the prostrate body of his true Chieftainess as if she mattered less than an abandoned hive.

Marimba did not feel Mbongo's hardened foot against her ribs. But she was not the zombie they thought her to be, for zombies do not have souls and hers remained intact. As always, it was filled with music and beauty and hope, with the fierceness required of a Warrior Princess and with the sexual appetites of a *Namirika.* Being a Human Immortal, she could hear the music inside her soul, and she could remember the pieces of her life, only she did not know that it was *her* music and *her* life. The drug had caused her to lose the *knowing,* and she could not speak, nor could she hear or see the present. She lay as if an infant in the gentle arms of her mother, *Amarava,* the exquisite Mother of Nations, and though she could not feel the blow from the foot of Mbongo, there appeared in her mind the memories of other blows.

She felt the rogue elephant's trunk in the small of her back, pushing her aside as he trampled upon her first husband, Zumangwe; she felt the blow to her temple as Simba the Lion leaped and brought her down before he took her second husband as his last meal; she felt the impact of her son Kahawa's war club on the back of her head.

In the same way, she knew nothing of being led into the light of the Immortal God Nangai, felt nothing when, ignoring all else, he greedily embedded his hollow talons into the flesh of her arm and siphoned into himself a goodly portion of her blood. She did not see his sores and blisters heal or watch the new limb grow where there had been only a stump.

Invigorated, excited by the fresh blood pulsing through his veins, Nangai at last looked closely at the Human Immortal.

"What have you done to her?" he asked of the wizard-lord.

"She is a zombie and will forever be at your service," the wizard-lord answered. "I am ready to claim my reward," he continued boldly.

Inside Nangai, flowing out of the tiny piece of Marimba's soul contained in the blood he had siphoned, came the music of a *makweyana,* the bow-harp which Marimba had invented, and the sound of her voice singing, *Carry my voice to the Land of the Gods/ Beyond the plains of Tura-ya-Moya . . .*

Nangai had heard such sounds only once before, in the land of the Wakambi, for there was no such thing as music or human song in the land of the Evil Ones. At that time, he had conspired with *Fesi* the Wolf, a great Masai warrior. Needing Marimba's blood, he had sent *Koma-Tembo,* son of *Fesi,* to scout the Land of the Wakambi. But *Koma-Tembo* had failed him. Though he mouthed the words, "I belong to Nangai. He commands and I obey," he had allowed himself to be captured by the Wakambi, and to be bewitched by the beauty and goodness of this woman, whom Nangai had not seen until this day.

Once warned, not even the Masai and a horde of demons had been able to capture Marimba. She had taken *Koma-Tembo*'s deadly bow and arrow and fashioned of it the *makweyana,* the world's first musical instrument. As the Masai approached, with Nangai behind them, she'd lifted her voice in a song of many verses, the first song heard in the world. He could not remember them all, but these words that flowed in his veins burned him as if with a lover's passion

. . . Carry my voice to the Land of the Gods
Beyond the plains of Tura-ya-Moya.

Tell those that rule all the stars up above—
Tell the mother of all the seas and the earth
Beyond the plains of Tura-ya-Moya:

Tell them that though the hyenas of death
Prowl without my kraal tonight—
Tell them that all these perils I'll face
And that I'll never cringe nor cower . . .

Terrified, the Masai had turned and run, giving her time to command her men to cut strips of kudu hide and the women to gather piles of round stones as shots. Placing these supplies in a strategic position, she'd said, "Never forget that I am your Warrior Princess." Having instructed her people on the use of her new invention, the slingshot, she'd led them in battle against the mighty Masai.

"May the gods punish me for what I have caused you to become," Nangai shouted as he stood in his cave by Lake Nyanza, so taken was he with her extraordinary appearance, with the music and song that rippled in his veins and with his memories of her bravery.

There came a shining light and the boom of thunder. A swirling mist filled the cave, a rainbow which formed itself into a giantess whom Nangai recognized as *Ma*, Mother of Stars. At once, he begged to be punished, and pleaded with her to allow Marimba to emerge from her coma.

"These vermin here," *Ma* said, pointing at the four wrongdoers, "shall be delivered unto the Viper Maidens. Though it is beyond me to understand what has caused *your* change of heart, you, Nangai, shall be demoted from god to ordinary High Immortal."

"And the woman?" Nangai asked.

"You will carry her back to her village. There,

among her people, the Wakambi, you will take her as
your only wife. If you rule the Wakambi with patience,
with wisdom, and with strength for a hundred summers, I shall lead you and your beloved Marimba to
a golden sanctuary which I shall prepare for you beneath the waters of Lake Nyanza."

When the Viper Maidens had feasted on the evil
humans, Nangai placed Marimba on his bed and held
her through what remained of the night. In the morning, he returned with her to her people and to her
son, Kahawa who had become desperate in his search
for his mother . . .

. . . Seated at the lake, Nangai—for it was he who
had loved Marimba for a hundred summers and who
sat with her now under the moon—heard again the
song that Marimba had played on the eve of her people's battle with the Masai.

Nangai felt ashamed. He held Marimba closer, begging her forgiveness, though of course he knew that
she could not hear him. Then, using the blessed gift
of knowledge which *Ma* had bestowed upon him, he
listened to all of the songs of Marimba's soul.

The music washed over his own soul, and his cleans-
ing was complete. He could see as if with an eagle's
vision. Like the bird of thunder which was able to see
the inner world of a buck hiding in the grasses miles
below, he could look fully into the past, and into the
inner world of his Warrior Princess. Excited by his
new ability, he began again to speak out loud.

"Though I had been High Lord of the Demons,"
he said, "I did not know of the curse placed upon you
by *Watamaraka,* the Mother of all Demons. Jealous
of your beauty and goodness, *Watamaraka* made certain that every man you married would die violently
within three moons of the wedding."

There had been so many things about Marimba
which Nangai had accepted without understanding and
which he now understood—the rogue elephant that
trampled her first husband, Zumangwe to death;

Simba the Lion taking her second husband as his last meal. He even understood why her son, Kahawa, had struck her on the back of her head with his war club.

It was this last which interested him most as *Ma* allowed him to see for himself what his past Evil had wrought.

Despite Marimba's new weapons, the experienced Masai were emerging the victors in their battle against her people.

"I think I must give myself to Nangai," she said. "I can bear no more blood to be shed in protecting me. I am the one he wants."

"NO!" Kahawa shouted. "I will not allow that to happen."

Seeing the determination on his mother's sculptured face, he approached her from behind and raised his club to her head, rendering her unconscious. Binding her with lengths of the kudu hide prepared for the slingshots, he hid her in a cave and rolled a heavy rock across the opening.

When he returned form his mission, he rid himself of the Night Howlers by hurling clubs and rocks into their burning red eyes. Then he faced Nangai himself.

"Show me where you have hidden your mother," Nangai shouted.

"You will not have her," Kahawa said, his voice strong though he was trembling. "If you were truly a god, you'd have found her yourself. I surely will not show you where she is."

Before Nangai could vent his fury upon the son of Marimba, there came through the night the sound of a new instrument, which became known first as the *karimba* and, later, as the *kalimba*. Accompanying it was the voice of Marimba, singing with such sweetness that the Night Howlers lost their scabs and became happy ghosts, the dead rose to dance, and Nangai returned defeated to the Land of Forever Night.

Such was the power of the sacred Song of the Kalimba, the instrument Marimba had built after being rescued from the cave where Kahawa had hidden her. Nangai had seen all of that with his own eyes. His ears had been too befouled with his own curses to hear the music and he had not seen what happened next from the darkness of his cave. He saw it now . . .

. . . Near Kahawa lay a sharpened ax. He bent to pick it up and used it to chop off his own right hand. Holding the bleeding stump on high, he begged the forgiveness of *Ma* and of his mother for having raised his hand against her.

"From this day forth, let this be your *siko,* your law," he said, his voice hoarse with pain. "If any among you should for any reason raise your hand against your mother, who carried you in her belly for nine moons and bore you, you shall cut off your own right hand."

As the night moved toward dawn, Nangai recounted all that he saw in his mind's eye. The words emerged as songs, so that when he was done, he had sung to Marimba all the melodies of her soul and of her heart.

Though she had not moved or interrupted, for the first time in a hundred years Marimba had heard her husband's voice. She had not tried to speak, but had listened instead as he sang the pictures of her life.

"It is time, my dearest husband," she said finally, taking Nangai's hand.

He stared at her, thinking he had gone mad. Lifting her in his arms, he sang of how, in the years that passed, she had fashioned out of the pieces of a snare the instrument of all instruments, named for her—the Marimba or xylophone. And of how she was named the Goddess of Music. And how, later, she fashioned the first drum from an old mortar and the fresh hide of a wildebeest and the *mukimbe,* a hand-xylophone, made of reeds.

When Nangai's voice trailed off into silence and the world of Lake Nyanza had returned to absolute stillness, Marimba again employed skills long gone unused.

Pointing at the surface of the lake, she sang of the golden sanctuary shining beneath the water, *"Beyond the plains of Tura-ya-Moya, deep in the heart of the Earth."*

HUNGER
by Nina Kiriki Hoffman

Nina Kiriki Hoffman has been pursuing a writing career for fifteen years and has sold more than 150 stories, two short story collections, two novels, *The Thread that Binds the Bones,* winner of the Bram Stoker Award for best first novel, and *The Silent Strength of Stones,* one novella, *Unmasking,* and one collaborative young adult novel with Tad Williams, *Child of an Ancient City.* Currently she almost makes a living writing scary books for kids.

The seventh time my father sold me, things changed.

My father was not an easy man to live with after the Goddess Demeter put a curse of insatiable hunger on him for desecrating her sacred grove. Groans came from him constantly, and he ate everything that looked like food, and, eventually, things that did not.

He was once king of Thessaly, before the hunger came on him; but he spent all our gold on mountains of flatbread and black grapes, figs, plums, dates, and pomegranates, eggs, smoked fish, and roast goat, and slabs of bacon, onions, and olives.

Taste did not matter to him. At first the palace cooks made huge meals for him, but they could not cook fast enough to keep up with Father's appetite. In the rage of his hunger, he went to the kitchens and ate uncooked bread dough and raw meat. He almost bit someone's hand off because she was holding an onion and did not release it fast enough. After that, the cooks fled.

My father ate my sandals. He ate dried flowers the slaves had arranged around the palace, and he even ate peacock feathers.

Mother left after Father ate all her undergarments and chewed the wax flowers off her favorite wig.

He would have sold the stones of our palace for handfuls of moldy grain. I managed to find someone who would buy the palace intact, but soon that money was gone, too, and we wandered the streets looking for discarded fruit in the gutters and begging lepta from strangers. We slept in a shack so miserable it had been deserted by everyone else.

I did not feel I could leave him; everyone else already had. I remembered the days when his eyes were clear, when he spoke to me of strategy and distant lands and art.

At night I lay listening to my father grind his teeth. His mind had vanished under the onslaught of his hunger. I was afraid to sleep; I had seen him salivate while staring at my toes.

Soon after that, my father sold me for the first time.

The man who bought me took me to his villa by the sea. He was old and harsh, but he only wanted me once a night, and during the day I played in the sand near the dark salty water. A host of slaves tended to the master's needs and the needs of the household, the vineyard, and the olive orchard. His cook made the most delectable things to eat; none of them were rotten; and my father did not try to snatch every morsel from my fingers before I could put it in my mouth.

Sometimes I thought of my father and wondered if my price bought him enough food to kill his hunger, even if only for a little while. I wished it so.

The honey cakes Theodora made every afternoon, the roast rabbit and fowl and lamb we had with bread for supper every night with sweet red wine, the dried figs and ripe apples always within reach filled out my flesh. When I pressed my fingers against my forearm,

I could barely feel my bones. My stomach no longer talked to me night and day.

I lived in a beautiful place where even the mosaics on the floor delighted the senses with shades and contrasts of brilliant glass colors. The air was warm here, and someone else did all the work.

And yet I had changed from starving freewoman to well-fed slave.

Some days I lay on the beach and scooped sand over my body, as though I could bury myself alive and emerge another person.

One day a large man rose from the waves and walked up the beach to stand at my feet. His beard and hair were the golden color of kelp, and his eyes were gray as fog. His skin was sunburned brown, and when he smiled down at me, his teeth gleamed like a slice of snow against a summer-baked rock.

"What are you doing there, daughter?" he asked in a deep voice.

The last thing I wanted to be to any man was a daughter. In the end I had liked that less than being a man's concubine. I did not know this man or what he might mean to me, so I said nothing.

"Did you know that this is a beach where gods wander?" he asked, and I shook my head. I had heard of places where gods and goddesses touched Earth and took mortal shape to wander among us and make trouble for those they encountered, and of other places where vapors issued from cracks into the depths, and gods' wills were made known to the sibyls who breathed the fumes, and emerge from the sibyls' lips in riddles and verses that only the wise could interpret.

Just such a place had been the grove where my father cut Demeter's trees for his roof braces. My father struck the first blow into an ancient tree that many had prayed to, and blood flowed from the wound. Then the goddess appeared as an old woman and begged him to stop, but he did not heed her. He had laughed and struck another blow.

I wanted no consort with gods.

I sifted more sand over my legs.

"Do I frighten you?" he asked, sitting beside me.

I slanted him a sideways glance. He frightened me, of course; but everything frightened me, more or less. Fear in me was a constant that only occasionally surged up into something sharp and prickling.

"Can you not speak?" he asked, and his concern seemed real.

"I can speak," I murmured without looking at him.

"What is your name?"

"Mestra." Once my name had meant something. No one used it anymore.

"Mestra. I won't hurt you," he said, and laid his big hard hand over mine on the sand. The heat in his hand surprised me. He lifted my hand and pressed his lips against my palm, and then a madness came over me so that I reached for him: he seemed to me like cold water in a desert.

What happened after was strange. It was as if I was not inside my body, or anywhere on Earth, but rather as though we were two liquids floating in some ocean, separate and then mixed together. It went beyond wine madness to someplace better.

For a while I was afraid to return to the shore. I stayed in the upper rooms during the day, embroidering borders onto robes and household linens, as I had been taught to do as a girl. After time passed and the ocean man did not come into the villa, I ventured out onto the balcony to do my needlework where the sun would help me pick out the patterns. Every day I thought about the liquid strangeness of melting into the man, and how I rose afterward in my own body without feeling at all hurt or worried.

It was ten days before I went back to the beach, and then the man came to me immediately, wet and glistening, as though he had been waiting and watching.

Days followed, all of a pattern: nights I went to my master, and days I went to my stranger on the beach.

A day came when the stranger sat beside me. "What are these marks on your shoulders?" he asked.

"My master beat me last night," I said. He had looked on me as I stood before him, naked; and he had touched me, and made me stroke him with oil and put my mouth on him; but his little stick had not lifted so he could poke it into me, and so he had beat me with a lash.

My stranger swam into the sea, came back with a small pottery jar, and stroked unguent into my shoulders and back. I felt soothed and comforted. We did not go to the mad place at all that day.

The next day, I had more marks. Even the ground-up corpses of insects could not make my master's stick rise. I hesitated to return to the beach. What if these blemishes proved to my stranger that I was not worthy of his attentions?

It was late in the afternoon when I finally went down to the water. He came and wrapped his arms around me, pressing me back against his warm wet chest. "This will not do," he said.

I shrugged in his embrace. What else was there?

"I am Poseidon."

I stiffened. What if I had done something to offend him? Would he curse me as Demeter had cursed my father? I could not think of any way I had been disrespectful to him except on the first day when I would not look at him or speak.

"I can give you the power of change," he said.

And so he taught me to turn myself into animals.

That night when my master called me in, and no undignified thing I did could make his stick rise, I watched him lift the lash to strike me, and I changed into a leopard.

He did not want me then; so I ran away.

I went to the beach and ran. Night was not dark! Stars shimmered in the night sky above me and all the scents were strong and inviting. I nosed small animals out from under the sand and ate them, crunching through shells to sweet, tender meat inside. I was free and wild. I danced in the wave edges, snapped at the foam. I raked my claws down tree trunks and leaped long distances.

Dogs caught my scent and barked as I ghosted past their masters' estates, but I only laughed, for they were tied up and I was free.

I slept on the beach and woke in my old body.

When dawn came, I was far from everything I had ever known; my leopard feet had carried me a distance I could not remember. I had passed other villas in the night, and gone through a forest that did not reach across the sand; and now, in the forest fringe, I could smell city smells, woodsmoke, body wastes, smithy fires and molten metal, meat roasting, bread baking, and the acrid scent of the dye works. I had no clothes or shoes and could not remember how to change back into a leopard.

I waited in the shadow of trees for a while, and saw the fishing boats put out from a harbor around a curve of beach. I wondered if Poseidon would be able to find me here. I longed for his embrace.

I waited out the day and the gnawing of hunger in my stomach. Images of honey cakes and the ripe red flesh of figs danced through my mind.

Even the little shellfish under the sand enticed me now, but I was not good at catching them, and I could not peel them out of their shells. I found a few dried apples on a tree in the forest where once an orchard had stood.

All day I waited, and my god did not come. He had told me that the other beach was a beach where gods wandered; perhaps there were many beaches where they never came, and this was one. Neither could I remember how to change into a creature that could be strong and brave and take care of itself in this world. As the sun lowered into the sea, I decided to go to the city.

I walked down the beach in twilight, following the little boats as they headed in after a day's harvest. I found the harbor where they went to tie up for the night and offload their fish. I waited until night had fallen entirely before I approached the docks.

On the beach where fisherfolk mended nets during the day I found a torn piece big enough to wrap around me. It did not conceal much, but it made me feel better.

One of the first people I saw in those dirty dockside streets was my father, gaunt and hungry, with eyes that burned. He stank of living too long with himself, and his clothes were filthy tatters. I would have walked on past, but he stared and stared at my face and said finally, "Mestra? Is that you?"

I knelt before him, holding my net around me like some captured thing. "Father. You look worse."

"I have nothing and less than nothing. How much my stomach hurts from starving! Can you help me?"

"I have nothing and less than nothing," I said. I touched his hand. Once he had given me a green pearl the size of my thumbnail, so beautiful I had spent half a day staring into it. We had traded it for a goat; but I still remembered the day he gave it to me.

"You have a father who needs you," he said, and because that was more than I had before I found him, I let him sell me again.

I knew my price would soon be gone, and my father's hunger would go unsatisfied. But maybe for a moment when he saw all the food he could buy, he would imagine it could satisfy him. Maybe that moment would be worth this.

The man who bought me this time was not so rich, and his villa had only one slave in it. She was glad of my help with household tasks; and he was not cruel to me, at least at first, though he wanted more of me than my first master had. Still, I spent some daylight hours on the beach.

Presently my god found me again. "Where did you go?" he asked.

I told him about my adventures as a leopard, my escape and not knowing how to find him again or how to change, and he taught me again how to be an animal. We spent sun-laden hours together. At night I went in to my new master.

For half a year all was well.

The something went wrong with my master's holdings, and his anger came out; his other slave was more valuable to him, so he struck me.

At least for a little while.

Until I turned into giant serpent.

I had not known the form I would choose; I found myself inside a strange body, and I saw that my master feared me. His mouth opened in a scream I could not hear, and he ran from me. I danced in that room where he had given me pain, danced with my scales sliding across the tiles, my tongue tasting the air of hints of sandalwood, cedar, and fear. How could a normal man master me? I danced my strange delight until the slave came in carrying a torch. She, too, was terrified, but she came toward me, brandishing her fire, and I fled out the window.

Before the dawn came I had swallowed a kid from my master's herd and found a place to hide and digest.

Sunlight brought me back to myself.

I made my way to the city.

This time, my father lay near death. For a little I considered walking away and never coming back, but he laid his hand upon my foot as I stood looking down at him, and I let him sell me again.

The seventh time my father sold me, things changed.

My new master took me home to the finest villa I had seen since leaving the palace. He gave me a slave of my own who dressed me and bathed me, rubbed me with scented oils, pumiced the calluses from my feet, ironed waves into my hair, and wound golden chains studded with jewels around my neck, wrists, and ankles. She perfumed me with essences of flowers and trees until I did not know myself.

Always when I went in to this newest master, I looked more beautiful than I had ever imagined possible, even when I was still a princess. Always this new master treated me as though I were a favorite wife.

A time came when I thought perhaps all my other lives had melted behind me, leaving me solid in this one so that I would never again have to remember the others.

Later a time came when my master Autolycus became displeased with me for some small thing, a pearl misplaced, perhaps, or one that did not perfectly match another.

The next night my slave, Lilla, did not put any jewels on me at all.

That night my master complained of the way my clothes draped about me, and the next night I came to him naked. The following night I came to him without any perfumes or oils, and the night that followed that I came to him with my hair unpressed and unbound.

This night I was just as I had been when he bought me at the market, except cleaner; if he complained of anything about me, I knew that as a woman, I would not be able to change it more to his liking.

"How rough your skin," he said, touching me. "How harsh your hair."

"I am as you asked me to be," I said.

"Yes," he said. He stroked his knuckle down my cheek.

"I have changed as I was directed," I said. "This is as essential a self as I have."

"And yet I have heard that you can change still more," he said.

"Oh?" My heart struck harder inside me.

"I have heard stories of men who thought they owned a woman but found that they owned a leopard, a serpent, a phoenix, a horned goat, a basilisk, a lion, a wolf."

"Strange stories,' I said.

"I heard that these men did not know what they had until they raised their fists in anger," he whispered to me. He stroked his knuckle down my other cheek, and then place his hand over my breast. "I wonder if there might be some other way to persuade you to change."

"Me?" I said.

"Are you not Mestra, daughter of Erysichthon?"

I stepped away from him, afraid of one who stared so deep into my history. "I am not," I said over my pounding heart.

"Are you not?"

"I am not."

He looked away a moment, then faced me. "Are you not Mestra Proteus?"

I could not deny it again; any truth thrice denied becomes a lie, with the denial becoming true.

I whispered, "I am."

"And do you change?" he asked.

I stared into his eyes and at first said nothing. I did not want to make this lie or truth. I wanted it to be unknown.

"Will you change for me? I do not want to hit you."

What will you give me? I wanted to ask. It was a strange thought. I did not want to give up my secret, my secret that could save me; what if I need it later? And yet . . . in my mind I was ready to bargain. A new thing.

"Change for me," he said, stroking my shoulders.

And so I did.

For Autolycus, I became a centaur.

He marveled, and thought me wonderful, even when I changed back into myself.

Later, when he was asleep, I lay and stared at the ceiling rushes. I thought about my lovers and my masters and their hungers. Some hungers fed me; because I satisfied their hungers, Poseidon had given me the power to change, and Autolycus had accepted my change as a gift.

I wondered if Autolycus would change the way the others had, and want to strike me when something went wrong. I still had change in me. I knew he could only master me so long as I let him.

He, too, had had thoughts in the night. In the morning he manumitted me, and when I was a freed woman, he asked me to marry him. I agreed.

We went down to the docks together. I did not know what I could do for my father: nothing could defeat the curse of hunger he lived under. Each time I had escaped a master and returned to my father, he had looked more gaunt and wasted, more fever-eyed and less in his own mind. Each time he sold me, I worried less about myself and more about him. Each time I wondered if he would be there the next time I returned.

This time was the last.

I gripped my husband's hand and stared. My father, dirty and skeletal, had pulled his foot up to his chest. He tugged his big toe closer to his mouth, and then he saw me.

"Mestra," he croaked. "What have you brought me?"

I gave him six loaves of bread. They disappeared inside him in an instant.

I thought, I can change. I can change into something so large it would take him a week to . . .

Then I knew I could not feed my father anymore.

We stared into each other's eyes for a long moment. He gaze dropped before mine did.

He lifted his left hand, thrust his fingers into his mouth, and bit down.

I turned away, pressed my face into my husband's

chest. I could not watch, but I listened as my father devoured himself, until even Autolycus could stand it no longer and we left.

There are some nights when I remember and long for the liquid fire of my unions with Poseidon. Then I think of unleashed hunger, and touch my husband's solid shoulder. Eventually sleep finds me again.

BOUDICCA
by Morgan Llywelyn

Morgan Llywelyn worked as a horse trainer, dance teacher, and a legal secretary before turning to writing. Her novels of legendary and historical Celtic heroes such as Brian Boru and Cuchulain have become famous all over the world for their attention to detail and characterization. Her recent novels include *Silverlight, Star Dancer,* and *Pride of Lions.* She lives in Ireland.

M ad. Mad, mad, mad. I am of course. Now. After Boudicca.

Once I was as sane as any man and more respected than most. A member of the tribe called Iceni, I also belonged to the intellectual class, the druids, who were revered by all the tribes of Britain. I was not a member of the inner circle of historians, lawgivers, and teachers who conducted our tribal college, yet men stepped aside for me on the forest paths and women looked at me admiringly out of the corners of their eyes. Even Boudicca did so, in spite of the fact that she was married to the king of the Iceni. Of course, that may be my imagination. Part of my madness.

Mine was the gift of divination. I could read the texts nature provided. By the whispering of leaves and the patterns of clouds I was able to foretell tomorrow. My saliva, spat into the breeze, shaped messages for me.

Some said it was magic.

In truth it was no magic, merely a talent, a gift of the head. My people brought offerings to pile at my feet, and in return I told them what they needed to know: were their mares in foal, would the grass recover from the drought, would they live long lives. They kept me busy and I enjoyed my status in the tribe. I served an important function; my head was valuable.

But not to Boudicca. She never visited me requesting divination.

She was proud, our queen. She claimed she could shape the future to her will. And for a long time, she did. Boudicca strode the earth as if she owned it and expected the grasses to bow down to her. When on occasion she failed to attend one of the rituals, the chief druid frowned and shook his staff at her, but she was impervious. Even his disapproval did not threaten her.

Like all of us, he secretly admired her.

From her strength the entire tribe of the Iceni drew strength. When Boudicca strode among us, tall and proud and arrogant, with her great masses of tawny hair hanging to her hips and her harsh voice like a war-trumpet, our hearts lifted. Forty sunseasons had tattooed her with freckles; forty snowseasons had drawn lines across her forehead. Our queen was a mature woman in her autumn, but we could imagine no winter ever claiming her.

Then, in the entrails of a dead stallion, I read her fate. I could not bring myself to tell her. The future I saw was unbearable to contemplate. As if some murky ooze were spreading outward from the swamp, a sense of foreboding came over me. For the first time in my life I resented my gift.

I sought other signs and took other readings, but the result was always the same. I drowned my fears in drunkenness; I walked the hills alone, and trembled beneath the stars until at last I convinced myself I had been mistaken. Druids are expected to be wise, but in refusing to accept the truth I was foolish.

Meanwhile Boudicca continued to float on the approval of the Iceni like some great swan on a lake, never looking down at the dark waters beneath.

The Iceni were a people of fluid shapes who dwelt intimately with nature. Then, a generation before the time of which I speak, the Romans had invaded the Isle of the Britons. They seized land, built towns that disturbed our forest gods and polluted our sacred waters, and demanded that the British tribes accept their authority. The armed might of the foreigners was impressive.

But we were warriors, too. Herders and farmers, we were also descendants of the Celtic warrior aristocracy. We bitterly resented the invasion; some of the tribes fought back.

The Romans won. The tribes they defeated were decimated and the survivors sold into slavery.

The Iceni were undecided how to respond to the invaders until our king, Prasutagus, declared we should formally acknowledge Roman authority in return for being allowed to live in peace. "We can continue to be guided by our own law," he said. "These Romans are not going to come into our fields and forests to see what we do. They are town people."

Prasutagus was not only a king, but also an old man and therefore credited with an old man's wisdom. The chief druid and the tribal elders supported his decision. If Boudicca disagreed, she never said so publicly. A wife was obligated to support her husband.

So we sent word to the Romans that the Iceni bade them welcome to Britain. Some Roman officers came to our tribeland, there was a little ceremony and a few speeches. The Romans said Prasutagus was a fine fellow with a vision for the future. Then they went away again.

For a while.

But as time passed, we observed that the Romans kept building their towns closer and closer to our territory. First their supply wagons appeared on our horizon; then their refuse was dumped in our meadows.

The Iceni tried to coexist with the foreigners. We even offered to share our wisdom, our knowledge of how to make nature work for us. But the Romans did not want what we could teach them. They scorned us as "barbarians." Imagine people who did not even have druids to keep them in harmony with earth and sky, scorning *us!*

Year by year, we watched Prasutagus bend the knee ever deeper to the Roman overlords until at last a dark muttering arose in the lodges of the Iceni. We resented. We smoldered. When we learned that a Roman army had wantonly destroyed the great college on Mona, the Isle of the Druids, a delegation of us went to Prasutagus and begged him to take up arms against the foreigners before it was too late.

I remember standing beside the council fire and watching the face of Boudicca. She and I were of an age, a full generation younger than Prasutagus. He was an old man who thought like an old man, and I saw the spark of contempt in her eyes when he refused to cry war.

"Rome is a fortress in another land entirely," Boudicca protested, speaking her mind in public at last. "We cannot see the Romans who live there. They cannot see us. Why do we allow any people so distant to have any power over us?"

"Because their power is here," her husband replied sadly. "In their warriors."

Boudicca lifted her arms, as strong and brawny as a man's, and held them high in the firelight. "My power is here!" she exulted. "I can match my strength and that of my people against any short dark foreigners!"

The young men of the tribe shouted and beat on their shields in agreement.

But Prasutagus would not listen. "I have no choice," he kept saying. "The gods are with them, their strength is too great for us. I have no choice."

At last she lowered her arms and stood, quiet if not docile, conceding to the will of the king. She knew the law. Boudicca was hot-tempered like all our race, but she was also a responsible woman. When she accepted, we all accepted.

I recalled the message I had read in the stallion's entrails but said nothing. Now I realize I should have. My silence at that time was my most terrible failure.

Within the change of the moon, Prasutagus was dead. He died in his sleep, an old man's death, and his two daughters wailed and sobbed and threw themselves across the battle-shield he had not carried for many years.

But Boudicca did not cry. She stood tall and proud, with something implacable in her face.

She is better off without him, I thought to myself. I never understood why she married him when she could have had any of us. Perhaps she wanted a husband who would offer her no competition. She certainly had that in Prasutagus, for all he was king of the Iceni. Boudicca was twice the man he was.

In the cubs of the wolf are mingled the spirits of both parents, however, and the daughters Prasutagus had sired on Boudicca were not as strong as their mother. They were comely and lissome, but neither of them was more than a face to look at and skin to touch. They were pale stars compared to the raging sun that was their mother.

At the next full moon, the chief judge of the tribe recited the will of Prasutagus aloud to his people. Even before he began to speak, I was aware that something was wrong. I could hear it in the night cries of the birds and the gurgling of the streams. The earth knew. The Mother always knows.

According to our custom, the druid lawgiver had memorized the king's wishes to the last detail so that he could repeat every word, every nuance, as if we were listening to the dead man speaking. That made the shock all the greater as he repeated, "I, Prasutagus, king of the Iceni, leave half of all Iceni land to the emperor of the Romans."

A howl of outrage reverberated through the tribe. Even I shouted; I could not help it.

The chief druid tried to calm us by saying, "The old king has taken the cautious path. He places us in the care of the Romans as a father bequeaths his children to . . ."

"No!" roared the crowd. "We are not his to give into slavery! And our tribeland was not his to barter to the Romans!"

Long-contained resentment boiled over like a cauldron on too hot a fire. "The Romans worked on him in secret," the old women claimed. "They took advantage of his age and addled wits. His will is not binding."

But the Romans thought it binding. They sent one of their generals to formalize the claim.

On a misty autumn morning Boudicca led the Icenian druids and elders to meet with the Roman. She intended to reason with him as one ruler negotiates with another. "There has been a misunderstanding," she told us. "We have dealt honorably with the Romans and never defied them; surely they will not seize our land now, not when we explain that it belongs to the tribe and cannot be given away by any individual."

Since the death of her husband Boudicca was leader of the Iceni, our Great Mother, second only to Mother Earth. How splendid she looked that day with her broad shoulders and her fierce eyes and her daughters on either side of her, testament to her fertility.

A Roman general arrived at the appointed time and place, accompanied by a large guard of swarthy men dressed in jointed metal. From beneath their helmets they looked out at us like so many predatory hawks. Their leader scarcely acknowledged Boudicca, nor did he offer her the gifts one leader customarily gives another. Instead he drew himself up to his full—and insignificant—height, and announced in a shrill voice,

"In the name of Catus Decianius, procurator of Londinium, and on behalf of Suetonius Paulinus, military governor of Britain, I proclaim this Roman territory!"

An infuriated Icenian hurled a spear. Its clever head slipped between the joints of metal armor and sank deep into the general's shoulder.

The Romans went mad then. They shouted at us as if we were a pack of wild dogs and attacked us.

Under Celtic law druids are exempt from battle. The wisdom in our heads is tribal treasure, too valuable to risk. So I was standing off to one side with the historians and the judges when more Romans appeared out of the fog and beat our tribal elders to the ground. Some of the soldiers ran over to where we stood and encircled us with drawn swords, penning druids like so many cattle. We could only watch helplessly as the Romans took their revenge.

They seized Boudicca, though it took six of their men to hold and subdue her. Then they tied her to a tree, stripped her tunic from her back, and lashed her with whips until she was covered with blood. Crimson gore matted her glorious hair. But she never cried out. Through it all she writhed against her bonds and kept twisting around to glare at the Romans. The look in her eyes should have turned them to stone.

When they tired of beating her, they spent their anger on her daughters instead. But not with whips. The girls were given first to the general, who managed to rape one of them in spite of the pain in his shoulder. But it was only a feeble attempt, what one would expect of a puny little man like that. Afterward, he gave the queen's daughters to his guards to use until there was hardly any life left in either of them.

This I stood and saw, while my heart turned rotten within me.

I can only imagine how Boudicca felt.

The Romans left the pride of the Iceni lying broken and bleeding on the breast of Mother Earth. Like a plague of locusts they swept through our tribeland, plundering and raping to show their contempt for us.

Boudicca's rage knew no bounds. She did not seem to feel the terrible injuries to her back; she was so consumed with fury that nothing physical could touch her. She and her daughters had been publicly outraged and her tribe humiliated.

When we learned that the Roman governor had gone to the far reaches of Wales, Boudicca announced a revolt. "Without its head, the Iceni shall break the snake's back," she said.

It was no small thing, declaring war on the Romans. For a generation they had been strutting across our island and shaking their spears in our faces. Nothing could intimidate Boudicca, however. The ignorant Romans, true barbarians, believed that death was the end, and so they were easily frightened. But we Celts knew the spirit was immortal. Only our bodies could be killed. There was no more the foreigners could do to hurt Boudicca than they had already done.

Now it would be her turn.

Even Boudicca could not challenge the Romans alone. When she needed help, she turned to me.

I was summoned to her in the gray time before dawn, when the spirits of the dead grow weary and stop watching us for a while. The fire smoldered on the hearth of the royal lodge; the air still smelled of the poultices the druid healer had applied to the injuries of the queen. Her daughters lay on their beds with their hair pulled across their faces in shame.

All I read in Boudicca's face was grim determination.

"The lion may look proud and disdainful in his tree," she remarked, "but it is the lioness who hunts."

If I had felt any sympathy for the Romans, I would have trembled for them then.

As I listened, she outlined her plans for attacking the Romans. Boudicca had no doubt that the Iceni would follow her, but she acknowledged that the support of the Otherworld was necessary as well. Nothing happens in the world of flesh that is not initiated by the world of spirit.

I started to tell her what I had seen of the future, and warn her. But when she turned her blazing eyes on me, I closed my mouth again. My vision must be wrong. The very sight of her convinced me that nothing could stand against her.

"Before I undertake to lead my people against these foreigners with their shaven faces, I must be able to assure them of victory," Boudicca said. "I will not commit our tribe to defeat. So from you I need a sign."

"Defeat and victory are two faces of one thing, great queen," I replied. "Like death and life, night and day. But I can tell you how to divine the outcome before the first engagement."

She leaned toward me then. I could smell her heated flesh and see the firelight trapped in her hair. "Tell me. Tell me, and you shall have the heads of our enemies as trophies!"

I concealed the shudder I felt. Something ancient and awful had come to life in Boudicca, for our people had not taken heads for generations.

Our warriors in all their glory, male and female together, went out to face the enemy. Plumes fluttered from their chariots; sunlight glinted off their spears. Boudicca personally drove a wicker war-chariot and carried the shield that had belonged to Prasutagus. She wore a tunic of many colors beneath a shaggy mantle fastened with a bronze brooch. A heavy gold torque encircled her neck, which she could swell like a man's in battle-rage.

I have never seen anything more beautiful than Boudicca on her way to war.

We druids accompanied the war party. Our poets and historians would see and mentally record everything that happened, to pass on to future generations.

I had a more immediate interest; I wanted to observe the results of our warrior queen's divination.

As was the custom, the families of the warriors followed in wagons containing their household goods. Whatever we did we did together.

Boudicca led the Iceni toward the nearest Roman outpost, a compound of plastered timber buildings with a wooden palisade. Before we reached the place, Boudicca signaled a halt within the shelter of a belt of trees. Then, according to my instructions, she loosed a hare from the folds of her tunic. "This hare is sacred to the goddess of battle," she announced. "Whichever way the hare runs, victory will follow."

The Iceni waited tensely as the little creature darted first in one direction, then another. I concentrated on the hare with all my might, clenching my fists so tightly that the nails dug into the palms until my hands filled with blood.

Blood is the best sacrifice.

Abruptly, the hare stopped and sat up. Its brown ears twitched once, twice . . . then it set off in a straight line for the Roman camp.

"Follow!" screamed Boudicca in her brazen voice.

Our warriors howled with sudden confidence. They fell upon the Romans and slew them all.

How splendid that first victory! How shining! The Romans bled and died like anyone else; they had no special magic. They were nothing to fear, merely foolish men who panicked and ran in terror when we unexpectedly descended upon them. We battered down their gates and their guards, we slaughtered them to the last man. We could not lose, for the goddess of war led us.

Boudicca led us.

That night she summoned me to her tent to thank me. Until the day I die I shall see her as she was then; magnificent. The heat of her skin, the firelight in her hair. . . . She was no young girl, Boudicca. But she gripped my two bloody hands and smiled at me the way a woman smiles at a man, and I left her tent to walk alone beneath the stars, dreaming wild dreams.

Like a fire in dry grass, the news of our success spread. The tribes of Britain need not bow down before the foreigners; land and honor were ours to reclaim. The warriors of the Trinovantes joined us even as the Roman officers in the east were trying to collect their soldiers from the scattered camps in which they were billeted.

Before they could do so, we marched on Camulodunum.

The civilian defenders of the Roman town made a desperate stand in the Temple of Claudius, where they hoped to hold out until the IXth Legion arrived to rescue them. They did not know that Boudicca had prepared an ambush along the roads leading to Camulodunum.

Our warriors cut the Roman legion to pieces. Unopposed, we destroyed the town and its two thousand inhabitants.

A madness seized us then, I think. Our warriors rampaged across the country, looting and burning Roman settlements. Any Briton who was suspected of being a Roman sympathizer suffered the same fate as the foreigners. As in the old days, there were trophy heads on poles and laughing and singing around the campfires. I was a druid, but for a brief time that summer I knew the joy of a warrior.

The tribe of the Durotriges, excited by our achievements, took up arms and overran the encamped II Legion.

Word of the growing revolt reached Paulinus. The governor returned from Wales at once and led a detachment of Roman cavalry toward Londinium.

Londinium lay directly in our path.

When Paulinus reached Londinium, he found its inhabitants paralyzed with fear. The procurator, Decianius, had already proved his cowardice by abandoning them to their fate and fleeing to Gaul.

"Even the mightiest of the Romans trembles at my name," Boudicca said to me, laughing.

I recalled the vision I had seen in the stallion's entrails. "Do not be too confident, great queen," I warned her. "Victory is the other face of defeat, remember. It would be wise to take care now, because . . ."

"Pthah!" she spat at me. In an eyeblink her fire turned to ice. "What are you trying to do, weaken me?"

I shrank away from her sudden and terrible temper, protesting my innocence. Perhaps if I had warned her earlier, when I first read the future, she might have been willing to be cautious. Now it was too late. And to be honest, the goddess of war had me in thrall as well.

"I have no doubts of your strength," I said, bowing low in acquiescence.

I could see my mistake. By opposing her, I had made her more determined than ever. I was but a man and she was a queen.

We marched on.

As Boudicca advanced, Paulinus abandoned Londinium to its fate and retreated toward the south, taking a number of citizens with him. Many of the town's inhabitants refused to flee, however, either because they were unable to do so or simply preferred to remain and fight for their property. Londinium was raw and new. It had no walls, no defenses; houses, villas, and warehouses sprawled across two hills on the north bank of the Thames. The location was ideal for offloading cargo from trading vessels, the source of Londinium's burgeoning prosperity. The Romans in their arrogance had never expected the cowed natives to attack.

But we were not cowed. Boudicca could not be cowed.

We set fire to the town and put its inhabitants to the sword. Some of our warriors visited upon the hapless Romans the sort of outrages that had been perpetrated upon our own people. When Londinium was a

forest of flames, Boudicca urged her people to move
on at once and attack Paulinus. But it was hard to get
the warriors to abandon pillage and rapine, for they
were mad with battle lust by that time.

"Why do they not obey me instantly?" a puzzled
Boudicca asked the chief druid.

"People will only follow a leader who takes them
in the direction they wish to go," he told her.

When we finally got underway again, the town of
Verulamium met the same fate as the others. Though
most of its inhabitants were members of the Catavel-
aunii tribe, they had given their allegiance to the Romans. We treated them as we had their masters. Again
there was an orgy of looting and the female Catavel-
aunii were hard-used. When their men tried to protect
them, they were killed without hesitation.

By now the druids estimated that some fifty thousand of the enemy had been slain.

Continuing to withdraw before us, Paulinus sent out
messengers summoning his remaining legions from as
far away as Deva. We intercepted some of the messengers, but others managed to get through. The Romans
were superb at the art of signaling over long distances.

I observed an owl flying toward us from the south,
presaging disaster. This bird above all others carries
dire omens. I felt obligated to warn Boudicca. "Through
wasting our days in taking vengeance, our warriors
have given Paulinus time to gather reinforcements," I
told the queen. "But it is not too late to turn back.
We have already won more than we ever expected."

She had grown haggard, and her eyes were sunken.
The campaign had been too long, I thought to myself.
Perhaps she would listen now. In her face I saw a
momentary softening which gave me hope. But then
she said, "Even if I wanted to retreat, I could not.
The people will only follow if I lead where they want
to go, so I am helpless."

I had never heard Boudicca speak in that fashion

before. The word "helpless" sank like a cold stone into my heart.

And so we went on to face Paulinus.

Roman and Briton met at the mouth of a narrow valley where the wily Paulinus finally chose to make a stand. The ground immediately ahead of us was open, encouraging the Icenians and Trinovantes to charge forward. The chariots went first. They were followed by foot warriors who ran in fine high fury, shouting insults at the enemy and brandishing their weapons. They made a great noise as was our custom in battle, but I observed that Boudicca was silent. She stood like a white oak in her lurching chariot, with her autumnal hair streaming behind her.

Above her I saw a raven swoop, hover, fly away.

"My queen!" I shouted in anguish. She could not hear me above the din of battle. I tried to shove my way through the throng and rescue her, but I could not get anywhere near her.

The Romans wheeled their cavalry in on us from both sides and proceeded to drive us into the valley. Sheer slopes on both sides held thousands of spear-throwers whose javelins rained death upon us. Then the Roman soldiers closed with us. In the press of bodies our warriors had no room to swing their greatswords; Roman shortswords sought their bellies. When it became obvious that we had no chance, some of our warriors tried to retreat, only to find the way blocked by the mass of our people in their wagons. The confusion was total.

By sundown it was over. Even the oxen who had pulled the wagons had been slain. Boudicca's two daughters lay dead among the warriors. They had fought, but not well enough.

At last I reached the queen's chariot, only to find it overturned and abandoned. I gnashed my teeth and tore my hair; I cursed my head that had not been wise enough to prevent this.

Then I found her. She lay almost completely hidden

by the chariot. Only a lock of her hair strayed out, lifting slightly in the rising breeze of evening so that it beckoned to me like a tawny hand. "Lie still, my queen, and I shall get help," I whispered.

"It is no use," she replied hoarsely. "One of my arms is hacked from my body."

"We can cauterize it with a torch. Our healers can . . ."

"No!" she interrupted me. "My people are defeated, my daughters are dead. Why should I wish to continue with this life? There is only one more thing you can do for me. Save me from captivity."

I knew what she wanted, in her position I would have done the same. Yet my voice trembled as I replied, "Do not ask that of me, great queen."

She stirred, restless with pain. "I do not ask. I command. The Romans must not be allowed to use my body as a prison for my spirit."

I went from her then and sought one of our healers. They always carry their stores with them; it was easy enough to obtain what I needed. Then I hurried back to the queen. I was terrified the Romans might find her first, but she was still concealed beneath the chariot.

I lifted it enough to be able to see her face.

She looked her age, and more, but she did not look like a woman about to die of her wounds. Boudicca was far too strong. That strength was her enemy now.

So I gave her the little vial I carried in my sleeve, then waited beside her while she drank its contents. Her lips twitched.

"Is it bitter, my queen?" I asked solicitously.

Boudicca favored me with her last smile. "Freedom is always sweet," she said.

They found me crouched beside her cooling body, beating my head with my hands. Or so I was told; I do not remember. Druids are supposed to have magnificent memories, but I have shed part of mine like a snake sheds its skin.

The Romans who took me captive thought I was mad and released me. The Romans believe the mad are god-touched. In time I made my way back to the land of the Iceni, though in truth it was ours no longer. Nor were many of my tribe left alive.

It is easy, almost pleasant, to be mad. I sit in the sun outside my lodge, and no one asks anything of me. On rare occasions when I speak aloud, I make little sense. I sit, or walk, or sleep as I will. Sometimes I plait my fingers. Sometimes I spit in the wind and make no attempt to divine anything from the spray.

I am just living out a life.

After Boudicca.

PESTILENCE
by Michael Scott

Michael Scott is an Irish writer who writes primarily horror and fantasy fiction. His novels and stories often have a strong Celtic thread woven into them, as does the following tale. Other novels by him include *Gemini Game* and *The Hallows,* as well as *The Tales of the Bard* trilogy, which includes *Magician's Law, Demon's Law, and Death's Law.* He lives in Ireland.

She was already falling when the slingshot-flung rock buzzed overhead; instinct, intuition, and too many years of surviving driving her down behind the skittish mount. The stone exploded off the cliff face, less than a handspan above the horse's head. It reared, metal-shod hooves pawing the air and Scathach rolled to one side to avoid being trampled. Another slingshot load—a metal ball this time—struck the saddle, slicing through the badly cured leather. The horse reared again, eyes wide, mouth frothing, prancing dangerously close to the edge of the narrow track. A third shot stung its rump, drawing blood, and the creature bucked, throwing off the supplies and blankets. Its rear hooves struck the ground hard, cracking the edge of the track, which sheered off. The horse screamed once, the sound high-pitched and human, forelegs scrabbling for purchase, before it slid over the edge and fell into the ravine below. It had stopped screaming long before Scathach heard it hit the bottom.

Two more slingshots rattled off the cliff face above her head, but Scathach didn't move; she knew her

attackers were unsure if they—or the prancing horse—
had got her or not, and were simply trying to force
her into making a move. The woman looked longingly
at the scattered remains of her pack on the trail almost
at arm's length. She could see the outline of the
Fomor blowpipe in the nearest bag . . . if she could
only reach it, she could hold off her attackers, or at
least reply to them. But the bag, for the moment, was
out of reach. If she made a move for it she would
reveal her location and expose herself to fire. The big
woman's hands went to the leather bag cinched tight
around her throat. At least she hadn't lost that. The
Lyonesse merchant who had employed her to carry it
northward had been insistent that it never leave her
presence. The swarthy southerner had then insulted
her by suggesting that she should not even attempt to
look into the bag, vaguely hinting that the contents
were cursed. Scathach wasn't interested; one of the
reasons she found regular employment as a courier
and guide was because of her reputation for honesty.

Scathach squinted toward the heavens; the sun was
low in the sky and storm clouds were gathering in the
north. It would be dark soon. Then she could slip
away. The woman smiled grimly. Once—when she had
been Scathach the Pitiless—she would have exacted
her vengeance on her attackers. But that had been a
long time ago; now she was perfectly content to escape
with her life. Cradling her head in her hands, she settled down to wait, idly wondering who had attacked
her. Brigands, probably. Since the death of Cuchulain,
her last protégé, Ireland had slipped back into law-
lessness. Pirates out of the Northlands, woad-daubed
savages from the east, blond-haired tribesmen from
the dark forests to the south had come across the sea
to seek their fortune into the now lawless land. Many
of them used slingshots, though it seemed unlikely that
they would have attacked someone like her—a single
rider, heavily armed, carrying no obvious baggage.

Brigands preferred their prey defenseless and preferably laden with baggage.

One of the native mountain tribes? Unlikely; they kept to the high valleys and rarely attacked travelers, and then only upon provocation. And they rarely used slingshots.

Army deserters? More likely. There had been mass desertions in this area over the past few seasons, western conscripts unwilling to fight for a cause they didn't understand, for a warrior-queen willing to sacrifice everything on a whim. Scathach's thin lips curled in distaste. She should have slain Maeve of Connaught when she had the chance all those years ago. If she had, then Ireland would have been a different place now, and many of the great heroes Scathach had tutored and trained in the arts of life and love and war would still be alive. When Cuchulain died, then the heart went out of her army and many simply turned their backs on her and walked away, leaving the battlefields strewn with their weapons and their honor.

The big woman nodded; she could easily imagine a small troop of army marksmen holed up in the mountains ambushing travelers. But if they were army marksmen they wouldn't have missed. She had seen army slingshooters bringing down a bird on the wing.

Easing her double-edged killing knife out of her right boot, she quickly mapped out her options.

They were depressingly few.

This was the high country on the borders of Ulster, unfamiliar territory to someone born and raised on the south coast. And even though she had traveled the length and breadth of Ireland and the lands beyond plying her weaponscraft, the only trade she knew, her travels had never taken her this far north, almost to the edge of the Ice Lands. Creatures that were little more than legend in the rest of the country roamed freely here; beasts that had become extinct in ages past survived in the hidden valleys and isolated caves. There were few human settlements hereabouts however, the Road Fever that had swept along the length of the Bothor Ri, the King's Road, in previous generations had devastated many of the towns and villages.

She spotted movement on the far side of the valley: across the ravine, hunched and twisted shapes scuttling through the undergrowth. She felt her chest tighten. Her opponents were not human. Were-folk, De Danann, Fomor, Fir Bolg, or Fir Dearg? She hoped not. A knife would prove little protection against an armored Bolg, and if she were up against De Danann or one of the Were-folk clans, she would not even see them coming.

A fist-sized green ball came sailing out of the sky and spattered against the wall almost directly above her head. She jerked back instinctively as thin green ichor dripped off the rock. Almost immediately, Scathach felt her gorge rise. The stench was indescribable: foul, bitter, a noisome mixture of excrement and urine, rotten eggs and rotting flesh. Moor pods. Another pod burst on the narrow path almost directly in front of her, sticky green pustules spattering across her jerkin. Ducking her head, Scathach gulped air and darted out onto the track, knowing that she had less than a score of heartbeats before the noxious fumes took effect.

Only Fir Bolg and Fir Dearg, the hairy stunted dwarves, could handle the moor pods with impunity . . . and this far north, both ate flesh.

The warrior snatched at her pack, and darted down the track, the edge of the path crumbling beneath her right boot. But even as she took her first staggering steps she knew she had inhaled some of the moor pod gas. The world was shifting, rainbow colors bleeding at the very edge of her vision, speckles of light dancing before her streaming eyes.

A slingshot chipped stone from the cliff face alongside her head, another struck her a glancing blow on the shoulder, numbing her entire arm, and then a puffy green ball exploded directly in front of her. Unable to stop her downward run, Scathach raced into its billowing cloud . . . and then stopped as suddenly as if she had run into a stone wall, and stood swaying. Then, slowly, she dropped to her knees and fell forward. With the last of her strength, she attempted to pull herself toward the edge of the ravine. Better to die clean then eaten alive. . . .

The face was hideous.

The hairless head was covered in leathery skin, the nose flat and piglike, the eyes yellow, speckled with broken veins, and the mouth was filled with tusks. "You should know that I am considered beautiful amongst my people." The voice was that of a young woman, high and pure, and all the more appalling because it issued from the creature's mouth.

Scathach struggled to sit up, grateful that the creature—neither Bolg nor Dearg though obviously kin to them—made no effort to help. The warrior felt sick to her stomach, her head thumped as if she had drunk a flagon of Gaulish cider and her right arm was throbbing. Drawing her knees up to her head, she pressed both hands to her throbbing temples and surreptitiously took stock of her surroundings. She was in a reed hut, circular in the Bolg fashion, but decorated with woven beads and knitted tapestries which were completely alien to Bolg culture. Beyond the walls, she could hear children's voices, the sounds high and clear against the gurgling backdrop of a fast flowing stream.

The monster moved forward and proffered a beautifully ornate stone goblet. "Drink. It will clear your head and stomach." She smiled at Scathach's hesitation, showing terrifying tusks. "If we had wished to harm you, we could have done so before now," she said reasonably.

Scathach nodded, dipping her head to hide her smile, knowing that some cultures took the baring of teeth as a threat. She sipped the green liquid. It was bitter, with a slightly chalky aftertaste.

"We make it from the root of the moor pods. It is only the fruits and pods which are poisonous; the leaves and roots have many medicinal uses."

"I feel better," the warrior admitted, straightening, turning to press her back against the wall of the hut. She was surprised to find her pack on the ground beside the straw pallet. She looked up at the creature. "I am Scathach," she said simply.

"And I am Moriath."

Scathach looked openly at the woman. She had traveled the length and breadth of Ireland, seen most of the myriad creatures that inhabited the land, but she had never encountered anything quite like Moriath. There was Bolg blood in her certainly, the Dearg Clan, too, in the shape of her head and the planes of her jaw, but her teeth were animal-like tusks, and yet her voice had all the pure tones of a De Danann mythsinger. She was wearing a long robe stitched and worked with countless thousands of beads and polished pebbles, similar to Tuatha De Danann fashion. Dearg and Bolg women usually went naked.

"I am of the Clan of Eriu."

"I've never heard of your clan."

"Few have," Moriath said simply. "We are a solitary people. We keep to ourselves, and have little commerce with the rest of the world."

"What happened on the mountain?" Scathach asked, leaning forward to drag her pack toward her. The woman made no effort to stop her.

"I'm afraid some of our young men got a little overenthusiastic. You will find everything is present," she added, yellow eyes flashing. "We are not thieves."

Scathach pulled out a small stone jar of salve and rubbed it on her grazed and scratched hands, wincing as the bitter astringent stung her flesh. But she had seen too many warriors lose fingers and even limbs because they hadn't cleansed even the simplest of wounds. "Do your young men usually attack lone travelers in the mountains?"

"Not usually," Moriath said. "But these are not usual times."

Scathach came slowly to her feet, swaying as the room shifted and spun around her. Moriath gripped her with a black-nailed claw, held her until everything settled. "You do not flinch from our appearance," Moriath said, "and yet I understand we are hideous to you."

"As I must be to you."

Moriath's smile was savage. "You are not pretty," she agreed.

"I spent two seasons sailing with the Island Bolgs. I never found them hideous. I had a Bolg . . . *companion* for a while," she said, choosing her words carefully. Rua had been more than a companion, but she was unsure how this woman would view such an attachment. In some of the Southlands, it was a capital crime.

"My people are cousin to the Bolg and the Dearg," Moriath said, turning away.

Scathach followed her to the door of the hut and looked out across a neat village of twenty huts, straddling either side of the fast flowing stream she had heard earlier. The village was enclosed behind a palisade of spiked furze. Children's squeals made her turn toward the water. Four children were splashing naked on the bank. Two were almost pure Bolg, another was hunched like one of the underground dwarves, and another had the flaming red hair of the leprechaun. The red-haired boy spotted the two women and came running up, moving around to stand behind Moriath, clutching her gown, peering at Scathach.

The warrior crouched and looked into the boy's bright green eyes. She smiled, keeping her mouth closed. "Hello? My name is Scathach."

"Mountain lady," the boy said, pointing to her and ran off.

Scathach straightened. "A fine boy."

"My son," Moriath said.

Scathach was unable to keep the look of surprise off her face. Bolg and leprechaun never interbred; the leprechaun clans had never forgiven the Bolg betrayal at the Second Battle of the Bridge.

"Look around you," Moriath said, walking away from the hut, forcing Scathach to follow her. "What do you see? You may be honest with me," she added.

"I see people, races, mixtures, the like of which should not exist," the warrior answered honestly.

"We are . . ." Moriath hesitated, ragged tusks chewing her lip as she sought for the proper word, "we are experiments."

Scathach felt a chill settle along the length of her spine. Such experiments had been outlawed since the Beast Wars.

"We are not freaks," Moriath said, "well perhaps we are," she added with a grin. "But think, in a generation, or two or three, if we can prove that the myriad native and magical races of Ireland can breed and interbreed, then much of the causes of conflict will have been removed."

Scathach's laugh was a harsh bark.

Moriath rounded on her, then abruptly stepped back, gaze fixed over the woman's left shoulder.

Scathach turned smoothly, hand falling easily to the knife in her belt. A human had appeared behind her. He was tall and thin, a shock of wild white hair contrasting sharply with skin the color of coal. The crimson jewel of one of the original De Danann Overlords winked in his forehead, and like most of his kin who had fled the Sinking Island of his birth, his age was unguessable.

"Our guest is a warrior, experienced in the ways of death and men. She knows it will not be so easy."

"In my experience people need little excuse for killing."

"True. But here," he spread his arms wide, "we are

trying to give them one less reason. Here we can see that many tribes and clans and their offspring can live in peace together."

"Attacking travelers is not very peaceful," Scathach remarked.

"Aaah, yes. There is a reason, but that does not excuse the action. I apologize. I am Alzion."

Scathach brought both hands together, thumbs to lips, forefingers touching the center of her forehead.

Alzion's smile was brilliant. "You know my race and customs."

"I spent four summers as bodyguard to the Boy King."

Alzion's smile hardened. He examined the scarred leather armor inset with metal rings and plates designed to turn a blade. Moving to one side, he examined the triple spiral tattoo high on the warrior's arm. "You are Scathach the Pitiless?"

"Once." The warrior stared into the man's black eyes. "No more."

Alzion nodded almost imperceptibly. "We all change. And how is my cousin?"

"He was assassinated three days after I left his employ."

"Aaah." There was a world of pain in the single word.

Scathach's smile hardened. "Those who usurped his throne did not live long enough to enjoy it," she said and turned away. "What brings a De Danann Overlord to this place?"

"What makes a warrior become a courier?" He nodded toward her leather bag. "Lyonesse work?"

"We all have our secrets," Scathach said, deliberately not answering his question. She looked around. "And this encampment is some secret . . ."

"Not for much longer," Alzion said. He reached for Scathach's arm, but his hand fell away when he saw the expression on her face. "My people are dying," he said simply. He led her to a hut that had been

separated from the others. He stopped before a white
line etched on the ground and pulled a cloth from a
bucket of pale white liquid. Pressing the square of
cloth to his face, he stepped across the line. Scathach
hesitated a moment before lifting a second cloth from
the bucket, covering her nose and following him.

The De Danann Overlord stopped outside the cave
and stooped his head to peer inside. Scathach looked
over her shoulder. There were six bodies in the hut.
At first she thought that they were dead, then she
realized that the blankets were moving slightly, fingers
twitching, veins throbbing. Moving inside, Alzion knelt
by the first body and gently lifted the blanket off a
young man. The medicinal square pressed to Scathach's lips suddenly tasted sour. The man's stunted
Dearg body was covered in weeping pustules.

"It started about ten days ago," Alzion said quietly,
wiping at the sores with a cloth. The man moaned in
his fevered sleep. "The elderly went first, we lost four
in one day, then we lost five children in two days. So
far the total is twenty-eight, and though the rate of
infection seems to have slowed down, we still lose one
or two a day." He tilted his head to look up at the
warrior. "The young men on the mountain weren't
trying to attack you today. They were trying to scare
you off." The De Danann's smile turned bitter. "Because you see, now you, too, are infected. And I'm
afraid that that means you can never leave this place."

Scathach always believed that she would die in battle. She had been little more than a girl—fourteen,
maybe fifteen summers—when she had had her palm
read by a cross-eyed crone on the eve of the battle
that would be remembered by history as Bloody Lake.
"I see you as an old woman, white-haired, withered,
with a sword in your hand, and a mound of dead at
your feet." There had been other rubbish about a husband and sons and daughters and riches aplenty, but

Scathach had believe none of that; she had wanted to believe that she would die an old woman.

Now she wasn't so sure.

She was more or less a prisoner in the village, free to wander around it, but not free to leave. Twenty-eight of the villagers were dead, six were dying, and another eight or ten were obviously ill. And yet the healthy remained to look after the others, even Alzion. But Scathach recognized the look in their eyes: an image she had seen in so many faces, the trapped, the besieged, the doomed.

The villagers were simply waiting for death.

Scathach walked along the riverbank with Moriath. The sun was low over the horizon, touching the distant mountains in purple, and the air was chill enough for the women's breaths to smoke even though it was still high summer in the lowlands.

"Have you ever had a disease like this before?" Scathach wondered.

"Never." Moriath shook her bald head. "The clan are remarkably healthy. Disease is relatively unknown here, and we've never experienced anything like this pestilence before. We grow our own vegetables and drink only from the stream." She lowered her voice and glanced over her shoulder. "Some of the people believe that we have been cursed, spell-cast, by the leprechauns, perhaps. The young men are recommending a sudden raid into their mining village to teach them a lesson, forcing them to lift the spell."

Scathach knelt by the water's edge, brushing the long grass with her fingertips. "I would not go up against the leprechaun," she said absently. "They are a formidable foe." She straightened, brushing her hands against her scuffed jerkin. "The people who first fell ill, show me where they lived."

Alzion was in the center of a group of heavily armed villagers when Scathach strode into their midst. One, a squat male with classic Bolg features, attempted to stand in her way; Scathach knocked him down without even breaking stride.

"I say we burn them out," someone shouted.

"Aye, block up the mines and smoke them out."

"Send marsh gas into the mines . . . that'll stop them."

"No!" Alzion's voice was a harsh rasp, but Scathach could hear the desperation in it. "We have no evidence that the leprechaun are behind this. None!"

"Only they know of our existence. It has to be them. Who knows what foul poisons they cook up in their deep mines. They have brought down this curse of pestilence on us."

"I say we burn them, burn them out. . . ."

"No!" Alzion shouted.

"You either stand with us or the leprechaun . . ."

"The leprechaun are not your enemy." Scathach used her battlefield voice, projecting a bark that could be heard all across the village.

"No one asked you." The speaker was a thickset Dearg holding a studded metal club.

Without hesitation, Scathach kicked him in the soft flesh beneath his chin, dropping him to the ground, writhing in agony. "If the leprechaun wanted to destroy you, they could have done so at any time. And if you go up against them, then they will destroy you. If you come with me, I will show you what has brought pestilence to your village." Pushing her way through the crowd, she strode away, not once looking back. Alzion hesitated a moment, before he ran after her. The rest of the villagers followed more slowly.

Scathach led the villagers along the banks of the stream, refusing to answer any of the De Danann Overlord's breathless questions . . . simply because she had no answers. If she had had the time she would have investigated her suspicions, but the mob had gathered too quickly, forcing her to act.

Scathach led them through the gathering gloom, and just when she thought that she might have been mistaken, she caught the faintest hint of foulness on the evening air, and knew, in that instant, that her supposition had been correct. She saw Alzion's nostrils flare and knew that he too had smelled the odor.

And then they rounded a bend in the stream.

Cathornach wurms were rare this far north, the horselike Dullahan even rarer. But ten days ago, the two creatures had met and fought. It was impossible at this stage to say who had got the better of the battle; neither had survived, and whatever wounds they had both suffered had been lost as their flesh had rotted away into the river where the fight had ended. Only the Cathornach's frill and the Dullahan's twisted horn and a portion of its skull remained as mute evidence of the battle. Scathach walked to the edge of the river and prodded the ivory horn with the tip of her boot. Bones, made brittle and soft by the rushing water, finally gave way, dipping the Dullahan's rotting head beneath the water. Pale fluids swirled in an oily pattern on the surface before they were dispersed.

"There is your pestilence," Scathach snapped, turning away. "No leprechaun poison, no magical disease, just nature." She looked at the villagers, "You would have gone to war—and been wiped out—over a pair of rotting carcasses." Shaking her head, she walked away. "You owe me a horse," she called back, "and supplies and water. Though not from the stream," she added.

THREE-EDGED CHOICE
by Ru Emerson

Ru Emerson is the author of more than a dozen novels, the majority of them in her *Night-Threads* series. Her other series is the *Nedao* trilogy, which includes *To the Haunted Mountains, In the Caves of Exile,* and *On The Seas of Destiny.* Recent books include *Huntress and the Sphinx* and *The Thief of Hermes.* She lives in Dallas, Oregon.

The current Baron of High Endsward was both ambitious and orderly, Liatt decided as she pulled a rough farm-woman's shawl over her head and stepped into the open food market. The barony had long been the butt of jokes, kingdomwide: a place where pigsties outnumbered hovels, where drunken inn-humor made much of the similarities between herders' daughters and the beasts they milked.

Whatever they had been in his grandsire's time, the current Baron Ognat's lands and city were clean and prosperous, the highland plateau holding a gaming-board of high-yield farms and herds, and a few quarries of gemstones. Liatt already knew that much, for reasons she preferred to keep to herself. But besides all that, she'd been with Gerik the Squat and his band of thieves the previous winter when the old fool decided to intercept High Endsward's tax payment to King Bhalor VI. To Bhalor's clerks at Castle Hold, in truth, because Bhalor was four hundred leagues to the north, leading the Kalinosan army against the Abitara's mercenaries.

Unfortunately, Gerik had forgotten the King's High-

way Guard was still very much in control of the Kalinosan roadways. He'd been hunted down, and seven
full moons ago, he and his entire inner council had
been executed. *Nice of him to pull such a stupid stunt
when he did,* she thought grimly as she eased through
the upper market, where a vigorous horse auction was
raising a din. *Those of us with any sense at all deserted
him as soon as we had our share of the take.*

The others had probably moved on to other bands
of thieves, or gone freelance, robbing drunks staggering out of taverns or snatching purses in markets
as busy and prosperous as this one. She, on the other
hand, had sized up the situation, decided road theft
was a self-eliminating occupation and gone in search
of something that paid better and was less likely to
cost her a hand—or her head.

Unfortunately, for a poor and plain young woman
of uncertain purity and a shadowy past, the choices
weren't that many, or that good. *I'm not bargaining
with my body ever again, unless it's that or starve, and
I absolutely will not herd or farm.* Older men with
good-sized holdings and no one to help work them,
no heirs, weren't picky about dowries *or* purity, but
they and their families wore themselves into their precious dirt. *Fine, if they want it. I don't.*

Besides, it would be a waste of the past two years:
Thanks to determination and wit, she'd earned the
right to take care of herself. Barely twenty, she knew
half a dozen good throws, was reasonably accurate
with a bow, and deadly with a thrown knife. Her size
worked in her favor for the rest; no one expected a
small-boned young woman to be strong or deadly, let
alone both.

It had taken time, half her share of the tax money,
and all her powers of persuasion to find someone willing to nominate her to the Assassin's Guild. Once the
Guild actually accepted her as a trainee, she'd moved
quickly into Apprentice Class. Only four others had
ever completed their ten preliminary kills as quickly

as she did, but for Liatt it was a test: the other four were all Grand Masters. And she wanted Apprentice level behind her. Apprentices had no say in the style of kill, suffered the presence of a Guildmaster at all times, and were paid only as much as the Master decided the work to be worth. Guildmaster Nykos reeked of onions, was notoriously stingy, and had strong views on how female assassins should work—either as bait or distraction, getting the mark drunk or in bed so someone else (male) could kill him.

Still, her seventh went down on her dagger, much to Nykos' annoyance: The mark had proved to be less drunk and more wary than he was supposed to be; she'd actually thrown the knife hoping for a distracting wound and been as surprised as anyone when the mark went down, dead before he hit the dirt. Nykos had petitioned the Guild to scratch the kill from her record, since she'd disobeyed his orders, but Aloric, the Journey who'd been going for his fifth, insisted she get both the point *and* the coin. The corner of her mouth twitched as she worked her way through a crowded grain market, eyes constantly moving, watching those around her. Aloric was somewhere well to the south these days—full Assassin and working the border between Kalinosa and Jaddeh. In the king's service, yet.

She tamped the thought firmly. *Probably die out there, too, Liatt. Life's short and brutish, doing what Aloric's up to. He wouldn't come back to you, anyway; he likes his women soft, pale-haired, and brainless.*

Journey level, she reminded herself firmly as the crowd swirled around her and the odor of roasting pig touched her nostrils. Journey was bearable: No Nykos, who was too arrogant to work with anyone but the readily cowed Apprentices. And while her first three Journey kills were accompanied, she'd had free choice of master, a set percentage of the coin—and a sense of responsibility for her acts: the master only intervened if she asked it, no matter what her peril. And now, with her fourth—

Fourth kill, Liatt thought, and a grim smile briefly quirked her mouth as she edged between two bakers' stalls and into a shaded square surrounded by tall dwellings.

From four through seven, she might be monitored, but effectively, she stood alone from now on. From this kill through ten, she'd still be working for stingy clients who paid less coin to have a Journey Assassin picked from the pool of talent, rather than a full-cost, full-title Assassin chosen by name. Liatt intended to earn *her* name well before her tenth Journey kill.

And not just a name for those Apprentice kills either, she promised herself. She'd been stunned when Nykos had made clear what her role was expected to be, even after Journey level. The fact was, however, almost all seventeen Guildswomen went out on "soften-up" assignments: to seduce the target or get him drunk, let someone else do the messy part. Most of those she'd talked to wanted nothing different. *Not me,* she promised herself again. *When I'm Guild, I'll have the title Assassin honestly.*

She turned left from the square and once again was part of heavy foot traffic; the greensmarket of Sward-on-Grau was in full swing, money and grocer's-goods changing hands everywhere. A small, dark woman clad in clean but shabby brownspun (bought first thing in the used-garb market at the edge of town), a basket of (stolen) eggs over one arm, shouldn't attract any unwarranted attention, she'd thought earlier, and it seemed to be true.

She'd already had opportunity to do what Grand Master Loryn impressed on his eager young Novice Assassins: Check the lay of the land, assess the potential danger from guards and dead end streets or market crowds, find the best exits, then go over things again, reassessing the situation once the purchaser of death at one remove named his or her target and handed over half the funds. Not every Purse (as the Guild called such buyers) was to be trusted—though it was both foolish and fatal to try to play tricks on the Guild. Even King Bhalor respected the Guild and its rules, imposing only a few of his own over them.

Liatt knew the best way to reach the impoverished and nameless tavern in the cheap quarters, where the Purse had agreed to meet her; she knew both the dangers and the safeties built into his choice.

For herself, at least.

By the time she reached the dry and crumbling fountain square where the tavern sat, she'd shed the cloak and eggs, and the hilt of a thin-bladed dagger rested comfortably against her palm, the rest of the weapon out of sight in her sleeve. There'd been some raucous drunks here late the previous night, including two who'd thought a short, slender woman in breeks to be an easy mark. She'd managed to avoid actual bloodshed, and she didn't intend to provoke a fight now; she doubted the Purse would want that kind of attention called to his Assassin. *Never hurts to be ready, though,* she reminded herself, and slipped through the narrow doorway.

The place smelled no better than it had the night before; if anything, the heat and lack of breeze made it worse. She ordered a mug of ale and settled her back against the far wall, where she could watch the decaying fountain and its square.

The ale itself was surprisingly good: dark, thick, and bitter. Except for the taverner and a filthy old man passed out beneath one of the benches, she had the place to herself. *Sometime between second and third bells,* the message had said. She eased one of her belts of throwing knives, quietly freed the two blades that pinched and settled them under her thigh, where they'd be easier to grab, then took single sip of ale before shoving the cup side. A sensible assassin kept a clear head and this was an anonymous client. Master Edon had narrowed the possibles to four, and "Tricky," was the best word he'd had for any of them.

He must think highly of me, to send me on such a kill even after I declined an overseer, she thought with satisfaction, and settled her shoulders against the wall to wait.

She didn't have that long to wait. Coarse laughter brought her upright and alert as a tall, raggedly-clad, and hooded person stalked imperiously through the square and around the dry fountain. "Slumming, yer lordship?" someone hooted from back in the shade; a chorus of jeering laughter followed. The ragged figure froze briefly, then spun about. More laughter as he suddenly seemed to recall himself; his shoulders slumped and head lowered, he moved with a stumbling, awkward shuffle, making his way into the tavern.

Liatt swore under her breath: The size and shape of the fellow was unmistakable, as was that walk of his. *Horta-Baron Ylfer, younger son—he used to be as arrogant as he was stupid, and that hasn't changed, I'll wager.* He wasn't on Edon's short list of likely purses, but unfortunately, Ylfer was trickier than anyone *on* the list.

She had a bad feeling about this kill, all at once. Nobles weren't supposed to make use of the Guild, by King's Decree and Guild rules and a noble agreement that came down to, "You won't and I won't." In actuality, the agreement meant nothing, and nobles did what they wanted, particularly now, with King Bhalor in the field. Ylfer was going to be bad news all around.

Particularly if his memory was any good.

She settled against the wall once more, daggers a hard presence under her right thigh as he stopped just inside the tavern door and swept the hood aside. His glance touched her briefly, moved on the shadowy interior, then passed dismissively over the fallen drunk and the taverner. He crossed to where she sat and gazed down at her through narrowed eyes.

Silence. He broke it finally. *"You're* what they sent?"

She shrugged, spoke in her lowest and most common-sounding voice. "You want a choice, you pay more for the privilege. Sit. I don't need a strained neck."

Eyes never leaving her face, he fumbled a bench under his legs and sat. The old drunk suddenly belched, snorted loudly and rolled onto his side, breaking the moment. "You have the proof?" Ylfer asked; sweat beaded his forehead and he looked nervous, all at once. For answer, Liatt slid one of the daggers from her sleeve, enough that he could see the Guild-marked handle, and pressed it back into place. But before she could say anything else, his eyes went wide. "By all the gods together, I don't believe it," he breathed. "You're the Ducina—Eleanora, Grand-Duke Harkin's lass!"

Damn, she thought tiredly. But the moment had been inevitable, here or elsewhere. She shook her head. "No. There *is* no Ducina, Grand-Duke Harkin no longer *has* a daughter; everyone knows that."

"Everyone knows he lost his fabled temper with her and wed her to the gods instead of my father," the young noble protested. "And I remember you, Ducina: the king's harvest banquet, three years ago."

"Unlikely. Members of the Assassin's Guild don't get invitations to royal banquets. Look at me, noble-man—I'm no pampered lady. No Ducina for certain."

Ylfer snickered, but his eyes were fixed on hers. Apparently he'd forgotten he was sitting with his back to the doorway of a shabby tavern in a bad part of his father's town and baiting an assassin. "You don't *look* like a ducina. Not the way she'd look now either. She should've known better than to tell old Harkin she wouldn't have my beloved papa; she's lucky the old brute didn't toss her out the window and into the river." He chuckled, eyes straying beyond her. "That was rich of him, selling her to the Sisters of Chastity— there's a name for you, considering how they earn their bread! Wonder how she felt about all those visiting priests . . ."

"Don't imagine," Liatt snarled and sprang; Ylfer gasped as her hip slammed down onto the table and her face was suddenly no distance at all from his. Between them, the tip of one of her slender-bladed daggers rested gently against his throat. She smiled coldly; he swallowed. "*My* name is Liatt—and if you're the one who made the contract, I need to know who and where, unless you'd rather wait here long enough for us to be seen together by someone other than those two." A jerk of her head took in the taverner, who was carefully not looking their way, and the drunk, who groaned, shifted slightly, and subsided onto his face again.

"Liatt," Ylfer whispered; he rubbed his throat as she settled back on her bench and stowed the knife out of sight, under her leg once more.

"Good," she replied softly. "Who and where," she reminded him flatly.

"My brother—"

He got no further; Liatt swore under her breath and the look on her face silenced him. "You know King's Law! The Guild gets good leeway for its business, but, damnit, taking part in a noble feud or killing a ruler or his heir is *not* acceptable!"

Ylfer eyed her nervously, but the set of his chin was defiant. "You don't know *who* he is, just that he's my brother; I haven't told you my name *or* his!"

"*You* may be stupid, but we're brighter than that," she cut him off. "The contract is void as of now, if that's what I say. The guildmasters will back me, and you'll still owe half the fee." He stayed quiet but he still had that stubborn look to him. *Damn,* she thought. But the young idiot was correct, he hadn't named names—his own *or* the chosen victim's. And she had reasons of her own to know the baron's heir to be a cold-blooded brute who'd make a terrible baron—worse than his father, who was at least a good administrator. *You swore from the time you left your father's halls you'd have nothing to do with politics ever again!* she angrily reminded herself.

An Assassin who wanted to reach a comfortable old age would remember that.

Ylfer must have taken her silence for agreement on some level; he began talking again, avoiding her eyes. "Say he's a man who owes me money, gambling debts—that's true, by the way, he's always been a lousy loser, ever since we were . . . since we first met," he finished hastily as Liatt cleared her throat. "He spends four nights of a five-day at a gambling den, the Blue Feather."

"I saw it earlier," she replied. "Only a fool would go to a place like that after dark, and whatever else he is, this *gambler* of yours isn't a fool."

"He has a reputation and certain skills with weapons; who'd dare attempt to rob him? Also, if the baron's heir—" She chopped a hand and he fell silent. After a long moment, she gestured for him to go on; he swallowed, licked his lips, and lowered his voice. "Your people aren't gods, they make mistakes and kill the wrong mark."

"Guild members who make mistakes like that—like *this*—don't earn or keep top ranking," she snapped. "I've got a career to think of here. If you want this—acquaintance dead, why don't *you* kill him?"

He sneered but he'd gone ashen under the neat beard. *He's afraid—no surprise there.* "Because that's not *my* training," Ylfer said. "People like me are the reason people like *you* have a calling, or didn't you know that? Now, a man emerging from the Feathery into the shadowy alley exactly at fourth night-bell . . . ."

"Be quiet so I can think," she growled and leaned back, tapping the tip of a dagger against her teeth as she thought. *It could work. I'd have to tell Master Edon the truth, because he knows my past, but that would be between him and me. He wouldn't give me away.* She didn't think he would. *Bottom line is, I get Fourth Journey Kill, and Kalinosa is rid of one of its nastier young nobles.* She eyed Ylfer with open dislike for a long moment, then slid the dagger up her sleeve and held out a hand. "Half the purse now, as agreed. No names mentioned. The other half—"

". . . on completion," he said as she hesitated over when and where. Her eyes narrowed. "I'll be nearby, did you expect anything else?"

"I shouldn't have," she mumbled. Of course he'd be there to watch; his kind always were. "I warn you, though: Any interference, anything you do to get in my way or get the attention of the guard: If I can't complete the contract because of your presence, you still owe the full purse."

"You'll get it," he said, and handed over a plain woven pouch. She hefted it experimentally and her eyebrows went up. Ylfer smirked. "Twenty gold crydantans and ten silver, half the purse now, as agreed. The other three cyrds are for—call it your trouble."

"There'd better be no trouble," she warned once again as she stuffed the purse in her shirt and leaned back. "You leave now—I'll make certain you're not watched." It was a good choice of words; the smirk was gone for good and a moment later, so was Ylfer. Outside, she could hear someone laughing, deliberately rude, as the hooded Horta-Baron stumbled past the dry fountain, but no one else seemed interested. Inside, the tavernkeeper was hammering the tap into a fresh cask, and the drunk was snoring softly.

Ylfer was no longer anywhere in sight. Liatt took another sip of her ale, set a copper next to the mug, and left.

The market was busier than ever, much hotter and muggier. She bought bread rolled around a highly spiced fish stew and ate it as she walked, moving without any apparent goal. By the time she'd finished the meal and rinsed sticky hands, the food market was nearly behind her—the armorer's booths just ahead. There'd been a matched set of dueling daggers at one that had caught her eye the night before. The Guild never begrudged its members coin bonus, and she had good use for hers.

The blades were still there—the weaponer at the far end of his counter, talking to a solidly built man in a broad-brimmed hat, but as she settled her elbows on the rough surface, he came up at once. "Still like the look of those, eh?" he asked.

"Price is still twenty silver?"

"Each," he reminded her firmly. "Here," he added. "Come back into the stall so you can handle them—blades like those, I can't allow out where they might be snatched and run with, you take my meaning. . . ."

"Taken," she assured him as she ducked under the counter and let him free one of them from the complicated knot he'd used to tie it to the center post. She knew all too well how easy it was for an accomplished thief to catch up expensive goods in a crowded market and vanish with them; *did it enough times myself.* At a distance the weapons had caught her eye; held, they were exquisitely balanced, the blades thin, beautifully edged. . . .

"Fine, aren't they?" the merchant asked finally. Movement out of the corner of her eye brought her around, but too late: The solidly built fellow moved faster than his bulk would've suggested, and he had her right arm in a hard grip; at belt level his free hand held a short, wide blade ready to use. The merchant faded back and eased out of the way.

"My man was right," the newcomer murmured. "He said my brother met with an assassin who wasn't what she seemed."

Hells, Liatt thought tiredly. She'd never have known the Fis-Baron; Ogaden was nearly twice the size he'd been the last time she'd seen him. Mostly fat, she thought, though he had muscle in his hand. His piggy little eyes hadn't changed, though. Or the intelligence behind them; it wouldn't do her any good to use the line she'd used on Ylfer. "Which of the two?" she asked finally. "I'm betting the taverner's what he seems, but that drunk wasn't." Ogaden smirked. "Now what? Keeping in mind that I'm a member of the Guild and . . ."

". . . and if you simply vanished, no one would be able to lay blame to me, would they?" he finished as she hesitated. "I know how to make a body disappear."

She looked down at the hand still hard on her right biceps, and eased the tip of the dueling blade between her sleeve and his fingers. He withdrew the hand. "I believe you. Since I'm still alive, I assume there's an alternative?"

He shrugged. "There is for most things, isn't there? You keep the purse Ylfer gave you, you dispatch Ylfer—"

"Let's avoid names," she said flatly. "You may not take Guild rules to heart, but I do."

"Always thought you were wasted as a duke's offspring," Ogaden said, and his smirk was unnervingly like his brother's. "I said at the time Father petitioned the grand duke for you that it would be a good match; he'd slap you once and you'd cut his throat that night. Would have saved me two years of heirhood. All right, no names mentioned," he went on evenly as she bared her teeth at him. "You keep the purse, and for an additional purse filled to match, you kill the man who sought my death. Three times that amount in total, if I can also persuade you to kill that man's father. . . ." She stared at him blankly, and he laughed. "Say that the one who stands to inherit the family goods grows bored with waiting, and add to that, the father in question has a new bride who supposedly carries his next offspring. And this bride is daughter to Duke Edryc, who, you may know, is duke of the lands encompassing all the local baron's holding. So if this female is growing a son, I might be—I probably *will be* supplanted. At best." Again that unnerving smirk. "Don't look at me like that—hells, what am I supposed to call you? You can't still be naming yourself Elea-ah—ah—?"

"It's Liatt," she broke in flatly.

"Liatt. Well, Ducina Khemi's father may have been less than a natural father, pledging his only daughter to a man who was wed before, is his own age, and has two sons. Still, the most prominent ducina in all Kalinosa had a father considerably worse; imagine sending your own blood to the so-called chaste nuns of—" Something about the look on her face stopped him. He shrugged. "I can only assure you, Baron Ognat is—"

"Save it," she hissed. "You're spending time, and I prefer not to be so much the center of attention. It's in your interests to convince me the man you want me to kill is less than human, and frankly, I don't care."

He laughed sourly and released her arm. "Point taken. Though I assure you I underestimate him, if anything. And you'd better not, if you're wise. Well, then. You agree to the task, the coin is guaranteed; manage things quietly, and the blades are yours—a gift from the grateful new Baron of High Endsward."

"And if I don't agree, I'm found dead in ditch?"

"Parts of you—perhaps," he replied carelessly.

She considered this briefly, her face expressionless but her mind a roil. Finally she shrugged. "I need to think it over."

"Think now," he replied flatly. "You agreed to Ylfer's plan, took his coin; I even know where you stowed the purse. And for what? A single Journey kill, a dark street in the midst of the city, where a guardsman—a handful of them, even—might be lurking?" Silence; he eyed her sidelong and she grimly gestured for him to go on. "Someone entering the hold via a balcony I can point out, just at fourth night-bell, takes little or no chance at all of being discovered: The servants are asleep, there are no guards in the family halls or apartments . . ."

". . . and if you've set me up, I'm in a damned unexplainable situation, aren't I? In that alleyway, I could claim mistaken identity—but not in the baron's apartments."

"I thought we weren't going to name names," Ogaden smirked. "And I could run you through, here and now, with the information my man brought me from that tavern—the Guild might protest but it couldn't legally act, and why would they, on behalf of a mere Journey assassin?" She turned away from him, staring across racks of blades without seeing them. "This way is sure, and if you don't trust my word—well, I don't exactly trust yours, either, do I? But I have no reason to get you into the holding, if I'm lying. There's every reason for me to want you there, and ready to act, if I'm not. And you have two more kills under your belt, instead of one."

She turned back to meet his level gaze and held out a hand. "One of the blades now."

"Both when you complete the contract," he began, but she shook her head, silencing him.

"One now—for the risk involved." He considered this momentarily, his attention brought sharply back to the moment; she had freed a sleeve-blade and the point rested against his belly, below the belt. "You can kill me, of course," she added softly. "Or try to. You won't come away unblooded, though. So I suggest a pact. You trust me as far as I trust you . . . which means you keep the front half of the purse you would ordinarily give me now. I get the blade."

He seemed genuinely startled, both by the weapon pressing against his trews and her choice. "Why?" he asked finally. "A wretched dueling dagger instead of a coin?"

"Oh, I'll earn the coin *and* the other blade," she

replied softly. She smiled, a turning of lips that didn't encompass black eyes. "Late tonight—fourth bell, isn't it? I'll meet you just after dark, outside the holding wall, south of the fourth guard niche, the one that's soot-stained from fire, you can show me this . . . 'special' entry. You'll be alone, if you're wise, because the night is more my friend than it is yours, and I won't be looking for more company than yours. As to the dagger—well, Fis-Baron, I like knives." She waited, but she knew she had him—his eyes were everywhere but meeting hers, all at once. He swore under his breath finally, flipped the beautifully balanced silver weapon end for end and held it out, hilt first. She took it, flipped her own dagger back into its sleeve cache and stepped back, gesturing with her new long-bladed toy. "After you," she murmured, and waited until he was gone, down the crowded passage between weapons stalls. The stall owner was eyeing her nervously. She held out the blade. "Gift to me from the man who chose your stall for a private conversation," she said.

"Ah—ah, so he told me."

"If you'd care to hold it for me, however . . ."

He was practically stuttering in his need to see her gone. "Oh, no, of course not—yours, if the—the gentleman says it is. The other—if you'd like it now, if you'd—"

"No, he set a bargain that I'll keep," she offered him a teeth-only smile that made him blink. "Pray your—your 'gentleman' does the same, sir." She brushed past him, dueling blade in hand, then ducked under the counter and merged with the crowd.

The blade was awkward to stow; too long for a sleeve or leg holder. *Should have taken the leather harness—I'll get it with the other blade, that's good enough.* It wasn't good enough, and she was irritated with herself: An Assassin who'd been at the business long enough would have thought that out before leaving the weapons stall and she'd feel stupid going back

for the harness now; the stall owner would think her
a fool. *Remember for next time,* she told herself angrily
and kept going. Properly mounted, the long blades
would cross between her shoulder blades and rest
nicely under her cloak, both hilts in easy reach. For
the moment, however—she finally tucked it under her
left arm, the hilt protruding from beneath her armpit,
the tip resting against her forearm and ribs, but since
the short cloak hid that side of her body, it didn't
matter.

She spent the next two hours making certain she
wasn't followed, then arranging for her horse to be
ready just short of daybreak, and finding a light meal
in a small bread-and-wine shop near the river. The
idea of eating never appealed much when she was
about to execute a contract—but the need for strength
and an alert mind was there, no matter what. Today,
she had to force herself to finish the bread and soup.
*Tonight, I take what I've always thought of as a real
contract: No quiet death by poison or by someone else
once I've compromised the mark and left him for someone with a blade; no thrown dagger across a shadowy
alley.* She'd never killed on a "real" contract before.
But everyone had a first; not everyone had an exciting
story to tell about the first either.

She wiped the soup bowl with the last of her bread,
took a second swallow of the sour wine that had come
with it, and left to find a niche overlooking the baron's
holding, where she could hide until full dark; she
needed to think—and plan.

The niche proved to be the flat roof of an abandoned smithy; the platform under her was rickety in
places, solid in one corner against the far wall, shad-
owed against late afternoon sun by a pile of brick and
other rubble. She sat with her back against a long
beam, feet drawn up, and rested her chin on her
knees, eyes fixed absently on the gray-stoned walls,
watching as an occasional marksman walked along a

sheltered ledge just down from the roof. The man, or men, seemed to be there for appearance—gods knew they didn't look very alert or interested in what they were doing, and the halberd one carried was an awkward thing that would be of little use as a weapon.

Trust no one, she thought, and grimaced. Master Edon had put her in an awkward position, all unknowing, in giving her the contract. *I did a better job of that, taking it, even after he said it wasn't one he'd normally give a Journey Assassin, even though the coin wouldn't pay for anyone above that rank.* Ylfer had complicated matters vastly by offering her an unexpected choice—and then Ogaden and *his* offer. . . . She shifted her weight and sighed quietly. The best thing to do right now would be to get her horse and ride out immediately, reach Guild quarters and tell Master Edon everything. A sensible, prudent Journey would do just that. *A sensible Journey doesn't have a past like mine, hasn't come up against two who'd know me by face, and doesn't have my reasons for liking the notion of killing snotty nobles for coin,* she assured herself, and settled back again.

Fourth bell would be just after middle night. A reasonably prudent Journey Assassin would be in place once full dark covered her steps, and she'd spend the time constructing possible events once she got inside— and also make certain Ogaden wasn't simply planning a surprise of his own. For her.

But fourth night-bell had come and gone, and she could make out a line of blood red along the eastern horizon; the opening spilled light onto the passage below and still no sign of Ogaden. *Damn,* she thought angrily. *I knew something would go wrong.* A sensible woman would leave now, before it got any lighter. But something didn't feel right; she eased from her hiding place and pulled herself up into the opening, swung her legs across the sill—and froze.

Light everywhere made her eyes tear: candles, lan-

terns, and on both sides of her, scented torches
mounted in wall niches. There was an unpleasant me-
tallic smell in the air; she pinched her nose to avoid
sneezing, stepped to one side, and blinked furiously.

All at once she could see the entire chamber—a
narrow reception room of some sort, no furnishings
but benches along the far wall—and she was sorry for
that fact: Ylfer lay nearly across her feet, a dagger—
one of *her* daggers, how was that possible?—clutched
in one parchment-pale hand. Two long strides away,
Ogaden sprawled on his back, lips drawn back from
his teeth in a hellish grimace, eyes wide. The throats
of both men were cut, ear to ear, and the floor was a
pool of dark red blood. Still liquid, she realized as a
slender red rill eased along a crease in the tiled floor.
Her heart seemed to freeze: just beyond Ogaden's out-
flung hand, another blade—this longer, more slender,
silver . . .

She stumbled back, set her shoulders against the
wall and, eyes searching the long room, began checking her various dagger-belts; her hands were trembling
so, it took much longer than it should have; the thread
of blood slowed, pooled in a crack. Nothing moved
now, except her hands.

One blade missing . . . that loose harness in her
right sleeve, but how had it slipped out without her
noticing? She kept her gaze above the floor, forced
herself to breathe slow and shallow. It wasn't helping,
much. She could only be grateful her last meal had
been hours earlier. The dagger was definitely gone,
not caught anywhere as it sometimes did. The other
blade—it was the match to the one she'd carried away
from that stall. The one Ogaden had promised her,
but he'd left it in the stall owner's hands!

She clutched her temples and tugged, hard, at the
hair over her ears. Whatever intrigues these two had
intended—well, the plots and counterplots had died
with them. But by whose hand, and why?

That is not your business, Liatt, she warned herself.

Getting out of this place alive—if only to report to Master Edon about the treachery wrapped around the contract—that was more important than getting to the bottom of two messy killings.

She swallowed bile. *I never smelled blood before—cuts, yes, small wounds, of course. But nothing like this!* Better to leave now before she lost whatever her queasy stomach still held.

But there was a door, she could see it now . . . half an ornate pair, shoved back into a hallway or the next chamber, and light beyond it. She hesitated as she passed Ylfer, then shook her head. "Leave the dagger, Liatt," she told herself flatly. "It's nothing to mark *you*, and there's no time for this."

A sensible Assassin of any class and cut (*do not think cut!* she ordered herself sharply as her stomach twisted once more) would be gone immediately; the window behind let onto darkness, the narrow passage led back to the street and no more than a hundred long strides away was the stable where her bay was currently housed. A clever Assassin in the midst of an assignment gone horribly wrong would be smart enough to be gone before anyone was aware of the need to look for the owner or owners of those two blades.

She backed toward the window, eyed the partly open door and sighed. Better to know, if there was anything to be known. If all else failed, Master Edon would want the information; she knew she wouldn't sleep without seeing that opening, knowing she'd had the opportunity and had been too afraid to act on it.

It was not quite as light in here; someone had recently burned a thick and cloying incense that at least covered the stench of blood, and there were furnishings everywhere: a long, narrow table with chairs at each end divided the room nearly in half, though there were other small benches, seats, and piles of cushions scattered seemingly at random around three walls. The nearest, fourth wall, had only a high-backed throne on a low, polished dias. With a jolt that made her chest hurt, Liatt realized someone sat on that throne, motionless except for an occasional gleam of teeth. She froze, right hand moving stealthily to let one of the sleeve-daggers down into her grasp, where she could throw it if need be.

But there wasn't time. The still, seated figure suddenly came to life, shoving himself to his feet and crossing to confront her all in one smooth, easy movement. With a shock, she realized it was Ogaden's father. Ylfer's father. A man her own (once) father's age, and supposedly once a suitor for her hand. Her eyes widened as he stopped just short of her boots: His fingernails were edged in dark red, and blood had splashed in his beard, streaking the shoulder of his soft shirt.

He smiled; it wasn't a nice smile. "You. It may surprise you to know I've kept track since your father turned me down flat as a suitor. And I wonder if he knows you still live—outside the holy house where he sent you, of course?"

There wasn't any point in attempting to feed this one a tale; he'd known her most of her years and she'd hated him for all of them. "Why would he care? Why would you?"

"I was heartbroken when he dismissed me as a potential mate, I assure you," Ognat's smile broadened; his eyes were pale brown, almost yellow, utterly without expression.

"I hear you've bought Ducina Khemi, and that she carries your child," Liatt said evently. "She's better suited to you than I could ever have been—if I remember her."

He laughed; his eyes were still flat, disconcerting. "I know you remember her. But yes, I find her cold, emotionless—if that's what you mean to say."

Liatt bared her teeth. "She *is* cold—like the rest of

Kalinosa's snotty nobles. Still—nowhere near as cold as your two sons, just now, I wager. But *you* wouldn't know about them, would you?"

"My sons? Oh, yes. Them. One of my newest guards just found them, both dead, more's the pity; two mismatched blades between them and blood everywhere. The poor boy couldn't say if they'd been quarreling as they so often do, and the matter got beyond mere shouting, or if they'd been attacked by someone—say someone fond of knives."

Cold certainty stopped her breath for a moment; one of his spies had overheard her conversation with Ogaden. *The blade-dealer, I'd wager anything on it; Ogaden paid him but Ognat paid him more!* Before she could speak, Ognat held up a hand and turned his head away. "Some news, Dhevyd?" he asked quietly. A dark-haired, blade-slender young guard came through the door she'd just used, her dagger in his hand, and inclined his head respectfully. If he was unnerved by so much blood and death, though, she saw no sign of it. Liatt's eyebrows went up; he didn't look a day over twenty—young for a household guard. He eyed her briefly, dismissively, and held out the bloody knife. The old baron didn't see it, or more likely ignored it; his eyes hadn't left her yet, but she doubted there was much here that escaped him.

"M'Lord Baron, there's nothing else to be found in there. Captain's gone back to the barracks, but he sent for your apothecary to view the chamber and settle the means and times of death, and told me to bring out this blade, for your examination. It's somewhat ordinary, but not . . . entirely."

Liatt opened her mouth, then closed it again as Dhevyd cast her another sidelong look. He handed the short blade over to the baron, who turned partly away from her to hold it to the light. *There was no one in that chamber when I came through it! No sign anyone had been there except the two dead, and whoever killed them! And both these men know that. In fact, I'd wager this pretty boy was right behind me when I came through the window. I'm being set up!* And there was nothing unusual about any of her throwing daggers, except the proof-dagger she'd shown Ylfer. Assassins used the most anonymous blades they could buy for assignments. But before she could voice any of that, Dhevyd pivoted sharply, snapping her silver-hilted dueling dagger from behind his back to bring it out and up, two-handed; the point caught the baron beneath the ribs and went in with appalling ease. Liatt stumbled back as her dagger fell from Ognat's nerveless hands; the guard stepped aside, taking the long weapon with him. The baron fell, dead before he hit the floor.

By the time the guard turned to face her, she had a matched pair of daggers out, one ready to stab or slash, the other poised to throw. "What in all the black hells was *that* about?"

The guard merely shook his head and tossed the long blade; it flew high, end for end, and dropped toward her. No deadly throw; it was most likely his intention to distract her and leap as her eyes left his. She let go the right-hand dagger to claw at the hilt, shifting her grip on the awkwardly long dueling blade and kicking the fallen dagger where he couldn't grab it.

She brought the silver-hilted blade to attack-ready; Dhevyd smiled faintly and drew his sword—half again as long and at least twice as heavy a weapon. "It's no business of yours, Assassin," he snapped. "You won't leave here alive, so why bother to tell you?"

"Maybe I won't," she jeered, but her heart sank. She had no sword-training at all, even a novice guardsman could probably skewer her without breaking a sweat. She set her hip against the long table for direction and balance, and began backing away from him. He smiled, the tip of his sword describing small circles as he came after her. "What—you're afraid I really might get away from you?" she demanded. He merely shook his head again and followed her down the table, sword at the ready but a prudent distance from her blade.

Maybe he's not that good, she thought suddenly. A half-skilled male of that age, holding a blade like his, should have launched himself at her, and he hadn't. Yet. She couldn't think of anything else to taunt him with, though. Not with that blade so close to her own throat. *Separate yourself from him; a barrier. . . .* She crouched as she backed two more steps, then sprang, her hip landing with bruising force on the long table; she rolled, blades well above her head the way she'd learned and came down on the balls of her feet, across the table from him. His mouth quirked briefly; she'd surprised him, she thought. *Keep him off guard,* she decided. But he surprised her by throwing himself forward, blade coming around in a furious arc; she caught his blade dangerously close to her fingers and the dueling dagger's hilt.

To her surprise, his blade rebounded and his eyes went wide. She had the advantage in upper arm and shoulder strength, then; she'd thought it possible. But more importantly, he wasn't as blade-trained as he wanted her to believe. She launched herself at him, counting on surprise. It worked; he fell back, tangled his feet together, and caught himself on the edge of the table as she rolled back across it. Before he could recover, the dueling sword slid between his ribs.

Blood covered her hands and she snatched them back, shocked by the heat and the smell. His lips moved soundlessly, mouthing something that made no sense to her dazed eyes; his eyes locked on hers as he went to his knees and then, mercifully, facedown onto the floor. Liatt clapped both hands over her mouth and stumbled back, eyes closed; a moment later, she swore fiercely, and scrubbed both sleeves over her face. Her hands felt disgustingly sticky; she held them out where she could see them. "If that's a real kill,

I'll pass on another," she told herself in a low voice that shook.

"You shouldn't," a resonant alto said, from somewhere just behind her; a fresh knife in hand, Liatt whirled, her jaw set and eyes tight. A copper-haired woman came through the draperies beside the dais and strolled over to the table; she was tossing a small gemmed purse from hand to hand. "You did what was wanted, even if no one set it out for you." Her eyes briefly flicked across the dead guard, and a corner of her mouth turned up. "He had nice hands, I'll miss him. But if he'd talked . . ." She shrugged, met Liatt's flat gaze. "I'd ask how you are doing these days, Eleanora—"

"That's *Liatt,* damnit," she growled.

The other woman laughed, baring perfect teeth in a humorless smile of her own. "Don't even bother, dear; even stupid Ylfer could name you at first glance, and you and I spent more time together than that."

"Not at *my* choice, Khemi," Liatt replied evenly. She raised her eyebrows, eyes moving down and back up the other's thin gown; she resheathed the knife.

"I suppose I should be insulted," Khemi murmured.

"You're a threat in your own way, but you won't get close to me, and I won't eat anything you offer. Weren't you blonde?"

"Don't be naive. I'm not a ducina, either—any more than you are." She held up the purse. "This is yours, by the way. Full price that both Ylfer and Ogaden offered you. But if there's any amount of coin you'd like from me, for solving the rest of my problem—"

"I'd like some answers, and *then* I'd like to get out of here, so I can tell my guildmaster what the hell happened here!" Liatt snarled. "Loss of a few coins won't hurt you, but I'd rather keep my head where it is."

Khemi's eyes moved from fallen guard to dead baron and back again. She finally shrugged. "Father wanted the barony reverted to him—but petitioning

King Bhalor would've taken coin and years he didn't want to spend."

"Why take it back? Ognat's done well by it—"

"His father was a lout, and his sons were worse—you know that. After *your* father turned down Ognat's offer to rid him of a daughter and her dowry, Father got rumor to him that I might be a better match. Poor stupid Ognat jumped on it, and I gained a husband." A cold little smile quirked her lips. "You shouldn't have been so stubborn, Eleanora; Ognat was a temperamental brute but nice to me—and generous." She brushed her fingers across a wide cuff bracelet, heavy gold studded with gems. "And because he was generous enough to have me named baroness when he and I wed—well, there's only one heir to the throne now. . . ."

"And her father's going to take it away from her," Liatt said. "I don't *believe* you set up something this—this—"

"It's all politics, Eleanora—"

"*No* politics, damnit! An that's *Liatt,* Baroness!"

The baroness shrugged. "If you prefer. Gods know you *look* older than Eleanora ought to. Consorting with peasants and brigands hasn't been good for your skin, dear."

"It's kept my skin intact, and don't play the fool with me, Khemi. Just tell me the rest so I can get out of here!"

"There isn't any 'rest.' " She tossed the purse; Liatt caught it. "It's my barony by law, but of course I won't want to stay here. Such unhappy memories, you know, my adored husband dead. And besides, Father and I have a bargain; the barony reverts and he sends his chief steward to Bhalor's council, to see if an agreement can't be reached to get the king a new wife."

"All that—all this—for *Bhalor?*" Liatt stared at her blankly, her hand automatically shoving the purse deep into an inner shirt pocket. "He's old, he's fat, he's—"

"He's king. He can have two heads, for all of me. All I need do is produce a heir for him, and my future's assured." She stroked the bracelet, then suddenly freed it and tossed it. "Keep it. The smallest crown Bhalor gives me will be worth twenty of that bracelet. Sell it, and you'll be able to buy face cream for the next ten years—if you live that long."

"Oh, I plan on it," Liatt said softly as she began backing away. "But remember who you're playing politics with, Khemi; they've had years to get good at it, and they can keep greed in check if they have to. I'm not so sure you can." She flipped up the bracelet, caught it again and clasped it on her forearm, dragging the thick sleeve down to cover it. "But I'll take this, with thanks." The baroness froze as a slender-bladed dagger flashed into view, the tip caught in Liatt's fingers. It thudded into the table, two arm's lengths away; Khemi stared wide-eyed at the swaying hilt. "A gift of at least equal value. Keep it close, Khemi; considering the games you're playing, you'll need it more than I will." Before the other woman could move or say anything, Liatt backed swiftly to the far wall and threw one leg over the nearest windowsill with a short drop beneath it. Her eyes fixed briefly and angrily on the fallen guard. "What a waste," she snarled, and dropped out of sight.

There was no sound of pursuit behind her. And moments after she gained the street, the lights in the throne room went out—Khemi's way of telling her that there'd be no "discovery" until the next morning. *Don't trust that; she's devious, like any of them. Lousy, politically-minded, sneaking, arrogant, snotty nobles.*

An hour later, Liatt had retrieved her horse from the stable and slipped out of High Endsward. "That's it," she told the bay as they clattered across a wide bridge over the Grau River. "I'm not cut out to be an assassin, any more than I was a thief. I won't play seductress or poisoner, I won't get involved with politics ever again—and killing people like that—" That boy's dark-fringed blue eyes would haunt her for a long time; the mere thought of so much blood turned her stomach.

But the alternatives still weren't good for a small, dark woman, even one with a costly bracelet and a thick purse: She had no family name or rank (*none I'd use*), no ongoing source of wealth. Realistically, Ylfer's coin would go to the Guild, bribing those like Nykos. "Nykos won't believe I was manipulated like that. He won't want to, and none of them knows nobles the way I do." She leaned sideways and spat angrily.

But an hour later, the sun rising just behind her, she grinned, suddenly cheerful. Three purses and four kills—three of them high-ranking nobles; she'd leave the Guild with her name intact, and she'd leave behind a legend that someone would have to work to equal. And Khemi's bracelet would be worth a fortune, even though she'd have to pry out the stones and melt the gold. Add to all that a pair of silver-hilted dueling daggers, one of them honestly blooded in a genuine fight. Now there would be time to decide what she *really* wanted.

Sword training, of course. Possibly the opportunity to journey south and join Aloric. But, then—if Bhalor was having the troubles rumors said . . . If he needed Aloric's kind up north but wasn't fussy about Guild affiliation . . . If there was a chance to ease into a company, learn real fighting, battle tactics . . .

But that was all days away. Just now, her choices were more personal and much more interesting: which road to take back to the Guild—which town, which inn. Wine or ale with her meat. Liatt laughed aloud, and urged her horse to a trot.

(This story is with thanks to Liatt, who came to life in 1988 at the ripe old age of forty-two and has wanted

THE JEWEL OF LOCARIA
by Jacey Bedford

Jacey Bedford is a new writer who lives in England. This is her first published story.

King Ahm'shiraz the Nearsighted of Locaria stood on the balcony above the palace courtyard and proudly proclaimed the birth of his first child. Queen Eradice stood silently by his side holding the small, precious bundle. She didn't smile, but nobody seemed to notice. The crowds cheered and whistled. In the foreground, dancers whirled the ritual steps of welcome for the baby princess.

The palace staff stood at a distance, beaming and grinning. The king's happiness was their own. Only the queen and Neryn, her loyal nurse, looked serious. They shared a secret, a secret so dangerous that it could split the kingdom.

A few days later, unnoticed by any, Neryn slipped away from the palace carrying nothing but a big, two-handled, soft canvas bag. The queen was asked why her nurse was missing when there was a royal baby to care for, but she simply shook her head sadly and said that Neryn had been called away to tend to her own family matters.

The new princess was named Alenza, and she grew to be beautiful and kind and everything a royal child should be. In due course, the king and queen made a brother, Prince Ludahr, for her to play with. Unlike most siblings, the raven-haired princess and the golden-haired prince became the best of friends as they grew into their teen years and approached adulthood.

Alenza was almost twenty when tragedy struck. King Ahm'shiraz the Nearsighted became King Ahm'shiraz the Blind. He awoke one morning with a terrible pain in his head, and though the royal physician was sent for, in less than a day his eyesight had clouded to a narrow tunnel then vanished altogether.

Throughout the Ten Kingdoms there was consternation. A blind king could not govern what he could not see.

Rostor of Ohenzee, Queen Eradice's father, spoke up for him at their council. His eyes might be useless, but he had loyal advisers and his mind was sharp.

He would be a weak link in their alliance against the Savage Hordes of Tixar, said Orman of Vascaar, who promptly attacked Locaria as if to prove his point. It was for the good of the Ten Kingdoms, he said.

Rostor of Ohenzee sent fifteen battalions to help Ahm'shiraz and the King of Lotarua sent twenty battalions to help Orman.

Seeing their ancient enemies in turmoil and knowing when they were on to a good thing, the Savage Hordes of Tixar began to mobilize their cavalry while they waited for the Ten Kingdoms to weaken each other with their squabbles.

In a cave at the base of a high mountain, where grassy hills gave way to bare rock, an encampment of mercenaries received the news of the fighting with optimism. It was a long time since their skills had been required.

"Nen? NEEHN?" Lorba bellowed into the dark of the cave mouth.

"En en en." His words echoed back.

"No need to bellock, yer great lummox. I ain't deaf." A wiry woman, well into middle age, came up behind him, carrying a bucket of water.

Lorba jumped and whirled round.

Nen laughed. "You'll have to do better than that, Lorba, if you want to stay out in front of them young 'uns. Time was, when you'd have heard me coming up behind you before I'd set off from the stream. You'd have smelled the water in the bucket and you'd have known it was me by the rattle of my beads. We're getting old."

"Not too old. There's a nice juicy war brewing. A war, I tell you. No more charity from the king when the winter drives the game off the reservation."

"A war, eh? War's a youngster's game."

Lorba drew himself up to his full height, which was considerable. "They might have the strength and the skill with arms, but they've not got the experience. They'll stand behind us a while yet, just you see if they don't."

"Hmph." Nen bustled past him to set the bucket down.

"Where's Zerilia?" Lorba asked.

"Hunting. You did a good job of turning her into a boy. She's never at home when I need her."

"I could never understand you babying her so much. She's got to take her place here. Have I ever tried to discriminate against her just because she's not my own? You wanted me to treat her different because her real father was some posh chap from the city?"

"I just said she wasn't built like the rest of the kids. She should have been left to follow her own ways."

"I did, Nen." A slender, raven-haired young woman stood in the mouth of the home cave. "No one forced me to do anything."

"See. I told you. You did a good job." Nen glowered at Lorba.

"And what was that about my real father?"

"Oh, nothing."

"You always said you didn't know who he was. Now you say he was some posh chap from the city."

"Well, there were a few possibilities. It was a wild party." Nen laughed it off.

"Fine." Zerilia shook her head. "But what would you say if it was me that came home with a baby and no husband?"

"I'd say you'd be lucky to find a man like Lorba to take care of you and treat your baby well."

"So don't complain when I want to be like him."

Lorba smiled indulgently as she dropped the brace of buck springers onto a slab of rock and gave him a hug around his prodigious middle.

That night, the talk around the fire was all of war. They passed the ale jug from hand to hand. Lorba swilled beer from it and handed it to his stepdaughter. She took a deep drink, belched, and passed it on. She was easy here in this rough company.

Women were not forbidden a place in their fighting force, but neither were they forced into battle if their preferences were to stay at home and make babies. Those male children with no taste for blood could become supply masters or armorers, or they could simply leave the reservation without rancor. There was no room on a battle line for those who were not prepared to see the job through at whatever the cost.

In the city, the people of Locaria prepared for invasion. Their armies were driven back almost to the outer defenses by Orman of Vascaar's crack troops. Without Ahm'shiraz at their head, it seemed their own men didn't have the heart for fighting. They seemed lost without their lord to follow. Blind as he was, Ahm'shiraz would have gone out to spur them on, but young Prince Ludahr, defying his mother's orders, took his father's place. The troops rallied 'round, and Orman was driven back and back and back, right into the waiting swords of the mercenaries. Caught in the crab's claw, Orman was soundly defeated and what was left of his army scattered to regroup on the border. Orman sent word that he would sign a treaty and make reparations, but he couldn't give back the one precious thing which had been lost.

Prince Ludahr came back from that last battle carried aloft on his shield like a hero. His bright eyes were clouded and his golden hair matted with blood from the blow that killed him.

A great wail went up from the people. First their king had gone blind, and now his son and heir was dead. "He gave his life to free us from the oppressor," they said. "A great hero," they called him, but his sister knew better.

"He was a frightened sixteen-year-old boy with a lot of courage and no sense." Alenza's face was pale and her eyes were red.

"He was a hero," Ahm'shiraz said between his tears. "A hero. My boy. My brave boy."

Queen Eradice had no words at all. She wept as though her heart would break.

The night after Ludahr's funeral, the king, once called Ahm'shiraz the Nearsighted, lately called Ahm'shiraz the Blind, became Ahm'shiraz the Farsighted, when he dreamed the dreams of a mage.

"It was as if I flew above this land," he recounted to his trusted council and his family. Those members of the palace staff who could find a space to stand were listening from the sidelines. "I flew like a bird. I saw again. I saw mountains, forests, cities, and towns. I saw the great waters of the Ohenzee which marks our border. I saw our own troops, tending their injured and burying their slain. I saw the mercenaries, who have long been allies, waiting to answer our call.

"And then I saw the armies gathered on our border. Not those of the Ten Kingdoms, but those of the Savage Hordes of Tixar. They wait to feed on the carcasses left by Orman of Vascaar. They rejoice in the losses we mourn, not just our own Prince Ludahr but all the children of the Ten Kingdoms slain in this foolish war. We should have been strong together; now we are riven apart, and Tixar will walk in and pick over our entrails.

"Then from high above, I saw Tixar himself. He stood whirling aloft something which caught the sun, split its rays and beamed them across the land, striking into the heart of that which he would take. It shone like nothing I have ever seen before. Then I dropped closer to the earth and saw that this glittering orb was set into the hilt of a sword of the finest smith-metal.

"Then I was borne aloft once more, through the clouds to a place so white that I could see nothing. There I heard a voice."

"A voice? A god-voice?" the chancellor asked.

"All I know is that I heard a voice."

"Tell us, Ahm'shiraz the Farsighted. Tell us what it said," a servant, enraptured by the tale and forgetting his place, called out.

"It said, 'That which was lost is soon to come home.' "

"That which was lost is soon to come home." The people gathered around whispered the words after the king.

"The Jewel of Locaria is the most powerful weapon of all."

"The Jewel of Locaria is the most powerful weapon of all," they breathed.

"The king's elder daughter must gain the Key to the Ten Kingdoms before Tixar bolts the door from the inside."

"The key to the Ten Kingdoms," they echoed.

"My lord, what does this mean?" the chancellor asked.

"It means . . ." Ahm'shiraz paused, "I don't know what it means. It's god-talk. But if we don't find out soon, we're heading for oblivion. *That which is lost is soon to come home. The Jewel of Locaria is the most powerful weapon of all. The king's elder daughter must gain the Key to the Ten Kingdoms before Tixar bolts the door from the inside.*"

"Could it be," said the chancellor, "that this Jewel once was ours and was stolen by Tixar's ancestors so many years ago that it's been forgotten? The Jewel . . . hmm . . . that must have been the shining orb you saw set into the hilt of the sword."

"So the sword must be the Key to the Ten Kingdoms." Ahm'shiraz was getting excited now. "And the king's elder daughter must gain it."

Ahm'shiraz the Farsighted was still a blind man. Out of all the court, he was the only one who was not looking straight at the ashen-faced Princess Alenza.

Queen Eradice spoke up for the first time since her son's death. Her voice cracked with emotion, and her knuckles were white as she screwed her hands into fists. "My Lord. Your son died on the battlefield in your place, would you have your daughter die, too? Would you take all my children from me?" She reached across and grabbed Alenza by the wrist and marched out, dragging the young woman with her.

"Mother. Mother, stop." Alenza struggled against her mother's grasp, but the queen, despite the fact that she looked delicate, had a grip like iron. She marched up the stairs and pulled the princess into her chamber.

"Out. All of you." She dismissed the servants with unaccustomed sharpness, then dropped the huge iron bolts behind them. Even so, she was not satisfied; servants were well known for their curiosity. In case someone was listening from the corridor, she ushered Alenza into her bedchamber and slammed the thick wooden door. Then she seemed to wilt. It was as though that one act of defiance had sapped her strength. Alenza caught her as she folded and eased her into a chair.

"Here." She took a goblet of water from the table and pushed it into Eradice's shaking hand. "Now tell me what this is all about, Mother. I have no more liking for the sound of this quest than you do, but I would not have run away in public."

"The prophecy was so specific. It called for the king's elder daughter."

"We don't know what it means. Maybe there's time yet for you to have another child. Perhaps the king will still have another daughter. My father didn't seem to worry about it. Do you worry in case he has a bastard child somewhere?"

"Alenza!" The Queen was shocked. "What do you know of bastards?"

"As much as most people. But I've never heard anything said against my father."

"And neither will you. The king is an honorable man. We might have had an arranged marriage but we have made a good match and we have both been faithful to it. Besides, your father would not endanger the kingdom by leaving bastards who may have a claim on the throne. Royal bastards are not allowed to live. Did you know that? And neither are royal twins, for the same reason. Multiple heirs to a throne are a potential danger to the kingdom."

There was a silence. Alenza looked at her mother. The queen was pale.

"This is not an easy tale, Alenza. I swallowed this secret many years ago, and it has sat like a stone in my belly. Even the king, your father, does not know this, but now you must share the burden.

"When you were born, you were born a twin, identical to your sister. I suspected I was carrying two babies, so I found an excuse to dismiss my doctor. When I gave birth, I did it secretly, with only the help of my own personal servant, Neryn, whom I had brought with me from Ohenzee when I married. I bore both babes without so much as a whimper, in case someone heard my labors and sent for a doctor.

If Ahm'shiraz had suspected a double birth, I would have had to give up the secondborn, and he would have been forced to cut out her heart as the law directs."

"He would have cut out the heart of his own child?"

"He would have had no choice. You know he is not

a hard man. It might have broken him to do it, but he is a king and he would not have failed in his duty."

"But you saved your child. Where is she?"

"I don't know."

"Don't know?"

"I saved her, but I couldn't keep her. For all our sakes, it had to be as if she had never been born. Neryn, my own faithful Neryn, took her from here, in a bag, wrapped in the afterbirth and bearing sheets, so none would dare to examine it closely. She promised to raise her as her own child somewhere, far away, where she might have a life of her own."

Eradice's tears flowed down her cheeks and Alenza brushed them away gently, seeing, for the first time, the vulnerability behind the queen's mask.

"Mother. Which of us was the elder?"

Eradice shook her head. "I don't know. Neryn gave me both to hold. How could I choose between? I put each of you in turn to my breast so that you both might know I loved you equally. Neryn had work to do to prepare the bag for smuggling one of the babes. When she came back, she asked which was the one she had handed to me from the right of the cradle and which from the left. I had been so dazed by the double birth that I had taken no notice of left or right, and in my arms I had swapped you from breast to breast.

"Alenza, if your father's dream is truly a prophecy, the quest may not be yours. You may not even be the elder."

Eight leagues from the city, the mercenaries camped 'round their own fire close to Locaria's army. Zerilia bound the wounds of her father and friends, not because she was the woman and nursing was woman's work, but because out of all of them she was the only one who had not received some kind of injury on that day. She had fought like a demon, her blade never still, seized by some kind of frenzy which seemed to cloak her in a shield of power.

Lorba had never seen anything like it. He had trained many mercenaries, but he had never before trained one who had the god-frenzy in battle. It was as if she couldn't be touched, even by the blood of others. He felt humbled in her presence.

She seemed not to notice. She told him off for being careless and stitched the flap of skin across his belly. Some of their number were dead, others badly wounded.

"Hire a qualified doctor, there'll be good payment for all this," Lorba shouted after them as they limped for home.

"How much have we earned?" Zerilia asked. "Enough to last the winter?"

"Aye and there'll be more yet. Tixar's not far away."

"Who's to stand against him? Will all the Ten Kingdoms come together?

"They might. Though I'll warrant Vascaar and Lotarua will want to see Locaria and Ohenzee take the brunt of his first attack."

"What of the other six?"

"It's my guess they'll all stand on the sidelines until they see how we fare."

"Can two kingdoms stand against the might of the Savage Hordes?"

"For a time."

Alenza was no warrior princess. She'd learned to read and to sing and to play the ricobar. She could beat the best of her father's court at chess, but she never quite knew whether that was because they patronized her. Being a princess required a sharp insight into motives and hidden agendas.

Animals were easier to deal with than humans. She could ride passably well. Horses didn't try to fool you because you were the king's daughter.

She ordered a suit of armor. The following day the Royal Armorer delivered one designed for a young man.

"It won't do," she said, as she walked around it and lifted the visor to stare into its cavernous depths. "I'm not saying it wouldn't protect me from some injury, but I could barely walk in something of that weight and . . ." She looked at the armorer. "Have you got a wife?"

"Yes, My Lady."

"Then go home and put your arms round her and remind yourself of what shape a woman is."

"Yes, My Lady."

"Look. I want something more like this."

Patiently she drew an undoubtedly female form with a female-shaped breastplate. The rest of the suit was lightweight and flexible.

"More like that," she said, "and no leg armor. Rig my saddle with thigh protectors. I don't intend to part company from my horse and if I do, I want to be able to run very fast."

"Is my lady sure about the, er . . . ." He held each of his hands, cup-shaped, in front of his chest.

"Very sure."

"And what about helm?"

"None."

"No helm?"

"No helm. It did my brother no good at all. A good sword will slice through a tin hat any day. My best protection is to stay instantly recognizable. If I'm going up against Tixar, I'm going to have to learn to fight. Send Euven to meet me on the training field."

"Yes, My Lady."

Euven was waiting for her as she'd commanded. He had with him a small training sword made of wood.

"Forget that," she told him, "I haven't got time to learn anything for real. Teach me how to hold sword without looking like I'm carrying a bouquet of flowers, and show me how to whirl it round and look impressive without cutting my own head off. If there's time, you can try and teach me to do something useful with it, but I don't guess we've got much time left. I hear Tixar is getting very close now."

"Alenza, what are you doing?" Two hours later, the king's voice cut into her sword swirling practice.

"I'm—learning—how—to—look—like—I—might—know—what—I'm—doing," she said, without breaking the rhythm of swing and thrust.

The king was holding on to Eradice's guiding arm. The queen whispered something to her husband.

"Child, no one expects you to go into battle," Ahm'shiraz said, more gently than he had ever said anything to her in his life before.

"If you are truly Ahm'shiraz the Farsighted, then you will know I have no choice. Tixar is breathing down our throats. Ohenzee and Locaria stand together, but the rest of the Ten Kingdoms are sitting on their brains and waiting. You can't expect our men to go into battle without a figurehead. Look how much better they fared with Ludahr leading them. I think they might fight for me."

She saw the tears leaking from his blind eyes. She wanted to rush into his arms the way she had as a child, but her childhood suddenly seemed a long way behind her. She hardened herself. *If I had been secondborn, he would have cut out my heart,* she thought.

"Besides," she continued, "the prophecy is very specific. *That which was lost is soon to come home. The Jewel of Locaria is the most powerful weapon of all. The king's elder daughter must gain the Key to the Ten Kingdoms before Tixar bolts the door from the inside.* If the sword that Tixar carries is the Key to the Ten Kingdoms and the Jewel of Locaria, set in its hilt, is a powerful weapon, and if I am to gain it, then all I have to do is wait. It is marching toward me. That which was lost is coming home."

* * *

The night before a battle is always strange. Some soldiers want to talk, others prefer to be alone with their thoughts. Zerilia sat with Lorba by the campfire.

Lorba had not dared to mention the god-frenzy that had carried her safely through the last battle. He loved his stepdaughter as much as he loved Nen. He hoped the god-frenzy was gifted to her. He knew that her birth had been special in some way, though Nen had never told him the actual details and he had been too respectful of her feelings to ask.

Eventually they rolled in their blankets and slept, though some time in the night, Zerilia must have crept closer. Lorba woke with her curled in his arms like a child. He smoothed her cropped black hair and prayed that the gods would give her a strong arm and a quick mind on this dangerous day.

In her pavilion, Alenza dressed carefully. She had leather body armor instead of chainmail. It wasn't as protective, but at least she could carry the weight of it. The armorer had followed her instructions to the letter and the armor was as snug as twenty pounds of metal could be. She drew her long hair into a severe plait and flattened it to her head. She wouldn't give anyone the advantage of a handle to catch her by. To please the armorer she had agreed to wear a leather cap to protect her skull from minor cuts and scrapes. When she was dressed she looked as much warrior as princess.

She stared in the glass and sighed. It was all a sham, but maybe if she played her part well, no one would know just how scared she was and how weak she felt. She wondered if real warriors felt like this on the day of battle.

Grimly she picked up her sword and marched out to her big gray war horse and her waiting followers. She mounted and clicked the leg armor on her saddle across her thighs. She took her sword and held it aloft, circling it to catch the early morning sunlight.

"Alenza!" one soldier shouted, and then they all took up the cry.

"Alenza!"

"Alenza. Lenza. Lenza."

It became a chant as she rode along the front row of troops. She had rehearsed a bold rousing speech, but she didn't need it. The troops would follow her. They would die for her. She prayed for their safety. She didn't want anyone to die for her, and she certainly didn't want to die for anyone else. This was what being royal was all about, putting the kingdom above individual lives and happiness, even your own. She came one reluctant step nearer to understanding how a father could cut the heart from his own baby.

The mercenaries, aligned with the regulars, took up the chant, too.

"Lenza. Lenza."

They were a rough crowd, coarse and brown, with work-worn armor and strong sensible horses. Her own gray pranced and posed. Alenza looked away from the mercenaries to steady him for a moment. When she looked back, she met the clear eyes of a young woman. Her face was dirt-streaked, as all the mercenaries' faces were, but a shock ran through her. It was like looking into a mirror. Alenza wanted to say something, but then she was past and left with no more than an impression burning in her brain. Identical. Twin.

Tixar could be seen up on the hill parading in front of his own troops. There were too many of them. Alenza knew that without the combined armies of the Ten Kingdoms, they couldn't hope to win. They might, at best, hold off disaster for a time.

They waited for Tixar's charge. Alenza would not go to him and meet him on the uphill slope. She saw the Hordes jump forward into a gallop just before she heard their full-throated cries of war. She held her hand up to steady her own troops. Meet Tixar on the level field.

Wait . . . Wait . . . Wait. . . .

Now!

Suddenly, they were roaring and racing toward each other, and it became impossible to tell horse from man or friend from foe. It was all blood and dust and flying stones. The crash of metal ate into Alenza's eardrums and the wild sound of screaming men and animals soared to a crescendo in the cacophony of rising sound. Yet somehow, in the midst of all the madness, she was acutely aware of herself, alive to the very tips of her fingers and toes.

Alenza swirled her sword high and screamed in battle rage. All thoughts of posing as the perfect figurehead on the great gray stallion were obsolete as adrenaline surged through her bloodstream.

A Hordesman felled her captain, and Alenza brought the sword down hard on his head. It was a lucky strike, the blade bit into flesh and bone, and he was gone beneath the feet of her war horse. She was aware that a grizzled mercenary had taken the captain's place by her side and that, to her right, someone was felling enemies like a farmer mowing hay with a scythe.

Even so, the day was going badly for Locaria. They were heavily outnumbered. There were familiar faces on the ground all around her. Too many faces. They were pushed back and back to the banks of the shallow but fast-flowing river. The mercenary never left her side. It was as if he were her guardian angel when all her own faithful troops had been cut down. They were back to back now, pressed close by some half dozen enemies.

"Zerilia!"

Even in the tumult she heard him call out. The whirlwind to her right edged closer and, in the storm of death, the young woman she had faced on the front line earlier in the day slaughtered her way toward them. Alenza slashed her own blade wildly at two attackers but felt the bite of steel through the leather of her armored boot, deep into her calf. There was no pain, even though she felt the muscle and tendons sliced open like so much butcher's meat. *That's going to hurt later,* she thought, and then her body failed her and she fell back into darkness.

"Lady. Lady!" Zerilia wiped mud and blood spatters from the princess' face. "Lady, can you hear me?"

"How is she?" Lorba called from the mouth of the undercut, riverbank cave where she was prepared to hold their sanctuary against all comers.

"She lives, but the leg wound is deep. She'll not walk for a while. Maybe never again without a limp."

The princess lay half in and half out of the water. Zerilia sat in the shallows of the stream with the princess' leg cradled on her knee. She already had the boot off and she was packing the wound with moss. Then she bound it tightly to stem the bleeding.

A soft moan announced the princess' return to reality.

"Quiet, Lady, you are safe for a time."

"You." The princess' eyes focused, even though her voice was shaky.

"Me?"

"You. Twin."

"What?"

"Twin."

"She's right, you do look alike." Lorba had judged it safe for a while and had come to lean over Zerilia's shoulder.

"Twins."

"She can't be serious." Zerilia had no looking glass of her own and was less familiar with her own face than Alenza was.

"Who is your mother?" the princess asked urgently. "Is she Neryn of the Ohenzee?"

"Nen. Her name is Nen." Zerilia said.

"Neryn. I've not heard that in twenty years, but it is her given name," Lorba breathed.

"Then you are my twin," Alenza said.

"Lady, I'm a mercenary."

"Listen. There's no time to spare. The prophecy was given to my father. The means to fulfill it has been given to me. Nothing happens unless it is for a purpose.

"Our mother birthed twin girls. One she kept and the other, a secret child, she sent away to save her life. Her friend and nurse, Neryn, took the baby to raise as her own. That's you. You are my sister."

Zerilia shook her head and sat, slack-jawed, while water swirled and eddied around them.

"Wake up, woman!" Alenza's words were a slap in the face. "You know of the prophecy?"

"Aye, Lady, who doesn't. *That which is lost is soon to come home. The Jewel of Locaria is the most power-ful weapon of all. The king's elder daughter must gain the Key to the Ten Kingdoms.*"

"The king's elder daughter. I don't know which of us is the elder, and neither does my mother. I only know that you have a better chance to gain the Key to the Ten Kingdoms. Here, swap clothing, take my armor. You must win through. You must be Alenza. Face Tixar and gain the sword."

Zerilia helped Alenza to remove her leather armor in the confined space and then pulled on the leathers, the breastplate and, to hide her cropped hair, the little cap. She left the rest of the protective metal plate. The sleeves prevented full arm movement and she needed all her skills now.

"The battle is coming to meet us. Hurry," Lorba said.

"Take her home, Father. Get her to where it is safe and her leg can heal. I'll do what I can here."

"You must win through." Alenza's eyes burned bright. "You must be a princess. You are Alenza now."

"I will fight, Lady. As to the rest . . ."

"Get the Key to the Ten Kingdoms, Take back the Jewel of Locaria. Bring back that which is lost. May all the gods go with you."

Zerilia, now looking every inch a warrior princess, rolled out from beneath the overhang into the stream and leaped back into the thick of the struggle over a mass of fallen bodies.

Sword in hand, she took two breaths to size up the state of the battle and picked her target. A Hordesman was wreaking havoc from the back of the princess' great gray war stallion. Zerilia caught him off-guard. She came up from underneath the horse and gutted the man with her sword point, then she hurled his dying body to the ground and leaped into the saddle.

The details of that day are not easily recounted. The whole picture emerged gradually and some deeds of bravery were never told at all. The war was not won, but the battle was not lost either. Some soldiers swore that they had seen the princess cut down, but when she reappeared, swinging her sword like a demon, they took up the chant again.

"Lenza. Lenza."

The princess fought like one possessed. She carved her way through the ranks of the massed enemy, leading loyal troops and mercenaries alike, until she was at Tixar's throat. The two crashed together and, they say, the ground shook. The princess would not be swayed from her purpose until at last a thundering blow delivered the sword into her hands and with it the Jewel of Locaria.

There was not one warrior in either army who did not know the prophecy and as the princess swung the sword, the Key to the Ten Kingdoms, up above her head, the sun came out and reflected off the faceted jewel set in its hilt. The rays of light pierced the minds of the Hordes and Tixar's men ran, carrying their injured lord with them. They didn't stop until they had regained the ridge upon which they had camped the previous night.

"Lenza! Lenza!"

Zerilia, though not a princess by upbringing, seized the moment. She whirled the sword into the air for all to see.

"The prophecy is fulfilled," she yelled. "That which is lost has come home. The Jewel of Locaria, the most powerful weapon of all, is here in my hand. The king's elder daughter has gained the Key to the Ten Kingdoms. Now, before Tixar bolts the door from the inside and extinguishes the light of the civilized world, will the Ten Kingdoms unite and drive him back into the slime from which he came? Send riders. Let all who will stand with us align on this field of battle. Let those who will not, lose the protection of the Kingdoms forever. Unite!"

"Unite!" The call was taken up.

In the days and weeks that followed, King Ahm'shiraz the Farsighted used his considerable political acumen and molded the Ten Kingdoms into one alliance. Even Vascaar and Lotarua came back to the fold, unable to stand against the powerful threat of the Jewel and the Key. The combined forces, with the warrior princess as their figurehead, drove out the Savage Hordes of Tixar, and peace settled on the land again.

In the Palace of Ahm'shiraz, the princess was praised and gifts were heaped at her door, but she rarely came out of her rooms, preferring solitude to celebration. They said she had the mark of the gods on her, so that she could only remember the prophecy and nothing else. She shunned the company of friends and family and even ate in her own room.

Her parents were delighted to have her back, safe, and they forgave her strange ways, rejoicing that it was better to have her back changed than to not have her back at all.

"Fulfilling a prophecy is a heavy task," Ahm'shiraz

said. "We can't expect her to be touched by gods and to remain as she was before."

She took to riding alone and she forbade anyone to follow her. One day she didn't come back.

The reservation looked almost foreign to Zerilia. The home cave was primitive. She had never missed the comforts of civilized city living because she had never had them before. Now she thought she might miss the mattress on her bed and the convenience of doors that closed against the chill winter winds. She was getting soft. She accepted the self-inflicted scorn.

"Zerilia!" Her father and her mother came running to meet her.

"Nen! Lorba!" She didn't have enough arms to hug them both at once but somehow she managed.

A figure, paler than most of the faces around the camp, followed Nen out of the home cave. She limped, but only slightly.

Nen and Lorba stepped back.

"Lady." Zerilia bowed her head.

"Sister."

Tactfully Nen and Lorba gave them some time alone.

"Let's walk." Alenza had been practicing every day. Nen had stitched her calf, and she had all but regained the full use of her toes, which she feared for a time had been damaged by the severing of nerve and sinew. "How are my—our—parents?"

"They are well."

"And do they . . ."

"Do they know about me? No. As I was a heroine, they forgave me all my strangeness, even my rough speech."

Alenza looked pensive. "And have you enjoyed being a princess?"

She wondered whether Zerilia could bear to give

up the luxury of the palace to trade places back into her own life.

"I can't deny that I have. I read your books and learned many things that would have been beyond the imagining of Zerilia the mercenary."

"And are you ready to give it up, or is this just a visit?"

Zerilia turned to Alenza, her eyes open wide.

"Do I have a choice?"

"There are always choices. You are stronger than I am, and I owe you so much. I couldn't stop you, and neither could I blame you if you wanted to take my place permanently. You've earned that right."

"I have learned much from your books. But I have not learned how to be a princess, and I will not know how to be a queen when my time comes to rule. Here." Zerilia took the sword from her scabbard and Alenza saw that it was the precious Key to the Ten Kingdoms. The Jewel of Locaria in the hilt was a deep endless blue.

"Ah, the magic sword."

"Take it. It's yours," Zerilia said.

"I suppose it is—or it would be if I was the elder daughter."

"If you are the only daughter, you will be both elder and younger combined," Zerilia said.

Alenza took the hilt of the sword; it felt warm in her grasp.

"Go on, then, get on with it." Zerilia held her head high. Her eyes were closed.

"What?"

"Cut out my heart. Don't say you haven't contemplated the need for it."

Alenza paled. She had thought just that. What would happen to the kingdom if Zerilia ever tried to make a legitimate claim to the throne? It might come at any time. She had been shown what life was like on the other side. What if she changed her mind and was no longer satisfied with living in caves and camps? What if she wanted palaces and servants?

Now she truly understood why her father would have been prepared to cut the heart out of one of his own twin daughters. The kingdom had almost been lost twice over. Was one life too high a price to pay for peace?

"Get on with it. My part in this is done. Would you have me turn my back to make it easier?" Zerilia bowed her head. "You have the Jewel, and the sword is most certainly the Key to the Ten Kingdoms, for it has brought all together as one, even Vascaar and Lotarua."

"And that which was lost has come home," Alenza said softly. "Zerilia, don't you see, this sword and the Jewel don't count for anything. It's you. You are the Jewel of Locaria. You are the Key to the Ten Kingdoms, you proved that when you united them with one single call. You are the one who has come home. Now I should just fade away and leave you to take my place. I'll bet you are the firstborn. If our mother had remembered her left from her right, you would have been brought up in palace and I would have lived in a cave."

"Whoever was firstborn, we can't swap. And you can't rule Locaria knowing I might change my mind and come and take your kingdom from you. If you don't use that sword now, you may regret it."

"And if I do use it, I know I'll regret it for all the rest of my breathing days. When our father eventually becomes Ahm'shiraz the Allseeing and goes back to his white place in the sky, I will change the law on twins, and we will rule together."

"Don't be silly. You've not shown lack of brains before—don't start now. Let's just come to an understanding. I'll be here if ever you need me, but don't come looking unless it's a dire emergency. I've had enough fighting to last me for quite a while. And, if you ever get the chance, tell our mother she made the right decision."

WARRIOR OF MA-AT
by *Kathleen M. Massie-Ferch*

Kathleen M. Massie-Ferch is the editor of two anthologies, *Ancient Enchantresses* and *Warrior Enchantresses*. Other short fiction by her appears in *New Amazons* and in a number of magazines. She lives in Verona, Wisconsin.

"Enough!" my pharaoh roared, silencing the two-dozen unruly voices. His ancient voice—diminishedby the years—carried throughout the marble-and-alabaster Hall of Audiences. He turned his piercing gaze toward me. At one time I had feared those dark eyes; now they worried me in a different way. I bowed and then faced the crowd, my tall staff of office before me.

"Who has come to petition the great god, Pharaoh, Lord of the Two Lands?" Nearly the entire elite gathering answered me simultaneously. I pounded my staff once on the stone stair to silence the many nobles, priests, and priestesses assembled on the main floor, five steps lower than me, and ten steps below Pharaoh on his golden throne. Only one of their number had remained silent throughout. Though I had never seen this woman—she had been a frightened child when she left court—I would know her in any crowd. I saw no softness in her amber eyes, nor did her pale complexion betray any hint of fear. A light blush reddened her high cheekbones, but from excitement, not shame. She was clearly her mother's daughter.

"The court recognizes Princess Nyt-akerti," I began, "daughter of Pharaoh, and daughter of Lady Nebt."

The young woman advanced three strides to stand at the base of the stairs. Save for her jewelry, she dressed more like a soldier than a princess. She wore the short linen kilt, tight leather vest, and costly weapons of an army officer. Nonetheless, there was no mistaking the feminine beauty of her curves. She bowed to Pharaoh, and her amber-colored braids fell forward, rattling softly from the many expensive beads woven into the long locks.

"Lady Nebt," Pharaoh called. An older version of the young princess stepped gracefully forward. She wore a gown of the finest linen and gold jewelry, as befitting a member of court. "Is this our daughter?"

"She is, Pharaoh. I ask you to forgive—"

Pharaoh both silenced and dismissed her with a slight wave of his hand. "Princess Nyt-akerti, how old are you?"

"I have seen the Hepu River flood eighteen times, Father." Her rich voice held no hint of her mother's foreign accent.

I thought Pharaoh looked ashen and weary. If he was, his voice did not betray any weakness. "It has been many years since anyone has brought such disorder to my audience halls. Priests and nobles yelling at each other. Why do you bring this here?"

"Forgive me, Father, that wasn't my desire."

"You've been absent from my court too long. I have forgotten where you've been."

"I serve Goddess Ma-at as High Priestess," the princess answered.

"What?" Pharaoh sought out another in the crowd. "Priest Saui-khu, is this true? Has one so young mastered all your teachings to become a full priestess?"

The old priest, Saui-khu, stepped forward slowly and bowed. "She has, Pharaoh. She took vows during the season of *akhit*, and has been a great source of pride for you."

"And you didn't think this important enough to tell me before now?" Pharaoh turned back to his daughter. "You have achieved great rank, yet you do not dress as they. Can you use that bronze sword at your side?"

"I can, Father, with great skill, and also the mace and spear. It is because of my skills with these weapons, and others, that I come here today. The priests and priestesses of Ma-at can teach me nothing more."

"Knowing the spells," interrupted Priest Saui-khu, "is not the same as being skilled in their use. You need time and—"

"Silence," I demanded. The pharaoh needed to rest. This much excitement would leave him ill. I would not allow that. "All will have a chance to speak, in their turn. Princess Nyt-akerti, you have come to petition the courts. Speak your mind."

"No, my Pharaoh," Lady Nebt interrupted. "Do not accept her offer." Other voices rose from the elite gathering.

Again I struck my staff on the stone step, demanding silence, before speaking. "Princess Nyt-akerti remain. All others leave." Once the room was free of disruptions, I nodded to the princess. Amongst the other nobles, she had seemed tall and strong. In the empty hall she now seemed more like the child I remembered; still she kept her back straight and head high.

"Father, I am a priestess of Ma-at. My oaths have bound me to the goddess for life. I'm honored to serve her, but I want to be released from my duties within the Temples."

"This, of course, is not to Priest Saui-khu's liking?"

"No, Father."

"Do you wish to return to court, then?"

"No. I wish to serve you against our enemy. As your daughter, I ask the right to fight in your army for Kemet."

Pharaoh leaned back in his golden throne. "It has been many years since these withered hands could hold a sword. Even if you are the most skilled of warriors with sword and mace, how can one more sword help? I would not see my daughter slain on the battlefield. We have men enough for that. And I cannot believe you are so knowledgeable in tactics to make you a general. Tactics take years and years to learn."

"I do not wish to be a general! I am your daughter and a priestess of Ma-at. I carry Narmer's holy gift within me. The goddess has—"

Pharaoh rose off his throne. "Silence!" he roared again. I rushed to his side to support him. The princess dropped to her knees and bowed low.

"I have seen a hundred floods of the great Hepu River! Do you think me a fool? I am Pharaoh, son of gods, and have not been blessed with Narmer's gift. You are not even my daughter by one of my queens. How is it you possess this great magic?"

Princess Nyt-akerti looked up. There was fear in her amber eyes. "But I am the daughter of a great god. I am your daughter. Narmer's magic is difficult to master. How could a boy of only six years be pharaoh and priest, too? Perhaps you weren't given this gift because you didn't need it to rule Kemet." Pharaoh leaned heavily on me and waited. She continued with more confidence and with a fire in her voice. "For ninety-two years we knew peace on our borders because of your firm hands and wisdom. Now for two years our enemies strike us, they test our strength to see whether the magic and power of Narmer still lives in the Two Lands, or if it has fled, so they may steal our farms and our food."

I encouraged Pharaoh to sit again. Princess Nyt-akerti climbed the steps and knelt at her father's feet. There was strength in her muscles as they rippled under her smooth, pale skin. Her hands looked strong and callused, indeed capable of using her weapons as she claimed.

"I have outlived most of my children," Pharaoh began, "and each of my four queens. I had thought the magic gone. Neter-kare is my heir by my third queen, yet he does not have this gift. None of my other sons possess it. Why the daughter of a foreigner?"

"The gods are not generous with their magical gifts. They returned the power to Kemet when you most need it, in the form of your youngest child. You need this gift now, and I am here."

"For many years now I have asked Goddess Ma-at to show me her truth, and then feared the gods no longer cared, until this morning when I walked in my garden. I saw a golden vulture fly in from the desert and land on the palace roof."

"Goddess Nekhbet," I whispered in awe.

"So I, too, believe," Pharaoh said. "The favor of the goddess has returned, even as my daughter has returned to me."

"Did you sleep in the palace last night?" I asked the princess.

"No, I arrived at dawn."

"As did the goddess," Pharaoh said softly. "Send for Prince Neter-kare."

Prince Neter-kare arrived quickly. His hair was more gray than black, but he was strong of arm and mind. When he, too, waited before his father, Pharaoh spoke again.

"It seems the servants of Ma-at are clothed in secrets, and I have only my daughter's loyalty to thank for enlightening me. Princess Nyt-akerti claims to possess the Gift of Narmer."

The prince shrugged his massive shoulders. "Having the power and using it are not the same. It would be simple enough to test her claims."

Nyt-akerti smiled. I saw satisfaction in her eyes as she turned and descended the steps to stand in the center of the Hall of Audiences. She removed her sandals and stood barefooted on the stone floor. With closed eyes, she remained very still for more than a minute, then shook her head. For a moment we only heard the soft rattle of the turquoise-and-amber beads in her hair. Then a tremendous volley of thunder exploded above the palace, the deep rumble reverberated through the hall.

"This is not great proof," Prince Neter-kare said. He spoke with a calm I did not entirely share.

The princess inclined her head slightly. "I would rather not waste the goddess' power."

"It is a rare sound over the desert," I added.

"And you can use that sword at your side?" Pharaoh asked again.

"Yes, Father. I had the best teachers. You paid for them."

"I grant your wish to leave the House of Ma-at, but not your vows."

She climbed the stairs. "I did not ask to be released from my vows. They are a part of my living *ka* and guide my every action. Besides, you would never trust me if I asked such a thing."

"I will not assign you to a combat unit. You will be on your own to help, wherever necessary, by using Narmer's magic. You will not go alone, but with a small company of warriors. Prince Neter-kare will select these men and command this band."

"Father?" the prince asked.

"You have been my heir for many years. You have served me well on the battlefields of war and court. You will go in my place, for I can no longer travel. You must see and understand her magic, so I might. Also, Lord Ipu-wer will accompany you."

I started. "My pharaoh, whatever you wish."

He turned to me. "You are my most trusted servant and grandson of my sister. You will see and hear all that happens and never hide anything from me, as others might."

I bowed. "I am honored by your confidence."

"And you will keep my daughter safe in ways the prince cannot, for you are very skilled in the weapons of court. And you speak the tongues of all our enemies." He turned to his daughter. "I am old, but not yet deaf to the voice of the gods. Our enemies are very strong and numerous. You are young, daughter, perhaps too young to fully understand our danger, and will think it more sport. So I will give you enough reason to want to win: Princess Nyt-akerti, if you speak the truth and end this war, I shall name you Horus."

"Before me?" Prince Neter-kare burst out. "Or as my queen?"

"Before you."

"Do you know what you are saying?"

"Yes, my wits are still solid. She will be the female Horus and my heir, but I would counsel her to take you as husband and consort, Neter-kare. You know the court as she can never know it. Nyt-akerti, if you are especially illustrious and strong in your fight against our enemies, I will name you co-regent and give you the honor of wearing the Double Crown and ruling beside me the last days of my life."

I watched a slight smile brighten the princess' face even as a cloud of frustration descended over the prince. I wanted to advise Pharaoh not to start a war within our borders while we fight invaders, but it was too late to turn back the words. And now I knew why he needed me with the princess.

From his belt Pharaoh removed a small knife and handed it to his daughter. She turned it over slowly several times. "There is power in this weapon. I feel it!"

"I thought you might. I cannot feel it, nor can Neter-kare. When you were an infant, I placed this blade on your chest, as I did with all my children. You let out a scream which brought every woman in the palace running to your side, though you were not harmed. This is the sacred knife of Pharaoh Narmer, fashioned from the thigh bone of God Osiris. Use it wisely; it is strong magic and the priests say it possesses the power to kill within its soft blade. If you fail me, I will not need to punish you; the Knife of

Osiris will do so. Yet if what you claim is true, this knife will make you Pharaoh. Go, destroy our enemy!"

Pharaoh commanded Prince Neter-kare to protect the princess. It was a wise choice to place him in charge of our company; the prince was well versed in the arts of leadership and had led our troops to numerous victories in his younger years. It was this success on the battlefields which had first attracted his father's attention over older, and less successful, brothers. We were a party of twelve men—one for each hour of the day or night. The choice of the holy number did not escape anyone's notice, nor the fact that Princess Nyt-akerti's presence disrupted the symmetry by being our thirteenth member.

Now I sat and watched the prince across the campfire. We camped in the ruins of an ancient temple near the caravan road on which we traveled. Clusters of limestone blocks and partial walls were left in random piles. They gave some measure of protection by shielding us from anyone passing on the nearby road. We had perhaps another easy day of travel before we got far enough into the Delta region to worry about the presence of our enemy. The others of our band, including the princess, had retired to their bedrolls.

"You have said little on all of this, Counselor," Prince Neter-kare asked of me, although he continued to stare at the small fire.

"A woman has never worn the Two Crowns before."

"Several of my sisters would have sent rivers of fear into our enemies' courts if they had become pharaoh, perhaps more so than I ever could. Your own late mother could negotiate a trade agreement with such skill even the mightiest thief thought her fair handed."

"Though I was young, I remember that treaty."

"They all had the misfortune of not outliving Father. I'm my father's fifth heir for the very same reason. Few remember that anymore. I think of these women and compare Nyt-akerti to them, and find this princess is lacking much. What does she know of state affairs? Of the forty-two nomes, she could name less than half of them and even fewer names of the families who lead each province. These men and women are the heart of Kemet's commerce, and its political strength. A pharaoh cannot survive without their support. What happens when conflicts arise between families and nomes? Who steps in, if not Pharaoh? And what does she know about farming? Can she survey the fields after the floodwaters have left?"

I smiled slightly. "She isn't stupid. She can learn these things even as you and I did, if they are necessary. This dark mood that hangs over your *ka* isn't like you."

"I've served Kemet all my life. Now when I am about to step out from my father's shadow, he tosses me aside for someone completely untried and a child! I disagree with him on how intact his wits are."

"Perhaps his age has caught up with his reason, perhaps not. Remember when she was very young, maybe only four years old? The women and children came running from the nursery, screaming of a demon."

"I remember. We found Nyt-akerti sitting on her bed with a giant cobra coiled under it. She was too scared to cry."

"No guard could get near enough to save her. Two men had poison spit at them and almost died. You calmly and carefully walked up to the cobra and talked to it softly for several minutes. Then you reached over and picked up the princess."

"It let me carry her away."

"Why?"

"Who knows."

"I do. I always thought that cobra was the Goddess Wadjet herself. The goddess let you near to show you that you are gods' chosen servant, even as Nyt-akerti is."

"I don't have Nyt-akerti's power."

"That doesn't matter. Nyt-akerti needs you. Kemet needs you still. Also, you promised the goddess back then you'd protect Nyt-akerti, just as you promised your father that yesterday."

"You are reaching too far, old friend."

"No, I'm not. You have always been the protector for anyone who needs it. The young gardener who forgot to water the queen's favorite tree. Or the maid who dropped a cherished ornament. You became the Crowned Prince to protect Kemet. Protecting this princess protects our beloved Kemet."

"I'm not so certain she is that important."

"Do you desire the Double Crown so much?"

"Of course I desire the crown. The lure of power is as tempting to me as to anyone, but you're right, not before Kemet—"

"Or is it you just don't like her? I'm not certain I do. She makes it challenging to even try to like her, by not letting anyone get too close."

He ran his hand across his freshly shaven head. "No, I'd welcome that challenge. She's beautiful and doesn't like to talk too much. I could get used to that in a wife. But the magic of Ma-at—that I do not trust. The magic has been gone for so long, its return seems more a trick. Are there secrets in her silence? Is she in league with the Temples to wrest power away from Pharaoh for themselves?"

"I never studied in the Temples. Their politics are odd. But I don't believe they support this use of the goddess' magic. You could see how even the thought of it frightened them, too."

"I don't trust that old priest. What did he really teach her? How can magic kill our enemy from a distance? Can magic alone give her enough knowledge to rule this land?"

"Why not ask me?" The voice came from the darkness behind me. Then the princess stepped into the light. She was dressed in a dark robe, a shadow against the cool desert night. "Ask me whatever you wish, and I will answer truthfully."

The prince glared at his sister for a few heartbeats,

then stood and left for his bedroll. I knew he wanted to say something, but I suspect he didn't trust his anger to stay hidden.

The princess laughed softly as she sat down. "He is afraid of me," she said. "I've seen it before."

"No, not you, never of you," I corrected. "I advise you not to laugh at him again. He is a very powerful man. He is a man of honor and left because you both carry swords and he didn't trust himself to just have words with you."

"When I am pharaoh—"

"*If* you become pharaoh, it will be because you have earned that right, as each heir has before you, including Prince Neter-kare."

"I have skills."

"Then concentrate on using them, not on the prize at the end. You will live longer. If you think the priests are happy with your actions, think again. Can you tell me why the priests didn't want Pharaoh to know about your magic?"

"No. It was years before I knew I was different from other novices. They kept me in seclusion, away from everyone but the older priestesses. And they kept me busy. I took up the sword because of a dream Ma-at sent me. That didn't please them, but I'd have it no other way. The same with coming to see Father."

"That strength will help you. You have many brothers left in court. If Pharaoh can so easily dismiss Neter-kare, perhaps Pharaoh can just as easily dismiss you. Or so they may think. Neter-kare is well liked in court."

"I trust no one."

"That may become a mistake. The men in this camp, including the prince, are not your enemies. The true enemy is out there in the night, waiting for us to err, then he will crush us. And if he doesn't, then you will have to face all the many problems of court and the Temples. You will have to learn how to trust and whom to trust. Perhaps that is the real reason your father sent you out here, as a test, not of your magic, but of you, the woman." With that caution I went to my own bed.

I awakened as the faintest glow of Re-Horakhti painted the eastern, desert sky. As I packed my bedroll, the prince came over to me and squatted nearby.

"What did you say to Nyt-akerti last night?" he asked softly.

"In effect, watch who you insult. Why?"

"She's gone?"

"Where?"

"Don't know. No one saw her leave."

"Her mace and spear are still here."

We stood and looked around. He then patted my arm and pointed west. We saw a dark figure move against the sand dunes. Our sentries saw it, too. Every man in camp had their sword ready, except the prince. Nyt-akerti walked up to Neter-kare.

"Where have you been?" His voice was soft, and not accusing. He gave her actions the benefit of doubt.

"I heard something in the sand." Her voice was low as she looked past us and to the horizon.

"What?" I asked.

"Don't laugh, but it sounded like a snake slipping over the dunes. A very big snake."

"You could hear a snake on the sand?" asked Lord Seneb, a son of the Am-pahue Nome. He was the tenth member of our group.

"No, no more than you could, which is why I knew it wasn't a snake. But I saw nothing, not even footprints in the sand. Yet I feel there is something out there."

"The moon is set," the prince said, "and it was a very dark night. It would be hard to see anything or anyone trying to hide. We must all keep watch on the land." He nodded once as if making a decision, then addressed us all in a clear voice in the growing light. "We near the coastline. The Shasu have been landing their ships along the beach and then gathering their forces. Once their army is assembled, they will select a town. We have at most a few days before they attack. Imet will likely be the first of many targets. The lives in the coastal villages depend on us, and our actions." He looked at the princess. "I chose these men before you because of their battle skills. Each is a prince of his home nome and would likely lead his own force if he left us. I have worked with them for years and know their skills and their limitations. You are the unknown. I will not have Pharaoh accuse me of hurrying your death by foolish means. We need to test your skills, Princess."

"I said—" Nyt-akerti began.

The prince waved her silent.

"Pharaoh ordered me to keep you safe. I need to see your skills, sister. Counselor Ipu-wer is the least accomplished of these men in the arts of weapons." He looked at me. "I mean no offense, cousin."

"I understand; my true skills lie elsewhere."

"Still he is well trained. Princess Nyt-akerti, I want you to fight our Counselor with sword. I'm not interested in blood, or in hurting the other. We save our strength for our enemy." The prince motioned for us to take to the sand.

"But—" she started to object again, but fell silent. The prince just stood silently with folded arms. I knew he would not argue with her.

I removed my warm robe and went to wait just east of the ruins, trying not to shiver. One of our sentries set four spears upright in the sand to mark the rectangular area of combat. We were surrounded by sand dunes. A path between the dunes led to the road we'd take at full light. Princess Nyt-akerti hesitated. She studied me, and then the others. She pointed to another man, closer to her own age.

"You are Ramose, correct?"

"Yes, princess, we are cousins," he answered.

"I will fight him," she stated.

"Why?" the prince asked.

"Because he is one of your best men. He is loyal to you, and he will think of me as your opponent if not enemy. Lord Ipu-wer thinks of me as a woman and princess. It wouldn't be a fair test of my skills."

"Ramose?" the prince asked.

"I am honored, although I don't think of the princess as an enemy. However, I have three older sisters, and a good memory. I have fought women before, even if not with a sword."

Princess Nyt-akerti removed her heavy cloak and stood on the packed-sand field wearing only a short kilt and leather vest. She took a fighter's stance with her sword positioned before her. Ramose was half again her weight, but still light in his sword-dance. He was more skilled with mace—I had practiced with him often enough—where sheer strength carried more killing power than graceful movement. Perhaps the princess saw that and thus chose him.

Ramose attacked first. The sound of his bronze blade as it struck the princess' filled the twilight. They pushed each other away, and then their swords clashed again. The blows came in rapid succession, each opponent testing the other's defenses. Nyt-akerti held her sword two-handed as if it were an extension of her arms, but Ramose's reach was longer in part because he could wield it one-handed. He was slower and more deliberate in his moves. Nyt-akerti moved like a pale cat in the dim light. Stray light glinted off her sword. It looked as if hieroglyphs ran down its center.

Ramose pushed forward, as Nyt-akerti retreated backward. Her movement took the fighters away from the ruins and up the slope of a dune. We followed. She turned aside each thrust with forceful counters. With every maneuver I found myself silently coaching her to move in a particular direction or manner; she seldom did. At the edge of my vision I saw Neter-kare pull one of the corner spears out of the sand, so the combatants wouldn't bump into it.

"His left side is weak," one of our men shouted.

"Quiet, Seneb," Ramose yelled. "She doesn't need your help!"

Ramose lunged forward. Nyt-akerti quickly spun around, lowered her sword and used Ramose's forward momentum to trip him. The big man twisted as he went down, trying to utilize his fall. He grabbed the princess' long braids and brought her down with him. It then became a wrestling match, the useless swords forgotten in the sand, with Ramose having most of the advantage by virtue of his extra weight.

"You're suppose to fight her, not sit on her, Ramose," someone added.

I looked up at the prince just in time to see him quickly aim and launch his spear at a shadow near the crest of dune where a temple block lay in the coarse sand. A low cry told us it had found a target. I was just behind the prince as we ran up the dune, swords ready. Ramose and Nyt-akerti were only a moment later in reaching the spot. Neter-kare rolled the body out of his dark robe. The armed man had the dark skin and curly brown hair of our enemy.

"He's Shasu, all right," Ramose said.

I looked around, scanning the horizon. "They never travel alone either."

"I don't see anything else out there," our sentry said. His partner backed him. They had been watching during the fight.

"We can't do anything if someone else slipped away," the prince said. We went back down the dune. The spears' owners retrieved the other three.

"Who next?" Nyt-akerti asked as she held her sword ready.

Neter-kare laughed. "I don't wish to tire you, sister, only test you. You move smoothly and with speed. And you didn't question my request for your *testing*. This is also a very good sign." He moved closer to her and took hold of her arm. She resisted at first and then let him position her in a fighting stance. "However, when you went down, you turned toward your right. If you had turned left, you might have been able to turn under Ramose and have broken free without going down. Like this." He demonstrated the movement.

She listened and watched. "Thank you, though I think I was a bit distracted."

"Battle is always distracting. You need to be aware of what's going on around you, but not let it take too much of your focus. Perhaps we rush to battle. If we stay here today and work on your technique—"

"We will have wasted a day," the princess added. "Nothing you tell me today can possibly make enough difference to take the risk. You said Imet has only a short time before the village is lost to the Shasu. We must move now, especially since our enemy may know we are here."

"Again, you show good sense. Can you endure in the heat of day?" he asked.

"I've never fought in battle, you know that, but I have practiced in full sun and won't wilt as a flower might."

"All right. We won't test your word further. In battle you should be able to hold your own, but we are a unit. We protect each other's backs. If you reach too far beyond your abilities just to prove your worth, or for fun, others may die with you. I will not have it. Understand?"

She nodded. Ramose came up behind her and lightly grasped her shoulder.

"If the fight had gone on a minute longer, Princess, you would have had me. I felt your knife blade against my back. Not many have won against me so quickly."

She smiled. "You have long arms, cousin."

"They compensate for my lack of height." Ramose rubbed his arms, as if cold. "Thank you for using your iron knife. I feared it was another blade out of legend."

"I have heard some legends as well. My other knife,

the one of bone, will never taste blood, in deference to legend, until I learn more."

"Prepare your gear," Prince Neter-kare ordered. "We leave at full light. Tonight we camp on the coast."

"And not in Imet?" the princess asked. "Why? How can we protect the village?"

"We stop the enemy before they land to diminish their numbers. Today we move inland, across the marshes, tomorrow you show us how you can destroy our enemy while they're still at sea."

She nodded and went to gather her few possessions. I did the same. On our backs we each carried our bedroll, and enough food and water for three days— the distance between the supply camps or army posts along our northeastern frontier in the Delta.

That night we camped among the jagged rocks along the coast. We could hear the surf pounding the beach. As a creature of the desert, I found it disquieting seeing water so vast, although knowing it couldn't be used was somehow reassuring. I took the first watch. It would take me at least three hours to relax enough to sleep as I quietly moved among the sharp rocks surrounding our camp. The young moon rested high in the sky; he had yet to obtain his full measure. Still, he brightened my path and eased my travel over the jumble of rough-edged boulders. I climbed around several massive rocks, turned the corner, and saw a shadow among the shadows.

"Who is there?" I whispered into the night while more firmly grasping my sword.

"It is me, Counselor," the princess answered. I moved closer to where she sat watching the ocean. It took a moment to realize what was different about her appearance.

"Princess, your hair!"

She touched the now-short locks with one hand and held the bead-strewn braids with the other. Even by moonlight I could see the flame color. "No one ever came so close to defeating me, just because of my hair. I doubt the Shasu would be as gentle as Ramose was. Never again."

"Your mother—"

She laughed softly. "Is not here. I'll send the braids to her if she misses them." Bitterness touched her words.

"We are not your enemy, my princess."

"Aren't you? You were all so pleasant today, but I don't believe any of you would want me as pharaoh before my brother."

"A woman pharaoh is unusual, more so than even a woman warrior, yet you still found a willing teacher. You'll become pharaoh as you became warrior, by earning the right. Somewhere along the path we will all accept your right, even the prince."

"Will he?"

"Yes, I don't doubt it. Not for a minute. We are children of Kemet, first. Bring peace to this land and none will stand against you."

"If I could be so certain!"

"Is being pharaoh so important to you? Is that why you went to your father? Or was it to help us against our enemy?"

She stood and looked out over the ocean. "This moist air does strange things to my thoughts. No, I came to Pharaoh because I wanted to help. Because I can help."

"I thought so. Love of Kemet runs strong even in your mother."

"This land is easy to love. It was only after Father offered me the Double Crown that I knew I wanted it. I was seven when my mother sent me away to the Temple. She never forgave me for being a daughter. She wanted a son to become Kemet's heir."

"You are too harsh toward her. She has always spoken highly of you. I have seen and heard her pride for you."

"Yet Pharaoh did not easily remember me."

"Sending you to the Temple was a victory for which she fought hard battles. If you were daughter of any other man, you would not have enjoyed so high an education. Did it occur to you that perhaps she didn't want anyone to really remember you until you could grow old enough to protect yourself? I don't know for sure if she knew you carried Narmer's magic. Maybe she suspected it. Twenty years ago, even fifteen, the court was not so friendly a place. The crown prince was sick, and then he died. Only Prince Neter-kare's firm hand kept order among the potential heirs long enough for Pharaoh to choose the next heir."

"You do want him before me!"

"That's not what I said. Neter-kare did what he did to protect Kemet. Pharaoh saw that and made the proper choice then. Perhaps now you are the proper choice. It's too soon to know. You have yet to prove yourself. I am willing to give you that chance." I looked at the ocean myself. So much untamed power in the waves, much like the princess beside me. "There is something you need to know which is little spoken of these days and which I'm sure your mother has never told you. No one would dare insult her so by bringing it forward. But I think you would understand her better by knowing. Your mother was a gift to Pharaoh. Her life as nobility has always been precarious."

"What do you mean?"

"She has no birthright to protect her. It is by Pharaoh's whim that she remains nobility and not slave."

"Father doesn't keep slaves."

"No, generally he does not. There are a few foreigners who remain so. Your mother did what she could to ensure you never share her uncertainty. As a priestess of Ma-at, and especially as a high priestess, you have earned special rights no one can steal—not even Pharaoh would dare anger the goddess so."

"I have always thought she didn't love me."

"She is not one to show her feelings easily, I think in that you are like her."

The young woman merely shrugged.

"I know her pride for you runs very deep. You are too quick to judge your friends and opponents."

"I don't know what a friend is. I never had friends in the Temple."

I wanted to comfort her, she seemed so young, but I knew she'd turn away from me, so I let her continue.

"I used to wake nights, alone in my room at the Temple. Sometimes I was so frightened. I had never been alone before. Then I woke one night, very afraid, to find a cobra in my room. It didn't matter that she could kill me, I took comfort in her presence, because I wasn't alone! Later I discovered she had a nest in the garden just outside my room. She never hurt me, never even came close to it. I could even touch her. She was the most beautiful golden color. Soon she was the only one I could talk to. She listened patiently every night.

"One day I was angry at an old priestess. She refused to let me practice with the bow or spear. She didn't like my training with any weapon. That night I was still mad and told the cobra I wished her dead. The next morning the priests found her dead. I was very careful about what I told my cobra after that. I'm afraid to want to be Pharaoh. I don't want to harm Father or Neter-kare."

"The power of the goddesses is in you. You are wise to be cautious. As Pharaoh, you cannot carry your heart in your hands for all to see, but that doesn't mean you can't allow some of us closer."

"Do you think Neter-kare likes me? Even a little?"

I laughed softly. "I think maybe. You're a challenge."

"Well, that is something."

"At some point you will need friends who are not goddesses, but human. Letting people close to you may not bring you any nearer to your goals, but you'll enjoy the traveling more."

"And if I'm dangerous to be near?"

"We are all strong warriors and can care for ourselves." I moved away and continued my patrol.

The Shasu's ship sailed parallel to the shore, just beyond the rocky reef, driven by stiff, predawn winds and her crew's determination. The ship was not as large as one of our battle fleet. She held only fifty men, maybe seventy. Still, with enough ships, they could assemble a large army on our very shores. A warm, salt-laden breeze filled the Shasu's sails and swept to shore, past the gray boulders hiding us from the ship's lookout. Princess Nyt-akerti, dressed in sand-colored robes, crawled out to the water's edge, where the sea left pale foam on the twilight-lit sand. Just out of reach of the hungry fingers of the rising waves, she took up her knife. The white blade shone in the low light, as she quickly carved hieroglyphs in the moistened sand.

I was as close as I could get to her and still be hidden by rock. Prince Neter-kare waited beside me.

"Do you think she has the power?" he whispered.

"The power, yes," I answered, "but this enemy is very strong, perhaps too strong."

A voice reached us from the shore. "Heka, he who is great-of-magic, fill my words with your power. Thoth, wise are you in magic, lend me your wisdom. Sand of Geb, hold me in your embrace that I may have strength to reach toward the stars of Nuut. Waters of Nun—" The princess' prayer faltered.

"Why has she stopped?" the prince asked.

She merely waited on the wet sand, head lowered. I left my hiding place and crawled to her side.

"What is it?" I whispered lest my voice carry on the waves to the passing ship.

"The priestesses taught me that my words were the magic and the magic was my words. I had only to write the words in my heart, and it would be so. This is Ma-at's truth, and Heka would make it so."

"Don't you believe it?" I asked.

"Yes, I believed it, but it seems so little—that I need more than just words. Look how big that ship is!"

"You need to know these men are your enemy. We're at war. If they are the victors, they will kill your father and brothers. Anyone who can lay claim to the throne. You and your mother will become their property—if they let you live."

Her amber-colored eyes were dark in the twilight, almost black. "Does that include you and the rest of our company?"

"Of course. They will wipe out the ruler and heir to every nome. If you have the power to protect Kemet, you must."

"Go back." She began to carve again in the wet sand as I retreated the beach. Her words followed me.

"Nun, hear your daughter, my enemy is in your watery embrace. Stay their course, smash their boat on the reef. Slay the hearts of those who would harm your people, for I, daughter of the North and daughter of the South, need your strength. Thoth may your words occur; Heka may your magic shine. Magic is my name. I made the spells in my heart—"

Her words were soft. The end of the prayer was carried away on the winds of Shu. Even so I wondered if it was sacrilege for me to hear any of it. She finished inscribing the last glyphs of her spell as the rising tide touched her writings. A hunger flowed through the sand! It surrounded and tasted me. Was I what it wanted?

"Do you feel that?" Prince Neter-kare asked.

"Yes! The power spreads with the retreating wave. Its strength fills the waters."

"I didn't believe she could," the prince said. "Look! It pulls the ship closer to shore! She didn't lie."

An alarm rose from those on board. The distance obscured the words. I felt the enemy's fear; it traveled across the waves with the magic. Seawater now covered all of the princess' spell, yet the glyphs remained distinct. They shone in the predawn darkness. I felt their powerful pull. I forced myself to stay where I was. The sound of wood scraping rock strained the air, but it was not the harsh crack of a deadly impact. Men rushed across the ship's deck, pulling on and adjusting wind-filled sheets. The sailors fought the spell-strengthened current.

The waves lapped over the powerful words again and again until their sharp edges blurred. Their image dimmed.

"The magic leaves us," the prince said. "We'd better leave, too."

Again the ship scraped the rocks, but this time the sound was softer, more a kiss than a blow. An encouraging cry rose from the ship and moved across rocks and waves. The sailors had cleared the worst of the hazardous shoreline. The waves continued caressing the beach and the princess where she knelt, soaking her robe. The sand was now free of marring glyphs, and the sailors, almost out of danger, proved stronger than her spell. Our enemy prepared to beach their ship.

"I've failed?" the princess cried. "No, the gods wouldn't do this, not to me!" The first rays of returning Re-Horakhti reached the wave-washed sands. Shouting men from the ship pointed to where Nytakerti knelt. I heard their word for sorceress on the wind. She did not move.

"Princess," I called out in a harsh whisper.

The prince waited only a heartbeat, then ran to her and pulled her to her feet. She braced against him.

"I would fight them here," she cried out.

"And you would die." The ship landed less than three hundred strides away. "We escape into the marshes and fight them there, if they follow." He pulled on her arm and they ran. We three scrambled over the rock and could hear our pursuers. About two hundred strides from the shore waited our ten warriors.

"What moves on the beach?" Seneb asked. "It feels as if the waves reach out to grab anyone who moves."

"It's the princess' magic." Neter-kare asked, "Are we safe from it, Nyt-akerti?"

"Yes, as long as we're on land," she answered.

"We are followed," Neter-kare told to the soldiers. "A dozen swords against over fifty men."

"Thirteen swords," Princess Nyt-Akerti said as she shrugged out of her wet robe to stand in her warrior garb. "We can remain here and fight. The rocks will hide us for a time."

"Not long enough."

"We can try!"

"I'll not lose good men to foolishness. We fight in the marshes. Only we know the safest paths. Many of them will drown or be bitten by snakes."

"Princess," I began, "can you call the creatures of the marsh to attack and slow their pursuit?"

"No—I mean yes—but they would attack all men, us as well as them. Creatures do not understand our wars."

An ibex cried into the waxing morning, as if warning us away from her nesting territory. We moved off the rocks and down onto the outer sand fields. A few of the Shasu scrambled after us in an effort to hold us until a greater number of their fellows could join them. Bronze rang on bronze in the growing heat. We spread out and ran through the tall grass fields toward the marshes. The prince wouldn't be baited to stand and fight. He urged us to hurry. The princess often lagged behind to fight. She saved me from greater injury twice when I slipped in the mud while fighting. Two of our men received minor cuts. We did not stop to dress the wounds.

Soon we were moving single file on paths through the tall, water-laden marshgrass. Seneb led the way; he had grown up in this nome. Although I could see nothing special about our route, little but our feet got wet. If someone veered from the path or slipped, the water rose over their heads. We hid from our enemy where we could. By midday we heard no more pursuit.

The day turned sweltering as the sun climbed past noon. It was a moist heat, the likes of which I had never known before. It stole our strength as we limped into the nearest army camp near sunset.

I waited atop a sandstone cliff beside my princess. Below, our army of five hundred men clashed with the forces of the Shasu king, Em-khet. His forces attacked first, but our men moved into the precise formations Prince Neter-kare had planned, brilliantly dividing the enemy forces, and weakening their greater number.

The noon wind blew hard into my face, robbing moisture from my skin. My hands looked as dark and dry as aged figs. The princess' skin had turned a painful red. There was still time to climb down the cliff path and rejoin our forces. She took a step, but stopped. Her dreams of victory were just that, dreams, unless all the gods supported her now.

"Help from the gods will not come easy," I said. "It must be won. Remember?"

"I remember." Her words were soft. "A balance between strength of arms and magic. This is Ma-at's truth. Ma-at's truth is my truth," she prayed.

"There is one aspect of your magic which I don't understand."

"Just one?" she asked. I could hear the gentle teasing in her words.

"On the beach, why didn't you encase your spell in a circle?"

"A circle? Why would I?"

"In every spell I have seen performed, the priests always encircle the magical hieroglyphs."

"They have never told me this. Why wouldn't they, if I need it?"

I shrugged. "Perhaps it isn't necessary." I suddenly felt chilled.

"What is it?" She took a step towards me in concern.

"What if the priests never told you because they wanted to control your magic and your power?"

"They wouldn't let me go into battle untrained?"

"They didn't want you to go at all!"

"Encircle my spell, I can do that. But how many times?"

"I don't remember, but several times, at least."

"Three is a holy number for the trinity of gods, but seven is more holy."

Nyt-akerti took a handful of sand and scattered it on the wind, testing Shu's strength. She moved toward the cliff's edge and threw another handful of sand in the air and spoke holy words. With her spell, the sand stayed suspended before her, oblivious to the pull of the earth, but not to the wind's, as its invisible fingers coursed around sand grains and through the priestess' short hair. I wondered how long the magic would last this time. She took up her holy blade, and quickly started carving in the sandy air the spell that might win this victory our army desperately needed.

"Heka, open your two eyes so that the Two Lands may see. I conjure by means of your magic. Strengthen Kemet's limbs from the power of our enemy. Goddess Tefnut, moisten their throats with the sweat of our foes." The hieroglyphs took shape in the sandy air, the wind curved around the figures and through them, widening the pictures. "Give us victory so that the deaths may stop, only in victory will both Kemet and the gods be strong. Give me this victory. Osiris, hear my plea. Neith, protect my warriors with your wings." Nyt-akerti then walked around her spell three full circles.

A battle cry rose up from below. Our men rallied around Prince Neter-kare. The pace of my heart quickened as I touched the war mace hanging from my belt. From below, the sound of mace on shield reverberated off the cliff face. Our smaller force held and even pushed the enemy back toward the great river, Hepu! Another cry went up from our men. The desert winds carried the song in its arms and intensified the call as our forces surged forward, though not as far as I hoped. I looked at her spell; it had faded. Much of the sand had been scoured away by the wind.

"If you stop the winds, your spell would last, but does it need the wind to carry the magic's strength to our men?"

"I don't know." She quickly threw more sand into the air, redrew her spell, and encircled it seven full turns. "Now, let's join the battle!"

"It's too dangerous!"

"Would you deny me this fight?"

"No, not I, but—"

"How can I rule men whom I refuse to fight next to in battle? Neter-Kare would never just stand here and watch them die for him, nor would you. How can I?"

The winds half-carried us down the steep path as if on Horus' wings, to stand with our army, in victory or defeat. Our band of warriors, led by the prince, fought nearest the cliff's base as the last block to protect the princess and her magic from the enemy. I began the next battle cry, our men's voices rising joyously in anticipation of their greatest victory.

Prince Neter-kare fought his way over to me. "You were to keep her up there," he nodded toward the cliff, "and safe."

"Was I?" I mopped the sweat from my brow and out of my eyes with my arm while scanning for my next opponent. "How can I deny her the joy of this fight?"

"The pharaoh said—" An enemy soldier came forward with raised mace aimed at the back of the prince's head. Princess Nyt-akerti's sword was there before mine, slicing off the warrior's arm with her powerful two-handed stroke. I finished the man with a stab in the chest.

"Brother," she said, "this is no time for tactical disagreements. We need every sword." She wore a grin more suited to a sporting arena and moved away to take on another warrior.

"Look up there," Ramose said from our other side. We followed where he pointed with his sword. A huge vulture soared overhead on the air currents. Sun glinted off its golden feathers. "Goddess Nekhbet protects the princess. Who can deny a goddess, with or without wings?"

"So she does," the prince answered. "Do not leave our little goddess' side, Counselor, Ramose," he ordered us, before the battle drew him away.

"How does he expect anyone to keep up with her?" Ramose asked me. We both fought to get near her again, and to stay there. It was as if she was Sekhmet, the warrior goddess, herself. The sun transformed Nytakerti's short locks into a crown of fire. Her bronze sword danced through the hot air, to fast for me to follow, but then I, too, had my own battles to fight and could not keep track of her or the prince for very long, lest I lose my head to some foreign mace. Only her battle cry reached me from time to time—it was deep like the beat of powerful wings on the winds.

When the battle finally slowed, I found my mace well-bloodied and many of the enemy dead at my feet, their painted bodies colorful under the bright sun. My sword had snapped in two in the belly of a foe early on. The princess' spell, long since vanished, had been enough help. She stood beside me, and the blood dripped from her own sword. We did not savor our victory long before we heard her name on the wind. Ramose called us. I felt my heart sink as we came closer.

Prince Neter-kare lay on the ground. Surgeons were tying off the deep gash in his left thigh. He would lose that leg, but the two deep slices to his abdomen drew the princess' attention. Each new packing of linen quickly became blood-soaked.

"Can you slow the blood flow?" she asked the surgeons as she knelt at his side.

"We are trying," one answered.

"Nyt-akerti," the prince said.

She took his hand in hers. "I'm here. We have won. Your battle plans were good. The saved our forces."

"I felt your magic on the wind," he began, "and in the blowing sand. It was stronger than before. It made me stronger. I never felt so powerful as I took on each warrior. I felt like a god out of legend." He closed his eyes for a moment to breathe through the pain. "Your talent grows with each use, but you have much to learn before you can be pharaoh. Trust in Ipu-wer and your men as much as you trust in the goddesses. You cannot save Kemet without their help."

"I will, I promise." Her voice was soft. I felt the tears welling within me even as I saw her eyes fill. She swallowed hard, trying to keep her composure.

"And once you are crowned, you must visit each nome and learn the names of the men and women who control each. You will need them to rule this land. Let Ipu-wer teach you how to survey the flooded fields. When you understand the farmers, your people will never go hungry."

"I will stand in the muddy fields with him and learn."

Prince Neter-kare nodded. "I saw Nekhbet flying over us as we fought. I knew she was there to keep you safe. You are the chosen of the gods and goddesses." He closed his eyes and his breath left him. None of us moved, save for the sobs welling in the troops around us. My own face was wet, as was the princess'.

She came to stand beside me as priests took the prince's body away. Her voice was a whisper at my side. "Do you think our people will ever love me as they loved him?"

"I think some already do, my princess," I answered, as Ramose came over to us. He placed a hand on both of our shoulders, sharing our grief over the loss of our kinsman.

The golden boat of Re had climbed well into the sky, filling the desert with his heat. Soon both armies would retire from the field to rest. I climbed the red-orange sandstone cliffs. She would be somewhere amongst this jumble of rocks. High overhead the vulture soared on the rising currents, always watching, protecting the one for whom I searched. Upward I trod under the sun's bright glare, waterskin resting against my leather vest. My new iron sword hung comfortably at my side—a war gift from my pharaoh. The sweat formed rivulets down my back and face. I looked from whence I'd come. Was even the Great Pyramid as high as this?

At the very summit of the outcrop sat Pharaoh Nyt-akerti, her fair legs crossed under her on the wind-blown sands. Wisps of sun-bleached hair escaped the thongs she had used to tie it back. The bright sun painted her locks more yellow than amber. Her amber eyes stared at the air before her, and I knew her vision saw a world other than the one in which I stood. Arrayed around her were dozens of figurines. One set of ushabtis clearly represented Kemet's warriors. Each figure portrayed the perfection and strength of her soldiers. Their weapons were held high, be it bow, mace, or bronze sword. The other figures were like the desert nomads we fought today; many of these ushabtis now lacked heads or limbs.

She still spun the weave of her spell, stealing the strength and will from our enemy. The power of the magic lent a shimmering to the hot air.

I would always see Nyt-akerti as my princess first, even though she had earned the title Pharaoh. Shortly after Prince Neter-kare's death, Pharaoh named his daughter the new Horus and crowned her co-regent with the Double Crown, even though the war was not finished. She had proved her magic, and the head of each nome supported her claim. It helped that the eight surviving warriors of our party sang her praises loudly. Ramose wrote a ballad in her honor. The beautiful poetry of his song surprised even me.

Pharaoh died that same season, entering the House of Death while he slept, and the longest reign of any Pharaoh ended after 94 years. It was whispered he could now leave his beloved Kemet because he knew she was finally safe. The comment brought a mist to Nyt-akerti's eyes. I knew she thought of Neter-kare and how the comment would hurt him. She finally understood how hard he had worked to keep Kemet safe while she grew up and learned how to use her magic in the Temple.

When my princess came from her trance, it was as if Re returned from behind a cloud, so intent was her gaze, and her smile. Her eyes shone brighter than the gold-and-amber bracelets adorning her arms. She reached for the waterskin without a word and drank deeply. I saw the vulture overhead soaring higher. She followed my gaze.

"The Goddess Nekhbet watches over you always. If I were to look, would I find a giant golden cobra among the rocks? Does Goddess Wadjet watch you, too?"

She shrugged. "The battle is done." Her voice was clear and strong for all her hours of silence. Her delicate hands moved slightly with each word.

"Good. The heat will drain our men. Later when the sun has sunk toward the west—"

"No, Lord Ipu-wer, it is finished, and done well. We have won!" She sprang lightly to her feet and looked out over the cliff's edge to where the battle had raged for so long. "I saw it in my vision. The goddess Ma-at has granted me my heart's desire—my final victory!"

I got up and followed her to the edge. I held only ten years more than her twenty, but had I ever been so young? Yes, but never so alive, until I came to serve her.

"My Pharaoh, certainly we must give some credit to our generals who implemented your brilliant strategies. General Ramose will want some of the glory."

She laughed, a sound as clear as the morning wind. "Our war plans were good, but not as good as my spell." She swept out her hand to encompass the numerous ushabtis. "Our men are strong, but not as strong as the goddesses and gods. God Shu brought the cooler winds to only our men. Goddess Ma-at hid our lack of strength from our enemies' eyes. But I will give Ramose much praise. He earned it, and more.

"It's time we find our army. The celebration tonight will be joyous. I wish Prince Neter-kare were here to share in it. Do you think he would be happy for me? Or would he yell at me and tell me what I did wrong?"

"Yes, he would tell you if you made a mistake, but he would raise his mug of beer high in your honor and be one of your strongest supporters. Kemet is strong and will remain strong by the grace of the goddess—"

"And her many swords," Nyt-akerti finished.

COMMON GROUND
by John Helfers

John Helfers is a writer and editor currently living in Green Bay, Wisconsin. His fiction appears in anthologies such as *Future Net, Sword of Ice and Other Tales of Valdemar,* and *The UFO Files,* among others. He is also the editor of the anthology *Black Cats and Broken Mirrors.* Future projects include coauthoring a fantasy novel and designing a role-playing game. In his spare time, what there is of it, he enjoys disc golf, inline skating, and role-playing games.

L aithen ducked as the arm of the *soran* whistled over her head, smashing into the tree trunk behind her. Using her momentum, she threw herself forward into a roll, the creature's massive foot just missing her.

A grunt caused her to look up at the monstrosity, and she noticed yet another arrow shaft sticking out of its neck. It looked up as well, spotting Sindar in the tree above it. The slim elf nocked another arrow into his short bow, fear visible on his pale features. With another grunt, the monster started climbing the tree after him.

Laithen watched the tree bend and sway under the *soran.* Sindar frowned and motioned for her to run. He readied his bow, aiming at the creature's head, which was large, shaggy, and looked like a cross between a Plainsman and a bear. It certainly had enough teeth. This thing, however, was faster than any bear had a right to be. Once surprised by it, the two elves hadn't had time to escape. Now Sindar glared at his sister again, urging her to leave.

Laithen had other plans. Grabbing her spear from where it had fallen, she let out a bloodcurdling scream and hurled the spear with all of her strength. It thunked solidly into the creature's back, but did not seem to injure it.

Distracted again, the monster's head swiveled and looked back down at her just as its hand, which could have covered Laithen's entire head, closed on another branch to pull its massive body higher into the tree. Fortunately, it chose a slim branch, which broke in its powerful grip. Off balance, the creature flailed for purchase in the tree, nearly knocking Sindar out of his perch as a clawed hand raked the branches where he had just been sitting. More tree limbs snapped as the oak gave way. With a loud bellow, the *soran* fell.

Laithen now had no time to regret her hasty action as she saw the huge shape hurtle toward her. She dove to one side, but not quite fast enough. A heavy weight slammed into her foot as both she and the *soran* landed in a shower of autumn leaves.

Swaying, Laithen rose to her feet and saw Sindar climbing down the tree. He jumped from the lower branches over to her, avoiding any contact with the now unmoving beast. Taking her by the arm, he said, "Let's go."

"But my spear—" she started to reply.

"Do you want to go digging around under that thing? Father didn't give that weapon so you could lose your life over it. We're getting out of here," the taller elf said.

"But, Sindar, we should kill—"

Again his exasperated voice cut her off. "I don't even know if that's possible. We're going. Now."

She shook off his hand. "I can walk just fine, thank you."

"Good," he replied, walking past her. "Don't fall behind."

Laithen looked at his retreating form, then at the *soran,* which happened to snort at that moment and then start moving weakly. Instinctively stepping away, she bit back a curse as she put weight on her injured heel. Remembering what she had said, she turned back and strode after her brother, ignoring the flare of pain every time she stepped on her wounded foot.

Koani heard the sounds of struggle in the distance, followed by a yell and a loud noise, as if a tree had fallen. Her ears pricked up, followed by her nose, which scented meat, as well as something else. She identified the rank odor as that of a kinkiller, which her pack avoided at all times. Still, the kinkillers sometimes left meat behind, which made investigating worth the risk.

Loping down the small hill, Koani headed toward the sounds of fighting, which suddenly ended with a loud yell and a crash which seemed to shake the trees around her. Animal sounds brought her closer to the scene, where she saw two of the furless ones communicating. The larger one moved to touch the smaller, but was shrugged off. Koani's head cocked as she listened to their incomprehensible barks and yips. With a final angry grunt, the tall one stalked off into the forest. The small one moved to follow, then stopped, wincing and favoring its leg. Steeling its expression, it strode after the tall one. Only then did Koani notice the kinkiller they had been fighting, even though its scent hung heavy in the clearing. The thing scrabbled at the ground, trying to rise. From where she was, the wolf could see the tan fur of the creature's underbelly. Koani just watched at the edge of the clearing, unaware of anything else until a dark shape hurtled into her, bowling her over.

Ending up on her back, Koani looked up to see Matsi, the female of their leader, standing over her, teeth bared and growling. Covering her nose with her paws, Koani exposed her belly, acknowledging the other's status. The conversation through their growls and yips was short and terse.

"Why do you watch the furless and kinkiller? Why are you not hunting?" Matsi asked.

"I thought they defeated it. When I looked, it did not move," Koani answered, all too aware of the thing's movement now.

With a violent shake of her head, Matsi made her position clear. "Kinkiller is death. Furless is death. No watch. You see furless, you run. You see kinkiller, you run faster."

Whimpering, Koani agreed. Only then did Matsi, after a final contemptuous glare, let her up. The two wolves swiftly left the monster far behind them, running to meet with the rest of the pack.

Laithen leaned against a tree and massaged her foot, which had now swelled to twice its normal size. Gritting her teeth, she tried to ease the stagskin boot off, only to wince as pain stabbed up her leg.

"Here, let me." Sindar had crept back to her in that annoying way he had, and was now kneeling to take a closer look.

"It's nothing, really," she hissed.

"Laithen, you've been breaking branches for the past hundred paces. Just relax and let me look at it." Gently kneading the heel of her foot, he winced at her gasp of pain. Going to a pouch at his side, he crushed a handful of leaves and let the fragments sift into her boot. Laithen felt a numbing warmth spread through her shin and foot, and when she tried walking again, it was without any difficulty at all.

He straightened and looked at her. "How's that?"

"Better, thanks." She smiled ruefully, her anger having dissipated on the walk.

"It should hold you until we reach Treehaven. You'd better have Nouri look at it. No doubt she'll want to fuss with it more." Sindar stepped back, waited for his sister to start moving, then fell into step beside her.

After a few minutes, Laithen broke the silence. "That was some fight, eh?"

Sindar shook his head. "Lucky neither of us were killed."

"Like you wouldn't have been if that *soran* had gotten its claws on you?" Laithen stated more than asked.

"It couldn't have gotten to me once I reached the top of the tree. I was trying to lure it higher, then I would have jumped off as the tree fell."

Laithen snorted. "And you call my plans foolhardy."

"It would have worked," Sindar said with infuriating calm.

Brushing a leaf off of her brown hide armor, Laithen said, "The warrior's oath—"

"Does not include fighting something you cannot beat. Since these *soren* have appeared, we haven't seen one dead yet, or even seriously wounded. They're twice as tall as our biggest warrior, and almost as fast. You saw how little effect my arrows had on it. You shouldn't even have been there."

Laithen pinned him with her gaze. "Why, because I'm the *Alfheim*'s daughter? That's a dagger that cuts both ways, brother. Besides, you're next in line for the crown anyway. I certainly don't want it."

"Yes, I know, but I'll still need you once that happens. Everybody knows, as you like to remind them, who the warrior is in the family," the lithe elf said.

"Sindar, you know I don't mean it like that." Laithen looked over to make sure he wasn't insulted, feeling relieved when she saw him smile.

"I know you don't. But it's true. As Father has often said, we are two halves of the same person. Together, we are whole. Anyway, if we don't discover a way to stop the *soren*, there won't be much of a kingdom to rule."

"Exactly, which is why we must track them down, take the fight to them."

Sindar shook his head. "No."

"But—"

"There are other ways than fighting," Sindar interrupted.

"What then? They avoid every snare we set for them and appear out of nowhere to attack us. Cold-season is almost here, Sindar. No one can go out to gather or hunt because they're always waiting for us, like what just happened back there. Our traps end up smashed and broken, with any food in them gone. The more hunting parties that go out, the more of them we encounter. If we don't find a way to get food for the coming snows, the village will starve."

Sindar whirled on her, his face grim. "Do you think I don't realize that? Your gift for stating the obvious is remarkable." Seeing her reaction to his sudden temper, he reined himself in. "Father has called a Council meeting tonight. We will discuss the matter and resolve it, one way or another." With that, he continued walking.

And that will mean leaving the forest, Laithen thought.

By the time the pack stopped moving, night had blanketed the woods for hours. On the way to the resting ground, Koani saw Matsi trotting alongside their leader Kamots. As she watched, both of them looked back at her, Matsi grinning, Kamots as calm as ever. Koani quickly looked away under their stares.

Once at the resting ground, the wolves all sat or lay on the ground, panting despite the autumn chill in the air. As always, Matsi and Kamots sat together, and Koani lay down away from the main group of wolves. While the rest of the pack accepted her, they did not go out of their way to include her, an arrangement which suited everyone just fine.

Kamots walked slowly into the center of the clearing. He turned, making sure every eye was upon him before beginning.

"This huntday, like many before it, has not brought

food for our bellies. The kinkillers still roam the forest, and have frightened off the meat we need to survive. We cannot drive them out either, as they are too strong to fight, even with the entire pack. Many of us lost packbrothers and sisters during those hopeless battles. If we do not move before the snows come, the pack will not survive."

The majority of the wolves yipped or nodded assent with their leader. Only Koani got to her feet and walked slowly into the clearing. Usually silent during the pack discussions, she was aware of every eye upon her.

"Brothers and sisters, it is known that you accepted me into your pack when I ran alone, and for this I thank you. But when I ran alone, I saw the world beyond this forest, and it is one we cannot survive in. The furless outside the forest advance closer every day, and where they go, everything dies. Animals flee, or are killed by the furless. The trees of the forest are taken from the ground in which they have risen, taken by the furless to make dens to live in. They will not exist side by side with us. They will take our young and kill them. They will kill us as well."

"The outsider fears the world beyond the forest. As long as the pack exists, there is no place we cannot survive." Matsi trotted up to stand beside Kamots. "If our leader says we move, then I say we follow."

"Follow to where?" Koani retorted. "The furless outside the forest are not like the furless here. Their stings can kill from far away, even farther than the furless who live in the trees. They watch for those like us, and when they see us, they leave bad meat, which brings on the drooling sickness that drives us mad. They are too powerful."

Matsi was about to retort angrily again, but was stopped by a touch from Kamots' nose. Gulping back her words, she waited for him to speak. When he did, his tone was calm.

"So, Koani, you would have us not leave the forest.

Of course, that would be preferable, but how are we to live? The kinkillers make hunting all but impossible. Our caches are gone, either eaten by us or found by others. The snows come fast, and all we have in our bellies now is hope. What is your answer?"

Remembering the scene she had come upon in the forest, Koani answered, "The furless ones who live in the forest. If we can ally with them, together we could fight the kinkillers."

For a moment, no one moved. The entire pack just looked at her. Then a chorus of voices spoke, their comments mingling together.

"Ally with the furless. You would have us run with those who wear skins of others. Barbaric," Matsi growled, walking toward Koani. Kamots advanced as well, barking to get the attention of the pack.

"Koani, as you said before, you are not of us, and perhaps where you come from, things are different. But here in the forest, we leave the furless alone, and they leave us alone. This is the way it has always been, existing without bloodshed."

"Yes, but does that mean that is the way it will always be?" Another wolf, Savre, said as he walked to the small circle. Savre was Kamots' brother, a slightly smaller black wolf. He was a taciturn one, aloof from the rest of the pack, but in a different way than Koani. His distance was accepted, the other wolves acknowledging that it was his way, and letting it pass. He never spoke up in discussion unless he felt it was warranted, and when he did speak, it always was. This time, he had also remained silent until he had heard the idea proposed. Now, he stood between Matsi and Koani, interrupting the hostility sparking between them. "Matsi said as long as the pack is together, it will survive. This is true, but only partly. If the pack cannot adapt to changing times, it will perish whether there are a few or many of us. This is the truth."

Upon seeing Savre take Koani's side, some of the younger wolves started to discuss her idea, while the older ones snorted their derision of the proposal. Kamots let the talk rise and fall for a few minutes, then yipped for silence.

"Our packsister has proposed an idea which brings with it much thought. Truly this cannot be decided in one evening. When the darkness passes, we will discuss this again. Then will we come to a decision. For now, rest and think about what has been spoken here."

The wolves fell silent, then walked to the sleeping area to huddle together for warmth. Koani turned to see Savre watching her, his face expressionless. Without a word, he turned and walked to the sleeping area. Koani started to follow, but stopped, realizing that rest was the last thing she wanted. Knowing Kamots wouldn't let her go, she joined the rest of the pack, lying in a large circle of fur and covering her nose with her paws. Because Koani was of lower status, she was relegated to the outside of the circle, with one side of her body exposed to the chilly night air.

After a long time, when the others' breathing had slowed to the cadence of sleep, Koani gently rolled to her feet and trotted to the edge of the forest. Looking back at the group of sleeping wolves one last time, she turned and ran into the forest.

Only one wolf saw her go. Savre, his head resting on his paws, watched her leave without alerting anyone. He stared off in the direction she had gone for a long time.

Laithen listened at the doorway of the large hut as the elders discussed what was to be done. She saw her father, the *Alfheim,* sitting in his carved wooden throne, listening to the debate rise and fall. Although she had every right to be at the meeting, she didn't bother, preferring action to words.

She smiled as she saw her father notice her and throw a sly wink while he listened to the speakers. Usually he would listen to both sides, then take the

best from both arguments and combine them, while
making each side think they had won. Laithen didn't
think it would be so easy this time.

Right now Sindar was pacing the council floor, trying to stave off the uprooting of the clan. Laithen
listened to him for a moment.

"—where else will we go? The forest is our home,
it has been provider for the tribe my whole life. It is
what we know. Without it, we will not survive."

"Sindar, your words are truth to all here. But an
even greater truth is that the beasts that now stalk the
forest threaten our existence even more. It may take
time, but we will endure, no matter where we may
go," Riko, one of the tribe's best hunters, said.

"We may endure, but at what cost? Must we leave
our homeland and wander, no longer able to—"

Laithen rose from her place and walked to the ladder, not wanting to hear more. Making sure her daggers were at her belt, she quickly climbed down and
ran into the forest. For a moment she could almost
hear Sindar's voice, warning her not to go into the
forest. *But they don't bother those who are alone,* she
thought, *at least, not usually.* She raised her head and
smiled. *Besides, there's nothing I can't outrun.*

There must be a way to stop these beasts, she thought
as she ran. When she was far enough away from the
village, she slowed to a walk, relishing her newly-
healed foot. Unfortunately, the news she had gotten
from the shaman hadn't been as good as the healing
herbs she now carried at her belt.

"Laithen, many in the tribe are arguing to leave
here, to go and settle in another part of the forest.
They feel the gods have left this place, and that evil
resides here instead," Nouri had said while tending to
her leg. She had listened as the shaman had talked,
her mind trying to come up with a way to save the
village from leaving, but had thought of nothing. Now,
back in the forest, she was coming up just as empty.

Short of killing one of them, there's not a lot I can

do, she thought. *And Sindar was right, it is foolish to fight something you can't beat. But does that make running away any better?* Laithen stopped, noticing for the first time where she was headed. If she continued on this path, she would eventually end up back where Sindar and she had fought the *soran* earlier that day. Shrugging, she decided to head back there, to see if she could find out anything about the things that had invaded the forest. *Besides, I want my spear back,* she thought.

After walking quite a way from Treehaven, Laithen was just about at the site where the battle had taken place. The forest was unnaturally quiet, with none of the usual insect or bird calls Laithen expected. A soft wind was her only companion now.

A few more minutes of travel brought her to the site. Other than the disturbed leaves and her spear lying on the ground, there was no sign of anything having happened here at all. Retrieving and cleaning her weapon, Laithen started looking around for any signs of where the *soran* had gone. Finding no trail, she examined the area where the thing had fallen.

Sniffing the ground, she was rewarded with an odor unlike anything she had ever smelled before. The scent was acrid, and made her nose tingle with irritation. A wet patch on the fallen leaves caught her eye, and she reached out a hand to touch the liquid. Sniffing it brought the same pungent smell to her nose. It was slippery and dark against her tan fingers.

Well, at least we know they bleed something, she thought. Just then her hunter's senses warned her of someone nearby. Laithen rolled backward to her feet and scanned the forest around her.

She didn't have to look very far. Without a sound, the *soran* stepped out from behind the tree and regarded her with dull eyes. Laithen's eyes widened as she realized just how silently it could move. Backpedaling quickly to get out of its immediate reach, she turned to run.

She had taken no more than a few steps when the *soran* landed right in front of her. Laithen was taken aback at how agile the thing was compared to when she and Sindar had fought it earlier.

Unfortunately, this information isn't going to help me when I'm dead. Knowing it was too fast to outrun now, she dropped into her fighting stance, spear ready, and waited for it to attack. Seconds later, it was upon her.

Koani trotted through the forest, aware of the eerie silence around her. The game that was usually out at night had gone to ground, fearing the kinkillers as much as the wolf pack did. Her belly rumbled, reminding her of the lack of food, and she hungrily sniffed the air, searching for something, anything, to eat.

Her ears, not her nose, detected movement ahead, and she quickly crept closer to see what was moving about.

In the familiar clearing ahead, she saw one of the furless ones facing a kinkiller. The smaller one was retreating before the monstrosity, which plodded relentlessly forward, brushing aside every attack the furless one tried. It's huge claw-studded hands would seem to score a hit on the small one time and again, but always, at the last second, the furless one would dodge aside or manage to parry the blow with its stick. The parrying wasn't as frequent, though, as the huge kinkiller often staggered the furless one with the weight of its fist.

Koani quickly turned and started walking around the clearing, watching the uneven combat all the while.

Laithen's arms windmilled in hurried attempts to keep the *soran* from killing her in one blow. Every time she had to block the beast's arms, it felt as if she was parrying a falling tree. Her own blows were deflected aside, and she could feel herself growing more tired.

Raising her spear for another block, she was surprised when the *soran* grabbed it out of her hands and hurled it across the clearing, all without pausing. Laithen drew her daggers and took aim, hoping to wound the thing enough so she could escape.

Without warning, a snarling blur of fur erupted out of the forest behind the *soran* and leaped at it. The *soran* staggered as the large animal slammed into it, ripping and tearing at its head.

The *soran* reared up, howling in anger and pain. It's paws reached up, grabbed the animal by the scruff of the neck, and slammed it down on the ground. The greatwolf, now that Laithen could get a good look at it, lay unmoving where it had landed. It looked stunned, but stared at Laithen with eyes that were bright and alert. With another howl of rage, the *soran* raised its massive paws to pulp the wolf's body.

Right when its arms started to descend, Laithen threw. The needle-sharp blade spun end over end and buried itself in the monster's neck. It reared back, screaming in agony, and clawed at the wound.

The greatwolf jumped to its feet and scrambled toward Laithen, who was also backpedaling. The creature's roar echoed through the trees. The wolf snarled back at it, standing in front of Laithen, who still held her one dagger. The *soran* lumbered forward, eager to tear into both of them.

Well, I saved the furless, but who's going to save me? Koani thought as she prepared herself for another attack. Catching the kinkiller by surprise had worked once, but she knew she wouldn't be so lucky a second time. Ducking and weaving, barking to distract it, Koani ran out to meet the kinkiller. *If the furless can use its stinger again, we might have a chance.*

It was a decision she regretted almost immediately. The kinkiller lashed out with one of its paws, aiming for her left flank. Koani dodged, but not fast enough. The beast's claws raked down her leg. Koani yelped in pain and leaped aside, landing in an untidy sprawl. The kinkiller loomed over her again. Koani waited until the last moment before she would dodge—

"Hey!" The shout took both the wolf and kinkiller by surprise. The two animals looked over at the small furless. Something whirled through the air, and the kinkiller was sporting another stinger, this one sticking out of its leg, just above the joint. The *soran* clutched at the wound and almost fell to one knee. It regained its balance, however, and ripped the stinger out of its leg. It started to take a step toward the furless, but stopped when it tried to walk on its wounded leg. It screamed again in frustration.

The furless held its long stinger in its other hand, and was motioning for Koani to come closer. Ducking away from the kinkiller, Koani sprang to the furless' side.

I can't believe I'm doing this, Laithen thought. Every instinct in her body was telling her to run as fast as she could into the forest. But she couldn't leave the greatwolf to be killed. After what it had done, she owed it that much. Only when she had stumbled over her spear lying on the ground had the barest glimmering of a plan formed in her mind, but it was enough.

The greatwolf left the screaming *soran* and bounded over to her. It was huge, standing at least four feet at the shoulder, its head at an equal height with hers. Laithen was relieved to see that the blow the animal had taken didn't seem to be hindering its ability to run. Their lives depended on it.

The *soran* had managed to turn itself around, and was trying to limp toward them. Praying that the wolf wouldn't attack her, Laithen vaulted onto its back. She fit perfectly. Grabbing a fistful of fur on the wolf's neck, she yanked hard in the direction she wanted to go. The wolf obeyed, sprinting for the far end of the clearing.

Once there, Laithen pulled on the scruff of the greatwolf's neck again. Her mount stopped so suddenly, that even gripping with her feet, she was almost pitched off. Nudging with her heels and twisting the fur she held, Laithen managed to convey to the wolf which direction she wanted to face. She tucked the spear under her other arm, the moonlight gleaming on the razor-sharp head. Pointing it straight at the *soran*, Laithen pulled the greatwolf's neck ruff forward while nudging with her heels. The wolf looked at Laithen for a moment, locking eyes with her. Laithen stared back at her and nodded.

Like an arrow, the wolf took off, heading straight for the *soran*. Laithen was gratified to see the *soran* stop for a moment, as if trying to understand what was happening. It grew larger and larger in her field of vision, until it blocked out everything else, even the sky. Laithen gripped the spear shaft so hard her arms hurt. Her legs burned from the effort of staying on the greatwolf's back. They were almost there, just another few steps—

The *soran* screamed again. Laithen answered back with her own roar, happy to hear the greatwolf growling beneath her. Screaming at the top of their lungs, the three met in the middle of the clearing. Laithen's last sensation was of hurtling through the air. She heard a primal roar, then darkness. . . .

Laithen awoke to something rough, warm, and wet sliding over her face. Blinking awake, she saw the face of the greatwolf right in front of her. She gasped instinctively and tried to sit up, crying out as pain shot up her leg.

Looking around, she saw she was still in the clearing. The greatwolf had moved a few feet away from her and was now crouched on the ground. Laithen searched for their enemy, and found it a few yards away.

The *soran* lay on its back, Laithen's spear sticking from its broad chest like a third limb. The bitter smell of its blood filled the clearing. Laithen couldn't detect any signs of life from the beast at all. She returned her attention to the greatwolf.

When the wolf shifted its weight, Laithen could see that it was favoring its right foreleg, which was oozing blood from a nasty cut. Its once lustrous coat was now dusty and matted. The elf held out her hands.

"Wait, wait, I won't hurt you." Her voice must have been sincere, because the wolf stopped squirming and looked at her. Laithen motioned for it to come nearer, her other hand reaching for the pouch of herbs at her belt.

The greatwolf limped over to her. Laithen shook some of the herbs out of her pouch and crushed them in her hand. She slowly reached over to the wolf's foreleg. It's gaze never strayed from her hand. Laithen had the impression that, had it wanted to, the greatwolf could have taken her hand off at the wrist with one bite. Laithen placed her hand on the injured leg, grimacing as the animal whimpered and stiffened in pain.

"Shh, I know, I know. It won't hurt much longer now." She gently rubbed the herbs on the leg. The wolf lay down beside her and let her finish tending the wound.

"There, that should hold it until I can have Nouri look at it. Doesn't feel like anything's broken, though," Laithen said. "Speaking of injuries, I suppose I should see how I'm doing." The wolf looked at her so seriously, Laithen felt like it understood what she was saying.

Taking a deep breath, she tried to straighten out her legs. The right one moved fine, but just touching the left caused another bolt of pain to course through her. Panting with the effort, she looked over at her new companion.

"Well, I guess we're both stuck here now. Sooner or later, they'll figure out I'm gone, once that pointless meeting is done." Thinking about the meeting made Laithen look back at the body of the *soran*. An idea danced around on the edges of her mind, but she couldn't grasp it.

A gust of wind caused her to shiver, and she moved closer to the greatwolf, burying her hands in its thick fur. The wolf curled its body around Laithen, spreading its thick tail across her legs. Soon Laithen was as comfortable as if she had been in her own hammock in Treehaven. The warmth of the greatwolf made her drowsy, and before she knew it, she was fast asleep.

Laithen jerked awake for the second time that night. Her head thumped on the ground, and she realized that the greatwolf had moved. Then she heard the low growling.

Looking up, she saw the wolf, teeth bared, standing over her. But it wasn't growling at her, but looking off towards the woods. Laithen turned her head.

Standing at the edge of the forest was a heavily armed party of elves, led by Sindar and her father. Three of them had arrows nocked and drawn, aiming straight at the wolf.

"Laithen, move!" Sindar whispered.

"No!" Laithen cried out. With an effort, she managed to rise to one knee, shielding the wolf with her body.

"Laithen, get out of the way," her father commanded.

"No father, the greatwolf saved my life," Laithen said. "Look." She gestured at the lifeless body of the *soran*. The *Alfheim* and the rest of the elves stepped into the clearing, her father motioning for the others to put down their weapons. Laithen reached behind her to soothe the still tense greatwolf.

"What are you talking about? Isn't that your spear in its body?" her father asked.

"Yes, but I didn't throw it. We—I mean—I was riding this wolf and impaled it on my spear," Laithen said. "I couldn't have done it without it, or her, I think."

Her father looked from his daughter to the greatwolf, and back. Only then did he notice that she hadn't gotten to her feet. "Child, are you injured?"

"It's nothing, I think I may have hurt my leg—" That was as far as she had gotten before the *Alfheim* picked her up, cradling her close to him.

"Until you have children of your own, you will never understand how worried I was about you. I'll give you the speech about running off in the forest alone once we're back at Treehaven. I know you can take care of yourself, but with these beasts around, no one is safe anymore," her father said.

His words had the opposite of their intended effect. Instead of hanging her head, Laithen looked up at him and nodded.

"That's exactly what I think, which is why we have to fight back."

There was silence in the clearing for a moment, then a few derisive snickers, which quieted immediately when the *Alfheim* turned his head toward the other elves.

"And just how would you do this?" Sindar asked.

Laithen pointed at the greatwolf before them. "With them. If we combine the speed and agility of the greatwolves with our weapons, we'll be able to combat the *soren* much more effectively."

Laithen's father looked at the greatwolf, who met his gaze with her own glowing golden eyes. "Hmmm," was all he said.

Koani watched the furless communicate among themselves, but her ears were listening for something else. She heard faint noises in the forest, and they were coming closer.

She saw one of the furless gasp and raise his stinger, followed by the rest, who surrounded the two that had been talking, trapping Koani inside the circle of furless. Looking in the direction they were aiming, she saw Kamots, Savre, Matsi, and the rest of the pack standing in the tree line, not moving, just watching. Koani looked back at the two furless that had been talking. The tall one motioned with his hand, and the others lowered their weapons again. He spoke again, and the warriors that had been blocking Koani's route to her pack moved aside, clearing a path for her. Koani looked at the two, then stepped forward and gently licked the face of the smaller furless. She turned and headed for her pack, moving slowly because of her tender foreleg.

"Are you all right? What was that all about?" Kamots asked when she rejoined the rest of her kin.

"I'm fine," Koani said, testing her leg. She was almost able to put her full weight on it already. "The furless are very skilled in the arts of healing."

Matsi shouldered her way forward. "You actually let them touch you?"

Koani watched Kamots, who was still staring off at the pack of furless. She chose her words carefully when she spoke. "Yes, it would seem we have much to learn from them about working together. We will have much to discuss when the darkness passes."

Kamots nodded, listening to the rest of the pack mutter excitedly about the dead kinkiller in the clearing. "So it would seem."

As the pack turned to head back into the forest, Savre trotted over to Koani. "Just what were doing in the forest with that furless anyway?" He asked with a grin that suggested he already knew the answer to his question.

Koani looked at him long and hard before replying with a smile of her own. "Finding common ground."

TWELVE-STEPPE PROGRAM
by Esther M. Friesner

Esther M. Friesner's latest novel is *Child of the Eagle*. She has written over twenty novels and coedited four anthologies. Other fiction of hers appears in *Excalibur, The Book of Kings*, and in *Fantasy and Science Fiction* and other prose magazines. She lives in Madison, Connecticut.

*S*ome days, Nir Mung-Mung reflected, *it just doesn't pay to be a eunuch.* He sighed deeply and shifted his weight in the saddle, as if trying to get comfortable, but it was really all for show. What was making him squirm wasn't the girth of the steed beneath him nor the design of the Garikkh-made saddle itself—a boxy contrivance intended to keep a warrior firmly mounted even if he were asleep, dead, or falling to pieces with decay—it was the sound of a woman's voice.

If you could call Princess Anuk'ti a woman, Nir thought bitchily. Now that his diplomatic mission to the Garikkh horde was essentially at an end, he felt free to give some of his uglier reflections full sway, even if he still didn't dare to voice them. *Her father, the yada-khango-Garikkh Otot swears that she's female—daughter of his favorite surviving concubine— but Lord Otot also told me that the stew was safe to eat. I spent* seven *hours out by the stink-trench, and I still don't feel so well. It wouldn't surprise me in the least if the old barbarian bugger couldn't tell his female children from the male. The gods know that all the Garikkh cubs I saw rampaging through the encamp-*

ment looked pretty much identical under all that filth and leather. Another explosion of guttural profanity from the gaudy palanquin farther back in the caravan made Nir wince. *From what I understand, the only time the Garikkh even bother distinguishing boys from girls is when the girls get pregnant or the boys slaughter all their siblings and take over the horde, like the yada-khango-Garikkh Otot himself did back in the Year of the Seven Willows. Merciful gods, let me have picked out one of the pregnant ones! My benevolent and compassionate Emperor will have my eyebrows sewn to my buttocks if I've botched this mission.*

He shifted his weight again, as if already feeling a ominous tickling sensation on his fundament. He hadn't asked for this assignment, but the Chief Eunuch had yoked him to it anyway.

"It's about time you stopped sopping up all the benefits of being a eunuch and started shouldering some of the responsibilities, my lad!" was the way that fat sow had put it as he leafed through the documents on his teakwood desk. "This is a simple enough task: Fetch back the royal Princess Anuk'ti of the Garikkh horde to wed the Emperor's heir apparent, Prince Floats-like-dandelion-fluff-upon-the-scented-waters."

"No kidding? Fluffy's getting married?" Nir's well-cultivated bushy eyebrows—considered a mark of beauty and status among his eunuch peers—rose high.

"Indeed." The Chief Eunuch was not at all disturbed by Nir's impertinent manner of referring to the Imperial prince. It was mild compared to some of the nicknames that the eunuchs had come up with for other members of the reigning house. "The Garikkh have lain waste the westernmost provinces of the Empire and are even now casting covetous eyes upon the heartland. Our armies are at present insufficient in numbers, training, and spirit to defeat them. Therefore we must engage in delaying tactics. Thus—at my suggestion—the proposal of marriage. The yada-khango-Garikkh Otot believes that if he gives us one of his daughters to become the prince's bride, his polluted blood has as good as achieved the Crane-and-Lion Throne."

"He wouldn't think that if he knew Prince Fluffy," Nir muttered.

"Which he does not," the Chief Eunuch reminded him, and for a wonder he did so without chiding Nir for having interrupted him. "This delusion suits us to no end. In the time it will take to effect the match, the Garikkh horde will observe a truce with the Lotus Empire. This breathing space will give us time to accomplish two goals: The upgrading of our armies to competent fighting strength and the insidious softening of the Garikkh horde's moral fiber, brought about by the seductive pleasures of the borderland cities they have already conquered and occupied."

Nir bowed his head. "A fine plan."

"Fine? No, brilliant. And all mine." The Chief Eunuch grinned. "Not bad, eh?"

An avid student of history (One of the advantages of being a eunuch was that you always had plenty of time to devote to reading) Nir knew that his boss' plan was only mediocre as far as such things went. It had been done and done again many times in the centuries since the gods themselves had mixed their own divine spittle with the blood of the Great Dawn Lion and the silver feathers of the Moon Crane to form the first Lotus Emperor. History taught Nir that the Chief Eunuch's plan would probably work as well as the wheel and for the same reasons: It was simple, practical, and showed absolutely no evidence of the wilder flights of imagination. However, history had also taught Nir that any eunuch who himself had an eye on the post of Chief Eunuch (eventually) would not live to realize that dream unless he kept his mouth shut except to repeat variations on "Yes, my gracious superior, your intellect dazzles my unworthy mind" as necessary.

Thus had Nir Mung-Mung replied to the Chief Eunuch as he accepted the scroll of his instructions and the goldstone token of his authority for the marriage embassy. He thought he'd said it quite humbly and sincerely. Sincerity was everything. His plans demanded that the Chief Eunuch go on believing that Nir Mung-Mung was the most subservient and obedient of his underlings. As Nir crawled backward out of the Chief Eunuch's presence, his mouth was full of dust bunnies, but his heart was full of joy over how thoroughly he had his master buffaloed.

Now, riding across the steppeland that separated the central Garikkh encampment from the border of the Lotus Empire heartland, the palanquin behind him spewing obscenities, he had his doubts. Although a eunuch's lifespan was long, a Chief Eunuch's was not. When a man had cut himself off from so much just to get a grab at political power, he often could not be content with less than the supreme measure of that power. The Bureau of Palace Management, otherwise known as Eunuch Central to the more physically complete (albeit disaffected, disgruntled, and largely disenfranchised) courtiers, was the vessel of that power. Eunuchs advised the Emperor, guided the Emperor, and jollied along the Emperor, but the Chief Eunuch was the one who got to play the Emperor like a three-stringed *blinga*. Therefore the Chief Eunuch generally lived better than the Emperor, but nowhere near as long; there was just too much competition for the job.

Yet for all that, the present holder of that cushy office had retained his place—and his life—for more than twenty years. His eyebrows had had the time to grow so thick and luxuriant that he could comb them back over his bald head for certain state occasions. Every time a likely successor arose among the subordinate hordes of palace eunuchs to threaten his status, the fellow inevitably met with some sort of catastrophe, usually bloody and fatal. Nir was nowhere near as bright as he was ambitious, but even he could detect something like a pattern there.

The only trouble was, he hadn't detected it soon enough, not until the long hours in the saddle gave him the leisure for such reflection. Now it crashed in upon him with all the revelatory impact of a swooning elephant. The match between Prince Fluffy and Princess Anuk'ti had been arranged by the Chief Eunuch and the documents requested the aforementioned princess *by name.* That was not the way such compacts were usually (and here Nir Mung-Mung trembled at the word) executed. In general, when the Lotus Empire deemed it advisable to bring alien blood into the family, one nubile barbarian was as good as the next. Why had this agreement mentioned Anuk'ti specifically?

The answer was so elementary in its deadly cunning that Nir's bowels went slack without benefit of Garikkh stew: The Chief Eunuch must have known what Anuk'ti was like from his spies just as surely as he knew she'd have the Lotus Prince for lunch once she was alone with him. Fluffy's death would be no great loss to the Empire, to be sure, but there was another element to consider, one more powerful than the Emperor's divine word, more lethal than the Empire's finest sword.

"The Empress," Nir breathed, and shuddered. If anything happened to her darling boy, that unspeakable woman would see to it that all persons directly or indirectly responsible for Prince Fluffy's demise lived only long enough to learn that *agony* has many, many levels of meaning.

All persons except *the Chief Eunuch,* Nir Mung-Mung thought. *By now he's had more than enough time to expunge his name from all documents concerning the match and to arrange the banishment of any of his servants who might be able to link him to it. Cruel, but I suppose it does keep secrets safe and household pension expenses down. But to do this to* me—! *And for me to have been so blind as to allow it! Why, that dirty, rotten, stinking, vicious—!*

It was more than he could bear. He jerked his steed to a halt, threw back his head, and unburdened himself of his newly formed opinion of the Chief Eunuch. He said—no, he *bellowed*—a word.

And *what* a word!

The intensity with which Nir Mung-Mung unexpectedly howled that word of supreme and blasphemous obscenity brought the entire caravan to a full stop, even though they were in the midst of the grassy wilderness with nothing in sight but more grass and more wilderness. It also silenced the ongoing litany of curses from the palanquin. The resulting stillness was absolute and, as such, rather terrifying. Imperial attendants flanking the palanquin—gently bred courtiers who had lost their physical capacity to blush within the first ten *nablaks* of the journey—stood exchanging apprehensive looks without daring to venture a peep through the heavy green-and-gold silk curtains.

"Do you think that's killed her?" a nearby mounted guard whispered.

"Gods grant it," his companion replied. Since both the speakers were themselves seasoned Garikkh warriors on loan from Lord Otot, Nir Mung-Mung found himself unable to chide them for their sentiments.

"I wouldn't be too sure of it if I were you," said their third comrade, a dough-faced young fellow whose riding leathers seemed ready to burst outward from the pressure of his belly. "The snake doesn't hiss before it strikes."

"The Perunian puff-adder does," the first man said. "It sort of whistles."

While the Garikkh guards fell to discussing the vocalizations of vipers, Nir pondered his options. He had to admit that he was himself more than a little startled by the abrupt silence his outburst had inspired in Prince Fluffy's sequestered bride. Had he mistaken the true nature of his charge? Did there lurk a sweet, sensitive, innocent princess behind that fishwife's tongue and those fighting skills worthy of a tavern brawler? Oh, what a gory scrimmage it had taken to force Anuk'ti into the palanquin in the first place! Had that free-for-all been a fluke?

Hunh! Not bloody likely. A passing sentiment was one thing, but the reality of memory quite another. Nir still remembered how the yada-khango-Garikkh Otot had laughed as the subsidiary eunuchs under Nir's command struggled to deal with Princess Anuk'ti's recalcitrance. "Poor baby!" he said in mock sympathy. "She doesn't want to leave her old dad." The dutiful daughter had left three of Nir's men so badly chewed over that they'd had to be left behind among the Garikkh horde for recuperation (hence the borrowed Garikkh attendants), and those who were fit enough to travel looked as if they'd been bathing with stoats.

Still, there was something ominous about the peace now fully settled over the palanquin. Nir decided that he'd better investigate. Trotting his steed back down the caravan line to the royal conveyance, he touched the curtains lightly and said, "Princess Anuk'ti? My lady? Are you all—?"

He never got to finish his solicitous inquiry. Strong brown hands heavy with rings thrust out through the curtains, grabbed him by the neck of his traveling robes, and yanked him into the palanquin before any of the attending guards could draw breath.

One of the Garikkh horsemen looked at his comrades. "You think we ought to—?" He jerked a thumb at the palanquin, silent once more.

"Well . . ." the second began.

"Are you *crazy?*" the dough-faced one blurted. The three of them settled down in their saddles to wait.

Inside the palanquin, Nir found himself in a situation most eunuchs seldom experienced. Flat on his back among the cushions, he gazed up into the hellish eyes of the Garikkh princess. She was thoroughly naked, except for the mounds of gold jewelry encircling wrists, ankles, neck, fingers, and toes. Straddling Nir's body, she brought her mouth down onto his and gave him a kiss that set his heart to racing and cleared his sinuses at the same time.

"I love you," she rasped when at last she broke the liplock. Her command of his spoken tongue was much more limited than her command of his physical one. Still, despite a terrible accent, she persevered: "You are only man for me. I will welcome your hot affections willingly. I will bear you many sons."

"Uhhhhh. I don't think so," Nir replied.

Anuk'ti's green eyes flashed. "Forget the puny Lotus Prince. I love you. I have gold. We will escape and live well. My thighs contain many heavens."

"Good for them." Nir's mouth was terribly dry, but he was terrified of how the Garikkh princess might interpret it if he ventured to lick his lips. "Your Highness, I'm quite flattered by your high regard for my unworthy person, but I'm also very much afraid that you don't understand—"

"I love you," Anuk'ti repeated for the third time. "What is to understand besides this? I love you. You I love. I have breasts that can smother small animals. Get me out of here and let our bodies kindle ten thousand grass fires as soon as we have outrun my father's men. Deal? I love you," she added once more, again with the same automatic intonation most people used to bless the health of a sneezer.

Nir did not reply at once. Lack of premeditation had plunked him down in the midst of this situation, and he wasn't about to make it any worse if he could help it. A hasty man would simply take the steer by the horns and tell Anuk'ti that he was a eunuch, go on to explain what a eunuch was, and what such a one could and could not do. He would wind down his little dissertation with a gentlemanly refusal of Anuk'ti's proffered passion based solely on the grounds of his own inadequacies and in no way reflecting upon the lady's innate desirability. He would conclude with the hope that two of them could remain good friends.

A hasty man would do that, and thus would become

with all good haste . . . a corpse. The princess didn't seem to be the sort of lady who had much truck with logic. Even though Nir's amorous experience was naturally limited, he had listened at enough palace doors to know that while all lovers claimed they wanted to be told the unvarnished truth in matters of the heart, the wise wooer came armed with varnish by the barrel.

"Austere and dreadful lady," Nir said in his most deferential voice. "The ecstacy which your words have stirred within my unworthy heart threatens to reduce that fragile organ to a pile of smoldering ashes. I am but a humble man of common blood, the child of many generations of starving peasants. A union of my miserable body with your own majestic person would blast me from the face of the earth as if consumed by the breath of dragons."

Princess Anuk'ti heard him out, her face contorted into a scowl capable of casting out demons. Nir had taken pains to speak slowly and carefully, in Anuk'ti's own tongue, so that there might be no chance of her misunderstanding his message, but to judge from the look she was giving him, the whole gorgeously phrased rejection had gone sailing over her head and out through the palanquin curtains.

The lady herself proved this conclusively by leaning back on her haunches, cupping one hand before her face, blowing into it, then demanding, "You are telling me I got dragon breath? If my father had not ordered his bodyguards to sneak away my favorite dagger, my best skinning knife, my three finest swords, and my nail file, I would gut you where you lie and drape your scrawny neck with your streaming entrails. Run away with me now. I love you," she added as an afterthought.

Nir swallowed hard, trying to maintain a clear head despite a stomach that was doing the Dance of the Fifty Grasshoppers. "I— If— We— All of those were *your* weapons?" he gasped at last. It was a pathetic utterance, a commonplace worthy of a village yokel.

He regretted it the instant he said it, and he closed his eyes at once, fully expecting his imminent death. The Garikkh princess had already shown herself to be an imposing fighter when armed with nothing more than the body the gods had given her. (Though during the Battle of the Palanquin she had augmented this with whatever came to hand, nearly garroting one of Nir's men with her emerald necklace and accounting for another using only a pile of camel dung).

"Of course!" Anuk'ti was proud of herself. "Those were only the best of my collection. I own many more sharp things, also clubs. I prefer daggers to swords, and you? Close work is good, rewarding, much more personal." She cocked her head at Nir coquettishly and added, "Or are you one of those sissyboy men, got to have long sticker to do the job?"

"No," said Nir, and tried to change the subject. "Refulgent sun of all female glory, the passion which your declaration of love has kindled within my worthless body will devour me without let or mercy if I do not find some way to display to you my supreme devotion. Therefore I beg, I plead, I implore you to permit me to make the utmost sacrifice any man can make before the altar of your beauty by denying myself a physical love which I can in no way merit and instead bringing you to the one union in all the earth that is deserving to receive your exalted pulchritude." He fell back among the cushions, panting for breath but looking hopeful.

The princess drew up one knee and drummed her fingers on the patella slowly. Her other hand bunched into a fist which supported her cheek. She regarded Nir Mung-Mung with much the same expression he had once seen on the face of Lord Trembling-breath-of-spring just before he dropped an unsatisfactory poet into the pit that held his pet tiger.

At last she sat up straight and asked, "Sheep or camel?"

"Er . . . I beg your pardon?" Nir was understandably confused.

"Which kind of dung was that you just handed me, sheep or camel?" she elucidated. "I'd say camel, judging by mass and quantity, but I'm just a simple barbarian lass and you're one of those slick talkers from the Lotus Empire. Who am I to question you? If you ask me, we can't overrun you with fire and sword soon enough, but no one *does* ask me." She sighed and flopped onto her back. "Fine. I tried. Never mind dumping more of your phony jabber on me; I'll come quietly, and I'll marry your squishy soft princeling, just like everyone wants. Mind you, I'm not giving any guarantees about how long the little twit's going to last once the honeymoon gets started, but right now I really don't much care. Don't let the palanquin curtains hit you in the ass on the way out." By some miracle, her accent and fluency in Nir's tongue had improved radically.

Nir noted this as well as the abrupt change in the lady's attitude. It troubled him more than her earlier attempted seduction/assault of his person. He was so bemused by this fresh mystery that he made no move to quit Princess Anuk'ti's palanquin, despite her charming invitation that he depart soonest.

This did not please the princess. "Well?" she snarled. "Do you need a hand—or a foot—out of here? Go. I want to be alone."

"My lady, your—your wish is of course my command, but—but—" Nir took a deep breath and blurted, "What's come over you? Where's all that 'Me Anuk'ti, me love you, we run away quick-quick' stuff you were pouring on before?"

"Oh, that?" Anuk'ti's scowl softened a bit. "First of all, I never lowered myself to the 'Me Anuk'ti' level and you know it, O Nibbler on the Lotus Emperor's Toenails. And if I did address you in . . . simpler fashion, it was only because you men always do seem to prefer your women heavy here—" she hefted her

breasts like a proud melon farmer, "—and light here."
She tapped the side of her skull.

The eunuch sucked air between his teeth and let it
out in a low whistle. "Who are you and what have
you done with the real Princess Anuk'ti? Same height
as you, same face, same coloring, likes bludgeoning,
likes to maim?"

"Would you prefer it if I maimed *you,* just to prove
my identity?" the princess inquired lightly.

"Not really."

"I didn't think so." She held up one hand, then
the other, studying her nails. In other women, such a
coquettish gesture might be seen merely as charming
self-absorption. When Anuk'ti studied her nails, she
put Nir in mind of a master assassin inspecting a portion of his arsenal. Reflexively he curled his legs
tightly beneath him, ready to spring out of the palanquin if she made the slightest questionable move. He
thought he was being very subtle about it.

"Calm down, I'm just checking for hangnails," she
drawled. "Besides, scratch-fights are dishonorable, fit
only for cats and children and my butterball of a
brother, Zhik."

"Honorable?" Nir repeated. He had heard much of the
Garikkh warriors' vaunted code of honor. Supposedly—
somewhere under all the wholesale slaughter and pillage and torture that the horde inflicted on those
towns unlucky enough to fall before them—there
were rules.

"Yes, *honorable,*" Anuk'ti shot right back at him
with some heat. "Does it surprise you to hear a
woman speak of honor in battle? Look, I was my father's favorite daughter—or that's what I thought until
the old goat turd shipped me off to marry Prince
Floats-face-down-in-the-goldfish-pond-if-I-have-it-my-
way. Anyhow, before Father did me dirt, he was a
jolly decent parent as parents go. When I told him I
wanted to be a warrior, he had his best retired general

give me weapons training. Of course I also received proper instruction in the Warrior's Code."

"Don't blame your father," Nir told her. "He had no choice; you were asked for by name in the official documents. For Lord Otot it was a case of either hand you over or forget about collecting the bride-price and getting one of his descendants on the Crane-and-Lion Throne faster and with less fuss than by war."

"By name? Me?" Anuk'ti's brows rose. "Why?"

The eunuch shrugged. "*I* assumed it was because once you got alone with the prince, you'd kill him." And, feeling in a confiding mood bordering on what-the-hell, Nir Mung-Mung explained all about the Chief Eunuch's methods for dealing with up-and-coming rivals before they came *too* far up.

Anuk'ti gave him another of those sheep-or-camel-dung looks. "Eunuchs," she said with some distaste. "In the name of the stallion-god Shtup-Shtup, what have you done to stir up one of those fat, lazy, wingle-less wonders? Why does he see you as his rival?"

Nir bridled. "First, not all eunuchs are fat. Second, if all eunuchs were lazy, life in the palace would be a lot more peaceful than it is. Third, princess or not, if you're going to mingle in polite Lotus Empire society, you will not call eunuchs 'wingleless wonders,' but 'Masters of the Jade Nubbin,' like everyone else. And finally, he sees me as his rival because I am. I want his job."

"You want to be Chief Eunuch? But— But to be Chief Eunuch you'd have to— That is, unless you already— Which means that you're a—a—" For the first time since he'd encountered her, Nir saw Anuk'ti blush. "Oh. I beg your pardon. When I said that bit about wingleless wonders I didn't realize you were a—a—"

"—a wonder?" Nir allowed himself to smile. "Then you must also realize why I could not accept your previous offers of amorous delight, dread lady."

"I know, I know," Anuk'ti said hurriedly. "Do we

have to talk about this any more? No offense, but I find this whole subject rather . . . creepy."

"Thanks *so* much," Nir said.

"But don't you . . . miss . . . not having . . . you know?"

The eunuch folded his arms and gave her a severe look. "I wasn't lying before when I told you I came from many generations of starving peasants. I tried starving for a while and I didn't like it, and since the Path of the Well-Grown Eyebrows is the only way to power and security open to a boy of my birth—no matter how bright that boy might be—I made up my mind to take it. We eunuchs are respected persons of the Imperial court, free to enrich ourselves as far as our wits allow, free to come and go everywhere, as we please. It may not be a perfect life, but you get regular meals and you meet interesting people. No one forced me to live it. It was my choice."

"Lucky you," Anuk'ti muttered. "At least you got to make your own decision. Maybe if someone had *asked* me about this match in the first place— But did they even bother seeing if I *had* an opinion? No. Oh, rat bones! I might as well come along quietly and marry your prince. And I won't kill him either." She looked up sharply at Nir. "That way you'll have accomplished your mission, the Chief Eunuch won't be able to touch you, I'll be married to the royal heir, and my days as a political pawn will be over. You know, I think I know *just* the morning-after gift I'm going to demand from my prince: The Chief Eunuch's head on a bed of parsley. *That* will teach him to try playing chess with my maidenhead!" Her smile was wide and bright, like the gateway to the first of the Fourteen Hundred Hells.

Nir sighed deeply. He admired the Garikkh girl's spunk, but his knowledge of the Chief Eunuch's many-layered wiles reminded him that despite her proud spirit and bold plans, she was still just as doomed as he. "Even if you don't kill your husband, there will be no morning-after gift for you. There will only be the headsman's blade."

"What?"

"A royal bride who fails to mark the wedding sheets with the Poppy of Chastity must be put to death."

"But I *will* mark the sheets! I'm a virgin. All that talk about what horseback riding does to you is just a lot of—"

"Even were you ten thousand virgins, your sheets would remain unstained. It takes two to pluck the Poppy."

Anuk'ti counted on her fingers. "Me. Prince Thingummy. Two. Where's the problem?"

"It's nothing personal. You are a very desirable woman, if I may venture a completely detached opinion, but the fact of the matter is that when it comes to the Pillow Arts and women, then our own, our esteemed, our beloved Prince Floats-like-dandelion-fluff-upon-the-scented-waters is generally to be found . . . elsewhere."

"Ahhhhh." Anuk'ti nodded. "Just like my brother Zhik. Bloody hell."

"Wrong adjective," said Nir morosely.

Anuk'ti was not one to accept defeat easily. "Hmmmm. You know, one bloodstain looks much like another. There's bound to be something sharp lying around the bedchamber. I could always cut myself and—"

"It wouldn't work. The prince would betray you. He just as cool toward this marriage as you, but he's going through with it because it's what his mother wants. Not even Prince Fluffy dares to stand against the Empress' will."

"If *she* wants me married to Fluffy, and he's scared of her, why would he rat on me and ruin her plans? It's not like I'd insist we make the Goat With Four Horns. I'd leave him alone and he'd leave me alone: The perfect marriage."

"I wouldn't know," Nir replied. "No more than you

would know that Lotus Empire tradition demands that after the Viewing of the Poppy, the royal newlyweds are kept sequestered in the prince's luxurious apartments until the bride shows proof positive of pregnancy. So. Would you care to tell me how you'd manage that, given what you'll have to work with?''

"Uh . . ." Anuk'ti was temporarily at a loss.

"Timing is everything," Nir told her. "If the match had taken place a year ago, your plan might have worked. Our prince does not *dis*like women—as companions—and you do have the advantage of fluency in our language, the Celestial Breath. He enjoys good conversation. Having a wife would have taken a great deal of pressure off him. You see, his mother refuses to believe that her son is . . . as he is. The two of you might have remained closeted together until thirteen hundred and ninety-nine hells froze over, and never a peep of protest from him . . . then."

"And now?" Anuk'ti asked. "What's so different about now?"

"Now," Nir said, "he's in love." As Anukti's mouth opened like a night-blooming flower, the eunuch continued: "Our beloved prince has a half brother, Devours-the-lightning, son of a concubine. An able fighter, he maintains a household consisting entirely of warriors—eunuchs and encumbered alike."

"Fighting eunuchs?" This was news to the Garikkh princess.

"Eunuchs make excellent warriors, highly valued by our generals. We have nothing to distract us."

"So the prince is in love with his half brother?" Anuk'ti shivered. "I'm getting that creepy feeling again."

"Don't," Nir directed tersely. "Prince Devours-the-lightning has no use for his more royal brother beyond target practice. Fluffy is enamored of one of his half brother's captains, and alas for you, his passion is reciprocated."

"Why alas for me? I don't care if he wants to spend

all his time trailing after soldiers. Gods witness, that's how Zhik spent his time when we were at home. His latest crush is a guardsman who—"

"Alas for you," Nir cut in, "because the protocols of marriage will separate our prince from his beloved until such time as he can present the court with a pregnant bride—fat chance—or until he can prove that his chosen wife has committed treason by faking the Poppy. The period of mourning for a royal bride— even one executed for treason—is two years; two years during which your grieving widower will be free to pursue his own interests without the possibility of a single peep of objection out of his formidable mother. Get the picture?"

Anuk'ti's face hardened. "I don't need to get the picture. I need to get a sword." She looked at Nir. "I don't suppose you could arrange it for me? I won't bother trying to bribe you with my body, but as you can see, I do have other tangible resources." She held up for his inspection the heavy gold chains around her neck.

"Tempting," Nir admitted. "And my plans for taking over the Chief Eunuch's job *do* look like they'll prove expensive. You can't hire a poisoner who's both effective *and* discreet on the cheap. But I must decline."

"Look, if it's because I called you a wingless wonder—"

"It's because I'll be dead," Nir forestalled her apology. "Otherwise I'd even be willing to get you that sword for free, smuggle it into the prince's apartments, the whole calabash. But as I said, I *will* be dead. Sorry to inconvenience you."

"You will *not!*" The princess was her old, strident self. "You'll have delivered me as ordered, mission accomplished. You'll be off the hook."

"Where I'll be is in seclusion also, pending the favorable outcome of your wedding night. They'll lock me away the moment this caravan enters the palace grounds. Another of our customs, dating back to the times before widespread employment of eunuchs in the Imperial service. It often took many months to bring a bride to the capital, and wise men understood that within that space of time certain . . . irregularities might transpire between the lady and her escort. The ambassador's head must answer for the bride's pur-loined virginity, therefore the ambassador himself must be kept locked up until proof of that virginity is made public on the morning after." He assumed an expression of fatalism. "Since the Chief Eunuch knows that your wedding night with Prince Fluffy *must* be unsatisfactory, one way or another, he will doubtless have me killed soon after I am sequestered. Why wait for the last minute?"

"I hope I get introduced to this Chief Eunuch of yours before the wedding night," Anuk'ti gritted. "I'll kill him, sword or no sword."

"My dear, I appreciate the thought, but—"

"What thought? I mean it. I know seven ways to touch a man so that his neck explodes. Oh, I'll die for it, I know, but since I'm bound to die one way or another, I might as well get some satisfaction out of it. Then Zhik and the others can ride back home and tell my father, and he can ride down on your stupid Lotus Empire and slaughter uncounted—"

"What did you say?" Unthinking, Nir grabbed Anuk'ti's wrist. "Zhik? Your brother Zhik? He's here?"

"Of course he's here," Anuk'ti replied, shaking off the eunuch's hand. "I told you. He's got a crush on one of the guards assigned to replace your ailing atten-dants. He disguised himself as a Garikkh warrior in order to follow his beloved. Gods, have you *seen* how ridiculous he looks in leather armor? Not that it'll do him a lick of good: K'haktar's about as interested in men as Prince Fluffy is in women."

"*That's* your brother? The pudgy Garikkh guard?"

Anuk'ti nodded. "He's going by the name of Kihz

to throw people off the scent. Brilliant, isn't he? He
thinks he fooled the whole horde when he sneaked
away, but frankly everyone knows all about his escape,
only no one cares. My father's got sons to spare; he
won't miss Zhik."

"Aha." Nir Mung-Mung's eyebrows came together
in thought so violently that they became entangled.
Later on he had to shear off a painfully large quantity
of hair to free one from the other, but it was a price
willingly paid. He beckoned Anuk'ti close and whispered in her ear.

Some time after that, Nir descended from the bridal
palanquin and approached one of the Garikkh
horsemen. Motioning for him to dismount, he drew
him away from the caravan and in a low voice said,
"You are discovered, Zhik. Your sister has betrayed
you. It is my duty to send you back to your father,
Lord Otot."

"No! Oh please, don't do that!" Zhik begged. "You
see, I love—"

Nir silenced him with a gesture. "Say no more. This
too, I know; I sympathize. I am not here to condemn,
but to help you. Hark! Heed my counsel. I urge you
to speak to the princess directly. Perhaps you can persuade her to relent."

"You mean . . . go . . . in there?" Zhik cast fearful
eyes at the palanquin.

"It's the only way," Nir assured him.

Thus is was that the plump Garikkh guard was seen
to enter the bridal palanquin, only to emerge some
time later visibly altered by his ordeal. For one thing,
his riding leathers no longer fit him quite so snugly
and he had deployed the dust mask attached to his
helmet. This latter occasioned much whispering among
the Imperial courtiers and the Garikkh guards alike
until Nir Mung-Mung hurried up to pat the fellow on
the back and croon in a carrying voice, "You poor
man! Scratched your face, did she?"

The guard nodded, and in a voice considerably deeper than before said, "Aye, the minx."

Nir patted the guard on the shoulder cheerfully. "Well, never mind. You just keep it covered up until we reach the capital. I promise you, everything will be *much* better then."

The guard's green eyes twinkled. "You betcha."

From the Jewel Annals of the Crane-and-Lion Throne in the Year of Admirable Crickets:

It is with all properly sanctioned emotions that this humble chronicler notes that our beloved Empress has followed her gracious lord, our beloved Emperor, into the Halls of Ten Thousand Eternal Delights. The cause of her death was accidental beheading at the hands of the former Garikkh guard and present warrior-eunuch known by the name of Kihz'anituk. This mischance occurred soon after His Imperial Majesty's passing (of natural causes) in the fourth year following the wedding and ritual isolation of his heir, Prince Floats-like-dandelion-fluff-upon-the-scented-waters, with the Garikkh princess Anuk'ti.

Given that our august Prince has not chosen to emerge from his apartments since his wedding night (although a bandaged hand was observed to fling forth an acceptably bloodstained sheet on the morning after), upon the Emperor's passing it was the wise decision of the Imperial Council to offer the Regency to our own respected Prince Devours-the-lightning (famous for his part in fending off the Garikkh horde at the Battle of Peony Mountain, the Standoff at the Five Dragon Cities, and the Phoenix River Compromise of the Twenty-four Thousand Bags of Gold). It was upon receipt of this news that Her Majesty the Empress, her common sense no doubt overwhelmed by grief, attempted to violate the sanctity of her son's marital seclusion.

If this humble chronicler may quote the words of

the eunuch Kihz'anituk: *She had to be stopped. So I stopped her.*

Given that the Heir Apparent has shown no interest in his mother's demise (indeed the prince's most recent response to inquiries from the Bureau of Palace Management has been *I'm happy! Go away and leave us alone!* followed by much giggling), the incident has been handled by Prince Devours-the-lightning, who has accorded the loyal Kihz'anituk a full pardon, thus:

Let all men within the boundaries of the Lotus Empire witness the debt of gratitude I owe my unworthy servant, the eunuch Kihz'anituk, who, since his arrival at Our court in the royal Garikkh bridal caravan, has chosen to serve me with singleminded devotion. Let all men further know that so loyal was and is this unworthy servant that, in an effort to avoid those distractions of the flesh to which common soldiers are subject, the Garikkh warrior Kihz'anituk voluntarily submitted to the process which has left behind nothing whatsoever of the male in this, my valued and constant (though of course unworthy) companion. Who among us would do the same? I didn't think so. In tardy appreciation of which sacrifice, may the wise men of the Imperial Council absolve my unworthy servant of all blame in this, as they value their revered and venerable necks. Not that I'm threatening anyone, mind.

The eunuch Kihz'anituk has since announced an immediate retirement from military service to His Intimidating Highness, citing understandable anxiety over a significant personal weight gain as the reason for this decision. Although the tendency of eunuchs to grow in bodily mass is well known throughout the Lotus Empire, the ever-increasing size of this newly evident bulge as to the eunuch Kihz'anituk's midsection moved the prince's unworthy servant to declare an instant departure on a pilgrimage of many months to pray at the shrines and temples for the miracle of divine deliverance.

There is much speculation in the corridors and gardens of the palace regarding the proper interpretation of the eunuch Kihz'anituk's parting words, uttered in that person's native Garikkh tongue, namely: *And not a day too soon! Talk about cutting it close.*

To which our revered, honored, and dread Prince Devours-the-lightning was heard to reply: *Ssshhhh!*

It is this humble chronicler's valueless opinion that when the aforementioned miracle comes to pass, it shall pass without public comment, no matter what form it takes nor how it may affect the shape and appearance of that lowly petitioner, the eunuch Kihz'anituk.

If this humble chronicler may dare yet once more to enshrine the golden words of our adored Prince Devours-the-lightning as he addressed the assembled courtiers following the departure of the eunuch Kihz'anituk: *And when my loyal companion returns, I don't want to hear one snide word out of you lot about any changes in the way he looks. Not one, do you hear me? The gods can do some really funny things to a body, you know, and to question the work of the gods is blasphemy. Have you taken a look at all the punishments for blasphemy we've got in the Royal Chronicles? And there's nothing there to suggest that a really religious ruler has to limit himself to inflicting only* one *of those punishments upon the miserable offender. He can inflict lots and lots. Do I make myself clear? Do you bunch of silk-frilled peacocks think you could manage to put a bridle on your gossipy tongues just this once?*

Sure they can.

This is going to be good.

Respectfully inscribed this day at the Hour of the Hamster, in the Brocade Chamber of the Bureau of Palace Management by the hand of Himself,

Nir Ming-Mung
Chief Eunuch

THE ROAD TO VENGEANCE
by Mickey Zucker Reichert

Mickey Zucker Reichert is a pediatrician whose twelve science fiction and fantasy novels include *The Legend of Nightfall, The Unknown Soldier,* and *The Renshai* trilogy. Her most recent release from DAW Books is *The Children of Wrath,* the third novel in *The Renshai Chronicles* trilogy. Her short fiction has appeared in numerous anthologies. Her claims to fame: she *has* performed brain surgery, and her parents *really are* rocket scientists.

Frigid night air washed through the city streets, howling between the closer-packed buildings of Genyana's south side. Princess Alexxa pulled her cloak more tightly around her. She tucked back long strands of black hair that had escaped her hood and the knot at the nape of her neck. A sword, smuggled beneath her cloak, slipped with the movement. She scrabbled to catch it, hands fumbling in the slippery satin of her blouse. The weapon tumbled, ringing against the cobbles. Moonlight glinted from steel.

Whispering a curse, the princess snatched up the sword and pressed into the shadows of a tailor's shop. She held her breath, sifting the sounds of city night. A discarded scrap of parchment, blown by the wind, rasped against stone. Crickets chirruped, a steadily rising and falling chorus. A distant dog barked twice, silenced by a shouted reprimand. No one seemed to have noticed her lapse, though she still felt the wary prickle of unseen eyes that had plagued her almost from the moment she had slipped from her palace window and dodged the posted watch.

Genyana appeared different in a darkness scarcely grazed by a crescent moon and a speckled blanket of stars. Buildings she had known since childhood, even the cottages of servants and the homes of friends, muted into forbidding dark blotches bathed in the eerie glow of moonlight. The warm press of happy people, the lighthearted chatter, the meandering chickens all disappeared with the dusk. For an instant, Alexxa imagined herself snuggled warmly beneath her blankets, soothed by the regular gentle snores of her nanny. A smile eased onto her features, immediately erased by need. Drawing herself to her full height, she deliberately banished the image. She had a job to do.

Alexxa continued walking toward the boundaries of Genyana, attentive for sounds of pursuit. On occasion, she thought she could hear a footstep, a scrape of leather against stone, a soft clearing of a throat. Always, she felt the same ominous sensation of being watched, yet when she turned to scan the roads and alleys behind her, she never caught a glimpse of another living creature. Even the mice seemed to have gone to ground for the night. When no one accosted her, she attributed the noises to echoes of her own movement, the feeling of overseeing to paranoia.

As Alexxa sneaked past the border sentries, her thoughts returned to her mission. She could not recall when the plan had first formed in her mind; it seemed rooted in eternity. For as long as she could remember, she had planned to seek her father on her twentieth birthday. And to kill him.

The idea brought a flash of white-hot anger that had barely dulled in intensity since age thirteen, when her mother had revealed the truth. Unlike her two younger sisters, Alexxa had not sprung from King Arno's seed. She had often wondered about the stick-straight black hair, so different from her mother's stiff red locks that braided so prettily and her father's and sisters' blond curls. More dense and solid than her willowy sisters, she had often lamented that her every bite packed excess weight on her hips and thighs, while they could eat freely and remain spectacularly slim. Her oval face, her high cheekbones, and her finely chiseled nose seemed to have come from nowhere, and her hazel eyes contrasted starkly with the blues and greens of the rest of her family.

Once past the borders of Genyana, Alexxa found herself on familiar dirt paths that led through the woodlands to the many farms on the outskirts. Chilled by night air, the metal of the sword grew icy, and her fingers cramped. Parting the folds of her cloak, she freed the weapon. Starlight glinted in pinpoints from the polished steel. She set it on the ground. Then, clamping her mouth into a grim line, she unrolled its sheathings from her pocket and drew out a leather belt tangled into the thong she brought to bind it. Nine months prior to her birth, raiders from Sarakas, the river town, had ransacked Genyana. Alexxa imagined her mother and other women struggling in panicked frenzy, helplessly pinned and ravished by foreign soldiers. Anger flared anew. She fumbled with the belt, fingers awkward from cold and rage.

A shadowy figure slunk from the edge of the forest to stand in Princess Alexxa's path.

Startled, Alexxa back-stepped with a gasp. Then, goaded by the anger still fiery within her, she snatched up the sword and waved it menacingly. Though she had taken no lessons of her own, she had diligently eavesdropped on those of her father and male cousins, practicing the techniques alone in her room. "Back away, stranger. Don't make me kill you."

The other did not obey but did not advance either.

Alexxa froze, impatient for her vision to adjust. Not only had the other come from a darker place, but the princess had the moonlight in her eyes. "Who are you?" she demanded, stalling. Discomfort and long silence gruffened her voice, which she appreciated. Beweaponed and partially hidden by her cloak, she might pass for a young man.

"You may call me Kazadim." The voice was definitively male, accented, and Alexxa could now tell that he stood taller by nearly a head. Dressed in a gray cloak with the hood pulled over his head, he remained as unrecognizable as she hoped she looked. A plain-looking scabbard held a large-hilted sword, and a dagger lay thrust through the opposite side. "What may *I* call *you?*"

Alexxa hesitated. If she revealed herself and she faced a Genyani ally, he might insist on escorting her back to the palace. A foreigner might capture her for ransom, though she doubted he would risk a war by raping and murdering a princess. Nevertheless, she tried to look threatening. "You have no need to call me anything."

Kazadim shrugged. " 'You There' seems inconvenient, but if it suits you—"

"I mean," Alexxa interrupted, "I intend to pass now and never see you again."

"What if I happen to be going the same way, You There?"

"Walk ahead or behind, then."

"As you wish." Kazadim made a broad gesture for Alexxa to pass, which she did, watching his every move. When he made no attempt to touch her, Alexxa finally dared to turn her back. As she headed along the crude roadway, the sensation of being watched intensified a hundredfold. Yet whenever the princess whirled, she found either an empty trail, lined by trees and brush, or Kazadim marching distantly and calmly at her pace, a shield slung across his back, a bow and quiver at his hip, and a pack dangling from his other hand.

As the night wore toward dawn, Alexxa found herself cold and tired. She had packed a minimum of gear: food, a change of clothes, a map, coin, toiletries, and a tinder box. Though she wore a sturdy woolen cloak, she wished she had also brought a blanket.

The path forked, and Alexxa took the right branch,

only to have Kazadim do the same. She quickened her pace as fatigue masked her thoughts and dragged her from steely determination to sulky irritability. She had considered this day for seven years, yet she still felt unprepared. She knew the route and could even review it on the road thanks to the birthday map from the king. She had considered the basics, yet inexperience seemed likely to prove the largest hurdle. Even the meager necessities she had thought to bring seemed too heavy. She had not slept well the past several nights, the excitement of this one keeping rest at bay. Soon, she would need to make camp or risk collapsing on the path; yet she wanted to lose her follower first.

As the false dawn painted the sky, Princess Alexxa slogged onward, every step a worsening burden. The longing for sleep became a burning need, and concerns for safety seemed to lose significance. She forced herself to continue until the trail branched, this time in three directions. Surely Kazadim's business would take him a different way than her.

Alexxa chose the rightmost fork, deliberately looking backward as the man approached her turning point. Though she expected him to take the same one she had, when he did so, she suffered an irksome pang of annoyance. "You're following me," she accused.

Kazadim glanced at the princess as if surprised to find her there. "It would seem so." He added carefully, "You look exhausted. Would you like to share my camp and food? Numbers bring safety as well as warmth."

Alexxa's eyes narrowed in distrust. *The only safety I need is from this heavily armed lunatic trailing me.* Drawing her sword, she shook it in warning. "If you come near me, I'll run you through."

"Ahh." Kazadim's shoulders rose and fell. "I'll assume that means you're not interested."

Alexxa sheathed her weapon. Picking a small patch of crushed-down stems not far from the road, she sat.

Rummaging in her pack for the tinder box, her hand closed on every other object first. Finally, she found the wooden box and drew it free. Opening it, she found the neat row of sticks she had placed there herself. The knife filled its accustomed depression, but the hollow beside it lay empty. The princess froze in horrified realization. Her memory zipped back to that moment in her room when she deemed the chunk of flint too battered for her long journey. The one she had chosen in its place now rested safely on her mirrored bureau where she had placed it knowing she could not possibly miss it there. But she had, and it meant she would sleep cold, in fear of wild animals.

Muttering another curse, Alexxa snapped the tinder box closed and replaced it in her pack. Too tired to eat, she cradled her head on her belongings and curled among the stems. She fell asleep almost immediately.

Princess Alexxa awakened with the aroma of cooking meat in her nostrils. She rolled to her back, imagining a breakfast of fresh eggs, bacon, and crusty bread. The corners of her lips tugged upward. Sunlight glared against her closed lids, and she jerked her eyes open. Now the light slanted into her eyes, blinding. She leaped to her feet, the sword slapping her side, blinking away colored afterimages that scored her vision of the roadway, trees, and a vast plain of weeds. Memory returned in a rush. Dirt and bits of stems soiled her cloak, but she no longer felt chilled. The acrid odor of a campfire joined the other smells. Her stomach rumbled.

Alexxa drew open her pack. The hard bread, smoked mutton, and withered fruit seemed desperately unappetizing compared to the wafting perfume of roasting fowl. Closing her pack, she sighed deeply. Had Kazadim intended to harm her, he could have done so easily enough last night while she slept like the dead. Gathering her things, she headed toward the enticing smell and hoped that his offer of hospitality still stood.

Alexxa expected a campfire to prove easy enough to find, yet she cast about for quite some time before she finally stumbled upon Kazadim's camp, nestled in a tree-lined grove. He crouched in front of a crackling fire, gnawing at a pheasant drumstick. The flames flickered scarlet over oddly-sculpted features nearing middle age. White hair hung to broad shoulders. Dark eyes full of wisdom studied her from beneath a fringe of pale bangs. The rest of the roasted pheasant sat on a stump, near the warmth of the campfire which still danced on its juices.

Kazadim lowered the bone, wiping his mouth with the back of his hand. "You There!" he said as if greeting an old friend by name. "What took you so long?" He did not wait for Alexxa to answer but ripped the other drumstick from the carcass and thrust it toward her.

Never heard of plates, forks, and napkins. Hunger got the better of Alexxa. Accepting Kazadim's offering, she bit deeply into the meat. Hot grease burned her tongue, but it barely slowed her. She ignored the man's curious stare as she ate with little more decorum than he had displayed. She did, however, wait until she had swallowed everything before speaking. "Why are you following me?"

Kazadim broke off the wings. "Where are you headed?" he asked as he offered one to her.

Caught up in eating, Alexxa started, "I'm going . . ." She caught herself, then deliberately looked him in the eye. "Where are *you* heading?"

Kazadim opened and closed his mouth, then admitted sheepishly, "All right, I'm following you."

The frank admission shocked Alexxa silent. For a moment, she even stopped eating.

"I wanted to know where a princess was going in the middle of the night."

"You—" Alexxa managed. "You know who I am?"

Kazadim smiled. "Everyone knows the royal family. You can't possibly know everyone. It gives us a distinct, if probably unfair, advantage."

Alexxa looked Kazadim up and down. His massive frame, impressive height, and straight hair better suited the mountain or river people. He would have stood out in Genyana. *As much as I do.* "Why did you ask my name, then? Why do you insist on calling me 'You There!' "

The ample shoulders rose and fell with casual ease. "If a princess wants to travel in disguise, who am I to interfere?"

"Not much of a disguise, apparently." Alexxa swept down her hood, spilling the black hair that had fallen from its bindings as she slept. "And you've interfered plenty."

"Only to try to make your journey more comfortable."

Alexxa had to concede that one. Taking her cue from his directness, and the success it had bought him, she fixed her gaze on the stranger. "You're not Genyani. Where are you from?"

Kazadim dodged the princess' gaze. "I'm not from anywhere. I'm a traveler, never staying in one place long."

Alexxa took a bite of pheasant, chewed, and swallowed. Refusing to take vagary as answer, she pressed. "Everyone comes from somewhere."

Kazadim looked back at Alexxa. "Ethnically, I'm Birindi. But I consider myself a man of the world."

Alexxa gnawed her way to the bone before addressing the oddity. "You've got a nice set of weapons for a vagabond." It suddenly struck her that she might have made company with a bandit. She banished the thought almost immediately. Kazadim had recognized her as the princess, must have realized she carried money, yet he had not bothered her or her belongings.

"I earn my way." Finished with his own wing, Kazadim drew his knife. He quartered the carcass with deft, practiced strokes. "Kazadim is a title, not a name. It means 'swordsman' in Birindi. People pay me to teach them to fight. Or to fight for them."

"You're a mercenary."

Kazadim frowned. "I consider myself a teacher." He hefted a piece from the pheasant. "I have joined causes, but money's not enough. I have to agree with them."

Alexxa amended her previous statement. "A mercenary with ethics and a conscience."

Kazadim's confidence slipped this once, revealing it as a facade. He glanced nervously around the clearing before changing the subject. "Do I get to know why a princess is creeping around the woods at night?"

Princess Alexxa considered several moments. As the hollow in her stomach filled, she became more aware of her greasy fingers and scorched tongue. "That depends on what you plan to do with the information."

"It depends on the information."

Stalemate. Alexxa sighed. Though under no obligation to speak a word to this stranger, she could see the advantage to his knowledge. "Let's deal."

"All right."

"I'll tell you what I'm doing after you've trained me."

Kazadim stared.

Misattributing his surprise to greed, Alexxa added, "And I'll pay you, too. As I can, anyway."

"No payment necessary." Kazadim spoke around a mouthful of meat. "The knowledge and the opportunity to guard you while you travel is enough." He added mischievously, "But if you can 'run me through,' you probably don't need my instruction."

Alexxa lowered her head to hide a guilty smile; her threat had been idle. "So you'll do it?"

Kazadim stared off into the forest, expression sobering. "Am I going to wake up some morning surrounded by Genyani swords seeking revenge for the abduction of a princess?"

Alexxa shook her head without raising it. Her mother's face filled her memory, the fierce glare of her pale eyes when she described the circumstances of Alexxa's birth. The princess' birthday presents had included the pack she now used for travel, and she had awakened to the sword left casually leaning in a corner. "My mother's known of my plans for years. I left her a note explaining that I deliberately left. She'll forestall a search." Though Alexxa had learned to discard bitterness long ago, she knew most would not mourn the loss of the misfit eldest daughter of Queen Shelnah. Finally, she looked at Kazadim. "When do we start?"

The man tossed pheasant bones into the fire, wiped his fingers on his britches, then rose with the grace of a cat. "Now."

Snow weighted the interweave of branches overhead, forming a roof that blocked the setting sun and brought darkness hours early. The arrhythmic thunk of wooden practice swords echoed from a familiar world of close-packed trunks and drifts. Seeing an opening, Alexxa lunged toward Kazadim's gut, only to find herself drawn into a trap. The instant she committed, the breach closed. His shield slapped her sword harmlessly aside, and cold wood brushed her neck.

"Damn!" Catching herself, Alexxa clapped a hand to her mouth.

Kazadim withdrew, grinning. "Where does a princess learn to talk like that?"

"Two months with a coarse, old mercenary." Alexxa stared at her own shield as if it had betrayed her.

"Coarse?" Kazadim repeated, with feigned offense. "Old?" He realigned. "I'm not too old to knock you on your insolent bottom, *lirada.*"

Princess Alexxa had grown accustomed to Kazadim calling her by the River term for student rather than title or name. In fact, she preferred it, uncertain how the people in the small villages they entered for supplies would handle a mixed-blood princess in their midst. Now, irritated by an icy wind cutting beneath her cloak as well as by her gross error, she could not help adding, "Two months into a journey that should take a month, and we're not even a quarter of the way to Sarakas."

"Patience, *lirada*." Kazadim glided into fighting stance, side toward Alexxa, knees slightly bent, weight balanced. "Competence takes time."

Alexxa assumed the proper posture, warily awaiting his first movement, attentive to the slush beneath her boots. "At this rate, I'll be twenty-one before we get there."

Kazadim flicked the sword toward Alexxa. "Would that be so bad?"

Gaze on his hands, the princess anticipated the attack, parrying easily. His silly question fueled her aggravation. "Yes." The promise to herself and, ultimately, to her mother smoldered inside her like an ageless and everburning flame. The obsession to which she had committed herself had become synonymous with the age of twenty. She cut for Kazadim's legs.

Kazadim dodged, then bore in with a flurry of attack, kicking up a shower of snow. He asked only, "Why?"

Forced to tend defense, Alexxa went silent. Kazadim's sword drummed against her shield. She managed a directed riposte through the web of wood he created.

"Why?" Kazadim repeated, retreating to avoid her blade.

No logic accompanied the answer, despite its intensive certainty. Alexxa had not yet explained even her intention to her teacher, and the ingrained need that had possessed her since she learned of the tragedy defied description. She answered the only way she could. "Because," she managed, and little more. "Simply because."

Princess Alexxa perched on the bank of the River Skarlaff, oiling and polishing until the steel of her sword gleamed. The joy of the previous night's practice hovered like the giddy aftermath of too much sweet wine. She had finally bested her teacher, scoring a "killing" blow through a wild and earnest defense. Kazadim had savored her triumph nearly as much as she had, loosing a whoop of joy despite certain bruising and grinning like a child with a new toy. Yet though she had slipped off to sleep battling an excitement that kept her heart rate quickened and tremors thrilling like spirals through her chest, Kazadim's features had wrinkled into a sorrow that seemed to confuse even himself.

Now, Alexxa sat listening to the river burbling its quiet and regular backbeat to the song of morning birds. Pink fled from the sky, chased by a late spring sun. Weeds rattled and danced in a pleasant wind that carried the scent of damp and greenery. The sadness that had seemed to affect Kazadim the previous night touched her now. In their eight months of travel, they had spent every moment together. Kazadim had insisted on near-constant teaching, and the need for competence had driven Alexxa to take full advantage of his dedication. Between lessons, they had exhausted every topic she could imagine, yet they still had much to say. When she spoke of her past, he hung on every word. In her moments of doubt, her times of homesickness and grief, he had listened without chiding or advising. Both had known from the start they would part ways in Sarakas. Suddenly, Alexxa realized she would sorely miss her teacher. And, apparently, he would miss her, too.

The clang of metal interrupted Princess Alexxa's thoughts. She turned as Kazadim approached, tossing her shield and pack to the ground beside her. The wind floated strands of his white hair like ghosts. The fine, Northern features she had once associated with savagery had become handsome for their familiarity. Her mother had helped her to see her own chiseled features as unique rather than merely different, and the spectacular grace with which Kazadim handled a frame that the folk in Genyana would have considered large and clumsy finally allowed her to accept the beauty inherent in her own build. He had done so much more than just teach her how to best the man who had so damaged her mother and made Alexxa mistrusted among people she should rule but never would. Kazadim had helped her accept herself. "Thank you," she said.

Kazadim gestured at the shield and pack. "No trouble."

Alexxa laughed. "I wasn't talking about bringing my things here."

The Birindi mercenary moved to stand in front of her. "No?"

"No." Alexxa rose to meet her teacher, still clutching sword and rag. "Thank you for teaching me so much."

"You're welcome, *lirada.*"

Alexxa shuffled her feet in the weeds, wishing she could find the words to make him understand the breadth of his teaching and the depth of her gratitude. She sighed, knowing they would go forever unspoken. "I never did pay you."

The dark eyes crinkled. "I told you I didn't want your money."

"I promised you an explanation."

"Indeed. That I will accept."

Alexxa cleared her throat. Unable to think of a preamble that would not dilute the significance of her revelation, she simply blurted, "I'm going to kill my father."

Kazadim only blinked, eyes still tensely lidded. "You're going to kill King Arno?"

Now it was Alexxa's turn to look surprised. Warmth suffused her, and she wondered if the traveling companion she had venerated a moment earlier truly deserved her mental praise. "Have you listened to nothing I told you?"

"Every word," Kazadim insisted. "But His Majesty

raised you since birth. He's loved and cared for you every moment of your life. Does he not deserve the title of father?"

"I meant . . ." Alexxa choked on the words, irritated that Kazadim chose such an important moment to worry for semantics and details. "I meant the bastard whose blood I share." The words emerged in a heated rush, fueled by a hatred that had simmered too long. Abruptly, she appreciated Kazadim's correction as much as she had condemned it only an instant earlier. "Whose straight black hair dangles from my head. Whose muddy eyes look out from a face not my family's. Whose blocky body—" The words dissolved into tears. She waited for Kazadim to comfort, wishing he would sweep her into his arms like a brother. He had shown sympathy before, gently stroking her hair as the winter wind stung her face and extremities and when the wish for home fires and nannies became nearly unbearable.

Now the warrior stood like a quiet fool, saying nothing, doing nothing.

The princess buried her face in her palms, sobbing.

Finally, Kazadim spoke softly. "How will you know him?"

"I'll know him." Alexxa felt a certainty she could not explain.

"How will you find him?"

Visions of a terrified Queen Shelnah, no older than Alexxa was now, filled the princess' head. Not for the first time, she felt the soldiers' hot bodies pressed against her, sticky with the blood of brothers and reeking of filth and sweat. Sorrow retreated before dark rage. "His accomplices called him . . ." The name clung to her tongue like a bite of thorned and bitter fruit, "Raygonir."

"Raygonir," Kazadim repeated. He closed his eyes, then opened them slowly. His next words emerged clear, unmistakable. *"Lirada, I* am Raygonir."

Alexxa looked at him, unable to speak: the hint of

residual pepper in his soft white locks, the soulful dark eyes, the Northern features, once alien, and now an obvious reflection of her own. The anger raged into an explosion. Without warning, she ripped the sword in her fist toward him.

Kazadim managed to draw and block in a motion. Steel crashed against steel, echoing, silencing the birds. The impact ached through Alexxa's fingers. Caught in a storm of hatred, she barely acknowledged the pain. She charged in with frenzied slashes that forced her teacher into desperate retreat. If he returned her strokes, she never noticed. Lost in all-consuming rage, she saw the world only through a red fog, needing revenge, needing absolution. Her blade rose, slashed, and fell repeatedly, hurling glitters of sunlight like lightning from the gods. Nothing mattered but the death of the man who met her feverish violence with deft parries and dodges.

Time passed in a vacuum. The agony screaming through overused sinews became insignificant background to the goading, unreasoning perfection of venom and wrath. Then, finally, Kazadim collapsed beneath her assault. Alexxa came to her senses with her sword poised over him, prepared to deliver the killing stroke. Only then she noticed the flap in his tunic and a welling line of blood over his ribs. Despite the minor injury and impending death, Kazadim looked unworried. The spark in his brown eyes stemmed from pride, not fear. He did not struggle or roll, simply waited for whatever end she chose to mete.

The princess crowed her victory through lips gone painfully dry. Her grip tensed on the hilt, and she imagined herself plunging the blade into his abdomen repeatedly, savoring the warm splash of blood, reliving a long-held daydream in her mind—but not in reality. There she remained stiffly in place as if some warped artist had replaced her with a perfect duplicate in granite. Pain and exhaustion overtook her suddenly, and she lowered her aching arms. Anger turned, once again, to tears. "Why," she whispered. "I have to know why."

"Why?" Kazadim repeated, his tone requesting clarification.

Realization struck as hard as the throbbing in Alexxa's arms. "You just claimed to be the one who attacked my . . ." she trailed off. ". . . because . . . because . . . you wanted to see how I would fare in the real situation. You risked your life . . ." She looked at Kazadim who sat cautiously but did not try to fully rise. Unfooled, she knew he could have leaped to his feet and back into battle from the moment she had hesitated instead of immediately killing him. He had been willing, perhaps even eager, to die at her hand.

"No." Kazadim studied Alexxa, stony-faced with sobriety. "I was a young man, younger than you are now, when I joined Sarakas' horde. Smitten with embellished tales of war. Full of dreams of glory." He sighed. "It wasn't what I expected. Men died. Friends died. Honor is the least of war. Celebrating victories in the daylight, you feel invincible. At night, every puff of wind becomes an enemy. You cling to one another in terror, afraid to die, certain you will, and try to pretend you're not afraid." Kazadim shook his head in obvious frustration. "You start to think, no, believe unfailingly that anything your friends do is right. If everyone you trust . . ." The mercenary's shoulders sagged. "It's impossible to explain. War makes even the worst things seem reasonable . . ."

Horror stole over Alexxa again, this time tempered by fatigue. "You *did* rape my mother. You are—"

"—the bastard who shares your blood." Kazadim's expression revealed the pain that facing death had not. "I'm sorry, *lirada.*"

The apology seemed woefully inadequate.

"I went back to Sarakas with the others, but I couldn't stay there. How could I brag about war achievements when I felt so evil, so unremittingly dirty? Back in the city, I realized I had had nothing in common with my companions except a distorted dream of glory and a fear of death. Experience stole even both of those from me, leaving nothing. I stayed five years before guilt drove me southward."

Alexxa ground her teeth, remaining silent. She wanted to stop him, wanted to shout that no justification existed for the cruelty he had inflicted—on herself and on her mother. But learning her own history proved too seductive to interrupt.

"I found your mother, learned of your birth, of your mother's marriage to the prince, now king." A slight smile bowed Kazadim's lips. "A good man, Arno, to follow through on a wedding plan despite your mother's condition. He made a better father than I ever could have." He met Alexxa's gaze, though it clearly pained him. "Five births from that attack, and the others all . . . 'died.' Mysteriously. Arno could have inflicted the same on you, but he refused to blame you for my mistake." He winced. "My act of evil."

Drained not just of rage, but of all emotion, Alexxa continued to stare.

"I left with a retinue of guards at my heels and a warning never to return. But I did. Repeatedly. I couldn't stop myself. I knew I would never earn forgiveness, but I had to apologize. I had to know what happened to you."

Alexxa found her tongue. "I suffered. I had to do everything twice as well as my sisters to get half the respect. And I'll never claim my birthright." She narrowed her eyes, daring him to say her "birthright" lay with him, not the king.

Kazadim did not do so. "I know. I suffered with you and appreciated that your parents had the closeness and words I didn't to help you through it. Genyana doesn't realize what it will lose by choosing a sister over you. I hope you'll use your experiences to help whoever takes the throne to see the world through the eyes of the maligned."

Alexxa stiffened. She had always planned to serve the kingdom as her sister's adviser. "You followed me from the castle."

Kazadim's lack of denial served as confirmation. "After a few years, the king and queen stopped trying to drive me away and ignored me. Eventually, the king gave me an occasional glance, a shrug, a rolling of the eyes. When you left the village, I had to follow. I had to know why and where. I had to keep you safe."

"And you didn't know I was looking for you?"

"No." Kazadim's expression turned pleading.

Princess Alexxa glanced at her hands, at the calluses that had formed since she began her sword training. *But Mother knew I was looking for you.* She thought of her birthday gifts and of the sword conveniently placed where she would find it. *Father, too.* Alexxa smiled at the understanding. *And they knew I would find you.* She had never loved her parents more.

Kazadim loosed another heavy breath. "I'm sorry." He turned toward his belongings and prepared to leave.

Before he could move, Alexxa hurled herself into his arms. For several moments, they embraced, his warm tears smearing onto her cheeks. At length, they separated, and Alexxa took Kazadim's hand. "Let's go home."

"Home?" Kazadim shifted uneasily.

"Genyana."

"Alexxa." Kazadim's fingers closed over hers. "I don't think I'm welcome."

"You are now." Alexxa smiled. "I know my parents. As you said yourself, good people. And they love me."

Kazadim still hesitated.

"Trust me."

Returning the smile, Kazadim did.

THE DREAMWAY PRINCESS
by Bill Ransom

Bill Ransom worked as a medic and firefighter before turn-
ing to fiction writing. He collaborated with Frank Herbert on
The Pandora Trilogy, which includes the novels *The Jesus
Incident, The Lazarus Effect,* and *The Ascension Factor.*
His most recent novel is *Viravax.*

Lula Kax let the norther pick a way for her through
the screams and the rubble toward the shattered
gates of the city. What was left of the city. She bent
and adjusted the brass rod in the waistband of her
skirt—she'd lifted the rod from the toilet at Martita's
when the soldiers said they wanted her for ques-
tioning. It wasn't much of a weapon, but the cold feel
of it at her waist gave her comfort. The norther
scooped up the dead dwarf's letters and a soldier's
weapon, then he said to Lula Kax: "Come with me,
we have no calendar to lose."

"We have no *time* to lose," she corrected.

"Yes," he said, "we have no *time* to lose."

He shouldered the weapon from its strap, then hurried her through the wreckage of the largest city in
the Roam. On the way, he picked up two backpacks
from the crushed table of a market stall. Among the
hissing ruins of the neighborhood market, where thick,
choking smoke mixed with the smothering odor of hot,
crushed fruit, Lula Kax and the norther stranger
stuffed their packs with food, water bottles, and
charges for the weapon. Lula had thought he was one
of the soldiers until the earth opened up, and the

norther left the soldiers behind in the grinding, snapping collapse of the dwarf's scrap-and-tin shack.

The norther didn't take her by force, and though he'd arrived with the two soldiers, he didn't arrest her for the death of the dwarf. The two soldiers had seen Lula Kax standing over the dwarf's body, but she had not killed him. She had not even known his name, though she passed him every day on her way to the market. But she agreed in a glance to follow the norther because he had the love letters that he claimed the dwarf had written her—letters which the dwarf had never sent. Letters that she hoped could lead her back to her people, if any of them survived outside the city walls among the raiders and the jaguar wars.

The dwarf's poor shack, the soldier's cuartel, all of Camellia Street shuddered, then lost its footing on the earth. Then the earth chewed raw stone into dust and spat it at the blackening sky. Now it dripped and plopped around them in thick, black globs. Yes, the earth shook down the city. But they were alive, and something true in the norther's blue eyes made her follow him. Lula Kax hesitated at what had been the city gates, and he urged her on with a flick of his hand.

"Walk it faster," he said.

She surveyed the wide expanse of land and the blackening sky ahead, the surrounding hills thick with trees and underbrush. Lula Kax and the norther would be exposed in the long trek to the trees, and from her youth she remembered all too well what that meant.

"What's the matter?" he asked. "I'm not going to carry you."

A soot-blackened old couple scurried past her, bumping her bulky pack and knocking her down. She tugged her skirt below her knees, struggled to her feet and choked back tears.

"I was ten," she said. "I came to the city when I was ten. I haven't been outside since."

"I know," he said. His gaze swept the horizon, and

he licked his lips. "I know what happened to you at the river."

Lula Kax was stunned.

He knows!

"We desire greatly to go now," he said.

She swallowed, adjusted her straps and corrected him.

"We *have* to go now."

He bowed slightly and swept a hand ahead of him. "Thank you," he said. "We have to go now."

As she followed, she felt the breeze against the bare exposure of her neck, and she imagined a blade slicing her skin with every step. She'd watched a raider kill her mother with a weapon just like the one the norther carried now. This norther was a little like the raiders: tall, fair-haired, and skinny, so unlike the dark-skinned, shorter people of her birth. He spoke her language poorly, but he did not frighten her as the soldiers did. He had frightened her when he was with the soldiers, but she was not afraid of him now the way she'd been at the dwarf's. Something in his blue eyes, in his tone of voice, reassured her that he was not a threat, but protection.

The norther stopped for a moment, and they both turned for a look back at what had been the City of Eternal Spring.

"That fog will attract raiders," he said. "We can't dream until the mountains."

"Smoke," she corrected. "Not fog, smoke."

"Thank you," he said again. He smiled for the first time in the few hours she had known him. "I have had no calendar—no, no *time*—to learn your language."

Smoke, black and putrid with the stink of charred flesh, roiled up from the city and spread out against the sky. Thick black blobs plopped around them and stuck in their hair and on their clothing. No more screams reached them from the city, just the occasional *whump* of an explosion. A few, like themselves, took their chances outside what remained of the walls. An old man in one group waved them over, but the norther didn't wave back. Instead, he sighed, hitched his pack into a more comfortable position, and started off for the mountains.

"Better not to group," he explained. "Easier for the raiders."

Lula Kax shouldered her pack, but she waited.

"Where are you taking me?"

He turned back to her and frowned.

"To your family," he said.

"My family is dead."

He wiped his sunburned brow with his shirtsleeve and smeared sooty sweat across his forehead.

"The people who cared for you are dead," he said. "Your *familia*, people of your blood, wait inside the mountains."

"There are no such people." She didn't know why he would torment her this way. She repeated, "My family is dead. I saw them die."

"Your family needs you," he said. He tapped the front of his shirt where he kept the dwarf's papers. "When we're inside the mountains, I will explain."

"Among the mountains," she said, "or in the mountains. Not inside the mountains."

He grumbled something unintelligible in his harsh norther tongue, then he strode up the hillside toward the valley that led to the highlands. She took a deep breath and followed. Neither of them looked back again.

The raiders hit them at dusk, just after the norther told her his name.

"They call me 'Mole,'" he said, "because I prefer the underground."

He scratched his back against a rock outcropping and yawned. He was about to speak again when something hit him on the side of his head, and a smelly, grunting body knocked Lula Kax to the ground. The first shock of fear galvanized a kind of lightning in her spine that shot through her arms and legs. Like that time at the river, her body knew what to do without

her. The raider pinned her chest and upper arms with
his forearm and worked her legs apart with his knees.
While his free hand fumbled at her underwear, Lula
Kax slipped the brass toilet rod out of the waistband
of her skirt. He tried to rip her underwear with a yank
that lifted his weight from her chest. She slipped her
arm free, and when he yanked again, she took a deep
breath and drove the rod into the corner of his eye.
He snatched at her arm as the rod crunched through
bone, and she wiggled it around. He said, "Ah!" once,
then tremors swept his body, and the rod made a sucking sound as she pulled it out. Hot pulses of blood
shot across her arms and chest.

The Mole's weapon crackled twice as she rolled free
of the twitching body. She crouched low, her feet
planted wide, and she breathed slow and deep. It was
as though she stood beside herself and watched what
her body was doing. Two raiders lay at the Mole's
feet, and he struggled with a third who twisted the
weapon and growled in frenzy. The weapon crackled
again, again. Mole hissed "Shit!"—the only norther
word she knew. Lula slid one step forward and kicked
the side of the raider's knee. It crumpled with a satis-
fying *pop,* and as he grabbed at it, she cut off his
scream with a snapping kick to his throat.

In a moment, after the gurgling stopped, all she
could hear was herself and the Mole breathing hard.
Her first clear thought was that the raider had touched
her below the waist, and she was now *mirame.* She
had to find someone of the Rom to help her cleanse
herself.

Suddenly, like that time at the river when she was
ten, when she killed the raider who killed her mother,
her head hurt so bad that she had to drop to her
knees. She pressed her forehead against the cool
earth, gasped and gagged, then lay on her side,
exhausted.

Lula felt a poke at her ribs. Another.

"Stay awake," Mole said. "You can dream in the mountains." He coughed, and a strange sucking sound came with it. "Get up."

No moon, and the dark curtain of her headache intensified the dark of the oncoming night.

"Get up," he repeated, and nudged her again. "I'm dead."

His breathing was faster now, shallower, and that same sucking sound whistled between each breath.

His silhouette sat propped against the rocks. She breathed deep to curb her nausea and crawled to him. He stuffed the envelope thick with the dwarf's letters into her hands. The envelope was wet and slick.

"Listen," he said. "No time to tell you everything. Letters are not to you. They are in code. Get them to your people in the mountains."

"But how? Where—"

"Up this valley. Above the trees. Make good time. Get to the stones . . . old piled stones. Dream there, and you will know everything."

"Let me see your wound."

"No. You desire greatly . . . you *have to* go. Do not dream . . . before you get . . . to the stones. Dreamways. That's how they . . . destroyed the city . . ." He sat up straighter, trying to drag in air. "You see . . . your body . . . knows what to do."

"But why me?"

"Your dream . . . will tell all. Go."

"No," she said. "I can't leave you here to die."

He reached for air in small, panting breaths.

"Don't . . . combat . . . with me," he whispered. "Jaguar country . . . I have to die . . . before I dream . . . or all is lost."

The *snap* of the weapon and its bright flash startled her. Mole toppled at her feet, his face in the dirt. She was already *mirame,* so she reached out and shook him by the shoulder. Nothing. Something scrambled in the rocks above her, so she stuffed the bloody envelope into her pack and picked up the Mole's weapon.

The grip felt familiar to her hand, but she did not remember touching such a weapon before. Her hands checked the charge, found it low. She emptied his pack onto the ground and her fingers swapped the low charge for a full one. She tucked the extra charges into the waistband of her skirt and shouldered her pack. By then the cone-nosed biting beetles had found her ankles and her headache pounded again, so she stamped her feet, sprinkled some dirt over Mole's head, and moved on.

Lula Kax sensed from the first that someone or something was following her: small, scrabbling sounds, a rustle near her shoulder, something like a muttering in the bushes. She was tempted to cut loose with the weapon, but that would be a waste of charges. She leaned her pack against a pine trunk to rest for a moment, and she realized that she could see in a way that she'd never experienced before. The way was clear before her—what she thought was a gravel wash was really a trail.

No moon, she thought, *and dawn is a long way off.*

The little hairs at her neck prickled. This sudden night-sight frightened her almost as much as the raiders. For a moment, her vision shifted as if she were in the branches of the tree behind her. She saw herself clearly, with her pack and the weapon, and she watched two raiders slipping up the trail behind her. They picked their way carefully, not hurrying, obviously following without trying to overtake her. A whisper came to her as though the whisperer stood at her shoulder.

If they find the place of stones, all is lost.

Almost before the whisper was over, they were upon her, and Lula Kax killed them both as naturally and as simply as putting on her sandals. She searched herself for remorse, for feeling of any kind, and found nothing but exhaustion. Though she wanted desperately to stay and to rest here, just for a few minutes, once again her body took over and her legs continued to haul her up the trail. And once again, something rustled and fluttered alongside her.

Lula Kax was so tired that she had reached the top and started down the other side without noticing. The cackle and caw of a crow snapped her out of her mind-numbed trudge. She shifted her pack, turned, and walked back to the rocky flat at the treeless crest. The first rosy finger of dawn lightened the horizon, and the crow called again. If fluttered its wings and hopped atop a small ruin of stones.

"A crow," she said, and dropped her heavy pack. "Was it you following me all night?"

The crow croaked an answer, then hopped and fluttered again atop the stones.

"So, is this the place that Mole sent me to?"

"Craaak!"

She walked over to the crow, and it didn't fly off. It stood atop a pile of stones that once must have been a wall encircling this part of the summit. Some of the stones had strange figures carved into them, and one stone, hollowed into a bowl, held water that oozed from a large stone just above it. She was desperately thirsty, so she drank the cold, fresh water until her forehead ached. Then she tore a fistful of dark bread from a loaf in her pack and tossed half of it to the crow. She could have sworn she heard it say "Thanks" in her mind, but it must have been her exhaustion talking.

"This place is pretty exposed," she told the crow. "It doesn't look like a safe place to sleep to me."

The crow looked at her, muttered something, then rose in a leap and a couple of wing-flaps to the top of the highest stone—a carved, weather-worn sentinel easily five times her height. There the crow set up a terrible ruckus, jumping and cawing and flapping its wings. Then it glided down beside her and pecked her foot.

"Ow!" She stepped back, and the crow muttered at her what could have been an apology.

"You'll keep watch while I sleep?"

"Craaak. Crk crk crk."

By this time she was so tired that she didn't have a choice. She found a spot within the circle of stones that she could crawl into with her weapon and her pack, where intruders could see her only if they were right on top of her. She set the pack up as a pillow and hugged herself tight against the chill. Now that she wasn't moving, she shivered with the cold, but the top of the sun broke the horizon, promising a warm morning. She hoped that this place was too high for scorpions and immediately fell deep asleep.

At first, she thought she'd wakened. The green-eyed, dark-skinned woman standing over her was beautiful; her expression, warm and loving. When the woman smiled, Lula Kax felt all of the chill of the night fall away.

"My child," the woman said, "do not be afraid. Your questions will be answered, and more."

"Who are you?"

The woman's image shimmered, and Lula Kax realized that she was an apparition or a vision.

"I am the one who gave you into good hands twenty years ago because there are those who would hunt you down. I trained you to fight when you were still in the womb by stealing the experiences of great warriors and placing them into your mind. I blocked part of your mind and put you in the hands of good people, so the enemies who ply the dreamways would not find you."

So, she thought, *Mole was right.*

She thought this calmly, and that surprised her.

"Yes, Mole," the woman said, and sadness washed her face. "There is much to reveal about him, but that must wait. He accomplished much, and he will be missed."

Lula Kax felt something happening with her head,

like a blindfold was lifted, locks were being cut away, and doors and windows opened.

"He said . . . he said my family was still alive."

"Yes," the woman said, "we are for now. But there is great danger, and this danger is not for us alone. This world and all who are in it will die if we cannot stop the one who hunts us."

"But if the world dies, he must die, too, no?"

"No." The woman shook her head sadly. "He is not of this world. A fabric separates our world from his. Each time he crosses, he weakens the fabric. If this fabric tears, and one world spills into the other, both are destroyed. We believe that he has ventured into other worlds that do not touch ours, and that he can escape there into other minds if necessary."

Lula Kax felt another burst of something bright flow into her mind.

"You are of my family?"

The woman's smile returned.

"My name is Afriqua Lee," she said. "I am your mother. And now you remember stories of Afriqua Lee and the Jaguar."

"Yes," Lula Kax said, "I remember. The Jaguar came in dreams from another world to steal the secrets of the Roam. His priests died in an old temple in the highlands."

"Yes," he mother said. "You sleep now in the ruins of that temple. We closed those entries to the dreamways, and we thought we killed the Jaguar. But other gateways opened, and the Jaguar escaped."

Lula Kax felt her heart galloping in her chest.

"What are these dreamways, these gateways?"

"We are on the dreamways now," her mother said. "We can connect through dreams, special dreams that cost us dearly."

"Why haven't I heard of this before?"

"Because very few have this gift—or, as some see it, this curse. Your body will tax you most painfully for this privilege. Others with this gift can enter your dreams, enter your mind, and they can alter or steal what's in there."

"Why have I never done this before if I have this gift?"

"You *have* done this before," Afriqua Lee said. "Before you were born. I took steps to protect you, to keep you safe and to let you get stronger, strong enough to hunt down the Jaguar and destroy him for good."

"Me?" Lula Kax was dumbfounded. "But how?"

"That is something only you will know. When you wake, you will be very ill. Rest there. When you're ready to travel, your guide will lead you to us. Do not sleep again until you have found our camp. The dreamways are many, but only a few are secure."

"I don't understand," Lula Kax said. "Where do I find my guide?"

Afriqua Lee smiled again.

"He's already found you," she said. "The crow will lead you home to the Romni Bari's tent—a title you will inherit soon enough. You will do no more laundry for the *gaje.* And I am most grateful that I have lived long enough to see you again, my daughter. Sleep flat and safe. I love you."

Her mother's face wavered, then disappeared.

My mother!

Lula Kax woke in the dark to a crushing headache that bloodied her nose and forced her to vomit before it was through with her. After that, her strength returned and she realized that she had slept at least one day and nearly through the night. She refreshed herself and shared a little more bread with the crow, who seemed none the worse for the long wait. Her mind reeled under the onslaught of images that her mother had sent her, but she understood now the struggle with the Jaguar and the inevitable part she had to play against him.

"Do you have a name?" she asked the crow.

"Cachaak," he said.

"Cachaak it is," she said. "Well, let's get to it."

She shouldered her weapon and her pack and followed the black bird down the other side of the highlands toward her family and her destiny.

BECOME A WARRIOR
by Jane Yolen

World Fantasy Award winner Jane Yolen has written well over 150 books for children and adults, and well over 200 short stories, most of them fantasy. She is a past president of the Science Fiction and Fantasy Writers of America as well as a twenty-five-year veteran of the Board of Directors of the Society of Children's Book Writers & Illustrators. Her most recent books are *Child of Faerie* and *Twelve Impossible Things Before Breakfast*. She lives with her husband in Hatfield, Massachusetts, and St. Andrews, Scotland.

Both the hunted and the hunter pray to God.

The moon hung like a bloody red ball over the silent battlefield. Only the shadows seemed to move. The men on the ground would never move again. And their women, sick with weeping, did not dare the field in the dark. It would be morning before they would come like crows to count their losses.

But on the edge of the field there was a sudden tiny movement, and it was no shadow. Something small was creeping to the muddy hem of the battleground. Something knelt there, face shining with grief. A child, a girl, the youngest daughter of the king who had died that evening surrounded by all his sons.

The girl looked across the dark field and, like her mother, like her sisters, like her aunts, did not dare put foot on to the bloody ground. But then she looked up at the moon and thought she saw her father's face there. Not the father who lay with his innards spilled

234

out into contorted hands. Not the one who had braided firesticks in his beard and charged into battle screaming. She thought she saw the father who had always sung her to sleep against the night terrors. The one who sat up with her when Great Graxyx haunted her dreams.

"I will do for you, Father, as you did for me," she whispered to the moon. She prayed to the goddess for the strength to accomplish what she had just promised.

Then foot by slow foot, she crept onto the field, searching in the red moon's light for the father who had fallen. She made slits of her eyes so she would not see the full horror around her. She breathed through her mouth so that she would not smell all the deaths. She never once thought of the Great Graxyx who lived—so she truly believed—in the black cave of her dressing room. Or any of the hundred and six gibbering children Graxyx had sired. She crept across the landscape made into a horror by the enemy hordes. All the dead men looked alike. She found her father by his boots.

She made her way up from the boots, past the gaping wound that had taken him from her, to his face which looked peaceful and familiar enough, except for the staring eyes. He had never stared like that. Rather his eyes had always been slotted, against the hot sun of the gods, against the lies of men. She closed his lids with trembling fingers and put her head down on his chest, where the stillness of the heart told her what she already knew.

And then she began to sing to him.

She sang of life, not death, and the small gods of new things. Of bees in the hive and birds on the summer wind. She sang of foxes denning and bears shrugging off winter. She sang of fish in the sparkling rivers and the first green uncurlings of fern in spring. She did not mention dying, blood, or wounds, or the awful stench of death. Her father already knew this well and did not need to be recalled to it.

And when she was done with her song, it was as if his corpse gave a great sigh, one last breath, though of course he was dead already half the night and made no sound at all. But she heard what she needed to hear.

By then it was morning and the crows came. The human crows as well as the black birds, poking and prying and feeding on the dead.

So she turned and went home and everyone wondered why she did not weep. But she had left her tears out on the battlefield.

She was seven years old.

Dogs bark, but the caravan goes on.

Before the men who had killed her father and who had killed her brothers could come to take all the women away to serve them, she had her maid cut her black hair as short as a boy's. The maid was a trembling sort, and the hair cut was ragged. But it would do.

She waited until the maid had turned around and leaned down to put away the shears. Then she put her arm around the woman and with a quick knife's cut across her throat killed her, before the woman could tell on her. It was a mercy, really, for she was old and ugly and would be used brutally by the soldiers before being slaughtered, probably in a slow and terrible manner. So her father had warned before he left for battle.

Then she went into the room of her youngest brother, dead in the field and lying by her father's right hand. In his great wooden chest she found a pair of trews that had probably been too small for him, but were nonetheless too long for her. With the still-bloody knife she sheared the legs of the trews a hand's width, rolled and sewed them with a quick seam. All the women of her house could sew well, even when it had to be done quickly. Even when it had to be done through half-closed eyes. Even when the hem was wet with blood. Even then.

When she put on the trews, they fit, though she had to pull the drawstring around the waist quite tight and tie the ribbands twice around her. She shrugged into one of her brother's shirts as well, tucking it down into the waistband. Then she slipped her bloody knife into the shirt sleeve. She wore her own riding boots, which could not be told from a boy's, for her brother's boots were many times too big for her.

Then she went out through the window her brother always used when he set out to court one of the young and pretty maids. She had watched him often enough through he had never known she was there, hiding beside the bed, a dark little figure as still as the night.

Climbing down the vine, hand over hand, was no great trouble either. She had done it before, following after him. Really, what a man and a maid did together was most interesting, if a bit odd. And certainly noisier than it needed to be.

She reached the ground in moments, crossed the garden, climbed over the outside wall by using a twisted tree as her ladder. When she dropped to the ground, she twisted her ankle a bit, but she made not the slightest whimper. She was a boy now. And she knew they did not cry.

In the west a cone of dark dust was rising up and advancing on the fortress, blotting out the sky. She knew it for the storm that many hooves make as horses race across the plains. The earth trembled beneath her feet. Behind her, in their rooms, the women had begun to wail. The sound was thin, like a gold filiment thrust into her breast. She plugged her ears that their cries could not recall her to her old life, for such was not her plan.

Circling around the stone skirting of the fortress, in the shadow so no one could see her, she started around toward the east. It was not a direction she knew. All she knew was that it was away from the horses of the enemy.

Once she glanced back at the fortress that had been the only home she had ever known. Her mother, her sisters, the other women stood on the battlements looking toward the west and the storm of riders. She could hear their wailing, could see the movement of their arms as they beat upon their breasts. She did not know if that were a plea or an invitation.

She did not turn to look again.

To become a warrior, forget the past.

Three years she worked as a serving lad in a fortress not unlike her own but many days' travel away. She learned to clean and to carry, she learned to work after a night of little sleep. Her arms and legs grew strong. Three years she worked as the cook's boy. She learned to prepare geese and rabbit and bear for the pot, and learned which parts were salty, which sweet. She could tell good mushrooms from bad and which greens might make the toughest meat palatable.

And then she knew she could no longer disguise the fact that she was a girl for her body had begun to change in ways that would give her away. So she left the fortress, starting east once more, taking only her knife and a long loop of rope which she wound around her waist seven times.

She was many days hungry, many days cold, but she did not turn back. Fear is a great incentive.

She taught herself to throw the knife and hit what she aimed at. Hunger is a great teacher.

She climbed trees when she found them in order to sleep safe at night. The rope made such passages easier.

She was so long by herself, she almost forgot how to speak. But she never forgot how to sing. In her dreams she sang to her father on the battlefield. Her songs made him live again. Awake she knew the truth was otherwise. He was dead. The worms had taken him. His spirit was with the goddess, drinking milk from her great pap, milk that tasted like honey wine.

She did not dream of her mother or of her sisters or of any of the women in her father's fortress. If they died, it had been with little honor. If they still lived, it was with less.

So she came at last to a huge forest with oaks thick as a goddess' waist. Over all was a green canopy of leaves that scarcely let in the sun. Here were many streams, rivulets that ran cold and clear, torrents that crashed against rocks, and pools that were full of silver trout whose meat was sweet. She taught herself to fish and to swim, and it would be hard to say which gave her the greater pleasure. Here, too, were nests of birds, and that meant eggs. Ferns curled and then opened, and she knew how to steam them, using a basket made of willow strips and a fire from rubbing sticks against one another. She followed bees to their hives, squirrels to their hidden nuts, ducks to their watered beds.

She grew strong, and brown, and—though she did not know it—very beautiful.

Beauty is a danger, to women as well as to men. To warriors most of all. It steers them away from the path of killing. It softens the soul.

When you are in a tree, be a tree.

She was three years alone in the forest and grew to trust the sky, the earth, the river, the trees, the way she trusted her knife. They did not lie to her. They did not kill wantonly. They gave her shelter, food, courage. She did not remember her father except as some sort of warrior god, with staring eyes, looking as she had seen him last. She did not remember her mother or sisters or aunts at all.

It had been so long since she had spoken to anyone, it was as if she could not speak at all. She knew words, they were in her head, but not in her mouth, on her tongue, in her throat. Instead she made the sounds she heard every day—the grunt of boar, the whistle of duck, the trilling of thrush, the settled cooing of the wood pigeon on its nest.

If anyone had asked her if she was content, she would have nodded.

Content.

Not happy. Not satisfied. Not done with her life's work.

Content.

And then one early evening a new sound entered her domain. A drumming on the ground, from many miles away. A strange halloing, thin, insistent, whining. The voices of some new animal, packed like wolves, singing out together.

She trembled. She did not know why. She did not remember why. But to be safe from the thing that made her tremble, she climbed a tree, the great oak that was in the very center of her world.

She used the rope ladder she had made, and pulled the ladder up after. Then she shrank back against the trunk of the tree to wait. She tried to be the brown of the bark, the green of the leaves, and in this she almost succeeded.

It was in the first soft moments of dark, with the woods outlined in muzzy black, that the pack ran yapping, howling, belling into the clearing around the oak.

In that instant she remembered dogs.

There were twenty of them, some large, lanky grays; some stumpy browns with long muzzles; some stiff-legged spotted with pushed-in noses; some thick-coated; some smooth. Her father, the god of war, had had such a motley pack. He had hunted boar and stag and hare with such. They had found him bear and fox and wolf with ease.

Still, she did not know why the dog pack was here, circling her tree. Their jaws were raised so that she could see their iron teeth, could hear the tolling of her death with their long tongues.

She used the single word she could remember. She said it with great authority, with trembling.

"Avaunt!"

At the sound of her voice, the animals all sat down on their haunches to stare up at her, their own tongues silenced. Except for one, a rat terrier, small and springy and unable to be still. He raced back up the path toward the west like some small spy going to report to his master.

Love comes like a thief, stealing the heart's gold away.

It was in the deeper dark that the dogs' master came, with his men behind him, their horses' hooves thrumming the forest paths. They trampled the grass, the foxglove's pink bells and the purple florets of self-heal, the wine-colored burdock flowers and the sprays of yellow goldenrod equally under the horses' heavy feet. The woods were wounded by their passage. The grass did not spring back nor the flowers raise up again.

She heard them and began trembling anew as they thrashed their way across her green haven and into the very heart of the wood.

Ahead of them raced the little terrier, his tail flagging them on, till he led them right to the circle of dogs waiting patiently beneath her tree.

"Look, my lord, they have found something," said one man.

"Odd they should be so quiet," said another.

But the one they called lord dismounted, waded through the sea of dogs, and stood at the very foot of the oak, his feet crunching on the fallen acorns. He stared up, and up, and up through the green leaves and at first saw nothing but brown and green.

One of the large gray dogs stood, walked over to his side, raised its great muzzle to the tree, and howled.

The sound made her shiver anew.

"See, my lord, see—high up. There is a trembling in the foliage," one of the men cried.

"You fool," the lord cried, "that is no trembling of leaves. It is a girl. She is dressed all in brown and green. See how she makes the very tree shimmer." Though how he could see her so well in the dark, she was never to understand. "Come down, child, we will not harm you."

She did not come down. Not then. Not until the morning fully revealed her. And then, if she was to eat, if she was to relieve herself, she had to come down. So she did, dropping the rope ladder, and skinning down it quickly. She kept her knife tucked up in her waist, out where they could see it and be afraid.

They did not touch her but watched her every movement, like a pack of dogs. When she went to the river to drink, they watched. When she ate the bit of journeycake the lord offered her, they watched. And even when she relieved herself, the lord watched. He would let no one else look then, which she knew honored her, though she did not care.

And when after several days he thought he had tamed her, the lord took her on his horse before him and rode with her back to the far west where he lived. By then he loved her, and knew that she loved him in return, though she had yet to speak a word to him.

"But then, what have words to do with love," he whispered to her as they rode.

He guessed by her carriage, by the way her eyes met his, that she was a princess of some sort, only badly used. He loved her for the past which she could not speak of, for her courage which showed in her face, and for her beauty. He would have loved her for much less, having found her in the tree, for she was something out of a story, out of a prophecy, out of a dream.

"I loved you at once," he whispered. "When I knew you from the tree."

She did not answer. Love was not yet in her vocabulary. But she did not say the one word she could speak: *avaunt*. She did not want him to go.

When the cat wants to eat her kittens, she says they look like mice.

His father was not so quick to love her.

His mother, thankfully, was long dead.

She knew his father at once, by the way his eyes were slotted against the hot sun of the gods, against the lies of men. She knew him to be a king if only by that.

And when she recognized her mother and her sisters in his retinue, she knew who it was she faced. They did not know her, of course. She was no longer seven but nearly seventeen. Her life had browned her, bronzed her, made her into such steel as they had never known. She could have told them but she had only contempt for their lives. As they had contempt now for her, thinking her some drudge run off to the forest, some sinister throwling from a forgotten clan.

When the king gave his grudging permission for their marriage, when the prince's advisers set down in long scrolls what she should and should not have, she only smiled at them. It was a tree's smile, giving away not a bit of the bark.

She waited until the night of her wedding to the prince, when they were couched together, the servants a-giggle outside their door. She waited until he had covered her face with kisses, when he had touched her in secret places that made her tremble, when he had brought blood between her legs. She waited until he had done all the things she had once watched her brother do to the maids, and she cried out with pleasure as she had heard them do. She waited until he was asleep, smiling happily in his dreams, because she did love him in her warrior way.

Then she took her knife and slit his throat, effi-

ciently and without cruelty, as she would a deer for
her dinner.

"You father killed my father," she whispered, soft
as a love token in his ear as the knife carved a smile
on his neck.

She stripped the bed of its bloody offering and
handed it to the servants who thought it the effusions
of the night. Then she walked down the hall to her
father-in-law's room.

He was bedded with her mother, riding her like one
old wave atop another.

"Here!" he cried as he realized someone was in the
room. "You!" he said when he realized who it was.

Her mother looked at her with half opened eyes
and, for the first time, saw who she really was, for she
had her father's face, fierce and determined.

"No!" her mother cried. "Avaunt!" But it was a cry
that was ten years late.

She killed the king with as much ease as she had
killed his son, but she let the knife linger longer to
give him a great deal of pain. Then she sliced off one
of his ears and put it gently in her mother's hand.

In all this she had said not one word. But wearing
the blood of the king on her gown, she walked out of
the palace and back to the woods, though she was
many days getting there.

No one tried to stop her, for no one saw her. She
was a flower in the meadow, a rock by the roadside,
a reed by the river, a tree in the forest.

And a warrior's mother by the spring of the year.

GOLDEN YEARS
by Lea M. Day

After being born, Lea Day evolved into an omnivorous reader. She thought the next logical step up would be to write. She grew up in Oregon, joined the Navy, saw the world, and then, to spite Thomas Wolfe and her family, came home again. She has the prerequisite cats to attend to, and hangs out in places where books are found.

Dearest Mum;
    It was nice to hear of your safe arrival at the shrine of Diana at Ephesus, and I think that this rest will do you some good. The girls loved the statues that you sent of Diana and the horses, and wonder when Gran will be visiting again. They so love your adventures.

The olive harvest looks good this year, and we have branched out and started a small fish paste sideline that is very promising. We are using that recipe that you brought back from that trip you and Dad took to the Inland Sea, so it is quite different from the usual fish paste around here. The olive harvest profits will cover most of the expenses including the pensions on your warriors. The other news that we have for you is bad. It's about the property investments that you and Dad made during the more profitable wars.

The worst news is that Thera did explode and destroyed most of the island. This included your villa and the surrounding property. On top of that, there have been a lot of earthquakes in Crete, and property values there have, pardon the expression, tumbled. In all, I would say that everything that you and Dad worked for is gone. All that is left is this olive farm, and it's not going to replace the revenues that you had planned on once you quit going off to war and pillaging.

Which brings up another subject. Mother, you are an Old Warrior in changing times. There are better small armies out there than you have had, and there have been advances in weaponry that well, frankly, have made you behind the times. Remember when the big change came when everyone went from copper to bronze? Well, this is even more so, now. It's Greek Fire and ramming Tirenes, and Science. It's not the good old days when you marched up to a town or palace, laid siege to it, and then carried off what you could. I have discussed this with the rest of the family, and we all agree that you need to slow down and take care of yourself, because without your health, you have nothing. We even went up to consult the Pythia about this, and talk about changing times! They have male priests up there, imagine that, men as priests. They claim that is because the Pythia speaks for Apollo, but, really. Call me old-fashioned, but how can they prove their purity as men? It's so much easier with women priestesses, and they can substantiate their devotion to the gods! Don't let me get distracted here, but even the Pythia foretold bad times if you went back out trying to earn a living as a Warrior Princess. And the cost for the oracle, I swear, it was twice as much as the last time we all went to see how Dad was doing in the Elysian Fields. (Well, that is where the Pythia said he was, though I do have some doubts every now and then.)

What Mikos and I have found is that there is a small villa outside of the seaport by the farm where Warrior Princesses can spend the rest of their days. I

found out about this from the farrier who does your
War Horses, and we went to see what he was telling
us about.

Mum, you are going to love this villa! Everyone has
a separate room, and they let you keep your arma-
ments and they have stable space for one horse per
resident. They provide two meals a day and they observe all the festivals and mark the anniversaries of
all the great battles. They were telling us about how
they were going to have a feast to observe the fall of
Troy, and they have some blind bard coming to recite
the story for everyone at the villa. It sounds great!
They have other activities, too, for the residents, battle
practice, tactic discussions, and best of all, they want
the residents to mentor some of the up-and-coming
warriors from the Academy in town. You won't be
sitting around on the stoa all day watching the goats
graze, you will have your days filled with things to do.
You will love the monthly practice battles that they
have with another villa up the coast that is for Warrior
Princes. It's all in good fun and they have a banquet
afterward, and any injuries are covered in their residents services.

The view from the villa is great. Yes, there is a stoa,
but it overlooks the town and the port below (did I
mention that the villa is on the top of a cliff?) and
you do have a great view. The town was raided by
pirates last year, and the villa is upwind, so when they
were burning the town, the residents of the villa could
watch the events as they unfolded without getting af-
fected by the smoke. I heard that they did get a small
force together to assist the town (and not the pirates,
that is just a rumor that someone put out). The residents were full of stories about that event; seems they
got more bumps and bruises getting the horses ready
than in actual hand-to-hand combat. Two of the ladies
even managed to get onboard the pirate ship and got

paid enough ransom to afford three years' fees at the villa. They also have an announcement for upcoming sunset cruises on the harbor, but they haven't finalized the arrangements yet. They have trips, too. This month they are going to the Swamp of Lerna to see the pure waters. They make sure that you aren't bored there.

I know, you want to ask who would be living in this villa. Well, they have space for twenty women there, but, I did notice that there were one or two men in residence. Yes, I did ask why there were men in a villa for Warrior Princesses, and they told us that there were instances where these men were Queens in their own right. Whatever, some of your old comrades are already there. I won't spoil the surprise by telling you who is there, but, remember the second Spartan campaign? Just think of it, you can talk about the times you had and not be bored with the mundane facts of pressing olives or how much milk the best goat is producing. They have the best bath I have seen. They have four pool attendants on duty at all times to assist the residents in their water activities and give massages by appointment. That, however, is an added fee, they say, and not included in the basic rates. They must be good, because they had women waiting for their turns. Those attendants are very easy on the eye and are quite attentive to the residents' needs, and always willing to engage in conversation. That was a good thing to hear because since you lost Dad, you really haven't had someone to converse with. We know that life on the campaign trail meant everything to you, and we don't want to take that from you. What we are doing is what is best for you Mum, and we want you to be happy.

We have asked them to hold a room for you when you get back from Ephesus, and we know that you won't be disappointed with it. I am sure that if Dad was still with us, he would want to move in there, too.

Other than that, Diodorus is doing well in his first campaign. We hear from him every now and then. They don't provide efficient couriers to bring the news home like you and Dad used to. Those glory days are passing quickly. No one takes pride in the battles and the hymn teachers like they used to.

The girls are getting so big, they both want to be boukoloi in the Mysteries this year, and that is another expense; that would be a choice calf or kid for the altar. I am not complaining as it is for the glory of Dionysus, and there is a chance that they will both be asked to be Priestesses. But then again, last month, they wanted to go off and write bad poetry about love and eternal devotion. I don't think that I should let them be going off to market by themselves any more. They are exposed to such radical notions about what is proper behavior. They need their Gran nearby to keep them focused.

We love and miss you,
Erigone

THE SWORD OF UNDEATH
by Felicia Dale

Felicia Dale is a musician based in Seattle, Washington. Other fiction by her appears in *New Amazons*.

Lesyen blundered through the undergrowth trying not to panic, though her heart was hammering in her chest and she trembled in every limb. She crashed into a sapling and nearly fell. She clutched at the rough bark and leaned her forehead against it as though it could tell her what to do next.

I'll never find her this way. Think, stupid, think!

The crows called louder, their voices sharp and insistent against the deep silence of the forest.

Lesyen set off again, turning toward the crows. The bushes thinned and an acrid reek assailed her, making her choke. A final effort and she burst into a small clearing. She blinked and coughed, rubbing away tears and taking shallow breaths.

Behrig lay motionless, stunned or unconscious. Behrig's sword, the Ne-Yeth, lay just out of reach, the leaf mold showing the scores her fingers had made in an effort to retrieve it. The lower half of the warrior's body was crushed by a glistening, pony-sized dark lump that was like nothing so much as congealed nightmare. Lesyen's neck hairs prickled and she would have turned and run, but she was too frightened to move.

There was a crow standing not far from Behrig's outstretched hand and another crow actually on her head.

The crow on Behrig's head probed sharply with its beak, once, twice. It swallowed its mouthful with an effort.

Rage broke the hold of fear and Lesyen darted forward, but the crows scrambled into flight before she could reach them. Her fingers closed on empty air. A strangled sound, half shriek, half sob, burst from her throat.

The crows in the treetops cawed angrily and then, with a whirr and a clatter, they flew away, their cries echoing strangely among the trees. Lesyen hardly heard them, so loud was her internal litany of self-abuse. Stupid, useless, too late to help even against something as small and weak as a crow. She wanted to kill something, break something, but she only began to tremble again.

Lesyen heard a small sound, a sigh, and she dropped to her knees beside Behrig. Was she waking? No, not yet. Lesyen stole sidelong glances at the creature that had felled the High King's greatest warrior.

It wasn't just the stench and proximity of the slimy thing that was so frightening, but its pure *otherness*. It had no apparent head, no eyes, no limbs. It had no more features than a clod of mud. Perhaps it had had more shape when it was alive. Lesyen wondered how it had moved without legs. It must have been quick to catch Behrig. Not quick enough to escape her, though, for the Ne-Yeth was stained to the hilt with a thin grayish slime. More of the slime oozed from several wounds in the creature's slick dark skin. The Ne-Yeth was unaffected though the slime had eaten holes in Behrig's clothing, etched her armor, and bleached the grass. Lesyen tried not to think of what it must be doing to her skin and flesh.

At least she wasn't dead; that much was certain. Whoever carried the Ne-Yeth could not die, Lesyen reminded herself, but the thought did not give her the comfort it had in the past. She had never thought of what this actually meant, but now, seeing Behrig's ruined body and her blinded, bloody face, Lesyen was sickened with a helpless fury that was beyond tears. To be so wounded and still be alive seemed the very heart of cruelty.

The hand that had dropped the sword lay palm up, the callused, wiry fingers curling gracefully. Only yesterday Behrig had pressed that hand on her shoulder as she spoke a word of praise for some small improvement in a lesson. Lesyen could not remember what she had done to warrant it, but the warmth of that contact had sustained her the rest of the day.

Lesyen took up the limp hand and kissed it. It was then her tears began to fall. The fingers stirred and tightened feebly on her own.

"Lesyen?" Behrig asked, her voice a croaking whisper. The blinded face turned toward her, and a grimace of agony distorted her features.

"Oh, yes," Lesyen managed to reply.

"Good. Just who I wanted . . ." Behrig's voice trailed off.

"What can I do for you? Should I go for help? The healers could—"

"Where is my sword? Don't touch it! But I need it . . ."

"It's right here— Oh, Behrig, let me go for help! I can't bear this!"

"No, no help. My sword. Take a stick. Push it to my hand. Ah, I can't see you. I wish I could. Brave Lesyen." Behrig let go of her hands and pushed at them to encourage her.

Lesyen forced herself into action. Scrabbling about in the fallen leaves she found a dead branch and with it maneuvered the sword under Behrig's hand.

The corners of Behrig's mouth turned up in a brief smile as her fingers clasped the hilt. Then the smile faded and she seemed to go deep inside herself where nothing, not even pain could follow her. Lesyen recognized the look, the trancelike quiet that came over the warrior at infrequent moments, sometimes in the middle of conversations. It was only a small part of the legends that preceded her like gulls riding the front of a storm wind.

Lesyen sat back on her heels trying to keep back her tears. She knew that if she began to weep now, she would be unable to stop. Behrig needed her, had called her brave, though she knew she wasn't brave at all. She was a weakling, a coward, stupid. Again the familiar chorus of faults tried to take over her mind, but with an effort Lesyen pushed them aside. No matter what she had been in the past, she must live up to being called brave by Behrig.

Abruptly, with a shock that obviously shredded her nerves with pain, Behrig was back. When she spoke, her voice was stronger than before, as if she thought her pain might soon cease.

"Of all my servants, of my companions, of my friends, you are the only one who followed me on this evil day. Why?"

"No one else saw what I saw," Lesyen said, her voice shaking despite all she could do to stay firm.

Behrig said nothing, so Lesyen continued.

"I saw you walking into a gray mist that seemed to swallow you whole, yet your sword shone through. I knew you were alone, and no one else saw the mist. It seemed evil somehow, so I went after you. I tried to make others come with me, but no one listened."

"No one?"

"Only Avendred, and he just laughed at me being frightened for you because, of course, he said you couldn't be killed so you were sure to be safe. I knew that, but still I had to go after you."

"Avendred . . ." Behrig's hand clenched weakly on the sword hilt. "No, I can't be killed, though I can wish to die. I wish so now. Will you help me? I never thought it would be you. I thought . . . You followed me so it must be you."

Lesyen was stunned. Help Behrig die? She couldn't die, Behrig must live, must let the healers help her. Surely there was something else she could do, anything but help her die. Then, with a terrible shock, Lesyen knew what Behrig meant.

"Lesyen—"

"No! It can't be me, I'm not like the others, I'm afraid of everything, I can't fight, I can't!" Lesyen knew she was gabbling and put her hands over her mouth to stop herself, but her mind squealed on, *This isn't fair, not me, I can't, I can't, I can't!*

"Lesyen, look at me! My body is ruined, but I can't die, I can only suffer and suffer and suffer until every bit of me is eaten away by this creature's blood, and even then—ah, I will never know peace. As long as the sword belongs to me, I am condemned to torment. I never thought it would be you, but you must be the one. You followed me as I followed the last one to carry the sword, as someone will follow you unless you are strong enough to destroy it."

"Destroy it?" Lesyen was shocked by the idea. The Ne-Yeth was like the ocean or a mountain, not something a mere human could destroy. A queer flutter of hope slowed her tears. "How?"

"It's not difficult. Any forge can melt it to a lump. When the shape is gone, so is the magic. I meant to do it myself, but there was always something to do first, someone to help, something to fight for . . ." Behrig's voice cracked, and she panted for breath. "Promise me you will destroy it right away. Don't wait, don't tell anyone. Otherwise they'll try to talk you out of it or beg you for help. But most of all, you mustn't use it. It will seduce you, and you'll end up ruined like the rest of us. It has always ended this way. Not again, not again."

Behrig seemed almost to be talking to herself rather than to Lesyen, as though these were familiar words she had thought many times. Or perhaps heard long ago, spoken by another. The thought chilled her.

"I promise," Lesyen said faintly, then more strongly, "I promise!"

The words seemed to call Behrig back from her

wandering. This time when she spoke, it was clear and direct.

"Then give me your hand. I must put it into your hand."

Lesyen reached out, then hesitated. It was all very well to promise to destroy the Ne-Yeth, but if she took it, Behrig would die.

"Oh, please, Lesy, please help me. You're not killing me, I would have been dead years ago except for the sword. Death will be a gift now, such a beautiful gift. I'll be safe."

The longing in Behrig's tortured face wrenched Lesyen's heart.

"But I love you," she whispered and was instantly ashamed that she should admit this, as if it might be an excuse, a way to escape the responsibility.

"I know. That's why you're here. Help me. You're the only one who can." Behrig's voice was so full of confidence that Lesyen thought her heart would break with pride and grief.

She took the sword from Behrig's grasp. Behrig smiled and took a deep breath.

Lesyen waited, but there was no word, no sigh of release, only silence.

The hilt of the Ne-Yeth was warm from Behrig's hand. Lesyen clung to this tiny remnant of the warrior's life, but the metal quickly adjusted to her own touch.

She felt no evidence of magical deathlessness, only a terrible fatigue that threatened to overwhelm her. Her vision swam and shrank until blackness swallowed the sight of the sword and Behrig's body. She didn't faint though she wished she could. Then she heard voices echoing faintly under the trees and in the space of a breath her vision returned. Those who would not follow before were coming now.

Lesyen got to her feet and without a backward glance slipped away into the undergrowth.

The bushes seemed to collude in her escape. They

no longer snagged at her clothing and tangled in her feet but parted effortlessly before her and closed softly behind her. She was out of sight before the first cries of disbelief, anguish, and suspicion rang out, and soon even these were left behind.

The Ne-Yeth was awkward in her grasp. Royal blood was no guarantee of talent and despite expert tutors and endless drills, she was still as inept as she had been at the beginning of her studies. Lesyen eyed the sword with annoyance. She could not appreciate its simple elegance or its grand history, it was only a burden to be destroyed as soon as possible. There was no easy way to carry it without a scabbard, but she could wrap it in her cloak. She did this, and the Ne-Yeth became an anonymous, oblong bundle. No one would know what she carried. She would throw it into a forge, and it would never hurt anyone again.

She tucked it under her arm and went on.

Lesyen walked until the sun was low behind the trees. She was hungry, thirsty, and lost, but she didn't care, only moving forward now out of habit and the fear of being followed and prevented from destroying the sword. She had wept until her eyes ached and her cheeks burned, until all her tears were used up. She stumbled on, sore-hearted and exhausted.

There was no path, only the leaf mold soft under her feet made fresh each year by the tall, silent trees. The peace of the endless avenues broken only by occasional distant bird song gradually calmed her, and her tearless weeping ceased.

The ground had been fairly level, but now it fell away, gradually at first, and then steepening until she was forced to pay close attention to her surroundings. The Ne-Yeth was hers now. If she fell and broke her neck, she would not simply die, she would lie and suffer as Behrig had and without the hope of rescue. She shuddered at the thought and slid to a stop, clinging one-handed to the trunk of a tree. The cloak had loosened and metal shone through a gap. She adjusted the cloak to cover the sword completely again and then paused to look around before going on.

It would be dark soon. Looking up, she saw a patch of sky, deep blue and cloudless. It might be cold to-night, but at least she wouldn't get wet. Behind her she saw only trees, but below her there was a path hugging the hillside. The sight gave her a queer pang of unease, but Lesyen set off toward it, sliding from tree to tree and trying not to fall.

At last she reached the path and stepped with a sigh of relief onto level ground. Then came the question of which way to go. The path curved tightly around the hillside and gave no hint as to which direction might be preferable. She looked at the sky again and thought hard about where the camp was and where Behrig had fallen. At last, not certain but almost so, she turned to face the south.

There in the middle of the path was Avendred. He loomed tall and ominous from the back of his war horse. Lesyen stared, for he seemed bathed in blood. She blinked, and the blood turned to rays of red sunlight pouring through a gap in the trees. The stallion arched his powerful neck and mouthed his bit making a pretty jingling noise like small bells. How could such a huge animal have moved so quietly? She must have been in a dream not to have heard them approaching.

Lesyen felt her courage sink into the soles of her feet.

"There you are at last," Avendred said. His voice was curiously toneless. "We've been looking for you for hours. Where have you been?"

"I, I was walking, I had to be alone," Lesyen stammered. She blushed under his scrutiny. Her heart began to hammer, and she heard herself saying faintly, "I got lost."

"Why, you silly child. You must be exhausted. Come on, I'll pull you up and you can ride back to camp with me." Avendred's voice acquired a tinge of sympathy mixed with annoyance. He smiled his beautiful smile and held out his hand, sure that Lesyen would obey him as she always had, as everyone did.

At one time she would have gladly, gratefully, accepted both the smile and his hand. But the smile did not reach his eyes, and the hand looked like it would rather strike her than help her. She shied back from him, just a step, before she could stop herself.

"I forgot you're afraid of horses," Avendred said. "Don't worry, Feredi won't hurt you. He's really quite gentle and won't mind a second rider a bit."

"No. That's all right. I'll just walk on a bit longer. I, I'm not ready for company yet. You go on ahead, and I'll come after."

"We'll go together," Avendred said and dismounted. "Let me carry your cloak for you, or perhaps you should put it on. The evening grows cool."

Again he reached for her.

Lesyen jumped back, and Avendred lunged swiftly after. The tips of his fingers caught the edge of the cloak, and he succeeded in pulling it part way from her grasp. Lesyen found the hilt of the Ne-Yeth under her fingers and automatically her hand went around it. The cloak slithered away, then hung forgotten from Avendred's hand.

"You! You have the sword!" he exclaimed. He stared at her and then laughed in disbelief. "Behrig must have been mad with pain to give it to you."

"Pain, yes, she was in pain, but she knew what she was doing," Lesyen said and sudden pride in the memory of being called brave stiffened her voice so that her words rang out without a tremor. The Ne-Yeth was heavy in her hand, but its weight gave her confidence.

"And what will you do with it?" Avendred asked in a tone calculated to soothe a suspicious mind.

Lesyen stared at Avendred's face and saw the ugly thoughts behind it as though his beauty was a clear glass window that hid nothing of the grim landscape on the other side.

Once she had loved him, or thought she did, though Avendred's thoughtless cruelty had caused her many sleepless nights. Now he was only one of the many who would try and take the Ne-Yeth from her before she could destroy it. She saw that he would do anything necessary to get the sword from her, even hurt her if it meant success. For a moment hate flared in her, acrid and caustic as the strange blood of the beast that Behrig had killed, but the words that blurted from her mouth had nothing to do with that.

"I, I'm a Hero now, like Behrig. I'm going to be famous and kill dragons and enemies of the High King and be in songs like she is, was, I mean." Lesyen was amazed at the way the lies poured out of her with only the one small hesitation. Where had such subtlety come from? She had never lied before. Again came the vague unease, but Avendred seemed a greater danger, so she pushed the feeling aside.

Avendred's smile had turned to a grin. He was drifting closer to her with an almost imperceptible stealth, but Lesyen was not unaware.

"You? A Hero? Nonsense, you know you can't even use a practice blade properly, let alone that great heavy thing. Give it here, you silly girl, such a weapon is not for you."

Avendred reached out again, but Lesyen jumped back and held the sword up as steadily as she could. Avendred eyed the blade without apparent concern, but he dropped his hand to his sides.

"You are being very foolish, Lesyen. I can't imagine that Behrig really meant for you to have the sword. She must have been desperate, poor thing. The Ne-Yeth should go to one who will use it properly."

"Such as yourself?" Lesyen tried to keep the irony out of her voice, but she need not have bothered, for Avendred did not hear it.

"Yes, or Evortra or Dannis, or anyone else like us

skilled in weaponry and aware of the risks and benefits of warfare. You're too weak and gentle, Lesyen. You don't have the natural fighter's talents. Behrig knew this; she said so when you first came to be trained. She said she thought you might someday gain the basic skills but that you would never be a true warrior. I don't know what she was thinking of when she gifted the sword to you instead of one of us."

Lesyen felt her eyes fill with tears, and her heart felt hollow and heavy as a stone. Behrig had said this about her? It was true; she wasn't very strong and she was afraid of being hurt which made her tentative in the drills and nervous around the horses. She knew she would never be a warrior. She would never be of any use to anyone, not the High King, not even her own family. She would always be the useless middle child, too plain to marry, to dull to come up with some original feat that would take the place of beauty or talent. . . .

Brave Lesyen, she heard Behrig's faint voice in her mind. *Just who I wanted. Dear one.*

Lesyen took a firmer grasp of the hilt and raised her left hand to help the right hold the heavy weapon steady between her and Avendred.

"I don't know what Behrig was thinking," Lesyen said. "But she said I was just the one she wanted. That's good enough for me."

Avendred changed tactics.

"Perhaps she saw something new in you in the last few days. I myself thought you were starting to make progress," he said. "And you come from good stock. After all, your father is a famous warrior and your mother is well known for her wisdom and skill in the ruling of her lands."

Without appearing to move, he had again lessened the distance between them. The tip of the blade wavered a hand's breadth from his chest, but he did not appear to notice it.

"Perhaps you could give the sword to me, or some

other one you trust, while you continue your studies. When you are worthy of it, the weapon would be returned to you."

Avendred spoke as though this was a logical possibility that had just occurred to him. He continued talking, but Lesyen no longer listened to him.

The sun had dropped near the horizon. Day was fading quickly; night would soon be in ascendance. Lesyen did not think there was a moon tonight. It would be a dark night with only stars to light it. If she could just slip back into the forest, Avendred would be hard pressed to follow after her in his heavy armor. She could hide easily in the shadows. She just needed to get back into the trees.

Perhaps some flicker of her intention showed on her face. Avendred pounced, one hand striking out and up at her arms to try and knock the Ne-Yeth away while with the other he grabbed at her clothing.

A flash of knowledge flared abruptly in Lesyen's brain. Her body moved swiftly, elegantly, and she was free of Avendred's grasp. She was so surprised that she was too slow to make use of her advantage, and instantly Avendred struck again.

The sword went sailing end over end and landed behind her on the path. With an eager, wordless exclamation Avendred shoved past her.

"Don't touch it!" Lesyen cried, too late.

There was another flash, this time from the sword itself and Avendred was flung as though kicked by his own horse. He landed on his back in the dirt, dazed but very quick to regain his feet. His face was twisted with fury, all his beauty gone. There was dirt on his cheek, a leaf in his hair. He drew his own sword and came at her, snarling.

"Give it to me or I'll make you beg like—"

Lesyen evaded his blow though she felt the wind of the blade stir her hair. She snatched up the Ne-Yeth. The hilt was hot and hummed with a silent vibration that filled her hands and ran up her forearms, exploding into her brain.

The world seemed suddenly still and distant. With a curious certainty Lesyen knew, that for her, time had stopped. It was like the pause between breaths, the rest between heartbeats. There was a murmuring, earnest but indistinct, like wind in treetops or waves on a shingle beach, the voices of a crowd all trying to speak to her at once. Lesyen could almost pick out separate words, individual voices, but . . . the unmoment was over. She heard the scuff of Avendred's feet behind her.

This time she moved deliberately, swinging the sword in a sinuous, glorious arc that felt as lovely and innocent as a dance step.

Avendred fell back in the dirt again. There was only a trace of blood on the Ne-Yeth, but blood poured from the wound in his neck and stained the pale surface of the path in a widening pool.

"You've been practicing," he said. He coughed.

Breath rasped in his throat, wet and labored, then ceased.

Lesyen's aching wrists could no longer stand the strain and she let the point of the Ne-Yeth rest in the dirt. She leaned on the sword and began to tremble with a tooth-rattling exhaustion that had nothing to do with physical fatigue. She stared at Avendred's body, at the blood that still ran from his wound though the pulse had stopped.

The sword did it, she thought, *it told me what to do. Besides, it's his fault. If he hadn't tried to take it from me he would still be alive.*

She knew this wasn't true. The Ne-Yeth hadn't told her to kill Avendred, it had only shown her how to do it. She had made the decision and acted all on her own.

Lesyen looked at the sword and slowly took her hands away from it. It fell over with a dull clang and lay gleaming dimly in the dirt. She felt sick and filthy, inside and out.

I lied, she thought. *I lied and I broke my promise not to use the sword, and now Avendred is dead.*

All her previous failures shrank to nothing against lying and breaking a promise. She might have been weak and cowardly, but she had never lied, never gone back on her word. She should have refused to fight, she should have run away. Even if Avendred had caught her and hurt her, she should have kept her promise.

Instead she had used the sword and murdered him.

Avendred was right, she thought. *I'm not a warrior. Warriors don't think of killing as murder, it's just business.*

But her heart beat faster at the thought that she had defeated Avendred in single combat. Granted, the sword had shown her how to do it, but she had actually struck down one of the High King's greatest warriors.

She really could be a Hero. She could take Behrig's place at the High King's right hand and continue Behrig's work for him. She would have her own armor, a war horse and a groom, her own standard and a servant to carry it, her own tent and servants to set it up and take it down for her, a cook, a maid. People would look at her with awe and say to each other, "That is the great warrior, Lesyen," and bow to her as she passed. Her siblings would pale beside her, and even her father and mother, for all their adventures, had nothing to compare to the Ne-Yeth. She would have no trouble getting a husband to add fortune and land to her family's holdings, but if she didn't want to marry, she could earn all the gold she wanted by teaching, as Behrig had done.

Her dream of being a warrior had come true. All she had to do was break her promise to Behrig, and her fortune was made.

Then she thought,

Who will I kill next?

It would not be as simple as "just" breaking a promise. It would mean death and pain and violence. Others besides Avendred would covet the Ne-Yeth, and like him, some would try to force her to give it up.

Lesyen had heard the stories of the duels Behrig had fought in the many years she owned the sword, and heard rumors of her scars. Lesyen shuddered, and the dreams of glory wavered before the reality of blood and pain. She was ashamed to see that she was as frightened of her own wounding as she was of causing the death of others. Why had she never thought of this before? It was a part of every warrior's life—how could she have ignored this for so long?

I always wanted to do something special, be someone important, well, this is my chance. Not exactly what I was thinking of but horses can't be riders.

Lesyen retrieved her cloak and the Ne-Yeth from the ground.

How odd, she thought. *The sword was still hot.*

She heard the shuffle of hooves behind her. A sudden chill made her scalp prickle and she turned around.

Avendred's war horse reared up on his hind legs not to attack but to stand, human like, on his back hooves. His shape blurred and shifted, swiftly became smaller, human, dark-haired . . .

"Mother?"

The figure smiled and reached out to embrace her.

Her mother, her real mother, had only one hand. This woman had two hands.

The Ne-Yeth tingled in her grasp and Lesyen let her body obey, raising the blade between her and the imposter. But the woman in her mother's shape, or whatever it was really, did not seem to mind the Ne-Yeth, only leaned forward and stretched out her arms farther in a peculiarly mindless way that made Lesyen shudder with sudden horror.

She heard more hooves on the path and a sudden glimmer of lamplight ran along the Ne-Yeth's blade.

"There you are! Oh, I'm glad we found you—" It was Evortra, her voice unmistakable after the hours of drill with her calling the figures.

Lesyen sagged with relief, and the tip of the Ne-Yeth dragged in the dirt. If Evortra was here then Dannis, her twin, would be here also. She was sure to be safe now.

"What in the world—" Evortra had caught sight of Avendred's body and the woman figure reaching, stretching her arms out so strangely long and jointless, prehensile . . .

Strike! the Ne-Yeth showed her how, *like this and this, and then—*

Lesyen half-raised the willing blade, but she hesitated, for over the slowly extending arms her mother's face still smiled fondly at her. Though her mother's eyes were never that dark or coldly luminous in such a weirdly beautiful way. Such lovely eyes—

"Look out!" Dannis and Evortra cried out together and Lesyen heard from behind her the rasp of a sword being drawn, the clap of legs to horses sides and the sudden drum of hooves. Then all sound ceased.

It was as though Lesyen stood in the middle of a terrific wind and yet no wind touched her. The bewitchment slipped from her and was gone.

Strike! the Ne-Yeth encouraged her, *Kill your enemy and escape unhurt. Like this—*

No. Show me a way to escape without killing.

There was a pause in the unmoment. Then came the burst of *how* and time was at its heels like a furious dog.

Lesyen twisted and fell back as the Ne-Yeth had shown her and exactly where she had been Dannis and the apparition collided.

The trap was sprung—the arms wrapped instantly around Dannis and jerked him from his horse. They fell to the ground and vanished as utterly as if they had never been.

Evortra made a strangled cry and fought to control her horse while Dannis' horse crashed into a tree in its fright. It staggered away a few steps and then stopped, panting and trembling in the dark under the trees.

Lesyen was frozen with horror and disbelief. She hadn't used the sword and still someone had to be sacrificed. What had happened to Dannis? Was he dead?

No. The Ne-Yeth was cooling in her hand, but still the answer came.

"H–he's not dead," Lesyen stammered as Evortra, in a terrible panic, jumped off her horse and dragged it after her as she went to the spot where Dannis had vanished.

"Dannis!" Evortra stared helplessly at the ground and then turned on Lesyen and grabbed her by the shoulder and shook her. "How do you know?"

"The sword—" Lesyen could hardly get the words out.

"You have to get him back!" Evortra exclaimed, and she glared at Lesyen in fury. There was the glitter of tears on her face. She let go of Lesyen's shoulder and turned away.

"What happened here? Why is Avendred dead? What was that, that creature? Oh, Dannis!" Then she fell silent.

Night had closed in and the lamp had gone out, lost in the struggle. The stars were bright in the sky, but their light was too fine to show more than the simplest things. Lesyen could see the path, the vertical lines of trees and Avendred's body stretched out not far away. Evortra was a dark shape next to the larger shape of her horse. She was getting something from the saddle. Presently there was the clink of metal and Evortra turned to Lesyen and held something out to her.

"It's the Ne-Yeth's scabbard," Evortra explained, her voice rough and tremulous.

Lesyen took it from her and managed to get the

sword inside the sheath. As the sword slipped into place, she felt a kind of muting of its presence. It was both a relief and disconcerting to feel a sense of separation from the Ne-Yeth, and she was dismayed all over again.

"Well, aren't you going to put it on?" Evortra asked sharply. "Come on, wear it properly. It's yours now, and you'd better get used to it."

Reluctantly Lesyen fastened the belt around her waist.

"Now, come on, help me. We have to get Avendred back to the camp. Can't leave him here for the crows." Evortra panted as she spoke as though every word was a sob. "Then you have to get my brother back for me. I don't care how long it takes or how far you have to go, but you'll get him back, and I'm going with you to make sure it happens. Oh, Dannis!"

They hoisted Avendred's body over Evortra's horse's back. Lesyen managed to catch Dannis' horse though it shied away from her in panic and only stopped when one rein twined around a branch. At the first touch the animal startled and nearly broke away, but then it submitted to her and seemed actually relieved to be under her control.

As Lesyen led it out of the trees and onto the path, she understood something of what it felt. She felt like Evortra's prisoner, and yet she had no desire to escape her, simply followed without question as Evortra led them away.

It was right that Evortra should demand the return of her brother, and it was right that Lesyen should feel compelled to acquiesce. She was responsible for Dannis' loss. If she had not moved out of the way of the apparition, but let it take her as it was meant to do, then Dannis would still be here.

Lesyen shuddered and wondered, ashamed, if she could have been brave enough to submit to that grasp and be taken who knew where and to what fate.

The Ne-Yeth dragged at her side, an awkward

weight that banged against her leg. It was no easier
to carry properly than it had been under her arm. She
wondered if she would ever get used to it.

I won't get used to it, she thought then. *I won't keep
it that long. I'll do my best to get Dannis back, and if
I survive, then I'll destroy it as I promised.*

Another voice, a very quiet one that spoke without
words, suggested that this might not be the right way
to go about things. She couldn't possibly rescue
Dannis without the Ne-Yeth to help her, she argued,
and pushed the quiet voice away and didn't listen to
it anymore.

THE LITTLE LANDMAID
by Sara Young

Sara Young was seven years old when she moved with her family to Bainbridge Island, Washington. As the new kid in school she spent many solitary hours playing on the beach near her home. "The Little Landmaid," her first published story, blends her passion for the environment with her early childhood fantasies.

First Mother Ocean invaded her sleep. They lived on the shore of Puget Sound, and her window faced the beach, so for a while it seemed as though all of her strange water dreams might have stemmed from leaving the window open.

She seemed an average eight-year-old girl; average height, weight, straight gold hair she preferred to wear long, but this was at a glance. If one looked closer, one would mark that her skin was moon-colored and nearly hairless, and her eyes were like twin pools of abalone that seemed, behind a childish curious gleam, to posses an infinity of wisdom. Her limbs were long and slender, and she moved with boneless grace. Her cheeks and lips were coral colored, and her hands and feet flawless white.

She was quiet, most said "introverted," and despite her obvious athletic build she detested any sport that involved running or jumping. She loved to swim, but unfortunately was allergic to chlorine. Her parents were uneasy about their oldest child for many good reasons; she seemed to get lost in herself, she had difficulty making and keeping friends, she had very little energy for a child her age.

Perhaps it was her baby brother that made her so
listless, they mused. After all, she was adopted, and
due to the wonders of technology, he was their own
genetic material. Perhaps their adopted daughter was
afraid that she was obsolete. Maybe they shouldn't
have been so open with her about her adoption. Perhaps if it weren't for their own guilt they may have
realized that their sad-eyed silent daughter was the
same sad-eyed silent baby who had won their hearts
eight years before.

No, her real problem was that she couldn't keep
away from the water. Mother Ocean, even the placid
Puget Sound, troubled her sleep. In dreams she went
out the window and walked into the water until it
covered the top of her head. Then her feet, calves,
knees, and thighs fused together and turned the color
of mother-of-pearl with the texture of dolphin skin.
Her fingers webbed. Others met her, and together
they swam near or far as their fins could take them,
and Mother Ocean whispered to her. She said *Darling
Morgan, I love you like no other, daughter mine, I love
you as only a mother can. You are my poor lost one,
stolen by my sister Dry Land. Tell me child, how goes
life in the World of Man?*

"Not well, Mother, not well. Their school can't decide if I'm brilliant or retarded, the other kids think
I'm a snob, and Mom and Dad think I hate my brother
Brandon. Sometimes he's a twerp, but he's only four
and I love him. I love all of them, Mother, but there's
just something in me that won't let me be at ease
there. I just don't seem to fit right."

*Of course not, my child, you are not like them. You
care about your adopted world, but one day soon I
will make you choose between us and come home. I
won't make you choose so young, but I must prepare
you for life here.*

With other sea-children she learned to speak in dolphin and sing in whale, and how to ride the currents
anywhere from the Baltic Sea to the Indian Ocean

and barely swim a stroke. Some nights they merely raced with the orcas and dove for oysters on the half-shell, other nights they were hard at work peeling barnacles off homes and herding salmon toward streams.

When it grew cold out, her adopted mother closed her window, but she still woke up damp and shivering with foot-shaped puddles across her floor. She was ashamed at first; this was another one of those things that made her "weird." She didn't know of any other little girls who swam in their sleep. Soon, however, she no longer cared if it seemed strange to others, since the only friends she had to tell lived underwater and in her dreams. She decided to study the phenomenon.

She found that it didn't occur every night. She put a piece of string in her window, and when she didn't dream the string was still there in the morning. She began marking the nights of nocturnal activity on her calendar, and found that she only went night-swimming while the moon was waxing. Even so, there were many waxing-moon nights when she stayed indoors.

Two years went by with two years' worth of tic-marks on seemingly unconnected growing-moon nights. Finally, for her birthday, her mother bought her a new calendar with the tides listed for each day. It took her six months, but she calculated that she only swam if the tide was still rising when she went to sleep. This accomplished, she knew which nights she could safely close her window.

Often she wandered the beach wondering if no one else could see the myriad dark eyes staring at her from beneath the water, their pale forms glowing like phosphorescence, their long hair winding around and behind them like kelp streamers.

She took off her shoes and dipped her feet in the water, and it was as if the Sound sighed ecstatically. She rolled up her jeans and waded in up to her knees, and shoals of salmon fry rubbed against her legs lovingly while seagulls exulted overhead.

The cuffs of her jeans got wet, so she decided that it wasn't so much more to wade in up to her hips, and then the hem of her shirt was soaked, so she continued until the water clucked her chin. Hands caressed her reverently, and hair swirled around her as voices cooed and sang to her, lips kissed her hair, and opalescent tails and ivory-pale torsos shimmered just under the surface, gently herding her toward deep water, the words calling her "Princess" and cajoling her home. She felt her legs buckle and her fingers begin to web, and left when the stunned realization echoed in her brain: "Awake?"

There came a day when she could no longer deny that she wasn't just dreaming. Beneath her rolled-up dripping cuffs her skin had turned mother-of-pearl mottled with returning flesh. She could just make out her companions' shining eyes as they reassembled under the rippling water, and hear their pleas to come back. There was Kingfisher, his long red hair staining the surface just like seaweed, there was Gwen, her white hair like foam, there was Nyadia, her violet tail iridescent in the wan sunlight. Morgan knew that she wasn't dreaming, and with this knowledge came a flood of questions. "Who am I?"

Mother Ocean answered *You already know who you are. My only daughter.*

"Where did I come from?"

My living body.

"Then why am I human?"

My sister Dry Land stole you from me.

"Why?"

She is a consummate thief.

It was natural, the most delightfully natural thing in the world to strip out of her clothes and let the cool compassionate brine close over the top of her head, to allow the others to drape her in white gold and pearls, walrus ivory and abalone, coral and shells. She allowed them to carry her to the Pacific Coast where they sat her on a throne of fossilized shark bones and the whales sang "All hail" and "Long live," and they danced until the tide changed and she needed to go home.

When she hauled herself onto the beach, her brother was waiting for her, shaping a mermaid into the wet sand. "Mom wants you to come in now," was all he said.

Three more years passed in much the same way. Morgan's education continued; she learned how to ride seahorses and raise the tide, shift the currents and control the weather. She could call hundred-foot swells and tsunami, hurricanes and monsoons, and then quash them again instantly. It was hard for a girl of thirteen not to feel dizzy with power, sometimes she would raise the waterline just to see the wonder in Brandon's face, sometimes she would sing him sirens' songs just to make him sleep and dream of the sea. Sometimes she would light a candle and sit in her window, dreaming of riding her seahorse around the Cape of Good Hope and sending her parents a postcard from Morocco.

Her seahorse was no gentle beast; not the meek little adornments of pet stores and doctor's offices. He was a primal force, Poseidon's prototype, shaped much like a Capricorn is with a mane of white, eyes burning red, and hooves of steel. He was the king of his herd, and in sudden gales sailors fainted before his cry, shuddered to see his mane froth before them, and died listening to his hooves thunder over their decks and masts, and as he drove their ships down into the waiting embrace of Leviathan. She loved her horse as many of her schoolmates love their dry and more placid counterparts, and named him Deception after her favorite place to ride.

Her life fell into a strange pattern; by day she was just a thirteen-year-old girl trying to keep up with school, and at night she danced and rode and held court for her friends. Sleep she saved for the last two hours of the night, and she found that this was all she really needed. Her body seemed indestructible.

One night, as she sat by her window, she heard a couple of humpback criers on their way to Neah Bay. They sang "Make ready, Your Highness, make ready, Court of Puget Sound, the King comes tomorrow, the King arrives tomorrow."

She ran down to the beach, meaning to follow them and ask what they meant, but they were gone too soon. Instead she asked Mother what they were talking about.

It is your betrothed, beloved. He hears that you have come of age and would like to know you.

"Betrothed? Mother, I'm thirteen years old. I'm not going to marry anyone for a very long time."

He has waited for a very long time already. It will not do to make him wait much longer. I think you will like the look of him. He was my first chosen child.

"So he's my brother, then?"

In a manner of speaking, but not in the way you mean.

"What's his name?"

Name? I believe he calls himself Leviathan now.

For the rest of the evening the water murmured "Leviathan comes," and Morgan went back to bed with no small amount of trepidation. Brandon came into her room bleary-eyed and asked her what the whales said. She answered "I have to get married soon."

"Can I come?" he asked hopefully.

"I don't think so," she sighed. Then she hugged him until she fell asleep.

It was the next evening when she met her betrothed. He had hair longer than twice his body-length and black as the *Titanic*'s hold at midnight, eyes green as froth and skin pale as foam, and his tail was black and green where the light hit it. There was in his smile and eyes and manner a way that spoke of the places where ships fall and fish have no eyes, a place where anything is possible only because nothing can be seen. She came to him wearing her jewels, her hair tied up in strands of pearls and ivory, her arms and waist bound up in white gold and abalone, and a giant moonstone hanging between her budding breasts, it caught the flicker of phosphorescence as she floated before her betrothed.

He said her name like a question, and she nodded mutely, unable to speak. He took her hand and introduced himself "Leviathan" and asked her if there was anywhere she wanted to go. She shook her head.

He said, "I know a place I think you'll like."

They swam north, her hand still in his, his lean body slicing through the water like a knife, letting her ride his wake. She caught the scent of his hair in the water, warm like a safe place to curl up and go to sleep. As they continued, the phosphorescence became brighter and more concentrated, until they came to a warm lagoon where the swirling lights were bright enough to read by. Then he took both of her hands, spun her to face him, and said, "I knew this was a good idea."

She smiled nervously at him as the tiny stars circled their faces and bodies, wondering what was expected of her, wondering if his sea-dragon smile hid as many secrets as it boasted. He gestured for her to sit in the bed of sea grass.

"You are worth waiting for," he whispered, kissing her cheek. She sighed, looked up, watched their hair mingle and slowly fall on top of them in a gold-and-black shroud. "You are so quiet. Are you afraid of me?" he asked.

"Yes." she murmured.

"Because of my age?"

"No." Then she looked in his face, and in his half-lidded eyes she saw the first man who ever set craft to water. "Yes."

"Is it because I change my shape?"

"Yes."

"Because I wreck ships?"

What? "Yes."

"Because we are to be married?"

"Yes. Definitely."

"Morgan, don't ever be afraid of me. There is no need."

"But—"

"And I can wait as long as you like."

"Thank you." She felt herself slump slightly, and they talked for the rest of the night. He told her about the last time he left the water, in the days before they took Atlantis, when he was allowed to breathe air. He told her about the battle, the horses rampaging across the continent, mountains crumbling in sluices of mud, buildings collapsing, all dry life fleeing in confusion and terror before their advance. She shuddered, asked him why he couldn't breathe air after that day.

"Because I let them get away. Because I warned them that we were coming."

"Who?"

"My family. My friends. Everyone I knew. They built fast ships and made it to other lands, and they told people about us, and they kept their technology and legends and used them to make land-men strong and brutal as those we destroyed. Men were never meant to have that much power. It's better here, easier to keep the balance where nothing can stay written down."

"She won't let you leave the water because you saved your family?"

"It's actually better this way. I don't have to question my loyalty any more. I know where I belong, and who I am. When the war comes, I'll be ready this time. I'll be thorough. It's much easier not to care about the world I'll be called on to destroy. And I like to eat ships, now that they make it easy."

"What if you try to leave the water?"

"I can't come back. I'll die." He turned on his side to face her and said "I'm frightening you again. Tell me, what do you do on Dry Land? What is it like?"

She told him about her parents and brother, explained to him about cars and jets, told him about science fiction and the reasons for Apollo 12, about NATO and freeways and dry ice and air conditioners and Nazis and cancer and television and bombs with half-lives.

He sighed and said, "Too much power. Way too much power."

When she came back to the beach, Brandon was waiting for her on the porch and the sun was nearly up. "Did you meet him?" he asked, tossing her a towel. She nodded as she stripped out of her jewels and dried off. "What was he like?"

"Perfect." she answered. "And scary."

It was easy to be fascinated by Leviathan. She dreamed of him when she wasn't in the water, and her grades fell and she became lethargic and dull, her eyes always far away. Her mother asked if it was a boy, and she said yes. Her mother, with a knowing smile, asked no further but suggested that she stop worrying so much and try to concentrate more on school.

The next time she saw her future husband it was two months later. She, Gwen, and Nyadia were racing with orcas when he appeared, quite suddenly, in front of them and said, "I have a task that needs a woman's touch. Hold on to me."

They agreed, and held onto his body as he swam so impossibly fast that the water seemed to part before him. Within an hour they crossed the Pacific to where the sun was just setting, and he let them go before a barely submerged spike of stone. In the distance there was a boat headed for the shore, glimmering in the red waning light.

Gwen was the first to understand, and propped herself up on the rocks and sang quietly to the ship. Her eyes hooded, her face turned placid and still, and she reached out to the ship as if to embrace it. Laughing,

Nyadia and then Morgan followed suit, circling the islet and leaping over it, singing, laughing, pale bare skin shining against the dark ocean. Slowly the ship came about, slowly she lumbered toward them, reminding Morgan of a sick dog on the make. The image made her laugh, and she wove it into her siren's song, asking them if they wouldn't like to prove otherwise. She could make out the men on board now, all staring at them in rapt fascination, watching them spin and churn playfully, abandoning the rock now, heading back out to sea, their voices mingling in a lullaby of tortured longing, a trance-weaving web of desire.

Their spell was broken by the sound of rock cleaving steel as the ship's hull struck the stone. The women disappeared beneath the waves to the lesser music of the hull tearing, the engines cutting, and sailors swearing in Japanese as they struggled to lower the life boats. Leviathan slammed their vessel hard on the starboard side, capsizing it and sending its contents spinning into the vast salty deep below. Morgan then saw something she would not soon forget: the bodies of dolphins circling down into darkness, blood swirling out of bludgeon-wounds, their glazed eyes frozen in perpetual terror.

"Why?" she stammered. "Dolphins are never anything but helpful and polite to people! Why do they do this?"

"Who knows why men do anything." Leviathan replied darkly.

Nyadia and Gwen laughed and sang to each other as they rode Leviathan home, but Morgan was characteristically silent.

The next night Brandon followed her down to the water's edge to catch a glimpse of his future brother-in-law. He was often disappointed, but the others had grown used to his presence. Nyadia even developed a crush on him, although Morgan told her he was far too young. "What's a few years to me?" she asked.

"A lot to him."

"Maybe. Maybe we can convince him to grow a tail like you do. He doesn't look right with legs."

Kingfisher laughed and grabbed Gwen's breasts from behind, kissing her neck and grinding his hips against her. People were much more licentious under water, but Morgan no longer noticed the difference. He said "Nyadia's just jealous of us. We all know no one but you can grow a tail." Gwen laughed and reached behind her, and he dropped out of the conversation.

"Why not?" asked Nyadia. "Mom says people used to grow tails all the time. We all came from Dry Land."

"Yeah, but that was before Atlantis," Gwen corrected.

"Yeah, before Leviathan messed it all up for us," Nyadia complained. "No disrespect intended," she amended. "Maybe if we could convince Mother Ocean to let one more grow a tail."

"You'd exhaust him to death," Kingfisher laughed, before Gwen kissed his mouth shut.

"Hmmm, let's see about that." She rocketed up to the surface and saw Brandon sitting in the driftwood, carving a mermaid into a piece of wood. Shining and bare-breasted she began to sing in a soft voice that only he could hear. His head cocked up, and then he dropped knife and wood and began walking methodically toward the water line, his eyes never leaving her pale form. He entered the water without noticing, soaking his tennis shoes, jeans, the bottom of his shirt, his arms reaching out to her in speechless supplication.

Morgan grabbed her tailfin and yanked hard, shouting "Stop it! He'll drown!"

Nyadia laughed musically, seductively, and kept singing, holding out her arms to him, calling him nearer and nearer. The water was up to his chin and lapping into his mouth, making him cough, but still he didn't notice. Finally Morgan leaped out of the water and knocked her down, and she giggled as she fell.

"He's just a little boy!" Morgan shouted.

"More like little man; did you see the look in his

eyes?" then she wavered under Morgan's glare and
said "All right, Your Highness. I'll let him go." With
that she swam out to Brandon, who was floundering
against a sudden cross-tide, and gathered him up in
her arms. She swam him back to the waist-deep water
and kissed him on the cheek before rejoining her companions. He walked the rest of the way up the beach,
and then stood staring at the water, his fingers brushing the spot she'd kissed.

"That was stupid, Nyadia," Leviathan scolded,
swimming silently to Morgan's side.

"Yes, Your Majesty," she agreed, trying to look
ashamed.

"Besides, we have important business to accomplish
tonight. Morgan, are you ready for your first battle?"

"What? What battle?"

"Up north. They've cleaned out a hundred miles of
water already. We have to get to them tonight while
we have the New Moon going for us. Great Mother,
this is going to be fun."

Their eyes shone with excitement, and Kingfisher
said, "Let's go."

"Hold on," he ordered, and they obeyed quickly.
Soon they were out the Straits of Juan de Fuca and
racing toward the Bering Sea, where Mother's entire
cavalry awaited them.

The horses were snorting and pawing just port of
the processing ship when they arrived, each with a
pale-faced and rage-driven rider, impatient for the raid
to commence. "Your Majesty, Your Highness, thank
you for your speed," said the Horse Captain, an older
man with a weathered thin face and gray hair longer
than himself and his horse combined. He was wearing
armor of plated shells; they all were. "Highness, your
horse is this way. Your Majesty, good hunting."

"Thank you," said Leviathan, before dropping out
of sight into the inky darkness below. Within seconds
Morgan sensed the presence of something dizzyingly
huge, something capable of swallowing aircraft-carriers in

just a few bites. She looked down and saw two gigantic green eyes staring up at them with blood lust and anticipation. Instead of vomiting with fear, she allowed the Horse Captain to lead her to her mount.

Deception was waiting for her with barely contained anticipation. His welcoming snort released a gout of foam, and his hooves danced and tail thrashed eagerly. On his saddle was armor of light silver and mother-of-pearl, plated to look like scales. "Haste, Your Highness," reminded the Captain.

"What am I to do here?" she asked, trembling with nerves as she pulled the sponge-padded tunic over her head.

"Use your instincts. Listen to Mother. We take the ship and sink her all hands down. We can't afford witnesses tonight. I apologize, but sometimes the distasteful is necessary. You may have noticed that we are nearly the only living things left in these waters."

She finished strapping on her wrist guards and breastplate, put on the heavy crown that would protect her temples against a fall, and said, "Ready. Mount up."

"Understood." He left her, and she raised her hand and gave the signal to begin back-bridling. As one, the cavalry yanked their mounts back, and the result was a building swell. Now they were looking down on the ship, listening to the panic on her decks as they saw the wave that was rising over their heads. They cut their nets and began securing the deck, and below them Leviathan positioned himself to catch what fell. He ate the nets in one loud chomp, and the sailors shouted, "What the hell was that!?" and feared for their lives. Still the swell built, eighty feet, ninety, one hundred, teetering now, without precision. It could fall at any time and kill everyone inside it, but they were well-practiced and well-balanced and Morgan wasn't done yet. She was waiting for a sign, so to release tension she let out a wordless shout that was taken up by all the others. Now the men on the ship were

screaming and crying and praying, and Mother Ocean
whispered, "Now."

She dropped her hand and they fell on the ship,
swamping it instantly. With inhuman howls they threw
the men into Leviathan's waiting jaws and ripped up
the decks, sending tools, components, personal effects,
and fish effluvia spinning into the tumultuous water.
The ship sank in less than two minutes, all hands down
in Leviathan's gullet. They reconvened and rode hard
to warmer waters.

She next saw Leviathan at the victory celebration,
glowing with health and energy, smiling and picking
his teeth with a bone. He grabbed Morgan around the
waist, kissed her lustily on the lips, and congratulated
her on a job well done. She shrank away, her terror
of him resurfacing. He laughed and said, "My gentle
love, you saw what they were, how they raped Mother
and left her empty. How can you grieve for men who
had no respect for life? Death was all they had in
them and all that was left for them. Tell me they didn't
deserve it." Then he leaned closer and said, "Tell me
you didn't enjoy it. I dare you." Then he kissed her
mouth shut, and they both knew it was true, but the
knowledge didn't bring the release he was hoping for.
Instead she backed away trembling, a cold place wash-
ing into her and making plans to stay. He felt the
water pulse around her and said "No, it isn't easy, I
do remember that, but it will become so with time."
Then he left her to brood while he cavorted.

The next night Leviathan came to her and said,
"You will have to choose soon. Everyone is waiting
for a wedding and a war, and before either of these
happen, you need to tell us your answer."

Morgan jerked away from him and said, "What if I
can't choose yet?"

"You don't have to choose right now. I'm just telling you what you already know." Then he leaned in
next to her ear and whispered, "Are you still afraid
of me?"

"Yes."

"Why? You know I'll never hurt you, and I'll wait as long as you want." Then, softly he added "Do you care for me at all?"

Touched by the vulnerability in his bottomless eyes, Morgan quickly answered, "Yes, I do care for you." Mentally she amended, "But I never want to be like you."

He had the answer he needed and smiled serenely. "Thank you. Believe it or not, it is important to me that you don't think I'm all monster."

And yet you are, my love. Unstoppable, furious, and beautiful in violence and pride and even insecurity. Why do I have to be so young?

When she came back, Brandon was waiting for her on the porch with a blanket and a cup of hot chocolate. "We heard about that ship on the news," he informed. "Jason's dad was on that boat."

Morgan stared at her feet. "I didn't know," she mumbled. "I'm sorry."

"No you aren't. And you shouldn't be either. It would have happened whether you were there or not, right?"

Instead of replying, she said, "They want me to choose now." She sat down naked on the porch. "I don't know what to do."

He stared at a sketchpad on his lap; a half-completed sea-dragon eating a Spanish galleon whole stared back up at him. He then looked out to sea and said, "When I was in Outdoor Ed they took us up to Deception Pass. There's an Indian story about it."

"Yeah? How's it go?"

"Well, there was this Indian princess, and one day a sea-king came up to the chief, her dad, and said, 'I'd like to marry your daughter.' The chief said, 'No way, I'll never see her again.' So the sea-king says, 'Tell you what; I'll send her back for a visit once a year. Now can I marry your daughter?' The chief agrees, and they get married, and she goes and lives underwater for a year. When she comes back, she's really happy to see her dad, and really sorry to go. Then another year goes by, and she comes back, and she's still real happy to see everyone, but she's quiet, and she's different. The next year she comes back, and all she can think about is going home again, and now she's really different. She even looks like a fish. After a few years she didn't come back at all, and they say it's her hair that makes the water swirl around like it does."

Morgan could have said that she didn't know of anyone living in Deception Pass, but instead she started crying and said, "I love you, Brandon."

The next day was Saturday, and she spent it pacing the shore, reluctant to change, just talking to Mother Ocean from the beach. "All the land, mother?"

As much as I can, daughter mine. And you will rule the new territory as queen.

"But why do you want it?"

Life came from me. It is mine to rule, not Man's. Not Dry Land's. She is too forgiving of Man; she will give them anything without protest. She lets them pervert her own body and destroy what it took her millions of years to create. She is too compassionate with such a dangerous animal. I am not so lenient, and my children are well governed. Don't Men speak of survival of the fittest?

"Dry Land didn't steal me because she's a thief, Mother. She's fighting for her life."

And losing, dear child. Don't forget that. Forsake me, and you, too, will lose. You cannot tell me that after all you've seen, you still believe She can hold us at bay. Even now she relents her waters to me, because Man has weakened her. She realizes that the balance must be kept. Even Leviathan, who also once had a human family, feels no qualms about this war. Your betrothed is older and wiser than you, and you would do well to emulate him.

"Only because you crushed him into compliance, because he couldn't make the choice you ask of me. Land may be a consummate thief, but you a consummate liar."

The ocean was silent, and instead filled her with visions of victory. Here were all the whales singing ballads to her bravery as Kingfisher toasted her at her wedding feast, and all the people of the Ocean cheered her. They dined on caviar in a submerged Space Needle, breathing champagne and clinking glasses of sashimi, laughing and arguing over who got to keep the copper pictures in the penny-pressers.

"You say I will be queen of all the new territories?" Morgan interrupted.

Yes. What of it?

"Then I decide where the boundaries are."

Silence. Then, grudging, *We will speak of this after the wedding.*

"There will be no wedding. I have a life on the shore where I may do as I please. I won't be anyone's slave, not Leviathan's and not yours."

There will be a wedding. I will not have a divided kingdom; I do not permit war between men in my domain.

"Then I choose where my kingdom begins and ends." Then Morgan had a conviction, and it felt like popcorn jumping inside her. "You need me. You need me to control Leviathan!"

Silence.

"It's true, isn't it! No war in your domain; why, you've spent a millennium making him into a remorseless killing machine. He's your bomb, and now you need me to deactivate him. The 'kingdom' is just an excuse. You need someone who can keep him from destroying what peace you achieve once you decide this war is over." She laughed at her own cleverness, and then said, "I also want to come back once a year to visit."

I could make another just like you. You aren't so important as you seem to think you are.

"Yes, except that he loves me, and you can't just replace one love with another. No one else could keep him from destroying your peace, and you know it."

You may have your visits for as long as Dry Land lasts. I suppose you wish to warn your family.

"I already have, Mother." Then she stood back and said *"And* I decide where the boundaries are. You can't have all the Dry Land. The balance must be kept, remember?"

We all decide where the boundaries are, starting with Man. I would keep the peace, but He would kill me entirely. We are all fighting for our lives, my darling daughter.

"Yes, Mother, and that is why we all need compassion. Let me say good-bye, and I'll come to you tomorrow."

The water was silent once more, and she turned to find Brandon staring at her from the porch, tears unshed making his eyes grow bright and round. She walked up to where he stood, put her arms around him, and said, "Don't believe everything they tell you in Outdoor Ed, kid."

He started sobbing in earnest, and howled, "You won't come back, I know it! Don't lie to me Morgan, I'm not a little kid anymore."

She said, "No, I need someone who can work it on this end. I can try to save your butts from down there, but people do need to keep their part of the balance. Otherwise it's like punching holes in your own life raft. I think you can help people see that."

"Quit making sermons. I won't see you for a whole year, and all you do is tell me a bunch of environmental crap."

She smiled because, at fifteen, she felt that she knew better than him how quickly a year would pass.

"Okay, no sermons, not tonight. But believe me, I'll come up with some great ones while I'm gone."

"You better." He sniffed, "I want to hear all of them when you come back."

I want you to hear all of them, and everyone else, too, thought Morgan as she led her brother into the house. I don't want to be the only one fighting for their lives.

SHE WANTS THINGS
by Bruce Holland Rogers

Bruce Holland Rogers won a Nebula for a novelette in 1997, the same year that one of his short stories was also a Nebula nominee. In addition to writing short stories and some unpublished novels, Bruce is a columnist for *Speculations* magazine and frequently speaks at writers' conferences. Among the anthologies he has written for are *Enchanted Forests*, *Witch Fantastic*, *Elf Magic*, and *The Fortune Teller*.

L apanqui heard about the Princess Tsotl before she ever saw her, for even among the Middle People, the princess was accounted fierce.

Among the people of the Unnamed City, she had another reputation, one that was best not spoken aloud, for the first time Tsotl came to the Feather Market, she took the wrong road. She would never say it was the wrong road. If she made her way to the market by walking through the jungle, then that was the way it ought to be done. She was a princess of the Middle People, and she did not make mistakes.

Yet every time she came to the Feather Market, it was by some different mistaken road.

In truth
this world began
in mistakes.
First Dreamer dreamed himself
out of the blackness
of Not Yet.

He
did not mean
to dream himself.
It was
an accident.

The Feather Market stood in the ruins of the Unnamed City. Merchants built their stalls with stones
that had once been a palace. Long ago, sun temples
had risen toward the sky. But Princess Tsotl's people
had defeated this country and taken many captives for
sacrifice. The city kept itself small and nameless, beneath further notice of the Middle People.

Over her armor of pounded bark, the princess wore
a robe of red and green feathers. This treasure on her
shoulders revealed her rank at once. There was no
excuse for failing to bow before her and speak respectfully. She carried her war club as another reminder.

After twice losing her way in the fruit market, she
found the street of the map sellers and went from stall
to stall. "Unfold that one," she commanded. "Now I
want to see those ones. Unbind them for me." She
read the place names on each map, Monkey Hills,
Smoking Mountain River, Mounds of Nine Jaguar.
None, it seemed, named the place she wanted.

"Perhaps if you said what you were looking for,"
said one map seller, "I could simply tell you if I had
it or not."

Her only answer was to raise herself to her full
height and lift her war club. She towered over the
man. The club's obsidian teeth glittered before his
eyes.

"As you wish," he said. One by one, he showed her
all of his maps. None was what she wanted, and she
gave him not even one faded feather for all his
trouble.

When Princess Tsotl came to Lapanqui's stall, Lapanqui was copying in bright colors the place names on

a faded original. The paints had taken days to grind
and mix.

The princess said, "Attend to me."

"In a moment," said Lapanqui, who had not looked
up to see who addressed her. "Let me clean my brush."

With her club, Princess Tsotl knocked over a pot of
blue paint. She said, "I am a princess of the Middle
People. You will attend to me *now*."

Lapanqui got to her feet. "Very well," she said.

"Lower your eyes when you address a princess.
Have you not learned to be discreet in the presence
of royalty?"

So Lapanqui lowered her gaze. She matched Tsotl's
impatience with calm, for impatience has been the
problem for this world from the very beginning.

First Dreamer dreamed himself into being
but he did not wake up.
In his sleep he felt a knot
a lump
a bump
growing out of his forehead.
In his sleep he felt it
and in his sleep he thought it was strange.
But still he did not wake up.

The bump in First Dreamer's forehead
cracked open like an egg.
Out came She Wants Things.
She turned herself into a hummingbird
and she flew around First Dreamer,
seeing what there was to see.
There wasn't much.
There was just First Dreamer
and the first grayness of creation.

She Wants Things was not satisfied.

Now
you must wake up,
she told First Dreamer.
Now
you must get busy!
Hurry!
Do as I say!

"This one," said Princess Tsotl, taking up a brittle map from the last stack. The map was made of many bark panels sewn together, like the panels of Tsotl's armor. It mapped part of the deep jungle, the shadow country. "This is the one."

"Careful how you hold it," said Lapanqui. "In two days, I can have your copy ready."

Princess Tsotl shook her head. "I must have it now. I'll give you nine heixtotl feathers."

"For the original? For a map as rare as that? The whole of your robe would not be enough to buy it."

"For such lies, I should cut out your tongue. A map for my robe? As if one such as you would know the worth of anything!"

"Two days. Twenty heixtotl for the copy."

Princess Tsotl raised her club. "A princess of the Middle People will have what she wants, and at the price she names."

And Lapanqui considered many things she might have said then, but she held her tongue. "Ten," she said.

Princess Tsotl counted out nine feathers. One of them was bent, but Lapanqui said nothing of it.

"Now," said the princess of the Middle People, "which way is south?"

Lapanqui, against her better judgment, took pity on the princess, at least enough to warn, "Those are dangerous lands there mapped. Avoid the places that bear the sigil of . . ."

"I know how to read a map," the princess said. "Just tell me which way is south."

The shadows at her feet could have told her. Lapanqui shook her head. "Have you ever been in the deep
jungle? Have you thought of hiring a guide?"

"You come, then," said Princess Tsotl.

"Not me," said Lapanqui. "I mean a real guide.
You can find one near the fruit stalls."

But Princess Tsotl raised her club again. "I am in
a hurry. You will serve."

> First Dreamer woke up,
> and She Wants Things told him
> to make a sun.

> Well, said First Dreamer,
> let me think
> about how it should
> be done.

> No time for that,
> said She Wants Things.
> Just get busy.

> First Dreamer rubbed his fingers together
> until they were hot,
> until they shot off sparks,
> and he blew on one spark
> to make a sun.

> The sun burned hot.
> Too hot.
> Even though She flew behind First Dreamer,
> She Wants Things felt Her feathers
> glow red.

> That first sun burned so bright
> that First Dreamer still saw it
> when he closed His eyes.
> There were no shadows anywhere.
> Before long that sun

burned itself up.
It went out
and left smoke.

That was not the way to do it,
said She Wants Things.
That was not it
at all.

They were just two days into the jungle when the
rains began. Princess Tsotl was not careful about keeping the map dry, no matter how often Lapanqui reminded her.

"It's my map," said the princess. "I will do with it
as I please."

On the afternoon of the fourth day, Princess Tsotl
took shelter under a rubber tree and unfolded the
map's panels. "Show me where we are."

The paints had run and bled together until the ruins
of Potonacal were indistinguishable from the Monkey
People Mounds. The green-painted river, instead of
following its orderly path, now washed generally everywhere. Bad enough to lose a map to royal thievery,
but to be close at hand for its destruction . . . Lapanqui could have cried.

"Where?" the princess said again.

"I can't tell any more," Lapanqui said. "How can I
read such a mess?"

"We're lost, you mean," said Princess Tsotl. The
feathers of her robe were matted together and splat-
tered with mud. She set down her club, then parted
her rain-soaked skirts, looking for some cloth that was
dry enough to wipe her hands. She caught Lapanqui
watching her. "Look away," she said. "Will you not
learn to be discreet in the presence of royalty?"

Lapanqui looked away.

"Your map is worthless," the princess said, "and
you're useless as a guide. See if I pay the six heixtotl
I promised."

"You promised eight. And how am I to follow a map that I can't read? How am I to guide you to a place you will not name?"

"Here," the princess said, pointing at a colorful smudge. "This is the place." She lowered her voice. "The Vale of the Two Most Ancient." Then she whispered. "The place of the gods. The place where I'll find First Dreamer and wake him."

First Dreamer was sleeping again.
She Wants Things flew around him
and called him awake.

Make a sun of light and darkness,
she told him.
Make a sun that is not so hot!

So First Dreamer made a second sun,
a sun that burned in the day
and cast shadows.
A sun that slept
at night.

Good,
said She Wants Things.
That's about right.
Now make creatures
who will praise us.

So First Dreamer made the jaguar
and the sloth,
He made the spider
and the toucan.
He made squirrels and bats
and ring-tailed cats,
raccoons and rabbits
and scorpions.
He made every creature
and a place for every creature.
He made the jungles and the mountains.

She Wants Things said,
Now let them praise us!

But First Dreamer had not given them speech.
The animals were satisfied with this world.
They were content,
but they could not
say so.

All right! said She Wants Things.
Start over!

So First Dreamer extinguished the second sun.
He gathered up most of the animals
to save for the next creation,
to save himself
some work.

With the third sun,
First Dreamer made people
out of clay.
They praised the gods,
just as She wanted,
but these clay people
dissolved
in the rain.

No good!
said She Wants Things.

"How do you know you'll find the First God in
this place?" Lapanqui said. "Vale of the Two Most
Ancients. That could mean anything! And look. It
bears the sigil of a place one shouldn't go."

"Many things that are dangerous to common people," said the princess, "are not dangerous to me."
She hefted her club. "Who could the Two Most Ancients be but First Dreamer and She Wants Things?
This is where they wait to begin creation again. I'm

going to wake up First Dreamer. I'm going to get him
to make a world in which the sun is not so hungry."

"If such a thing could be done," said Lapanqui,
thinking of all that war had cost her city, "don't you
think it would have been done by now? If First
Dreamer could be awakened, don't you think She
Wants Things would have made him stir?"

"It took me to think of it," said Tsotl. "It took a
princess." She smiled. "When the sun does not require
captives for sacrifice, then think of all the slaves I'll
have! How rich will my robes be then! I'll wear them
once and burn them."

"Ah," said Lapanqui. "That's well worth waking the
gods for."

The princess gestured with her club. "Get going,"
she said. "The gods await me."

For the fourth sun,
First Dreamer made people
out of wood.
They had short wooden arms
and flat wooden faces.
They were stubborn.
They had voices,
but they refused to praise
the gods.
Refused!

She Wants Things
was angry
with these wooden people.
She whispered to their tools,
to the cook pots and baskets and hoes.
She Wants Things
stirred up the possessions
so that one morning
the grinding stones said to the wooden people,
All day long you grind our faces,
so let's see how you like it!

The baskets said,
All day long you stuff things into us,
so let's see how you like it!
The axes said,
All day long you smash our faces,
so let's see how you like it!
And the tools ground and stuffed and smashed.
The tools pried and sawed and shook
until the wooden people were all dead
except for a few that First Dreamer
turned into monkeys
and one or two
who hid
themselves where
First Dreamer did not see them.

You can do better,
She Wants Things told First Dreamer.

First Dreamer had been awake a long time, now.
He'd been kept busy with making worlds.
He was getting tired.
In a hurry, He made the fifth sun.
In a hurry, He brought back the animals.
In a hurry, He made flesh people
who praised the gods.

She Wants Things
was satisfied
for a time.

But First Dreamer made some mistakes.
The sun He made in such a hurry
could not sustain itself.
It needed sacrifices
to keep burning
to stay bright
to be hot.

That's not right,
said She Wants Things.
That's not
what I had in mind.

But First Dreamer had gone back to sleep.
There was no waking him,
no matter how She called,
no matter how She flew about his head.

So this fifth sun that we live under
needs to be fed victims.
That is why war is holy.
That is why we feed hearts
to the sun.

First, Lapanqui smelled smoke. Then she and the princess came suddenly upon the milpa, a clearing where long rows of corn grew taller than Lapanqui had ever seen corn grow before. The beans that climbed the stalks bore pods as long as a war club. A digging stick taller than a man had been tied to a tree. Now and then it wriggled, as if struggling against the ropes. The smoke was coming from a cave, and from inside the cave there also came a sound like logs grinding back and forth over stone.

"What can this be but the Vale of the Two Most Ancient," said the princess. "Inside that cave, First Dreamer sleeps."

"Then what's that sound?" said Lapanqui.

"What else could it be but First Dreamer snoring?"

"And why are the corn stalks so tall?"

"Is First Dreamer not a giant? For the first goddess sprang from his head."

"If he sleeps, then who tends the corn?"

"She Wants Things must tend the corn."

"And if First Dreamer sleeps all the time, when does he eat the harvest?"

"Stop asking so many questions and go look into the cave."

"Me?"

"The god may have guardians. I should know what they are so that I'm prepared for them."

Lapanqui shook her head. "Let us be patient," she said. "Perhaps whatever is inside the cave will show itself."

But Princess Tsotl raised her club. So Lapanqui ventured into the open space of the milpa.

"Don't *you* wake the god!" the princess warned her. "It is up to *me* to tell him how the world must be changed!"

Lapanqui threaded her way through the corn stalks and stood at last outside the cave. The grinding sound continued without a pause. Keeping close to the wall, she stepped into the darkness. She could just make out the glow of embers against the cave's far wall.

Suddenly, the grinding ceased. Something rough-skinned clasped her in the darkness and lifted her high. A voice rumbled, "Light, brother! Stoke the fire! I have something!"

Flames leaped up among the embers, and Lapanqui could see who held her. He was man-shaped, more or less, with short arms and a thick neck. The features of his face were flat and close together, like a child's first wood carving.

"Ah, at last we have one," said another voice. "At last we have you, little mother, little princess. At last you've come."

He was another wooden giant like the first.

"How long we've waited since the gods turned against us," said the first. "How long we've been alone, awaiting our bride!"

Now the flames were bright enough to let Lapanqui see the floor of the cave, the mounds of kernels and the little piles of corn meal. "You were grinding corn," she said, "with your hands."

"Only way to do it," said the second giant.

"Can't trust a grinding stone," added the first. "A broom and a digging stick are dangerous enough."

Only then did Lapanqui notice the broom that was tied to a pillar of the cave. Like the digging stick, it twisted against its ropes, trying to free itself. "But how do you cook the meal?"

"Can't. No jar for soaking, no pot for cooking. Can't trust 'em."

"Eat it raw, that's what we do. Beans, too. That's what we've done for all this time. But all that will change. A hard life it's been."

"But now," said the other one.

"Yes, now," said the giant holding Lapanqui, "you'll make bowls that don't bash. You'll make grinding stones that don't smash." He tugged at her skirts, examining her. "You'll serve us, and we'll father a generation on you."

"Tie her so she won't wander off," said the other giant. "Here, I'll bring rope."

"But I'm flesh," Lapanqui protested. "See how soft my skin is. I'm not like you."

"Poor thing," said the giant who held her. "It's true."

"I'm not of your kind. I can't be to your taste."

"That's true as well," said the other. "I feel no stirring when I look upon her, brother."

"We'll have to make do," said the one who held her, bruising her legs as he rubbed them.

"Ouch!"

"Perhaps you'll roughen up with time."

"I doubt it," Lapanqui said. "What a shame that the wooden woman I met just outside the milpa can't be coaxed to come to you."

"A wooden woman?" The giant dropped her and started for the mouth of the cave.

"Wait!" cried his brother. "How is it that we never saw her before? This is a trick!"

"She's very shy," said Lapanqui. "You should let me speak to her."

*   *   *

"What did you see?" asked Princess Tsotl.

Lapanqui considered for a moment, then took pity upon the princess for a second time. "Giants of wood," she said. "We should leave them alone."

The princess narrowed her eyes. "The snoring stopped. Did you wake the god?"

"The giants were grinding corn with their hands."

Princess Tsotl hefted her war club. "You're lying. How did you get those bruises on your legs? Tell me the truth, or die!"

So Lapanqui said, "Very well. I tried to trick you. The god lies sleeping in the cave. I got him to stop snoring, but I couldn't wake him up."

"Of course the god wouldn't wake for the likes of you. How were you bruised?"

"The god has guardians, just as you supposed. They're made of wood."

"Of wood? Is that all?" said the princess, "I've armor to deal with that." And she tapped her rough bark armor with the butt of her club.

"But they'll tear your robe," Lapanqui said. "They'll ruin your fine feathers."

"Then you'll keep the robe safe while I battle the guardians," said Princess Tsotl. She started to take the robe off, then said, "Lower your eyes! Haven't you learned yet to be discreet in the presence of royalty?" She carefully folded the robe and gave it to Lapanqui to hold. "Stay here!" she commanded. Her wooden armor squeaked a little as she strode to the cave to change the world, to make it more to her liking.

Waiting at the edge of the milpa, Lapanqui heard nothing for a long time. She crept a little closer, and then to the very mouth of the cave. That's when she heard Princess Tsotl cry, "Put me down! Put me down! Can't you see I'm a princess?"

"Indeed you are," boomed a voice. "Our little princess."

"She's made of wood!" said another voice. "How nice and rough she is!"

"How good to have you here at last," said the first voice. "How good to meet you, little mother." Then, a little softer, "She *is* rough. I feel myself stirring, brother. I feel the sap rise."

Lapanqui crept away then, for she had learned to be discreet.

ONE TREE HILL
by R. Davis

R. Davis lives in Green Bay, Wisconsin with his very patient wife Monica and his beautiful daughter Morgan Storm. He writes both fiction and poetry, and holds a B.A. in English from the University of Wisconsin-Green Bay. His current projects include a book-length manuscript of poetry entitled *In the Absence of Language* as well as numerous short stories and a fantasy novel. Other stories by him appear in *The UFO Files* and *Black Cats and Broken Mirrors*.

> *"Quos amor verus tenuit, tenebit."*
> *"Those whom true love has held, it will go on holding."—Seneca*

Just before sunset, General Sharia Shaynok knelt at the top of a small hill overlooking the dusty, empty road she and Gavin had just traveled. Marked on her map as One Tree Hill, it acted as a grassy support for a large, ungainly, and extremely old cottonwood tree. The road had no name that Sharia knew of, and for now, it remained empty as it meandered toward the northwest. Sharia knew that the soldiers she and Gavin had been eluding for the past two days would soon be coming down the nameless road. They were like dogs on the trail of a deer, she thought. No matter how they had twisted and turned, they had never been far behind. The lead they had now was the best she had been able to manage, and it wasn't much.

Rising from her knees, Sharia rolled up her map and, with a last look at the road, went to check on the exhausted horses. A barely audible groan from the base of the tree stopped her in mid-stride. Sharia knelt down, her armor creaking, and took Gavin's hand. She smiled down at him. "Rest a while longer, friend. We have some time yet before they get here."

Gavin stared up at Sharia with his intense gray eyes, and a cough briefly racked his lungs before he spoke. "Sharia, we don't have time—you have time. I'm played out." His voice had a wet sound to it, and Sharia knew blood was in his lungs from the sword cut he'd taken while they were escaping.

"Don't be silly. Your wound isn't that bad." Sharia looked over at the horses as she spoke. "In a few minutes, we'll both be riding out of here."

Gavin regarded Sharia with a slight grin that somehow managed to offset the pallor of his face. "Sharia, listen to me. The wound is bad enough. I'm slowing you down." He coughed again, and Sharia pulled a cloth from her belt pouch to wipe away the thin trickle of bright red blood that ran down his dirty chin. "Besides," he said, "not even a healer could help me now. I've torn something inside." He paused, trying not to cough. "Last night, I think, during the ride."

Sharia uncorked her waterskin and held it to his lips. She poured a small amount into his mouth and watched him swallow with a grimace. After taking a sip for herself, Sharia replaced the waterskin on her belt. "Listen, I'm going to go check on the road and the horses and—"

"Sharia, wait!" Gavin tried to sit up and collapsed back onto his cloak which Sharia had used to cover the ground.

"Yes, Gavin, what is it?" Sharia again took his hand.

He said nothing for a moment, just stared up at her as though he were parting the past with his eyes. "Sharia, we're a long way from the markets of Soursic. How, in the name of the gods, did we ever manage to get here? To this place, I mean? It certainly wasn't what we expected." He blinked and shuddered as though cold, although the air was hot and dusty. It was late summer and the plains were browning under the sun.

Not replying, Sharia ran a hand caked with dirt and blood through her short-cropped brown-and-gray hair. She rocked back on her heels and looked at Gavin. For a moment, she could see him as he was on the day she had bought him in the markets at Soursic—handsome and angry, his black hair shining in the noon sun as if to make a mockery of the barely modest rag he wore. She had never wanted, nor even looked at, the other men offered. Had it not been against all tradition, Sharia knew she would have married him. But that could never happen because he was a slave-companion.

The slave-companions were bred and genetically engineered by the science wizards of Soursic to be many things; advisers, help meets, sometimes lovers. As a high ranking general, it had been Sharia's right to buy him. She had needed an assistant to help her conquer this land for the empress, one who could lighten the burdens of interim rulership and advise her on matters both political and military. Gavin could do both. The personal history sheet she'd looked at prior to buying him indicated that Gavin's genes from the maternal line went back through five generations of warriors. He had often sparred with Sharia, demonstrating that he had been well trained with both spear and long sword.

But it was the paternal gene Sharia had found most compelling. His father had once been a tactical adviser to the empress herself. It was his plan that had placed the empress in a position of strength unrivaled on the continent. Gavin had been trained to assess situations by his father. That is, with a calculating eye toward success. During their discussions, Sharia found him to be her match in both political and military discussions. He was brilliant, and Sharia considered him her best and wisest investment in the war effort. It was only later on, in the hard light of war, that Sharia began to realize that Gavin was much more than an investment.

Sharia did not have a husband, for so long as she remained an unmarried princess, the possibility of an alliance marriage to one of the other noble houses still existed. Gavin himself would have appreciated this political reality had she talked to him about it. But she had not. Nor had she ever touched him or made even the briefest mention of her growing feelings. First, because she felt that his body must belong to him, regardless of his status as a slave. He wasn't, she thought, property to be used as she wished.

Second, and though it seemed both wasteful and silly now, she hadn't the courage. Sharia laughed to herself. A general, she thought, afraid of rejection by a man! But during this war, Sharia had realized she wanted him, and found herself unable to say a single word about it.

"Sharia?"

"Sorry, I guess I was woolgathering." Sharia saw him smile and wondered how long he had known of her feelings for him. "I will tell you what I think, Gavin, but then we must go. The soldiers will be here soon, and I'd prefer to be gone." She squeezed his hand, and admitted to herself that he was the only thing besides war she had ever really loved. Now it seemed as though she might well lose both. The war was already lost, and Gavin was badly wounded—perhaps dying. She looked down the hill, heard the wind blow across the leaves above her head, watched it make distant dust devils on the road. The sun would be gone within the hour.

"Gavin, you know as well as I how we got here. It happens to even the best generals from time to time. We made errors in judgement about the people here. We thought they could be conquered one province at a time, with minimal casualties to ourselves. Mostly, we didn't think they would organize a rebellion so quickly, and certainly not at my headquarters!" Sharia shook her head, remembering how her outrider sentries had warned her at the last minute. Falling at her feet, the messenger gasped out her report with her last breath: "The castle is surrounded, and we're hopelessly outnumbered. Escape if you can!" Now Sharia sighed. "We just made too many mistakes. I should've known better, should've trusted my instincts. Damn, I'm tired."

Gavin said nothing for a minute, waiting to make sure she was through. "It's not entirely your fault, you know. I, too, thought we could take this land easily. I'm your principal adviser, and a portion of the blame is mine." He paused, looking up at the tree. "It's pretty here."

"Yes, Gavin, my friend, it is. But it's time to go. The soldiers will be here soon, peasant dogs that they are." Sharia rose to get the horses, then stopped and looked down at him. "Gavin, I . . . I want you to know how sorry I am about all this. I—"

"Shush, Sharia, I know." He coughed several times, and waited for the spasm to pass. He wiped his lips off, and smiled a red smile. "I know, Sharia." His eyes locked with hers for a moment, then he added quietly, "And that is enough."

Sharia did not hear his last mumbled comment as she turned away. Walking toward the chestnut-colored mare that Gavin had been riding, her thoughts turned to escaping the soldiers and this land. Her empress would—probably—forgive her failure here, although Sharia would insist that she send another general, someone younger and more bloodthirsty, to retake what had been lost. This land would be taken, but not, she thought to herself, by me. She was going to retire. Once Gavin was better, she would say to hell with allegiances, alliances, and tradition. She would marry him, and devote her remaining years to more peaceful pursuits. She was, as she had told Gavin, tired. Occupied with her thoughts, mainly how Gavin might not be able to ride, Sharia concentrated on tending to the exhausted mare. She did not see how he was watching her.

Gavin coughed again, several times as he watched Sharia work. He did not, however, let it interfere with his own. In his mind, he was counting the number of hours to the coast and escape. He know the statistics well for travel by horse, even for a tired one. He also knew he was dying—physician skills had been part of his training. Knowing this, and knowing that he was slowing Sharia's escape made his decision easier. He decided, in a way that seemed awfully detached to himself, that admitting his feelings was painful. He knew he loved Sharia, wanted to be with her, although it was unheard of for a general to take a slave-companion as a husband. He also knew that escape, given the numbers and the circumstances, was nearly impossible for them both.

He could not tell her to go. She would see it as quitting, which came hard to her. So he would just do it. To save her, and perhaps it would be enough for him to know that she lived and had loved him in her own way, in what time they had had together. It might even be enough to commend his soul into the next world, where all warriors could feast at the high table.

Reaching a trembling hand down to his right thigh, Gavin stared up at the fading light through the leaves, and unsheathed the dagger Sharia had given to him before starting this doomed campaign. He did not look at it, or at her, fearing that he would lose his nerve. Clenching his sweaty, shaking fist around the dagger hilt, he breathed a final prayer for Sharia's escape and his own soul. As another coughing fit shook his frame, he kissed the tip of the blade with his bloodied lips, raised and reversed it, and drove it with the last of his strength into his own chest. He died with a barely audible groan. In death, Gavin was smiling, his face stained only a little by the tears he had not known he cried.

Sharia turned when she heard Gavin's groan and the dull thud of a dagger piercing flesh. The blood drained from her face as she saw the hilt of a dagger protruding from his still chest. For a moment, she looked around wildly for an unnoticed enemy. One great, horrified inhalation later, Sharia's scream echoed across One Tree Hill and into the barren plains beyond it. She fell onto her knees beside him and gathered him into her arms.

Sharia cried in spite of herself. I am, she reflected as she rocked his body, the conqueror, conquered. After what seemed a long while, she looked back down the road, now barely visible in the last light of day. In the distance, a dust cloud was moving in her direction. It was then that Sharia knew what she should do, what she must do. Gavin had been right, she knew that he thought escape impossible.

She laid Gavin's body on the ground underneath the cottonwood tree. She wiped his dirty, peaceful face, pulled the dagger from his chest with a sob, and gave him the kiss she should have given him before he died. Sharia covered his body with her own cloak, royal emblem over his still heart as though he were nobility. Turning away toward the horses, she stripped the saddle off the mare, then her own mount. Slapping them both on the hindquarters, she sent them trotting down the hill. Some lucky peasant would find them, and perhaps thank the gods for his fortune. Sharia would not be needing her horse anymore. She was done running.

The first stars became visible in the eastern sky, as Sharia, with a watchful eye on the approaching dust cloud, pulled her sword from the scabbard and began to polish it. She dusted off her dirty armor as best she could. She knew she would be fighting in near darkness, the only light that of the stars and the red crescent moon that hung low on the horizon. Because she held the higher ground, she would be at a slight advantage. Sharia smiled at the oncoming soldiers, though they couldn't see it yet. She waited, and reflected on how many of them she could kill before she herself died. Untrained as most of them were, she thought, there would be a large harvest for old lady Death tonight.

A short time later, the first of the peasant soldiers saw the gleam of her sword in the dark, a brief reflection of light from their torches. Sharia waited for them. As they approached the hill, Sharia called down to them. "Well, dogs, I see you've finally caught up. So come, then! I will kill many of you, perhaps all of you, for this is the price of his death and mine!"

The leader of the soldiers, an ungainly man with a wandering eye, answered her. "Nay, General. Surrender yourself. You're already defeated. Your army is gone, you have no horses, and no escape. We'll be merciful." This last remark was greeted with a few stray chuckles from his men.

"Come up, dog-leader," Sharia said. "I've a mercy of my own for you. Or are you a coward?"

The leader stared up at the dark figure on the hill. He could hear the few pieces of scavenged armor his men wore creak as they wondered if he would stand being called a coward. He motioned to several of his soldiers. "Go up there and get her. Kill her if you have to."

From the top of the hill, the soldiers could hear Sharia laughing softly. "I'm waiting, leader of puppies!"

The three selected soldiers started up the hill while the others watched. The leader said nothing. The first clang of metal on metal rang out earlier than he expected—Sharia had met them partway. The silhouettes were hard to make out, only the sounds of warriors grunting, the clash of swords, and then silence. One figure remained standing in the dark. "Boys," the leader called, "did you get her?"

Suddenly, three heads landed one by one at his feet. "Hardly, peasant. I'm not surprised you sent children to do an adult's job. If this is your best, I'll still be here come sunrise!" Sharia laughed again, a mocking sound.

The leader of the peasant soldiers motioned to the others with him to come closer. In a harsh whisper he said, "That's it, then. We rush her together. She can't take all of us." His voice shook only a little, then he raised his hand high above his head. When he lowered it, he and all thirty-one of his men rushed up the hill with a roar. Sharia watched them come, raised her sword in a traditional salute, and did indeed begin to reap a great harvest.

She killed the leader first, her dagger finding the white blob of his wandering eye easily in the dark. The leader, whom Sharia did not even have a name for, fell with a scream. Three others died before Sharia had been injured at all. She killed a fifth peasant at the same time as she took a slice on her left arm, leaving it dangling uselessly at her side. Two more died nearly as easily, but Sharia knew she was starting to slow. She had lost a lot of blood now, and was surrounded. They seemed to be striking from all sides at once, the way dogs will do when they've cornered the deer. Sharia's breath came in quick gasps. "Come on, you mongrels. Come on, you little boys. Is this the best you can do?" She smiled in the darkness. Her once strong voice bubbled weakly in her lungs.

The peasants fell on her with a final roar, and General Sharia Shaynok died without making a sound. The wind blew, and the peasants waited for sunrise to bury the dead. When they found her body, not one word was said.

Some three years later, underneath a fully blossomed cottonwood tree, a young girl found a dagger on One Tree Hill. It was encrusted with old blood and dirt, half-buried beneath a pile of weeds. She did not know the story of General Sharia Shaynok, nor had she heard of Gavin, the slave-companion who had died with her. The girl only knew that somehow this place was special. It had a mark of peace on it. And so she went there to watch the sunset over the road while cottonwood blossoms flew through the air like summer snow. She polished her dagger, letting the light catch on the still-bright blade, and dreamed of one day being a princess and a warrior.

STRAYS

by Megan Lindholm

Megan Lindholm has explored many facets of fantasy fiction, from urban fantasy in *The Wizard of the Pigeons* to historical fantasy in *The Reindeer People*. She has also collaborated with fellow author Steven Brust on the novel *Gypsy*. Recently she began a new cycle of books with *Assassin's Apprentice, Royal Assassin,* and *Assassin's Quest,* written under the pseudonym Robin Hobb. She lives in Washington with her husband and four children.

Lonnie Spencer looked like a boy. She sat on a rusty bike, one foot on the curb, the toe of her other ratty sneaker in the gutter. She had scabby knees, a smoking skull on her baggy sweatshirt, and a baseball hat backward over her chopped black hair. "What's wrong with that kid's face?" was my second thought when I saw her. My first had been to avoid him because he looked like he'd kick gutter water at you just to get it on your school clothes.

As I edged past, she spoke in a clear girl's voice, "Take a picture, it'll last longer."

I had been staring. I'd never seen anyone my own age with a big scar down her face. It ridged her Native American skin, pulling her cheek and her eye to one side. It was hard not to stare. So I looked down and saw the Barbie doll lashed to the front of her bike. It had a fur skirt and one boob. Her clumpy hair was tied back with gold thread. A tiny wooden bow was slung over her shoulder.

"Amazon." I said without thinking.

"Yeah!" Lonnie grinned and suddenly didn't look so scary. "She's an Amazon warrior. That's why I cut off her tit. So she can shoot a bow better. I read that they really did that."

"I know. I read about it, too."

Our eyes met. Connection. We both read, and we read weird stuff, stuff about women who were warriors. It's so simple, when you're a kid.

In her next breath, Lonnie announced, "I'm a warrior, too. I been teaching myself martial arts. Ninja stuff, swords and pikes, too. I want to learn to shoot a bow. Scars are okay, on a warrior. Hey. My name's Lonnie Spencer." She stuck out a grubby hand. She had a boy's way of doing things. "What's yours?"

Her hand was scratchy, scabs and dirt and dry skin. "Mandy Curtis."

"Mandy, huh. Bet you get teased a lot about that in school. Handy Mandy. I hate school. All the teachers hate me, and the kids tease me all the time. 'Cause of my scars, you know, and because I don't dress like they do. They think if you don't have the right kind of clothes, you're nothing. Lower than shit."

Her words spilled forth. I sensed she needed to talk but didn't find many listeners. I'm a listener, like my mom. She says it's our curse, to have total strangers tell us their darkest secrets. I glanced at Lonnie again. Not many of the girls I'd met at school would want to be seen talking to her. My clothes were a lot better than hers, and I was still having trouble making friends.

I kept walking. I was supposed to come straight home from school every day. We were new to this neighborhood, and Mom was jumpy. Our building was okay, but two blocks away was a commercial strip, and the apartments that bordered it attracted what Mom called "a rougher element." Mom had never defined that, but I looked at Lonnie and knew. She coasted her bike alongside in the gutter as I walked. "I didn't get my scars in a fight, though," she volunteered abruptly. "My mom threw me through a picture window when I was two. She was pretty drunk, and I was fussy. That's what she says, anyway. Cut up my face and cut my leg muscles, too." She watched for my reaction. Her words challenged me. "That's why I limp when I walk. They had to put over a hundred and seven stitches in me. After that, they put me in a foster home, until my Grandma came and got me. Now Mom has me."

Kids ask the questions that adults swallow. "Why do you want to live with someone who threw you through a window?"

Lonnie lifted one shoulder. "Well, you know, she's my mom. She went to counseling. And the court says it's okay, and Grandma is getting pretty old. So." Again the one-shoulder shrug.

So. That could sum up a lot of Lonnie Spencer. So.

The conversation lagged awkwardly. Mom wouldn't want me hanging around with Lonnie. I knew it. I think Lonnie knew it, too. But I was as desperately lonely as she was. "You go to Mason School?" I asked her, just as she exclaimed, "Oh, no! Not Scruffy, oh, man . . ."

She hopped off her bike, letting it clatter into the gutter. Without a look at me, she hurried to a sodden calico body at the edge of the street. I followed her, reluctant but curious. Lonnie crouched close over it; I stayed back. The cat's mouth was open, white teeth and a sprawling tongue. I wouldn't have touched that sunken body with a stick, but Lonnie stroked it, smoothing its soggy fur.

"I hope his next eight lives are better than this one was," she said quietly.

"You really believe a cat has nine lives?"

"Sure. Why not? One old lady, a foster mom, she told me if a cat really likes you, it can give you one of its lives. Wouldn't that be something? Get to live a cat's life?"

I looked at the dead cat. "Doesn't look like he enjoyed it much," I pointed out.

"I can think of worse lives than being a stray cat," she said darkly as she unslung her backpack. She pulled out a can of neon orange spray paint. The balls inside it rattled like dice as she shook it. Then she outlined the cat's body, meticulously tracing each leg and the tail, even the jab of an ear against the pavement. She surveyed her work, then capped the paint and put it away. Without squeamishness, she picked up the little body and moved it to the grassy strip between the sidewalk and the street. The orange outline of the body remained on the pavement, a grim reminder. I was speechless.

Lonnie wiped her hands self-consciously down her shirt. "I don't think people should just hit a cat and forget it," she said quietly. "This way, whoever hit that cat has to look at that outline every time they drive past. I put the bodies up off the street and some city guy comes and picks them up instead of the next fifty cars making him mush."

"Do you think we should try to find his owner?" I asked in a hushed voice. In a macabre way, I relished the idea of being the bearer of such sad tidings.

"Naw," Lonnie said dismissively. She looked down at the dead cat with bitterness. "Scruffy didn't belong to anyone except himself. A stray disappears, no one wonders about it." She shrugged into her backpack. As she picked her bike out of the gutter, she added, "I figure it's something I owe them, in a way. My loyal subjects should not be left dead in the street. I done all I can for him, now."

"Your loyal subjects?" I asked skeptically. Being weird is okay unless it's fake-weird. A lot of kids pretend to be weird just to impress other people. I wondered about Lonnie. Maybe even her scar story was fake, maybe she'd just been in a bad car wreck.

She gave her shrug again. "I'm Queen of the Strays. Even my mom says so. Which reminds me, I'm supposed to be picking up some junk for my mom. See you around."

She was already pedaling down the street. When she hit puddles, muddy water rooster-tailed up her back, but she didn't avoid them. Fluorescent cats and a one-boobed Barbie. Genuinely weird, I decided. I liked her. "Yeah, see you," I called after her.

I got home just as the rain resumed. I called Mom's office and left a message on her voice mail that I was safely home. I dumped my books in my room and went to the kitchen. Not much in the fridge. There used to be little microwave pizzas or pudding cups when Mom and Dad were together. Not that we're starving now, just on a budget. I grabbed an apple and some cheese. Then I watched television and did homework until Mom got home. I forgot about Lonnie until late that night. I thought about rain soaking the cat's body and hoped someone had picked it up. Then I thought about all the live strays, shivering in the rain. Lonnie was Queen of the Strays. I wondered what she had meant, and then I fell asleep.

Three weeks passed. I didn't see Lonnie. I watched for her, in the lunchroom at school or when I saw kids on bikes in the street, but I never saw her. Then one day, walking home from school, I found two outlines of dead cats in the street. The paint was bright and fresh.

I had reached the front of our apartment building and was fishing my key out of my shirt when Lonnie yelled to me from down the block. I waved back and she came in a lopsided run. She favored her right leg. As she came, I realized that her whole body twisted that direction. It hadn't been so obvious when she was on her bike.

"Hey, Mandy," she greeted me.

I was surprised at how glad I was to see her. "Hey, Lonnie! Long time, no see. Where's your bike?"

She shrugged. "Got stole. My mom left it out and someone took it while I was gone. She didn't even notice until I asked her where it went. So." She paused, then changed the subject. "Hey. Look what I made." She pulled a little drawstring bag out of her shirt. It was hanging around her neck on a string. "This is my new, uh, whatacallit, omelet."

"Amulet," I said reflexively.

She tugged the bag open. Inside was a little princess doll from a McDonald's Happy Meal. Like the Barbie, it was missing a boob. As it was dressed in a ball gown, it looked very peculiar. Lonnie shrugged at my frown. "It doesn't look as good as the other one."

I changed the subject. "So. Where were you, then?"

She shrugged again as she replaced her amulet. "CPS came and got me, 'cause I missed so much school. They stuck me in a foster home, but they couldn't make me go to school either. So now I got a deal with my social worker. She lets me live with my mom, I stay out of trouble and go to school."

"I didn't see you at school today," I pointed out. "If you live around here, you should go to Mason."

"Yeah, I *should,*" she conceded sarcastically. "But even when I'm there, you wouldn't see me. I'm in the special ed classes at the end of the hall."

"But you're not retarded!" I protested.

"Special ed isn't all retarded. There's deaf kids. And ADA. Hyperactive. Emotionally disturbed. They got lots of names for us troublemakers. They just shove us together and forget about us."

"Oh," I said lamely.

"I don't care." She smiled and wagged her head to show how little it bothered her. "Mostly I just read all day. They don't bother me, I don't give them any grief."

"Well." I glanced up at the sky. "I've got to go in. I have to call my mom as soon as I get home from school."

"Oh, latch-key kid, huh?" She watched me stick my key in the security door. "Well, after that, do you want to hang out?"

I stopped. "I'm not supposed to have friends in when Mom isn't home," I said awkwardly. I hated saying it. I was sure she'd take it as an excuse to ditch her.

"So who's going to tell?" she demanded with a superior look. I quailed before it. Knowing I was going to regret this, knowing I'd have to tell my mom later, I unlocked the door and let her in ahead of me.

Our apartment was on the third floor. I was painfully conscious of Lonnie limping up the stairs. There was an elevator at the other end of the building, but I'd never used it. I felt almost ashamed that my body was sound and whole and that the climb didn't bother me. As I unlocked my door, I automatically said, "Wipe your feet."

"Du-uh!" Lonnie retorted sarcastically. She walked in just like a stray cat, with that sort of wiggle that says they're doing you a favor to come in. She stopped in the middle of our living room. For an instant, the envy on her face was so intense it was almost hatred. Then she gave her shrug. "Nice place," she said neutrally. "Got anything to eat?"

"In the kitchen. I've got to phone Mom."

While I left my message, Lonnie went through the refrigerator. By the time I got off the phone, she had eaten an apple, drunk a big glass of milk and poured herself a second one, and taken out the bread and margarine. "Want a sandwich?" she asked as I turned around.

"I hate peanut butter, and that's all there is," I said stiffly. I'd never seen anyone go through a refrigerator so fast. Especially someone else's refrigerator.

"There's sugar," she said, spreading margarine thickly on two slices of bread. "Ever had a sugar sandwich? Mom used to give them to me all the time."

"That's gross," I said as she picked up the sugar bowl and dumped sugar on the bread. She pushed it out in a thick layer, capped it with the other piece of buttered bread. When she lifted it, sugar dribbled out

around the edges. Her teeth crunched in the thick
layer of sugar. I winced. I imagined her teeth melting
away inside her mouth.

"You ought to try it," she told me through a mouthful. She washed it down with half the glass of milk,
sighed, and took another sandy bite.

As she drained off the milk, I suddenly knew that
Lonnie had been really hungry. Not after-school snack
hungry, but really hungry. I had seen the billboards
about Americans going to bed hungry, but I never
grasped it until I watched Lonnie eat. It scared me. I
suddenly wanted her out of our house. It wasn't all
the food she had eaten or the sugar mess on the floor.
It suddenly seemed that by living near people like
Lonnie and having her inside our house, Mom and I
had gotten closer to some invisible edge. First there
had been the real family and home, Mom and Dad
and me in a house with a yard and Pop-tarts and po-
tato chips in the kitchen. Then there was Mom and
me in an apartment, no yard, toast and jam instead of
Pop-tarts. . . . We were safe right now, as long as Dad
sent the support money, as long as Mom kept her job,
but right down the street there were people who lived
in cruddy apartments, and their kids were in special
ed and were hungry. That was scary. Mom and I
weren't people like that. We'd never be people like
that. Unless . . .

"Let's go hang out," I said to her. I didn't even put
her glass in the dishwasher or sweep up the sugar.
Instead, I took a pack of graham crackers out of the
cupboard. I opened it as we walked to the door. She
followed me, just like a hungry stray.

I felt safer as soon as I shut the door behind us.
But now I was stuck outside with her on a cold and
windy day. "Want to go to the library?" I offered. It
was one of the few places Mom had approved for me
to hang out on my own. Even then, I was supposed
to say I was going there and phone again when I
got back.

"Naw," Lonnie said. She took the package of graham crackers, shook out three and handed the stack back to me. "I have to pick up some junk for my mom. But we can do my route before that. Come on."

I thought maybe she had a paper route. Instead it was her roadkill route. Lonnie patrolled for animal bodies. The only one thing she found that day was a dead crow in the gutter. It had been there a while, but she still painted around it and then moved the body reverently up onto the grassy strip. After that, we stopped at two dumpsters, one behind Burger King and the other behind Kentucky Fried Chicken. They had concrete block enclosures and bushes around their dumpsters. There was even a locked gate on Kentucky Fried Chicken's, but it didn't stop Lonnie. She made a big deal of waiting until no one was around before we crept up on them. "Warrior practice," she whispered. "We could get arrested for this. You keep watch."

So I stood guard while she went dumpster diving. She emerged smelling like grease with bags full of chicken bones and half eaten biscuits and a couple of cartons of gravy. It amazed me how fast she filled up bags with stuff other people had thrown away. At Burger King, she got parts of hamburgers and fries. "What are you going to do with that stuff?" I asked Lonnie as we walked away. I was half afraid she'd say that she and her mom were going to eat it for dinner.

"Just wait. I'll show you," she promised. She grinned when she said it, like she was proud of what she carried.

"I've got to get home soon," I told her. "Mom sometimes calls me back, and I didn't say I was going out. I'm supposed to be doing homework."

"Don't sweat it, sister. This won't take long, and I really want you to see it. Come on." She lurched along faster.

She lived on the other side of the main road and back two blocks off the strip. The sun goes down early in October. Lights were on inside the apartments. The building sign said Oakview Manor, but there were no oaks, no trees at all. Some boys were hanging out in the littered parking lot behind the building, smoking cigarettes and perching cool on top of a junk car. One called out as we walked by, "Hey, baby, wanna suck my weenie?" I was grossed out, but Lonnie acted like he didn't exist. The boys laughed behind us, and one said something about 'Scarface.' She kept walking, so I did, too.

At the other end of the parking lot, three battered dumpsters stank in a row. Beyond them was a vacant lot full of blackberry brambles and junk. Old tires and part of a chair stuck out of the brambles. The frame of a junk pickup truck was just visible through the sagging, wet vines. Lonnie sat down on the damp curb and tore open the bags. She spread the food out like it was a picnic, tearing the chicken and burgers to pieces with her fingers and then breaking up the biscuits on top of a bag and dumping the congealed gravy out on them. "For the little ones," she told me quietly. She looked around at the bushes expectantly, then frowned. "Stand back. They're shy of everyone but me."

I backed up. I had guessed it would be cats, and I was right. What was shocking was how many. "Kitty, kitty," Lonnie called. Not loudly. But here came cats of every color and size and age, tattered veterans with ragged ears and sticky-eyed kittens trailing after their mothers. Blacks and calicoes, long-haired cats so matted they looked like dirty bath mats, and an elegant Siamese with only one ear emerged from that briar patch. An orange momma cat and her three black-and-white babies came singing. They converged on Lonnie and the food, crowding until they looked like a patchwork quilt of cat fur.

They were not delicate eaters. They made smacky noises and kitty 'ummm' noises. They crunched bones and lapped gravy noisily. There were warning rumbles as felines jockeyed for position, but surprisingly little outright snarling or smacking. Instead, the overwhelming sound was purring.

Lonnie enthroned on the curb in the midst of her loyal subjects smiled down upon them. She judiciously moved round-bellied kittens to one side to let newcomers have a chance at the gravy and biscuits. As she reached down among the cats, the older felines offered her homage and fealty, pausing in their dining to rub their heads along her arms. Some even stood upright on their hind legs to embrace her. As the food diminished, I thought the cats would leave. Instead they simply turned more attention upon Lonnie. Her lap filled up with squirming kittens, while others clawed pleadingly at her legs. A huge orange tom suddenly leaped up to land as softly as a falling leaf on her shoulders. He draped himself there like a royal mantle, and his huge rusty purr vibrated the air. Lonnie preened. Pleasure and pride transformed her face. "See," she called to me. "Queen of the Strays. I told you." She opened her arms wide to indicate her swarm and cats instantly reared up to bump their heads against her outstretched hands.

"Oh, yeah? Well, you're gonna be Queen of the Ass-Kicked if you don't get up here with my stuff!" The voice came from a third floor window. To someone in the room behind him, the man said, "Stupid little cunt is down there fucking around with those cats again."

The light went out of Lonnie's face. She stared up at him. He glared back. He was a young man with dark, curly hair, his T-shirt tight on his muscular chest. A woman walked by behind him. I looked back at Lonnie. She had a sickly smile. With a pretense of brightness in her voice she called up, "Hey, Carl! Tell Mom to look out here, she should see all my cats!"

Carl's face darkened. "You mom don't got time for that shit, and neither do you! Stupid fucking cats. No, don't you encourage . . . ." He turned from the window, drawing back a fist at someone and speaking angrily.

Lonnie's mom, I thought. He was threatening Lonnie's mom. We couldn't hear what he said. Lonnie stared up at the window, not with fear, but something darker. Carl leaned out again. "Get up here with my stuff!"

Lonnie stood up, the cats melting away around her, trickling away into the shadows. A lone cat stayed, a big striper, winding and bumping against her legs. She didn't seem to feel him. Shame burned in her eyes when her glance grazed me. This was not how she wanted me to see her. She reached up to grip the little doll strung around her neck. Her eyes suddenly blazed. She squared herself. "I didn't go get your stuff." She put her fists on her hips defiantly. "I forgot," she said in a snotty voice.

Carl's scowl deepened. "You forgot? Yeah, right. Well, you forget dinner or coming in until you get it, Lonnie. And it better not be short, or I'll throw you outta *this* window. Get going, now!" He slammed the window shut. Across the parking lot, the boys laughed.

She stood a moment, then stuffed her hands in her pockets and walked away. The striper cat sat down with an unhappy meow. I hurried to catch up with her. It was getting really dark. Mom was going to kill me. "Lonnie?"

She didn't look back. "I got to go," she said in a thick voice.

I ran after her. "Lonnie! Lonnie, your cats are really something. You really are the Queen of the Strays."

"Yeah," she said flatly. She wouldn't look at me. "I got to go. See you around." She lengthened her stride, limping hastily away.

"Okay, I'll look for you at school tomorrow."

She didn't answer. Darkness swallowed her. Rain began to fall.

Before I got home, the headlights of the cars were reflecting off the puddles in the streets. I hurried upstairs, praying that Mom wouldn't be home yet. She wasn't. I hung up my dripping coat, kicked off my wet sneakers and raced into the kitchen. The phone machine was flashing. Six messages. I was toast.

I was cleaning up sugar and listening to Mom's frantic, "Mandy? Are you there? Mandy, pick up!" when I heard her key in the front door. I was still standing in the kitchen looking guilty when she found me.

She looked me up and down. The lower half of my jeans and my socks were sopping. "Where have you been?"

I could have lied and said I was at the library, but Mom and I don't do that to each other. And I needed to tell someone about Lonnie. So I told her everything, from the one-boobed Barbie to the cat-carpet and Carl. Her face got tight, and I knew she didn't like what she was hearing. But she listened, while we fixed dinner. We didn't have to talk about dinner. Wednesday was spaghetti. I chopped mushrooms and peppers, she chopped the onions and smashed the garlic. She put the water to boil for the pasta, I sawed the frozen French bread open and spread it with margarine.

By the time everything was ready, she had heard all about Lonnie. Her first words were pretty hard on me. "I trust you to have good judgment, Mandy."

"I don't think I did anything wrong."

"I didn't say you did wrong. I said you used poor judgment. You let a stranger in while I was gone. You left without telling me where you were going or when you'd be back. If something bad had happened to you, I wouldn't even have known where to start looking."

"Why do you always assume something bad is going to happen? When am I supposed to have friends over? I can't have them in while you're gone, and I can't go out with them. What am I supposed to do, just come home and be alone all day?"

"You can have friends over," my mom objected. "But I need to know something about people before we let them into our home. Mandy, just because a person is your own age and a girl doesn't mean she can't hurt you. Or that she won't steal from us."

"MOM!" I exploded, but she kept on talking.

"Lonnie is probably a nice kid who's just had a hard time. But the people she knows may not be nice. If someone knew that I'm at work all day and you're at school, they could rip us off. I certainly couldn't afford to replace the stereo and the television and the microwave all at once. We'd just have to do without."

"You haven't even met Lonnie and you're judging her!"

"I'm not judging her. I'm trying to protect you." Mom paused. "Mandy. There's a lot of Lonnies in the world. As much as I'd like to, I can't save them all. Sometimes, I feel like I can't even protect you any more. But I do my best. Even when it means . . ." She halted her words. Then she spoke gravely. "Mandy, if you hang out with Lonnie, people will treat you like Lonnie. Not that Lonnie deserves to be treated like she is. In fact, I'm sure she doesn't. But I can't protect Lonnie. All I can do is try to protect you."

She was so serious that my anger evaporated. We sat at the little table in the kitchen with our dinner getting cold between us. I tried to remember the big table in our old dining room with the hardwood floor and the wallpaper. I couldn't. "Mom?" I asked suddenly. "What is the difference between Lonnie and me?"

Mom was quiet for a long time. Then she said, "Maybe the difference is me. Someone who cares fiercely about you."

"Lonnie loves her mom, even if she did throw her out a window."

"Lonnie may love her mom, but it doesn't sound like her mom cares about her. It doesn't sound like anyone does."

"Only her cats," I conceded. "And half of them are deaders." And me, I thought. I care about her.

In the end, we made compromises. I could have

Lonnie over if I told Mom she was there. Mom had to get Lonnie's phone number, address, and her Mom's name. If we went out, it had to be somewhere like the library, not just to walk around. I had to call Mom before I went and when I got back. I had to stay out of dumpsters. And I wasn't allowed to go to Lonnie's house.

"But why?" I ventured.

"Because," Mom said darkly, and that was the end of that.

I looked for Lonnie at school the next day. I even went to the special-ed rooms. No Lonnie. Three days later, I found one cat-body outline, but I couldn't tell if it was new or old because of all the rain. I was afraid to go to her building. Mom was right, it was a tough neighborhood. But on the fourth day, I screwed up my courage and took the long way home from school to walk through her neighborhood.

I saw her from half a block away. She was standing at the corner of a convenience store parking lot, her arms crossed on her chest. There were three boys facing her. Two were our age, one looked older. They had her bike.

It was so beat up I wouldn't have recognized it, except for the Amazon Barbie. One of the boys sat on the bike possessively while the other two stood between Lonnie and the bike.

"I don't care what he said," Lonnie told them. "It's my bike, and I want it back." She tried to circle, to get close enough to get her hands on the bike, but the two boys blocked her lazily.

"Your dad said we could have it." The boy on the bike was cocky about it.

"Carl's not my dad!" Lonnie declared furiously. "Get off my bike!"

"So what? He said we could have it for picking up his junk for him. Gave us ten bucks, too." There was a sneer of laughter in the older boy's voice.

I froze, watching them. They moved by a set of

unspoken rules. Lonnie could not physically touch the boys, and they knew it. All they had to do to keep her from the bike was to stand between her and it. She moved back and forth, trying to get past them. She looked stupid and helpless and she knew it. A man walked up to them and stopped. My hopes rose.

"It's a piece of shit bike anyway," one of the boys declared laughingly as they blocked her yet again.

"Yeah. We're gonna take it down to the lake and run it off the dock into the water."

The light changed. The man crossed the street. It was as if he had not even seen Lonnie and the boys and the bike. He didn't even look back.

"You better not!" Lonnie threatened helplessly. She darted once more at the bike. And collided with a boy.

"Hey!" he pushed her violently back. "Keep your hands off me, bitch!"

"Yeah, whore!"

Suddenly, in the physical contact, the rules of the game had changed. The boys pushed at her. Lonnie cowered back and the one on the bike rode it up on her, pushing the wheel against her. Now instead of trying to grab her bike back, she was trying to back away from it. The other boys touched her. Her face. "God, you're ugly!" Her chest. "She ain't got no tits, just like her dolly! Your momma cut them off, too?" Her crotch. "Whoo, whoo, you like that, ho?"

Across the street, a bus stopped and two people got off. They walked away into the darkness. Cars drove by in the gathering dusk of the overcast October evening. No one paid any attention to Lonnie's plight. Deep in my heart, I knew why. She was already broken, already damaged past repairing. If you can't fix something, then don't worry about hurting it even more. The boys knew that. She wasn't worth saving from them. It was like jumping on the couch that already had broken springs. She was just a thing to practice on.

"Stop it, stop it!" She flailed at them wildly, trying

to slap away the hands that darted in to touch her insultingly, pushing, poking, slapping her face. She had forgotten she was a warrior. She was just a girl, and that was a boy's game. She couldn't win it. Leaves in the gutter rustled by. I was so cold I was shaking. So cold. I should get home, I was cold and it was getting dark and my mom would be mad at me. One of the boys pushed her hard as the other one rammed her with the bike. She fell down on the sidewalk and suddenly they ringed her, the bike discarded on the pavement as they sneered down at her.

Some tribal memory of what came next reared its savage face from my subconscious.

"No!" I suddenly screamed. My voice came out shrill and childish. I flew toward them, gripping my book bag by its strap. A stupid weapon, my only weapon. "Get away from her, get away from her!" I uttered the word I knew Lonnie could never say. "Help! Help me, someone, they're hurting her! Help! Get away from her!"

I waded into them, swinging my book bag, and they suddenly fell back. Abruptly their ugly faces turned confused and surprised. Like magic, they were only boys again, just teasing boys who always push you as far as they can, especially if the playground teacher isn't around.

"Look out, it's Wonder Woman!" one yelled, and a man who had come to the door of the Seven-Eleven across the parking lot laughed out loud. They grabbed the bike and ran away, shouting insults at one another—You pussy! You wimp! You sissy!—as they ran. No one came to help as I took Lonnie's hands and dragged her to her feet. The knee of her sweatpants was torn and her backpack was muddy. There was mud on the side of her face, too.

"Are you hurt?" I asked her as she stood. I tried to hug her. She slapped my hands angrily away.

"They got my damn bike! Shit! Shit, shit, shit, why didn't you grab the bike while it was laying there!"

Her eyes blazed as she turned on me. I fell back in surprise before her anger.

"I was worried about you! The bike wasn't that important!"

"That's easy for you to say. A bike isn't the only damn thing you've got!" She lifted her sleeve to wipe mud off her face. She might have wiped away tears as well. I stared at her, speechless. I thought I had been brave, almost heroic. She seemed to think I had been stupid. She glanced up from examining a bleeding scrape on her knee and knew she'd hurt me. She tried to explain. "Look, it's like this. If we had got the bike, we would have won. Now I got all bruised up and I lost, too. So they'll tease me with the bike again. I got to fight them all over again tomorrow."

"I think it's dumb to fight for that bike at all," I said quietly. "You could really get hurt. The bike isn't worth it."

"Yeah," she said sarcastically. "That's what they teach us girls. Don't get into fights over stuff. It's not worth getting hurt over. So guys keep taking stuff from us, knowing we won't fight. Those guys, if I don't fight them to get my bike back, then they'll take something else from me. And something more. They'll keep on taking stuff from me until I have to fight back. Only by then it'll be too late, because I'll never have learned to fight, so whatever it is that I finally fight for, they'll just take it from me anyway."

Her logic was torturous, and I shied away from her conclusion.

"Like Carl," she added bitterly. "I didn't fight him at first. He moved in. He eats our food and uses our phone and leaves the house a mess. He took my home. He took my mom. Shit. He even took my bike and gave it to those guys. Now he thinks he can take anything he wants, and I won't fight. He's probably right, too."

"I know I probably can't beat those boys," she admitted a few minutes later as we walked slowly down the darkening street. "But I can make it cost them something to pick on me. They can hit me and knock me down, but they know I'm going to fight back, hit back. So maybe they'll go find an easier target. I know, everyone says that if you avoid a bully or ignore him, he'll go away. But that's bullshit. They don't. They just grow up and become your mom's boyfriend. Dead cat."

I don't know how she saw it in the dark. Black fur in a black gutter, but she saw it. She opened her pack and took out her spray can and inscribed his neon orange memorial on the pavement. She scooped up his body carefully and set it at the base of a no parking sign. "Still warm," she said regretfully as she wiped her hands down her shirt. "Poor kitty." Crouched over the body, it was like she spoke to the cat. "Carl gave them my bike. That's like he gave them permission to pick on me, take stuff like me. Like I don't matter any more than a dead cat in the gutter. Run over me and just keep going." She smoothed the cat's rumpled fur a last time. "God, I hate Carl," she said quietly.

More conversationally, she added, "You know what really pisses me off? That Carl gave them my bike *and* some money for picking up his dope. He never gives me nothing for picking up his junk. I just have to do it. So that if someone gets caught with it, it's me. He told my Mom, if I get caught, they won't do much, because I'm a kid."

"But doesn't your mom . . ." I began.

"Long as my mom gets her junk, she'll believe whatever he says," Lonnie said sadly. "Since Carl moved in, it's like I'm mostly invisible. She doesn't even yell at me any more. The only time she talks to me is when I bring the junk home. She always thanks me. That's the only reason I do it." Her eyes swung to mine. "And *I* still talk to *her*. Carl's always telling me to shut up, but I don't. I tell her about my cats, I told her about you." In a quieter voice she added, "I tell her she shouldn't be tricking just to get money for

junk. That's how I fight him. Maybe I won't win, but
no one can say I didn't fight." She gave her one shouldered shrug. "I won't stop either. Long as I keep
fighting, he can't say he won."

When I got in, Mom was waiting for me. Her face
was white. "I damn near called the cops," she hissed
at me. "You didn't call me, I came straight home,
there's no sign of you . . ." Then she burst into tears.

I was stupid. I told her where I'd been and what
had happened. When I was done, she just sat there
on the couch with her face in her hands. She spoke
through her fingers. "God, Mandy. You have no
concept . . . look. Sweetie. You can't get involved in
this. You just can't. Drugs and prostitution and abuse
and . . . No. Mandy, you have to stay away from her.
You must."

"I can't." I was telling the truth. "I can't just abandon her. Then she'd have no one! I have you, but she
doesn't have anyone but a bunch of stray cats."

Mom got up and walked into her room without a
word. That really shook me up. For a minute I thought
that was it, that she was so mad she wasn't even going
to talk to me any more. Then she came back with a
little red tube in her hand.

"This is not a toy," she told me severely, as if I had
asked to play with it. "This is a serious weapon. Pepper spray. You point it like this, push this catch down,
and then spray it. It will make anyone back off long
enough for you to run away. Don't stick around and
try to fight, just get away. And use it only if you are
really in danger. Never for a joke, never as a threat.
If you have to, use it. Other than that, don't even tell
anyone you have it."

"There's two," I said out loud as I took them.

"Give the other one to Lonnie," she said. She
walked to the window and peered out through the
curtains. She talked to the night. "Show her how to
use it. But after that, you are not allowed to see her

any more. Do you understand? This is as much as we can do for her. No more."

I couldn't argue with that voice, but I wondered if I would obey her. "Mom," I asked quietly. "If you had been there tonight, if you had been me . . . would you have used it on those boys?"

"No. Boys your age are just . . . Well, maybe, yes. Yes." She hesitated. "I don't know," she admitted. "Mandy, I don't know, I wasn't there, you weren't the one being threatened . . . If Lonnie had just walked away, if she hadn't challenged them . . ." Her voice trailed away. She didn't know either. How could I know when to fight back if my own mom didn't know? In a quieter voice she added, "I have to get us into a better place. I have to."

I didn't see Lonnie for a while. I took a different route home from school, used a different door into my building. I pretended that if I didn't see her, I wasn't avoiding her. I liked her, but her problems were just too scary. I tried not to think about her, but my hand kept finding the extra vial of pepper spray in my coat pocket. Then one afternoon at four o'clock, I turned off the TV and put on my coat. I wrote Mom a note. I left the apartment.

It was dark, but at least it wasn't raining. I walked fast, glad there were no boys hanging out around her building tonight. I wondered how I'd know which door was hers. I wondered if I'd have the guts to knock. But I didn't have to. Lonnie knelt on the ground by the dumpster. The single parking lot light illuminated at least a dozen orange outlines of cats on the pavement. As I watched, another one slowly formed on the ground in front of Lonnie. I went to her.

The area around the dumpster was littered with sprawled cat bodies. A terrible noise was coming from Lonnie as she painted around them. "Uh, huh, huh"; the noise people make when they can't cry. I was afraid to get too close to her. She crawled to the next cat and began outlining it.

"What happened?" I whispered into the darkness.

She looked up, startled. Even in the dimness, I could see she was broken. "I don't know," she choked out when she recognized me. "I don't know. They weren't hit by cars, they weren't killed by dogs. They're just dead. I just don't know." She sank down in defeat on the dirty pavement. "My strays. My loyal subjects." Her hand rested on one dead cat like a benediction. Behind her, a small kitten mewed questioningly in the bushes. "I got nothing left," she told me sadly. She shook her head. "I fought and I fought. But I still lost. In the end, it all got taken away." She seemed to get smaller.

"Lonnie!" Carl called from the window. He leaned out, craning to see her. "Lonnie, you down there? You got my stuff?"

It was the wrong time to ask her that. She came to her feet like a puppet hauled up on its strings. "No!" she screeched back. "No, I don't!" Then, in a plea for understanding, "Carl, my cats are dead! Something killed them." Her voice broke on the words.

"Oh, no, really?" His voice shook. "That's awful, Lonnie. That's just terrible." Then he laughed out loud, and I knew he'd been holding it back all along. "Well, maybe someone poisoned the fuckers so you'd quit wasting time on them. Quit sniveling and go get my stuff. Now!"

Her hands flew up to her face in horror. Speechless, she stared into the darkness beyond the dumpsters. When she dropped her hands a moment later, her painty fingers had left fluorescent stripes on her cheeks.

I couldn't believe what happened next. She didn't even look at me. She limped straight to the door of her building. She obediently went inside. Lonnie had stopped fighting.

The kitten found me. I felt her tiny claws in my sock. I picked her up. She was skinny and her little mouth opened hugely when she cried. "You've got the wrong person," I told her. I set her down and walked away.

Then I heard the sound. Not a shout. A roar, like the roar of a lioness, wordless in her fury. It came from the window above. Carl yelled back but it was a startled shout, full of dismay. I couldn't see much, but I saw her shadow crash into his, her fists pummeling at his face and chest. For an instant I thought that she could win. But it was still a boy's game. I heard his answering roar of anger. He seized her by the upper arms, lifted her off her feet, and threw her.

She hit the window. The glass shattered, flying out like a cloud of diamonds. Lonnie fell with it, twisting and yowling.

I did a stupid thing. Somehow I had the pepper spray in my hand and I pointed it up at the window. Lonnie seemed to be falling forever. I saw Carl look out as she fell, I even saw the shock on his face, heard someone else in the room behind him scream. Then I squeezed the button and enveloped myself in a cloud of pepper gas. Carl was too far away. Even finally knowing when to fight, I thought to myself, was not enough. People like Carl still won. Blinded and choking, I fell to my knees as Lonnie struck the ground. Broken glass rang in a brittle rain with her.

Everything in the world stopped. I didn't kneel by her, I crumpled. I tried to touch her but I couldn't. I wasn't Lonnie, to touch death without fear. Then she lifted her head. She looked at me and her mouth opened. As if she moved a mountain, she turned her head. Her lips pulled back. With her last breath, she snarled up at the window that framed Carl.

Summoned, the cats came. The queen's loyal subjects poured forth to her call. They came in a wave that became a tide. From the bushes in back of the dumpster, from under cars, from everywhere, they came. They flooded the parking lot. A score, a hundred, five hundred fluorescent orange silhouettes lit the night as they answered her call. I saw Carl stagger back from the window. Like living flames, the cats licked up the side of the building, over the sill and through the broken glass. The rumble of their snarls was like a big truck idling. The parking lot was darker when the last one disappeared inside. The hissing and spitting and caterwauling from up there almost drowned his screams.

Mom's headlights hit me just about the same time the cats poured out of the window again. Like molten gold or streaming honey, they flowed down the side of the building. They engulfed Lonnie and me. I felt the warmth of a hundred small bodies, the soft swipe of velvet paws as they rushed past and over me to get to her. I swear I saw them, and I swear I felt them.

They purred all over Lonnie, they marked her with their brows, they bumped her with their fluorescent noses. They nudged and they pleaded and they nagged, pushing at her body. They kneaded it with their paws demandingly, scores of little fluorescent paws pushing at her yielding flesh, making her smaller and more compact, recreating her in a new and perfect image.

The Queen of the Strays sat up groggily. She blinked her great amber eyes. She lifted a velvet paw to swipe at her tabby face. She stood and she stretched, showing me four sets of razor claws and four powerful legs attached to a lithe and perfect body.

"Lonnie?" I asked incredulously.

The cat shrugged one shoulder.

In the next instant, Lonnie was gone. The tidal wave of fluorescent cats retreated, and she padded off in the midst of them. The great orange glow surged into the blackberry tangle. Their light dwindled as they faded into the thorny jungle of vines. Then it winked out. Lonnie was gone, and my mom was there going, "Oh, my God, my God. Get in the car, Mandy. Right now. Get in the car."

I did. We were halfway home before I noticed the tiny black-and-white kitten that was stuck to my sock like a burr. When I put it in my lap, it curled up and began to purr.

I don't know what Mom saw that night. She says I had pepper gas in my eyes and that I couldn't have seen anything. The papers said that a junkie whore got mad at her pimp and cut him to ribbons with a razor. The papers never even mentioned Lonnie.

No one ever wonders what happens to strays when they disappear.

I hope her next eight lives are better than this one was.

DEBRIEFING THE WARRIOR/
PRINCESS
by Elizabeth Ann Scarborough

Elizabeth Ann Scarborough won a Nebula Award in 1989
for her novel *The Healer's War,* based on her experiences
as an Army nurse in Vietnam. She has collaborated on four
books with Anne McCaffrey, three novels and one anthology, *Space Opera.* Her most recent novel is *The Godmoth-
er's Web,* which uses Native American folklore as a
backdrop. She lives in Washington with four cats, Popsicle,
Kittibits, Trixie and Treat.

The reincarnation of King Arthur Pendragon
opened wide blue eyes and gave Merlin the Magician a mischievous look as the great wizard assisted
Arthur's reincarnation up from the coffin. The former
king handed Merlin the lily which had been borne on
the breast of the last, best little black frock, the only
one in the former king's collection of which the press
had no photographic record. The lily became Excalibur, which it had always been, through Merlin's en-
chantment keeping a low profile befitting its place in
the life of its renovated owner.

"You look ravishing, my dear," Merlin said with a
gallant bow as the former king straightened the frock's
ever-so-slightly belled skirt so that it fell into a more
graceful shape. In looks, Merlin resembled less a court
magician than the therapist the king had most recently
employed. Or was it the astrologist? Merlin seemed

to shift ever so slightly, just when the king felt certain of the answer. But Merlin had always been that way.

The reincarnated king had been disoriented from the time the lid of the coffin opened, the face of the legendary magician appeared, and the king once more set foot on the royal home of Avalon, the little island in the lake to which Arthur had retired until once more needed by Britain. Once the former king's size five strappy black stiletto-heeled sandal touched the soil, everything came back. Actually, the sole did not literally touch the soil, which was buried in layers and layers of colorful floral tributes that made the king feel rather less like King Arthur or his most recent self and more like Dorothy of Kansas in the poppy field outside Oz. But nonetheless, Arthur-that-was remembered all of the past, from centuries ago until the present day, when the mourners had tearfully departed and taken up the little bridge.

Arthur's reincarnation gave Merlin an exasperated look from under the famous fringed lids shyly shielding the luminous blue eyes. "You did *not* make it easy on me this time, did you, old chap?" the king's reincarnation chided.

"But, er—my *dear* Arthur—you *had* complained that when I was turning you into all of those creatures to teach you how to see the world as they did, I ought to have turned you into a woman so you could understand Guinevere. Your wish is—"

"Even so. It made everything so bloody difficult. And you married me off to Lancelot this time and made Guin look like an overbred species of hound. I don't see at all how I could have been expected to accomplish anything with such handicaps."

"Nonsense, my dear," Merlin said, spreading a magic carpet beneath a stately oak. "You had all of the weapons any woman would need in her arsenal to accomplish the task. You are now considered to have been the most beautiful and womanly lady in the world, you reached the age of nineteen with your virtue intact, were given noble birth but not the kingdom, as formerly, and won the future king—that is— Lancelot—almost immediately. And the people were mad for you."

"Well, yes. Funny how one's reputation improves after one is deceased, don't you think?"

"Ah, but that is not reputation, my dear. That is legend. And legend has always become you. Or rather, you have always become legend. I can't see that it was that difficult to figure out."

"You might have named me Ursula, so I would have recognized myself," the former king complained.

"A rose by any other name may still smell as sweet, as that actor chappie said, but I can't see great men swooning over an 'Ursula,' nor Manchester housewives identifying with her problems. And you *were* given the name of the Roman goddess of the hunt. Surely that was some sort of clue."

"Hardly," the former king said with a slight snuffle of his longish aristocratic nose, the single feature of the lovely face which saved it from the vapid too-cute prettiness it would have had given, say, a button nose. "*Loads* of upper class British school girls are named the same thing, and I didn't even *like* to hunt. Not for a real fox anyway. And it seems the boars and bears and elk have mostly disappeared. Somehow a hunt is just not the same thing riding the hounds to a scented floor mop. And I found that I no longer cared as much for horses as I formerly did when surrounded by my terribly equestrian in-laws. How on earth did you expect me to accomplish anything when you'd sent me back as Cinderella, or rather," she said with a nod to the coffin, "Snow White perhaps. Why could I have not been more like that Xena person on the telly? There were so many times I should have loved to kick some arse—or at least a bloody camera. But my gym didn't offer martial arts courses, I'm afraid. And if it had done, I don't think the instructor would have allowed me to take it.

"He always acted as if I were some sort of porcelain doll and he might have broken me. Funny that it was ultimately that sort of protectiveness that *did* break me," and the former king patted the side of her face, which, being a spiritual sort of face at this point, was once more perfect, including the framing coiffure, which had not a single curl arranged in anything but charmingly casual fluffiness. "You might at least have showed up in this life yourself. I could have used a bit of magic."

"A *bit* of magic?" Merlin cried incredulously. "My dear leige-lady, you were invested with more glamourie than is to be found in all of the realm of faerie. Furthermore, all manner of masters and mistresses of artifice and illusion attended you constantly while you were in your royal role and afterward, your own magic had become mature and you no longer needed such minor magics. In fact, you gave them away, which I don't understand entirely, but magic isn't at all what it used to be."

"I suppose when you look at it that way . . . you know, now that I remember who I was—who I am, it comes to me that the feeling I had when I was being chased by the photographers was quite familiar."

"In *our* day many people still understood that taking one's image is to steal part of one's essence," Merlin said with a huff. "Nowadays, with all this rationality, people seem to discount the damage that sort of thing can do."

"Hm. I grant that just a snapshot here and there, or even a great many of them, such as the ones I have of the children, aren't a harmful thing. It was the great quantity of them, the way they were always around me, so that my eyes never stopped being blinded by flashbulbs—I felt as if I lived in a world where the sun was a bloody strobe light most of the time, to tell you the truth—it was as if, trying to photograph my every movement, every activity, every mood, they were trying to suck up my soul!"

"That's exactly right," Merlin said. "That's precisely what they were doing. Once they had it, you would no longer be a threat to their plans, you see."

"Er—of course. Merlin, old dear, have you been reading back issues of *The Mercenary Magician's Militia* magazine again?"

"Certainly not! That was simply investigative curiosity. You know I like to keep up with the times."

"Oh, yes," the former king agreed, her dimples showing. "*And* the *Independent and* the *Herald.*"

"Droll, my dear, very droll indeed," Merlin said with a huff, his hand reaching up to smooth his beard as if it were ruffled feathers. "But you do have serious enemies, you know, and though your friends and loved ones have always been the ones to deal you the most painful blows, Morgan le Fey and Mordred are still your undoing."

"Merlin, I will not have it said that either of my current children in any way resemble Mordred."

"Perish the thought!" Merlin said with genuine horror. "They are in part new souls—we do have those from time to time, you know—but retain some of the essences of Sir Gawain and Sir Percival, your most valiant knights."

"Please don't tell me my former mother-in-law is Morgan le Fey. It simply won't do, old friend."

"Not at all. She is actually your devoted foster brother, that conservative and somewhat hide-bound fellow, Sir Cai."

"That explains a lot," the former Arthur said with a pensive, downcast look. "Cai always did try very hard but lacked—I don't know, imagination, perhaps, to try new things, to come out from behind his stuffy traditions and simply be the splendid fellow he was. Her Majesty is a bit like that. A good sort but afraid to commit herself publicly to a sincerely comforting word."

"Ahem. Let's not be too harsh, my leige. Sir Cai, now as well as then, was a warrior of the old school.

Afraid? Not a bit of it. Never a braver soul walked the earth. You are the exception, who can wade into battle, be wounded, and show your wounds—Excalibur can heal them only when they are evident. And strangely enough, others wounded as you are learn that if their wounds show, they also may be healed. But before you held the sword or married into the family, depending on the lifetime under discussion, Cai did things the old way. One would not show one's wounds, as to do so would seem to one's enemies a sign of weakness and make one's followers afraid."

"But my mother-in-law never wielded a claymore or charged into a line of enemy soldiers," Arthur-that-was protested.

"Not those things, no, but she was in a war, as was her consort, and the two of them behave as soldiers and sovereigns of old, in the same way that Cai behaved. Your mother-in-law, if you'll recall, my dear, once drove ambulances during the war. She and her consort and her mother were all present during the blitz. Her wounds could not be showed and so never were they healed. The Americans have a phrase for such emotional injuries now, I believe . . ."

"Post Traumatic Stress Disorder," the princess who had been a king offered with the informed confidence with which she did her most important work. "Some of the fellows who were working with the humanitarian organizations to remove the landmines were American veterans of the Vietnam conflict. They explained it to me. It's a form of what was called in my mother-in-law's day 'shell-shocked' or 'battle fatigued' except that it has not until recently been recognized that the condition manifests itself in different ways and to varying degrees."

"Your mother-in-law's and Cai's manifestation, then, as you would have it, resides in the stiffening of the upper lip and spine, and in the taking of refuge in saying nothing that can be construed as weakness to their enemies or fallibility to their followers. They become panicked when called upon to do so, you understand."

The newer, comelier version of Arthur looked momentarily chastened. "No, I'm afraid I was so busy being hurt by their reticence and coldness that I did not understand. Poor Cai! A stouter heart never beat, of course, but it seems he never really has been able to be himself, even as a woman."

"Precisely," Merlin said. "No, I don't believe you ever met Morgan le Fey or Mordred in this life, but they have passed along their philosophy to many, and their minions were those who were trying to soak up your spirit with their pictures."

"Tabloid owners, surely not! That's not enough power for them."

"It was enough to do for you, my dear," he said gravely.

"True," she admitted.

"They also manufactured arms—such as the land-mines you came to oppose. That, more than anything, was your undoing, you know."

"Well, I'm glad to hear it was that rather than what the press was reporting. Such an idiotic way to die."

"Hmmm—I suppose a philosopher might question whether it was more idiotic than dying on the sword of your own son."

"I do—er—get the point," the once king and princess giggled. "And wouldn't it have been ghastly if I had actually died by my own hand or from my bulimia?"

"Oh, that," Merlin said. "I'm afraid I must claim some responsibility for that. You see, I knew that in this present transformation of yours, you would be learning all about being a woman—including both power and powerlessness. I thought it best, after the way you ended your last life, to start with the power-lessness, so that once you gained your power, you would have the understanding you needed for your work. All of the evils that beset woman—lovelessness, betrayal by one she loves, being hostage in an 'enemy' camp totally in sympathy with her husband, weakness, illness—"

"The very same evils that afflicted me as a man, except for the 'enemy camp' bits, I seem to recall," the past king said.

Merlin/the therapist/the astrologer smiled proudly. "Yes, the very same ones. Isn't it amazing. And you thought you didn't understand women in your last life!"

"Maybe not, but when I was King Arthur, I didn't feel so bloody powerless ALL the time, only when it came to Lance and Genny."

"That was because, as a man, you learned of your other powers first, before you felt the weakness. With women, it is usually the other way around. Most of them enter into their power only after they've gone through the perils of mating, of having children, that sort of thing."

"Oh really?" the king's reincarnation smiled mischievously. "And just when did you learn so much about women?"

"Who do you think was running the women's crisis center that you claimed did you so much good?"

"I thought you said you weren't there because of all the hairdressers and such."

"No, I said it was they who helped cover you with glamourie, a job I had to attend to without any assistance whatsoever when we last met. This time I was not present as a magician. But I was, as formerly, there to advise you when you needed me—or when it seemed that you might possibly listen."

"I'm listening now," the former king said, cupping his comely chin in a shapely hand attached to a slender arm whose elbow rested upon a much-admired knee. The fallen trunk of a tree formed an excellent seat. "And I admit it. I've made a mess of things both as a king and as a princess. Do tell me what comes next."

"I think first perhaps you should be aware of what's coming now," Merlin said. "Have you any idea what a sensation your death caused?"

"Snuffing it at my tender age? Well, yes, I suppose that would upset the 'company'—bowing out before I was properly dismissed." The bitterness in that statement drained out of the king, and it was with true misery that the former monarch added, "And the boys will be devastated, I'm afraid. Oh, dear. No one but my former husband to guide them."

"Before you distress yourself further, perhaps you should have a look at something. We'll have to do it the old-fashioned way since there are no electrical outlets on this island and I quite neglected to bring my battery-powered television."

Merlin/the therapist/astrologer led her through the little stand of trees to the edge of the water. The sun was just setting, painting the still pool pink.

"I seem to recall that Avalon was a magic island covered in mist and surrounded by the sea," the king said. "This is nothing but a folly my grandfather constructed to enhance the grounds of the family estate. This body of water is simply an ornamental man-made pond. *Hardly* the sea."

Merlin stopped by the shore and indicated another conveniently placed log where the once-king could rest. "Where in the water it actually is and how large or small it appears to others are matters of no consequence to the magic isle of Avalon. It goes where it wishes and appears however it is pleased to appear. And while this water is fresh and has never, it is true, belonged to the sea, at least since those ancient times when the globe was covered with water, it was, long before your family was founded, long before the Romans came, a natural well and from that well came a scrying pool. At one time it even had a dragon to guard it, but he went on to become the chairman of the board of a large multinational energy corporation, I believe."

"Nevertheless, I have the strangest feeling that you are going to tell me the pool still scrys?" Arthur-that-was asked.

"Bravo," Merlin said. "Most astute. Not that I would expect less from you, my dear."

He waved his hands first in grand gestures, and then rather as if he were clicking a remote control, and images began to appear in the water.

To Arthur the vision in the water would have been amazing had it not been for the most recent incarnation, when the format of the scenes that appeared was a sometimes irritating occurrence. As it was, Merlin flipped forward rapidly, through the days of coverage, the constant droning of the newscasters, the reportage on the car crash, the hospitalization, the—death. And afterward, so many pictures familiar all over the world.

Then, the most amazing part of it all, the response of the kingdom to the death—the piles of flowers, the tears, the quiet anger at those in power for their un-kindness. To fill in the gaps, the press even had to provide coverage of the important work most recently done—the stroll through the minefield, the comforting of the sick and wounded.

The pictures of the funeral amazed the once king. The queen herself waiting on foot with all of the royal family around her. No pomp, no jewels or state robes, just black clothing, more than any family nowadays usually did for the deceased ex-wife of an eldest son. When the caisson carrying the coffin went by, the monarch bowed her head, as did the rest of the family. The family humbled by the outrage of the kingdom at the lack of care given to the one member of the royal family widely loved and admired.

"That's vindication for you, surely," Merlin said. "You see, you were loved."

"I see," said the former king in a small voice. The heartfelt eulogies of the country were a blur compared to the single word on the little bouquet placed on the casket, a gift from a half-orphaned son.

"A bit late, of course," Merlin said. "But these things always were. You see, you made a tremendous impact. Did tremendous good. Made an impression that may last through time, much as your initial one did . . ."

"Why?" the princess who had been Arthur asked. "I mean, why so much? And why did I become me after having been a legend for uniting the country?"

"Why, to reunite it of course. It's fallen on dreadful times since colonial days. No *esprit de corps,* so to speak. No focus. By your well-spent life and early death, by the love you commanded from your people, you provided that focus, suggested peacetime campaigns that were worthy of royals and commoners alike. Whereas in your first life, you united the kingdom by war, in the most recent one, you united it, as you see, with love. An amazing feat. Everybody loved you."

"Yes, particularly now that I'm out of the way and no threat to anyone," the celebrated deceased said, with an understanding of reality that might have surprised those who had considered the most recent incarnation pretty but shallow and perhaps a little stupid.

"No need to be so unhappy, surely?" Merlin said. "You wanted love, and what do you call this?"

"I should have liked something a bit more personal, is all," the once-king, presently crowned by the press as "queen of hearts" sighed. "Here I am the darling of history, scholars, writers, thinkers, statesmen, from the first life, and in this one, the whole kingdom, and yet Guinevere, who was the only woman I loved when I was a man, didn't love me enough to keep from betraying me with another man, and my former husband, when I'm supposedly the most beautiful and admired woman in the world, preferred that horse-faced—" The warrior/princess wanted to cry, but the tears dropping into the pool and messing up the reception didn't feel real. "Just when maybe I might have found someone to love me best—well, it's ironic, isn't it, that after all the times I tried to take my own life, when I finally felt I had something to live for—some*one* to live for—we're both killed."

"Hearing what those people have to say, seeing their faces, can you not feel their love?" Merlin asked.

"They didn't know me, though, did they? I mean, I could be nice to them, take care of them, even love them, for the time I was there but what about if I had needed something from them, would any of them have done more than *he* did?"

Merlin shrugged. "Perhaps. There are other givers in the world, not so celebrated as yourself, but givers nonetheless. The problem is, you see, that your sort never gives to one another. You look for those who need you. Genny—who was well on her way to becoming the sort of princess you are today when you married her. She might have made a loveless match with an older man who would have slain her for her betrayal, but you, who fought battle after battle to unify a nation, allowed her to love, even when it hurt you. And your former husband, though he needed another woman, has never understood how to earn the love of those who need him until he married you. He failed you, it's true. But you drew his attention to the matter." Merlin nodded at pictures of the gentleman in question answering subjects addressing himself and his sons by first name, replying gently and humbly to their condolences and remarks. "He has mourned other men he thought were his teachers but you, my dear, have been his greatest tutor of all."

"Bully for me."

"Indeed," Merlin said, smiling. "For no matter the personal cost, in both lives, you have always battled for what was right, even if it was yourself you had to battle. That is why I'm here, you see."

"I don't see at all. Am I dead for good now or what?"

350 Elizabeth Ann Scarborough

"Or what," Merlin answered. "What, indeed? And who, why, how? You see, as afterworlds go, none of us have it exactly right—it's somewhere between what we druids once believed, the beliefs of the American aborigines, those of the Judeo-Christian factions, and those of the Buddhists. Bits of each. Even a little of Valhalla, if going someplace to hang about feasting and telling battle stories with other warriors interests you?"

The former king and princess gave a delicate shudder.

"I rather thought so. That's the traditional hero's reward but I, as a major druid, archangel, bodhisattva, and general spiritual higher-up, have been empowered to offer you a chance to finally get what you want from life, next time around."

He stirred the waters and showed a sort of apartment building where two children, a boy and a girl, walked from separate doors, met, and continued walking together, the boy taking the girl's books, she smiling lovingly. The scenes shifted as they grew older, married, had children, and filled each other's years until a great catastrophe swept the land, burned cities to the ground, caused seas to boil, the land to burn, the children to die, and the two people to be killed together when their home collapsed on them. "There. You can have that if you like. Happily ever after. Genuine true heterosexual marital love. With children. Also loving. Just what you've wanted all along."

"Well, yes," the hero of two lifetimes said. "But the end. That was so tragic. What a dreadful thing to happen to such lovely people. Couldn't something be done about that bit?"

"Well, yes, of course, it could," Merlin said. "But *they* could not do it. They know nothing of statesmanship or warfare, nothing of diplomacy or the needs of the many. I hate to say it, but they only know the needs of each other and their children and their jobs, which are fairly straightforward and undemanding so that there are no stresses or undue strains on their happiness. They can be saved only by an honest leader whose complete and selfless attention is on the larger picture, whose loneliness turned into selfless love of country and people, who—"

"You mean me," groaned the warrior and princess. "I could save those people, if I'm—not them. That's it, isn't it?"

Merlin nodded.

"Oh, well then," the warrior/princess said. "What shall I have for a magic sword this time, and where will you be when I need guidance?"

Merlin swirled the waters again and showed the hero enough of destiny to tempt, reassure, and possibly, to compensate for all of the rewards and riches that could not fall to one whose heart had to belong to the people.

Don't Miss These Exciting DAW Anthologies